The I

MW01126425

The Perfect Boy
© 2008, 2014 Mark A. Roeder

Cover Photo Credits: Model: Wrangel and Background: Vlue on Dreamstime.com.
Cover Design: Ken Clark

ISBN-13: 978-1497473522
ISBN-10: 1497473527

Printed in the United States of America

Acknowledgements

I'd like to thank Robbie Ellis-Cantwell, Ken Clark, Kathy Staley, and David Yates for proofing the original version of this manuscript and James Adkinson for proofing this revised edition. I'd also like to thank Ken Clark for the great new cover.

Dedication

This book is dedicated to Jeff Morgan. Thanks for making my trips to Fort Wayne fun.

December 2003
Toby

"Martin Wolfe! Stay away from me!"

Play practice was just letting out. Krista and half the cast of *A Christmas Carol*, including me, of course, were coming out of the auditorium when we heard the distant, frightened voice. Only moments later, there was a scream, followed soon by the doors to the gym bursting open and slamming against the walls. Josh Lucas tore through the doors as if the hounds of hell were pursuing him. His eyes were wide and crazed. He didn't even notice the throng coming out of the auditorium.

Ian rounded the corner from the other direction. Josh spotted him and screeched to a halt.

"No!" Josh screamed. "I'm sorry! I won't tell anyone! Call him off! Call your ghost off! For God's sake! Please!"

Ian grinned.

Josh gasped, toppled over backward, and hit his head hard on the floor. He lay motionless. His eyes were closed. The crowd gaped at his still form. Krista ran to him. She raised his wrist and checked his pulse.

"He's dead." She looked directly into my eyes. "Oh, my God. He's dead!"

Ian's grin faded, and the color drained from his face. He stared down at the dead football player in horror.

Two Months Earlier —October 2003

"Down!" I said shoving Cedi back into the chair.

"Grrrrr."

"She's just gonna color and trim your hair Cedi, not shave you bald."

"But I love my pink hair!"

"You promised Jordan you would dye it black. You can change it back to pink later—or blue, or purple. I think purple was my favorite."

"Yeah! That looked cool! Didn't it mate?"

"Sit!"

Cedi stood up again. The boy could not sit still. I swear I was going to have to smack him on the nose with a rolled-up newspaper. We'd been in Clips & Curls for ten minutes, and the poor beautician had yet to touch his hair.

"Come on Cedi. Clara came in late just for you. Hold still!"

"Sorry," said Cedi, looking over at Clara.

"No problem, cutie," Clara said as she smacked her gum.

Clara was barely out of high school, and I think she had a thing for Cedi. He is quite a little hottie in an unconventional way; slim and sinewy with greenish blue eyes that appear violet at times and medium length, curly hair of an unknown color. I don't know the last time anyone saw Cedi's natural hair color.

"I'm definitely not getting paid enough for this," I said more to myself than anyone else.

"What? You're getting paid to spend time with me? Noooooo!" Cedi wailed.

"Calm down, hyper-boy. Jordan hired me to get you ready for your first appearance on stage with *Phantom*. Why he thinks I can handle you I'll never know."

Cedi started to get up again, but I pointed my finger at him.

"Stay!"

Cedi held still long enough for Clara to get to work. As she washed his hair, I wondered how I'd gotten myself in this mess. Well, I knew how; Jordan gazed into my eyes and asked me, that's how. Besides, overseeing Cedi's transformation into a more or less normal boy wasn't that big a task—or rather wouldn't be if Cedi could sit still more than five seconds without being sedated. He was trying to cooperate and yet still squirmed in the chair as Clara washed his hair.

Cedi behaved fairly well—at least by Cedi standards—but I was glad to see him back to his old, overactive self. I knew his breakup with Thad was hard on him, even if Thad had dumped him for his own good. Cedi and I had shared our sorrows over our recent breakups. I was going to miss Cedi when he was gone, and his departure was coming up all too soon. After the upcoming concert at Phantom World, Cedi would leave on tour with *Phantom*. There were little more than forty-eight hours before we had to say goodbye.

An hour or so later, Cedi was finished. Clara twirled him around so that he was facing the mirror.

"What do you think?" she asked.

"I'm gorgeous!" Cedi said.

He jumped up out of the chair, hugged Clara, and led her around the room in an impromptu dance. Clara obviously didn't mind.

I'd never seen Cedi with a normal hair color before, but he looked hot. Clara had not only dyed his hair black, but trimmed it in such a way that it looked wild and yet not messy.

Cedi paid Clara, gave her a big tip, and then we stepped out onto the sidewalk.

"So, what do you want to do on your last night of freedom?" I asked.

"You mean before I'm surrounded by bodyguards, screaming girls, and paparazzi?"

"Exactly."

"Um... eat my weight in pancakes!"

"Café Blackford then?"

"Yes! I'm buying, since I'm gonna be rich now!"

I laughed.

"Good, then I'm ordering something really expensive."

"There is nothing really expensive in Café Blackford Toby."

"Drat!"

"Drat? You Americans definitely talk funny."

"Well, you British drive on the wrong side of the road."

"Do not!"

"Do too!"

Spending time with Cedi was like babysitting a ten-year-old at times, but he made me laugh.

Autumn had come to Blackford, but it was still warm enough outside. I drank in the scent of the fallen leaves as Cedi and I walked side by side. Part of me, a big part, wished he was staying, but I knew he had to follow his dream. Touring with *Phantom!* How cool was that?

We reached Café Blackford without incident and were soon seated away from the windows near the fire.

"I feel as if I never truly got the chance to explore Blackford," Cedi said as we perused the menus. "I feel like I just got here. Now I'm leaving."

"You'll come back; after all, your aunt lives here, and then there's Thad."

"Yeah," said Cedi, a bit sadly. He was still smarting over his breakup with Thad T. Thomas, Blackford's resident celebrity and the author of a series of very popular vampire novels.

"Cheer up. You're going on tour with *Phantom*. You're not allowed to be sad."

Cedi grinned. "You know I always dreamed of being in a group like *Phantom,* but I never thought I'd get to be a part of *Phantom.* It's unreal."

"You're unreal, punk."

Cedi and I looked up. Chase Simmons, football jock, former nemesis, but now friend stood over us. It was too bad Chase didn't go for guys. He was a hottie; dark hair, dark eyes, and nice muscles.

"Sorry, I have no time for losers," Cedi said.

"Then what are you doing hanging with Riester?"

"Funny!" I said.

"Sit down, steroid-boy," said Cedi. "We were just about to order."

Chase joined us. Not that many weeks ago I thought of Chase as a badass who might enjoy rearranging my face, but things had changed—thanks to Cedi. The jocks had done their best to give Cedi a hard time, but he had a unique way of handling abuse; he refused delivery.

Our waitress arrived soon to take our orders.

"I'll have the pecan pancakes and the strawberry pancakes. And bacon!" Cedi said.

"There is no way you can eat all that," Chase said.

"Just watch me!"

Chase ordered a triple cheeseburger and fries. I opted for a banana-nut waffle and bacon.

"So, you ready to be a big hotshot rock star?" Chase asked.

"I was born a rock star!"

"Sure you were," Chase said. "I remember you back in the old days when you were nothing more than a little punk."

"The old days?" Cedi said. "You've only known me for three months!"

"Yeah, like I said."

"I'm excited!"

"You're always excited," Chase said.

"I don't think I could sing in front of all those people," I said.

"Come on Toby, you've performed in front of an auditorium full of people!"

"That was acting. It's not the same."

"I can't wait!" Cedi said.

"Well, the concert at Phantom World is the day after tomorrow," I said.

"Yeah. It's gonna be a blast!"

Cedi, Chase, and I talked and laughed while we waited on our orders. The few girls who were in the café came up to our table and asked for Cedi's autograph. Chase watched enviously.

"What a waste; all those girls interested in *you*."

"Hey. I like girls! I'm only half gay, you know."

"Jealous, Chase?" I asked.

"Yes!"

Cedi laughed so loud everyone in the café stared at us for a moment.

"Don't worry, Chase. Cedi will be gone soon, and then the girls will turn their attention back to you."

"Yeah! They'll be willing to settle for second best when I'm gone!" Cedi said.

Chase crossed his arms and shot Cedi a menacing look. Had he meant it, it would've been scary. Chase had a load of muscles and could've snapped Cedi like a twig.

Our food arrived, and we got down to the serious business of eating. The portions were rather large at Café Blackford, and I couldn't begin to finish mine. I watched in amazement as more and more of Cedi's pancakes disappeared.

Chase finally pushed his plate away, leaving part of his burger and a good many fries. I ate about two-thirds of my waffle and half my bacon. It was as much as I could manage. Cedi's pecan pancakes were gone, and Chase and I watched as he devoured his strawberry pancakes and bacon.

"I can't believe it," Chase said when Cedi pushed his platters away. "I would have bet a hundred bucks you couldn't eat all that."

"And you would have lost!" Cedi said.

Cedi paid for all of us. Chase and I escorted Cedi back to his aunt's house. We were his unofficial bodyguards, protecting him from wild, teenage girls. Luckily, none spotted us on our walk.

"Remember Cedi, you're supposed to be at Phantom World by 11 a.m. tomorrow," I said.

"Aww, and poor Toby will be stuck in school."

"True, but I'll see you at the concert in a couple of nights."

"Good night guys!"

"Night, loser," Chase said.

"Night, Cedi."

Chase and I went our separate ways. I was truly going to miss Cedi. Blackford would never be the same without him.

Daniel

I zoomed down the sidewalk toward the school, my backpack dangling from one shoulder, my dark hair flying. Major distraction. I jerked my head to the side, my skateboard hit a rock, and I went tumbling into a small knot of skaters and Goths who were seated on a concrete retaining wall.

"Smooth move Peralta," Ian said, frowning as he helped the others push me up onto my feet.

"Hey, that rock ran right out in front of me! It could have happened to anyone."

"Yeah, sure," said Auddie Mason, my best girl friend but not my girlfriend, if you know what I mean.

I hoped no one noticed what caused me to wipe out; the cute boy chatting it up with Becky Wayne and Cindy Erickson. I was soon to learn his name was Cole Fitch, but at that moment his name didn't matter. My heart beat faster as I looked at him. I had to tear my gaze away from his curly black hair and green eyes before my friends got wise. Only Auddie seemed to notice me checking out the new boy in school, but then only Auddie knew I liked boys.

I stole another look at Cole as he walked away. The first day at a new school was an unsettling experience for most, but Cole was so completely at ease it was as if he'd been there all along. This had to be his first day. A boy like that could not have escaped my notice since the beginning of the school year. No way!

I hate to admit this, but I stalked Cole as he moved through the hallways of Blackford High School. I had to get a closer look! Cole was a vision of masculine beauty. He was hot enough for the cover of a teen magazine. He wasn't muscular like the football jocks but rather was slim and sexy. Likewise, he wasn't tall. He was about my height, 5'10", but it suited him perfectly. Cole looked like a boy-band escapee, and I suspected he'd been created for the sole purpose of driving me out of my mind with longing. I wanted a poster of him to tack up on my wall.

I stared at Cole while he worked the combination on his locker. I couldn't help it. When I came to my senses, I jerked my head this way and that, checking to see if anyone noticed me gawking. I wasn't out, and being tagged as queer at B.H.S. could be dangerous to my health. Everyone was going about his or her own business, but I had to watch myself. A slipup like that could cost me dearly. That was the trouble with beautiful boys like Cole Fitch; their looks made them dangerous. They could cause boys like me to reveal more than we wished. I tore myself away from Cole and headed for my own locker.

"Hey Daniel, what's up?" Toby asked.

"Um, nothin' much." I sure couldn't tell him about stalking Cole.

"Happy Birthday."

"You remembered?"

"Sure."

"Hey, I'm having a party tomorrow tonight—just a few friends. Everyone is dressing up, because it's Halloween," I said, grinning. "You can come if you want."

"I would love to, but I can't. My parents have saddled me with handing out Halloween candy to juvenile delinquents."

"Aww, that sucks."

"I would like to get together with you some other time."

"Cool."

"Awesome," Toby said, smiling. He stood there for a few moments as if he wanted to say something more, then he bid me goodbye.

I felt guilty for not inviting Toby to my party sooner. The truth was I simply forgot. We hadn't been hanging out together all that long, so I was still getting used to the idea. Toby was cool. He always greeted me in the halls and smiled at me. He was a nice guy and there were precious few of those around. Toby had been kind of detached and sad recently. That's why I'd started hanging out with him more. I didn't like to see anyone in pain. I was glad I'd made the effort. We were fast becoming friends.

I slammed my locker and headed to class. Okay, you're going to think I'm a total freak, but there's something I should tell you before we go any further. You'll probably want to quit reading about me and chuck this book in the trash, but I can't live a lie. Yeah, I live in perpetual fear of being tagged as queer, but I'm not talking about that. I have a HUGE secret. I like school. I mean I *really* like it. I like English. I like algebra. I love world history. I love literature! So yeah, I'm a freak. This is your chance to jump ship if you can't handle it.

Okay, now that the losers are gone, he-he, we can continue. You know how I just said I love literature? Well, I had another reason to love it when I arrived for my third-period class. The desk between Toby and me had sat empty since it was vacated by Cedi. He was leaving to go on tour with *Phantom* in a couple of days. Yeah, sounds unbelievable, right? But it's true! If you don't believe me check out MTV or any music magazine. It's big news. Well, Cedi touring with *Phantom* is big news, not the fact that he used to sit beside me. Anyway, I'm getting way off topic, so it's time to tell you what was so great about literature, other than reading *Emma* by Jane Austen. Sitting in the desk recently vacated by Cedi was none other than my personal heartthrob! Cole Fitch!

I learned Cole's name when Mrs. Corlett announced it to the class, along with the fact he was a new student. As if we didn't know! Toby eagerly eyed Cole from where he sat on the other side of him. Most of the class eyed Cole. The girls practically drooled. Some of the guys frowned, suffering no doubt from a clear-cut case of jealousy. Personally, I enjoyed the scenery.

Cole looked in my direction and, gasp, smiled at me! I swear my heart pounded as though I'd been running in gym. I grinned back. Thankfully, Cole looked away again before I had time to go goofy. He had such dreamy green eyes. Swoon!

The next delightful surprise of the day came at lunch when I discovered that Cole had the same lunch period as I did. I didn't dare sit with him. I was permanently assigned to the skater table. I don't mean officially assigned, but seating wasn't random in the cafeteria. Each little group had its own territory. The jocks had their tables, the artsy crowd had theirs, we skaters had ours, and so on.

Even if I had the nerve to sit by Cole it was impossible. Girls swarmed around him like bees—bees who'd just discovered the most beautiful flower in existence. A few guys sat near him too, or rather near their girlfriends who were sitting near Cole. The guys eyed Cole suspiciously. Yeah, they knew competition when they saw it. They knew their girls would run to Cole if he snapped his fingers.

"You're drooling," Auddie whispered in my ear.

"I am not!" I said, quickly wiping my mouth, just in case.

Auddie giggled. I looked around to make sure no one had overheard, but Auddie was discreet. She would never place me in danger. My friends were cool. Some of them, like Ian, were way out there. All of us were outsiders. I feared I'd become even more an outsider if my buddies knew I drooled over boys instead of girls. I'd have to join the burnout table—if they'd have me.

The skater table was occupied by Jake Patrick, Andy Straus, Ian Babcock, Auddie Mason, and of course, me. We were a small group, but we stuck together. Auddie always sat next to me. A lot of people thought we had something going, something physical. We didn't. I wasn't interested in Auddie like that, and besides, we'd been friends so long it would've been weird. Jake sat across from me. He was kind of funny, but he was often quiet. It made for a weird combination. Sometimes, he wouldn't say anything for the longest time, and then he'd crack us all up. Andy, another of our crowd, usually had his nose poked in a skating magazine. He was forever making us look at pictures or reading us facts about skaters. Rounding out our little group was Ian Babcock. Ian was not only a skater but also a Goth.

The Goth table was adjacent to the skater table—well, it was the other end of the same table. There weren't that many skaters or Goths at B.H.S. Ian sat right in between, forming a bridge between the two groups. Ian was a double dose of bizarre. He wore only black. His hair was black and touched his shoulders. Ian wore a leather collar with spikes and studded leather bracelets on his wrists. He also wore lots of chains and necklaces. He had an earring dangling from his left ear and black makeup lining his eyes. Ian didn't smile, at least not much. He has this ultra-serious, angry look to him most of the time. Some kids are afraid of him, but he's actually rather cool. You just have to get past the spikes to get close to him.

I eyed Cole as I ate my fish sandwich. I had to fight to keep from sighing out loud. If I was allowed to design my very own boyfriend, I couldn't have done better. Cole was perfect. Okay, I know no one is perfect, but wow! I didn't even see how anyone could stand to be *that* handsome.

I looked around the table, checking out the looks of my friends. Jake and Andy were far from good looking. They were both on the scrawny side and just not that hot. Ian was rather handsome in a scary sort of way. The black makeup he wore around his eyes hid his features, but his good looks still came through. I had a secret crush on him. I was afraid he'd punch me if he knew I thought he was hot. Auddie was good looking, but she was a girl, so she was no good for comparison with Cole.

I looked at Cole again. My heart sank in my chest. I didn't have a snowball's chance in hell with a boy like him. Still, I could dream. I could hope. I could fantasize. I planned to do a little fantasizing later that night. I was going to need to in order to release the tension in my groin. Okay, I realized that might be T.M.I. (Too Much Information), but I'm a teenage boy, so...

I caught only a few glimpses of Cole the rest of the day, which was just as well. I was in serious danger of outing myself by drooling over him. I had to get myself under control.

Cedi

I yawned and looked into the mirror over the bathroom sink. The stranger who stared back momentarily startled me. I turned my head from side to side while still keeping my eyes on my reflection. Black was a rather tame hair color, but I guessed I'd get used to it. It was the only real concession I'd made to join *Phantom*.

I think the guys were right. Phantom's fans probably weren't ready for a boy with pink hair. Besides, it was only hair. No one was asking me to change my personality. I could still be me.

"This is it Cedi. Today is the day," I said to my reflection.

All the papers had been signed, and for the next several months I was officially a member of *Phantom*. Somehow, that made all the difference. I had practiced with Jordan, Ross, and Kieran already, preparing for the upcoming tour. Today would be my first practice as an official member of the band.

I looked forward to the concert. I would be performing on the very stage where it all started not so long ago. A freak accident injured Kieran, and I found myself on stage with my idols. Now, I was returning to that stage not as an outsider but as a member of the band.

It was Jordan's idea to give an unscheduled concert before we began the tour. He didn't say so, but I know the concert was for me. It was a chance to play for my hometown crowd and to perform for friends. True, I'd lived in Blackford not quite three months, but this was my home as much as, or more so, than England. There wasn't much that frightened me, but I was glad there would be some friendly faces in the crowd my first time out.

This was actually my second time, but I was in such a daze during my first performance that it seemed unreal. Everything had happened so fast. This time would be different. We would even be playing a special version of *Do You Know That I Love You* with me on the violin. I couldn't wait!

My life had changed dramatically. Such a short time ago, I'd gone to school with Toby, Chase, and the gang. Now, I'd soon be heading out on a cross-country tour, living my dream. Thad was right. I was insane to think of passing up the opportunity of a lifetime. As much as it hurt, I knew Thad did the right thing when he dumped me. Despite his comments to the contrary, I knew it was a great sacrifice on his part as well. I'd never forget what he'd done for me.

I stripped off my top and boxers and climbed into the shower. This was going to be some day.

I arrived at Phantom World about 10:30. The park was closed for the season, and the rides were eerily silent. A small workforce moved about, shutting up the rides and booths until the park reopened in the spring. Only the large amphitheatre was alive. I quickly made my way there to join Jordan, Ross, and Kieran.

I heard the sound of an electric guitar as I neared. It was probably Chad getting the instruments ready for our practice session. Chad was a blast—a real California surfer dude, or so I'd thought until I found out he'd never been to California except with the band. He sure sounded like the surfers in movies. Every other word he spoke was "dude."

I spotted Kieran on the stage as it came within sight. I was still getting used to being so close to my idol. Kieran was a god; no one could play the guitar like he could. Of course, he couldn't play now because of the accident. That's why I was here. Until his arm mended, he wasn't allowed to touch a guitar.

At first I could barely speak to Kieran because I was overwhelmed by his presence. Thad said Kieran was the only person in the world who could make me speechless. Thad was right—again. I was loosening up around Kieran. At least he seemed real now. Before, it was as though my mind couldn't quite comprehend he was really speaking to me. It was as if I was in a dream. The dream had become reality, and Kieran and I were even becoming friends. It was a bummer he wouldn't be with us for the tour. Since he couldn't play, he was taking some time off to be with his fiancée, Natalie.

As I drew close to the stage, I could see Jordan drinking a mug of something, talking to Chad and a pretty strawberry blonde. I struggled to remember her name.... Samantha; that was it, although everyone called her Sam. She helped Chad with sound. Ralph was nearby. Now *there* was a lucky guy. I couldn't even imagine what it would be like to have a partner like Jordan. Of course if I could've had my pick of the guys, I would've chosen Kieran. That was an impossibility because Kieran was hetero.

"Cedi!" Ross yelled when he spotted me. He ran toward me, hurtled himself off the stage, and jumped into my arms. I tried to catch him, but Ross was considerably larger than I was. We both crashed to the ground.

"Ross! You idiot!" Kieran yelled. "If you hurt our new guitarist, I'm gonna kick your ass."

"He has no sense of humor," Ross whispered loudly enough that Kieran was sure to hear.

I smiled and shook my head. Ross was a ton of fun. He was also wicked cute, especially when he smiled.

"How are you this morning, Cedi?" Jordan asked.

"Excited!"

"The same as always then," Ralph said.

"Ohhhhh, donuts!" I said, spotting the big box on the table at the side of the stage. I grabbed up a crème-filled maple long-john and took a bite.

"There's hot English Breakfast tea, as well," Ralph said.

"Hot tea? Now you're talking!"

I made myself a mug of tea, nice and sweet with plenty of sugar and cream.

"You British and your tea," Ross said, taking a swig of his Coke. "Are we going to have to break for teatime every day?"

I giggled. "Only if you want."

"Hey, I like hot tea, and I'm not British," Jordan said.

"Well you're just plain weird," Ross said.

Ross leaned in close and pretended to whisper, although he spoke loud enough for all to hear. "He even likes guys instead of girls."

"Like that's a secret!" I said.

"What gave me away?" Jordan asked. "Was it the press conference or my boyfriend?"

"Both," I said.

Jordan was most definitely gay. Kieran was obviously not. I wondered about Ross. Even back in Britain, the tabloids were filled with stories about his sexual exploits with members of both sexes. There were lots of photos of Ross coming out of clubs, eating in restaurants, attending plays, and so forth. Sometimes he was with a girl, sometimes with a guy. The tabloids always played it up if he was spotted with a male. These were the same papers that claimed a B-52 had been found on Mars and that Noah's Ark had been spotted floating off the coast of Japan so I didn't know what to make of the stories. Ross was definitely a hottie. He could probably have any girl or guy he wanted.

I pushed the matter from my mind. What did it matter? Why was I even thinking about it? I took a sip of tea and then bit into my long-john. Ross grinned at me mischievously.

"Okay guys," Jordan said. "I think we need to run through *DYK* with Cedi's violin sections. We don't have that one down yet and I know Chad and Sam are still working out the sound levels."

"And I'm having trouble switching back and forth between the guitar and violin," I said.

"Our bass guitarist can handle the guitar sections once we're on the road. You won't have to worry about that after this first concert."

I was glad to hear that. While I liked rushing back and forth between instruments, I was a bit concerned I'd screw up. There was precious little time between the sections. It would be cool when the backup musicians joined us. I knew the sound would be richer. I was glad they weren't present on the day I filled in for Kieran; otherwise, it would've been the bass guitarist replacing Kieran and not me. I would never have gotten the chance to play with *Phantom*.

Kieran couldn't play, but he could still sing. We'd been practicing a song that featured Kieran in the lead. I'd never heard it before, but it was eerily beautiful. It was called *Nemesis* and was all about this guy and his greatest enemy, who turned out to really be his friend. The song brought to mind images of knights in shining armor, dragons, and mythical creatures. It was almost magical.

"Ready guys?" Jordan asked when we'd all finished pigging out on donuts.

"Jordan is a slave driver Cedi. Get used to it," Ross said as he headed for his drums.

I picked up my electric guitar, and Jordan stood behind his keyboard. Ross started the beat on his drums, and we began to play.

Something came upon me when the music started. It was as if I wasn't the same Cedi anymore. It was a bit like the feeling I'd had when I looked into the mirror earlier that morning. I was me and yet not me. I felt transformed, as if I'd changed from Clark Kent to Superman. I became lost in the music. I became the music. During our practice, there were only Chad, Sam, and a handful of workers around, but it didn't matter. The music was magical whether anyone was there to hear it or not.

The magic intensified when we reached the first violin section. I couldn't count the times I'd listened to *Do You Know That I Love You,* and there I was putting my own mark on it. My addition melded in smoothly, as if it had been there all along. I almost couldn't believe I was standing on stage with Jordan, Ross, and Kieran. It was a dream come true.

"We may have to cut a single of that," Jordan said when we'd finished the song. "Or put it on the next album. That's extraordinary, Cedi."

"Thanks!" I said, grinning like an idiot no doubt.

We practiced the rest of the morning and broke for lunch a little before one. Lunch was served in the flat on top of the Graymoor Mansion. I loved the view from up there. One could stand and look out over the entire park.

"Pizza!" Ross yelled as we entered.

Steaming hot pizzas were just being set out on a long table. Yes! I could really get into this whole rock-star thing!

Chad, Ralph, Sam, and the crew joined Kieran, Ross, Jordan, and me. We were one big family. The guys were as friendly to the crew as they were to each other—perhaps more so. Jordan clearly ran the show. When he talked, people listened, but he was mostly just one of the guys. Everyone made me feel right at home.

After three Cokes and several slices of pizza, I was revved up and ready to go. Ross challenged me to a duel with bread sticks, and we fought each other while Chad laughed and Jordan and Kieran rolled their eyes.

"I should seriously be getting paid for babysitting," Jordan told Kieran, but I saw him grin.

"Well at least now Ross has someone to play with."

Ross glanced over at Kieran and arched his eyebrow. I darted and jabbed him in the chest, a bit too hard because my bread stick broke. Ross grabbed his chest as if wounded.

"Now I have you," he said and unleashed a vicious attack. Soon, I was on my back giggling as Ross finished me off, using his breadstick like a dagger.

"You guys are too weird," Ralph said.

"But you know you love us Ralphie!" Ross said, jumping up. He ran to Ralph and planted a big kiss right on his lips. Ralph wiped his mouth with pretend disgust.

"Okay children, we need to get back to work," Jordan said.

"So what's up next?" I asked.

"We're giving interviews the rest of the day."

"Interviews?"

"Yeah, to publicize the upcoming tour," Jordan said. "Cedric, why don't you stay back with me for a bit while the others go on. I'll give you some pointers."

"Watch out Cedi," Ross said. "Jordan is a predator. More than one boy has lost his virginity when he 'stayed back' with Jordan."

"What makes you think I'm a virgin?" I asked.

Ross arched his eyebrow again—at me this time.

"Ross, go away," Jordan ordered.

Ross growled, but left. Everyone else departed as well.

"I'm guessing you've never been interviewed before," Jordan said.

"No."

"Just remember, you don't have to answer all the questions—or any of them if you don't want. Most of the questions will be fairly standard. In fact, you'll get sick of hearing them over and over. You're new, so a lot of attention will focus on you. You'll probably be asked about how you feel about joining the band, what it's like to work with us, what musical experiences you had before, etc. Some of the questions can get very personal, so don't be afraid to say "no comment," or tell the reporter you won't talk about that. Sometimes it's necessary to be very firm. Most reporters are fairly cool, but some get overly aggressive and ask questions about things that are no one's business. How much you want to share about your private life is your business. Remember that some things can and will be taken out of context, so watch what you say."

I felt a bit intimidated.

"Don't worry Cedric. You'll do fine. It's a bit scary the first couple of times, but you'll get used to it. It's the price of fame. There will only be a few reporters here today. We'll do the really big press conferences when we start the tour. Most of the reporters here today are from local radio and TV stations. There's even one from your old high school."

I nodded.

"You ready?"

"Yeah!"

I followed Jordan down the stairs and across the park. We chatted about the upcoming tour, the tour bus, the hotels we'd be staying in, and more. When we neared the stage I was no longer quite so certain I was ready. There were only about a dozen reporters, but there were four big cameras, and one was from MTV!

As soon as Jordan and I stepped onto the stage, most of the reporters descended upon us. I felt a sense of panic. Jordan held up his hands.

"I'm sure you're all eager to talk to our newest band member, but take it easy on him. You'll all get your chance for a one-on-one interview with Cedric. How about you first?" Jordan said, pointing to a girl I recognized from school. She always hung out at the skater table.

Jordan had a commanding presence, and the reporters listened to him. I think his promise that everyone would get one-on-one time with me, and presumably the rest of the guys, set the reporters at ease. I was thankful my first interview was with the Blackford High School newspaper. I had no doubt Jordan picked out the B.H.S. reporter so I could ease into my life in the spotlight.

"Hi Cedi. I'm Auddie," the girl said.

"Yeah, I remember you."

Auddie looked over toward Jordan, where he was speaking in front of a camera.

"It's rather overwhelming to be around them, isn't it?" I said.

"Yeah."

"Why don't we sit over here?"

I led Auddie to one of the tables that had been set up on the stage. We both took a seat. Auddie was visibly nervous.

"So what would you like to ask me?" I prompted.

"Oh. Um... what does it feel like to join *Phantom* for the tour? Were you a fan before you met them?"

I began speaking, and my lack of ease completely disappeared. Auddie didn't ask any personal questions. She stuck with questions about the tour, the music, and how I felt about it all. By the end, we were talking and laughing as though we'd known each other for a long time.

The next reporter was from a local radio station. The station broke into its programming to do a live interview with me. It was a little freaky to know lots and lots of people were listening as I spoke, but I soon forgot about that and just talked.

Talking in front of a camera took a bit more nerve, but I liked it! At the end of my first TV interview, I ran up to the camera, stared right into the lens and shouted, "Come and watch me on stage!"

Everything went more or less smoothly until the MTV reporter asked me a totally unexpected question.

"You've been seen with novelist, Thad T. Thomas. Is it true the two of you are dating?"

How the hell did MTV know about that?

"No. I am not dating Thad T. Thomas. I'm not dating anyone."

"But you have been seen with him."

"Yes. As you probably know, Thad lives here in Blackford. I've lived here a few months now. I've met a lot of great people. I haven't had the chance to hang out with as many of them as I would like, but I have been able to spend time with a few like Thad and some of the guys from my high school."

Thankfully, the reporter didn't press me on the Thad issue. Instead, he asked what it felt like to leave high school and join *Phantom*. I thought I'd handled the Thad question quite well. He'd dumped me, so I could truthfully answer that we weren't a couple.

The questions continued. Jordan had accurately predicted most of them. Even with so few reporters I found myself answering the same questions over and over again. Luckily, the Thad question came up only once. It was a reminder that my private life was no longer quite so private as before.

The funniest questions involved my hair. I was asked why I'd dyed it black, did I plan to grow it long like Jordan and Ross, and what was my natural color? Jordan rolled his eyes at me when the reporter wasn't looking. I was sure he'd had more than his share of hair questions.

It was time for supper by the time all the interviews were wrapped up. I was starving.

"I had no idea doing interviews would take so long," I said to Ross as we walked back toward the flat.

"That was nothing. Sometimes, it takes all day. Just wait until you do your first photo shoot. You'll be bouncing off the walls."

Kieran, Jordan, and Ross were beginning to feel kind of like my big brothers, at least so far as in taking me under their wings. I wasn't that much younger than they were. I was eighteen and they were all about twenty-two. Ross actually seemed more like he was fourteen, except for the fact he was sexy as hell. He often acted like a little boy, but he had a man's body and such a nice bum! Mmm.

I had supper with the guys—steak this time—and then we practiced a bit more. I was worn out by the time Ralph drove me home. It had been an incredible day.

Toby
Halloween 2003

"Who's the new dude?" Eddie asked.

"I think his name is Cole," Krista said.

I turned my head. There was Cole. Wow! Was he hot!

"We should've asked him to sit with us," Eddie said.

"Why?" Orlando asked, clearly bewildered. "Are you hot for the new boy Eddie?"

Eddie scowled.

"Look at all the babes swarming around him. I bet we could have sold seats next to him for ten bucks, easy. We should merchandize that boy before someone else does," Eddie said.

Krista groaned, but I silently thought I would've gladly paid ten bucks to sit next to Cole at lunch. The value of my seat in literature had skyrocketed. It had been cool sitting next to Cedi, but my proximity to that stunning piece of eye candy named Cole Fitch was beyond price.

"Guys who are that good looking are freak shows," Eddie said. "It's not normal."

"Then you're in no danger of abnormality," Orlando said.

"Screw you Gamboa!"

Practically every girl in the cafeteria was gazing at Cole with adoration. Several of them hovered around him.

"Females! Just look at them. Like moths to the flame," Eddie said.

"Well, he is hot," Krista said.

"Probably stuck up," I said.

"I'd like to find out," Krista said.

"I'm so glad I'm not cursed with abnormal beauty," Eddie said.

"Yeah, that was a real close one for ya, wasn't it Eddie?" Orlando said.

"I repeat. Screw you Gamboa."

Orlando laughed. It had been quite a while since I'd seen him as much as smile.

The voices of my friends faded as I became lost in my own thoughts. It was Halloween and I was single. I'd been single every Halloween of my life, but I'd hoped this one would be different. I looked toward Orlando. Until recently he'd been my boyfriend, but Kerry had taken him away from me. Orlando and I still weren't talking, at least not directly. We sat near each other at lunch and interacted through our shared friends, but we didn't speak. If we passed each other in the hallways our only communication was with our eyes. Neither of us knew what to say. Orlando no doubt felt guilty for cheating on me. I was still angry and hurt, but I also understood. That's not to say I was the least bit happy that Orlando dumped me. Yeah, he dumped *me*. After he cheated on me with Kerry, I should've dumped him. I was willing to forgive him and talk things out, but Orlando wasn't interested. He broke up with me because he knew he would only hurt me again. Orlando couldn't keep his hands out of Kerry's pants so he dumped me to spare me more pain—but it still hurt.

Orlando must have felt me looking at him, because he turned and met my eyes. His smile disappeared.

I looked over to Daniel's table. He was sitting with his skater friends and laughing. I hadn't noticed him much while I was dating Orlando, or even before, but I was crushing on him now. Daniel was having a birthday party in a few hours. I wished I could be there, but I'd already promised to watch the house. I'd spend my evening at home handing out Halloween candy to witches, goblins, and ghouls. So pathetic.

After lunch, I headed for my locker. My lunch period was the very last lunch period, so my day was mostly over. There were only three periods left. My favorite class was eighth-period drama, which was only an hour away. Just yesterday, Mrs. Jelen had delivered the delightful news that this year there would be a winter play. *Peter Pan* had been such a hit that we were doing *A Christmas Carol* for the holiday season. Before, we had done a fall and a spring play, but nothing in the winter. I'd been landing leads left and right—Oliver, Tom Sawyer, Peter Pan—but that was about to come to an end. I was a good actor, but I couldn't see myself playing Scrooge. I had already decided not to try out for the part. It was time to let someone else have the lead. Besides, if

I took a lesser role this time around, I might be able to land the lead in the spring play.

As I walked down the hallway, I gave serious thought to what character I wanted to portray. Marley perhaps? Scrooge's nephew might be more fun. Tiny Tim? No, I don't think so. I couldn't see myself leaning on a crutch saying, "God Bless us, every one." Oh well, there was time yet. I didn't have to decide right away.

Kerry locked his eyes on mine as he came around the corner. He smiled as if he didn't have a care in the world. He mocked me with his eyes and the smirk on his handsome face. I *hated* Kerry. He ruined the relationship I'd had with Orlando. If it wasn't for him, Orlando and I would still be together. Kerry didn't care about relationships. He didn't care whom he hurt. As long as he got what he wanted, he was happy.

"Hello Toby," he said as if I was his best friend.

"Drop dead, fucker."

I wanted to beat Kerry senseless, but I didn't stand a chance against him or his muscles.

"Ohhh, still bitter I see. You shouldn't try to compete with the big boys," Kerry said, groping his crotch. "You'll never win."

"Eat shit and die."

Kerry laughed at me. His laughter pissed me off. I was no threat to him and he knew it. Kerry dismissed me as if I was nothing.

I didn't often use such language, but Kerry made me so mad I couldn't see straight. The truly weird thing was that his sister, Krista, was my best girl friend. She also didn't get along well with Kerry. Besides being an all-around jerk, Kerry had also broken up Krista's relationship with Orlando. Krista and Orlando dated before Orlando and I were a couple. It's a long, complicated story, and I don't want to get into it right now. The moral of the tale is that Kerry is an asshole.

I missed Orlando. I missed him holding me and kissing me, but there was no point in looking back. What I'd had with Orlando was gone. If he ever freed himself from Kerry's spell, then perhaps we could be together again, but who knew if that would ever happen? I was no longer sure I wanted Orlando back. Some words, once spoken, can't be taken back. Some acts, once performed, can't be erased.

I actually had fun handing out treats Halloween night. Pathetic, huh? I'd felt pretty wretched after Orlando told me our relationship was over. There's nothing like getting dumped to send your self-esteem crashing to the ground. I wished I were still a kid—blissfully ignorant of romantic relationships. If I was a bit younger, I could have been hoarding candy instead of passing it out. Mackenzie was out on the town loading up on sugar, no doubt. He'd probably be bouncing off the walls when he returned. My little brother was nearly too old for trick or treating, even though he was immature. He was fifteen going on six. I envied him his last Halloween as a child.

Mackenzie returned at ten when the official time for trick or treating was over. I left him in charge of greeting stragglers and went for a stroll. The atmosphere outside was windy and spooky, perfect for Halloween. I walked down the sidewalk, stopping to admire jack-o'-lanterns sitting on porches and grinning through windows. Cotton ghosts hovered in the trees, and scarecrows guarded the entrances to homes. There was a nip in the air, and I settled into my flannel shirt and warm jacket.

As I walked, I thought about Daniel and Cole. It was time to pick myself up, dust off my pants, and get back on the horse. I didn't have a good track record when it came to finding myself a boyfriend. When I finally landed one, I couldn't keep him, but I couldn't give up. Orlando wasn't the only guy around. Just because we'd crashed and burned didn't mean my future was hopeless. I wondered if there was any chance that Daniel or Cole liked guys. I wished I knew. When God was handing out gaydar, I must've got in the wrong line. Oh, how I yearned for some out gay boys in Blackford!

I could come out myself. Krista, Eddie, and, of course, Orlando knew. Mackenzie had known for quite a while. My parents knew too. Mom had caught me making out with Orlando. That had worked out better than I would've suspected. The few who knew my secret were cool with it, but that didn't mean my classmates would feel the same. I was no Cedi. I couldn't fend off abuse by wildly counterattacking. I might not get beat up if guys like Josh Lucas found out about me, but then again... In any case, I wasn't ready to become the school homo.

I wished I could risk it. Then maybe another gay boy would reveal himself and ask me out. Coming out required a little more courage than I possessed. Someday I'd do it, but not yet.

I'd have to land a boyfriend the hard way. Daniel and I were becoming friends, so perhaps I could draw us closer and then test the waters. I had to do something. I'd spent enough time wallowing in self-pity and sadness. Hmm, what would Cedi say about that? Probably, "Get off your bum and go find yourself a bloke!" I laughed to myself. I could actually hear Cedi's British accent in my head. I wondered how Cedi was doing. I had little doubt that he was having the time of his life. I was the one I needed to think about. It was time to start over. I might go down in flames—again—but I had to try. It was time to see if I could make Daniel Peralta my new boyfriend.

A chill went up my spine. I halted. I turned and caught a glimpse of a ghostly apparition, a dead boy with a noose around his neck. I shivered. I saw him only for a moment, but that was more than enough to freak me out. I was sure it was nothing more than a late trick or treater, or perhaps someone returning from a party, but he seemed to float rather than walk. I could swear he'd passed right through a hedge. My eyes were playing tricks on me. Perhaps the atmosphere was a bit too spooky on this Halloween night.

Daniel

After school, I walked Auddie home through a whirlwind of falling leaves. My backpack was slung over my shoulder, and my skateboard was tucked under my arm. We were less than a block from B.H.S. when Cole drove past.

"Wow!" I said. "A Corvette!"

I stared after Cole. I couldn't believe my eyes, but he was driving a red Corvette convertible.

"How can a high-school kid afford a $50,000 car?" Auddie asked.

"Rich parents," I said.

"Either that or he had one hell of a paper route before he moved to Blackford," Auddie said.

"Cole has it all," I said.

"Are you jealous, Daniel?"

"Maybe, but mostly I'm in awe. I can't even imagine what it would be like to look like he does, wear clothes like his, be *that* popular, and drive a Corvette! He's like a god."

"Wow, you're hotter for him than I thought."

"Oh, like you wouldn't lock lips with him in a flash if you got the chance! Hypocrite," I said, laughing.

"I wouldn't pull away if he tried to kiss me, but there's little danger of that."

"Don't sell yourself short. You're beautiful."

"If I'm so beautiful, why don't you try anything with me?"

"You know why! I'm gay! And, we've been friends forever!"

Auddie giggled.

"Every girl should have a gay boy friend."

"I heard the school is going to start issuing gay boys to all the girls beginning next semester. The trouble is, there aren't enough of us to go around."

"Well, I've already got mine."

"You know the main problem with Blackford?" I asked.

"I'm sure you're about to tell me."

"It has no out gay boys. There are a few suspected queers, but no one is really out—now that Cedi is gone."

"You could be the first, Daniel."

"No, thank you. I like my face the way it is—unaltered."

"Cedi seemed to get along okay."

"Well, he was crazy! Everyone was afraid to mess with him."

"Yeah, like the time he pretended to be Josh Lucas' boyfriend."

"If you remember, Cedi did get his ass kicked for that."

"True, but it didn't slow him down."

"Well, I'm not Cedi. I'm not that bold. If I get tagged as queer, I'll be a punching bag for guys like Josh."

"I'd protect you."

"Yeah, having a girl fight my battles for me will make me look real manly," I said, flipping my hair out of my eyes.

"Well, you don't have to be out, but I do wish we could find you a boyfriend."

"That's makes two of us!"

"I wouldn't mind having one myself."

"At least you can look without worrying about getting a fist in the face for your trouble."

"True."

"Perhaps you should go after Cole before some other girl grabs him up."

"As if I had a chance. Maybe you should go after him."

"Yeah, right! Cole Fitch? Gay? I don't think so."

"He could be gay."

"Could be, but what's the chance of that? Ten percent? Those are not good odds. You've got a ninety percent chance that he's straight."

"He is gorgeous," Auddie said. "He has great taste in clothes. He's incredibly neat. He could well be batting for your team."

"I wish, but if wishes were horses then beggars would ride."

"I bet you want to ride Cole."

"I can't believe you said that!" I laughed.

"Maybe he's bisexual. We could both ride him."

"Yeah, I'll take him on odd-numbered days. You can have him on even-numbered days."

"We're being terribly shallow," Auddie said. "We're both yearning for Cole because he's so good-looking. We need to search for substance, someone who is good and kind and loving."

"Hey, I am searching for substance. I'm just gonna fantasize about Cole while I'm doing it."

"You're terrible! I know what you'll be doing while you fantasize about him."

"Don't go there. Don't pretend you haven't already undressed him in your mind."

"I've done no such thing!"

"Well, I have and he's hot!"

Auddie laughed. She leaned over and gave me a kiss on the cheek as we reached her house.

"I'll see you at seven."

"Bye, Auddie."

Auddie walked up the brick pathway to her home. I continued down the sidewalk but turned at the sound of my best friend's voice.

"Daniel."

"Yeah?"

"Happy Birthday!"

I grinned and went on my way. I was terminally single, but at least I had one very good friend.

***

My birthday party was a blast! There were only five guests, but I'd rather have my real friends over instead of a bunch of kids I barely knew. Auddie was there, of course, dressed as Morticia Addams. Andy Straus came as a dead skater. He actually didn't look all that different than usual, except that his face was painted grayish-white. He looked cool, nonetheless. Jake came as Frankenstein. He looked really cool, even if he was way too short for the monster. Ian came as a dead boy with a noose around his neck. His bluish-white face paint made him look totally creepy.

"The ghost of Martin Wolfe?" Auddie asked when he arrived.

"Hey, you got it," Ian said.

"Martin Wolfe. There's a name I haven't heard since the sixth grade," I said, looking rather sharp in my vampire outfit.

"Who the hell is Martin Wolfe?" Jake asked.

"You remember, the seniors used to freak us out by telling us the ghost of Martin Wolfe would come for us and drag us away," I said. "It was back when we started at B.H.S. The older guys told us that Martin hated sixth graders."

"Oh, yeah!" Jake said. "I'd forgotten."

"You know, there really was a Martin Wolfe, and he hanged himself right in our school," Ian said.

"There was never a Martin Wolfe," Jake said. "That's all made up. It's like the clubfoot story at the summer camp my parents made me attend a few years back."

"I heard he was real," I said.

Jake laughed. "Happy birthday, Daniel."

Everyone joined in and wished me a happy birthday. I grinned.

"Let's have some pizza!" I said. "Then cake!"

We wolfed down pepperoni pizza while rock music played in the background. We talked and laughed and cut up. Even Ian joked around and laughed. He was a much happier person when he was alone with friends.

My birthday cake had a spooky theme, which was not unusual considering that I was born on Halloween. Of course, there were some cracks made about that, but I was used to it. The cake was a large graveyard with marshmallow tombstones. There was even a mausoleum and gnarled trees. On top of the graves, it read, "Happy 16th, Daniel."

I know birthday wishes aren't supposed to be revealed if they are to come true, but I'm sure you can guess what I wished for—someone with curly black hair and green eyes. 'Nuff said.

My skater buddies were always a lot of fun. Most of the time we skated, but sometimes we got together to party. By party I don't mean drugs, sex, and alcohol. I had seen the other guys drink a few beers, but most often they went for Sunkist or Pepsi. I'd tried beer once myself. Yuck! As far as I knew, none of us was into drugs. Ian might have experimented, but if he did, he never talked about it. As for sex, I was a virgin. Jake claimed to have screwed a girl at camp, but the rest of us thought it highly unlikely. Andy made no such claims, but he had this little smile that crossed his face if asked. I suspected he had been with a girl. Ian didn't talk about sex. If he talked about anything, it was skating or music.

All of us talked about skating. Ian was totally kick-ass on a skateboard. Andy and Jake were awesome too. Auddie could skate as well as any of the guys. I knew how to handle a board better than the average guy and had no trouble keeping up with my buddies. I also had a cool name for a skater. As far as I knew, we weren't related, but Peralta was a big name in skating. He was one of the guys who made skating what it is. He was around even before Tony Hawk.

My party broke up a little before eleven. I walked Auddie home. She had no need of a man to protect her, but we liked to walk and talk. I valued all my friends, but Auddie meant the most. We shared things with each other that we shared with no one else.

***

"Stay away from my girl, pretty boy, or you're gonna get hurt."

I recognized the voice of Adam Henshaw, one of the football players, before I even rounded the corner. I stepped into view, and there were Adam and Mike Bradley, another muscular football jock, holding Cole up against the lockers.

"Adam! You'd better get out to the parking lot. I saw some of those auto-shop guys messing with your truck!" I said.

"Those fuckers!" Adam yelled. "Come on, Mike!"

The pair bolted down the hallway. I grinned at Cole.

"Let me guess," he said. "You made that up."

I held my hands out and bowed my head.

"Daniel Peralta at your service."

"Hey, thanks dude. Those guys were gonna mess me up."

"Are you okay?"

"Yeah. You came at just the right time."

"I forgot my backpack, so I came back for it. I don't usually hang around after school's out for the day."

I was such an airhead sometimes. I was halfway home before I noticed my backpack wasn't swinging from my shoulder. I was glad Auddie wasn't along to see what a dufus I was, although she already knew.

"Not on any sports team, huh?"

"No. I did do the school play, but that's over. We performed *Peter Pan* this year. I played the exciting role of a lost boy."

"I'm far too busy for extracurricular activities."

I almost couldn't believe Cole Fitch was talking to me. I was weak in the knees. He was so cute!

"You might want to make yourself scarce. Adam and Mike will likely come back when they find out Adam's truck is safe."

"No. Jocks aren't that smart. They'll assume I beat it out of here, so there's no hurry."

"Well..." I didn't quite know what to say. Actually speaking to Cole was overwhelming.

"Thanks again for saving my butt. If you hadn't come along, those guys would have kicked my ass."

"I'm glad they fell for it."

"You think fast on your feet."

"It's a necessary talent for those of us who can't bench press our own body weight. If you can't be strong, you've gotta be smart."

"Exactly. Hey, let me give you a ride home. It's the least I can do for my hero."

I must've turned completely red. I felt as if I could fly. Cole Fitch actually called *me* his hero.

"You don't have to do that."

"I want to. Besides, you can protect me with that sharp mind if any other bullies are around."

I laughed.

"Where's your locker?" Cole asked.

I pointed up the hallway.

"Okay, get your backpack and I'll drive you home."

I quickly retrieved my pack. Cole and I walked through the nearly deserted hallways. I couldn't help but steal a few looks at him. It was no wonder guys like Adam feared Cole would steal their girls. Cole hung back while I scanned the parking lot for any sign of Adam or Mike. I gave him the all clear, and he joined me.

"You know those guys will probably come after you again. You'd better watch your back."

"Not to worry. I'll take care of Adam and Mike. They caught me unawares, but I won't let that happen again."

"Be careful Cole."

"Don't worry about me. I know how to take care of myself."

I didn't voice my thoughts, but I was thinking how he'd come within an inch of getting beaten to a pulp. I didn't see how he could "take care" of Adam or Mike.

"So, are the football twins the main badasses here at B.H.S.?"

"They're near the top, at least. There are quite a few guys around who it's best to avoid. I mainly avoid trouble by not drawing attention to myself."

I looked at the handsome boy walking beside me. There was no way Cole Fitch could fail to draw the attention of others.

"I don't like bullies," Cole said.

"Who does?"

"Good point."

"Wow," I said, looking at Cole's Corvette.

"Like it?"

"What's not to like? How did you afford a car like this?"

"Well, don't tell anyone, but it was a couple of years old when I bought it. Dad paid for most of it."

"Your family must be rich."

"Dad and I do okay."

"Your mom doesn't live with you?"

"She's dead."

"I'm sorry."

"Don't worry about it. Get in."

I didn't know what I would do if my mom died. Cole's life looked perfect from the outside, but I guess he had troubles like all of us.

I climbed into the sleek sports car, running my hand along the leather interior.

"This is the sweetest car I've ever seen in my entire life."

Cole grinned and it increased his cuteness exponentially.

"It's a babe magnet."

"I don't think you need a car to help you attract girls."

I froze. Had I actually told Cole, indirectly, that I thought he was hot?

"Thanks," Cole said, grinning at me. "You're not so bad yourself."

"Please. I'm borderline ugly."

"Hey, don't be down on yourself man. You're okay. I'd even say you're cute."

Oh my gosh! Cole said I was cute. My heart pounded in my chest.

"So which way to your house?" Cole asked as he pulled out of his parking spot.

"Hang a left. It's only a few blocks."

Even though it was a bit cool, Cole put the top down. His curly black hair flowed in the wind. How could anyone stand being so handsome?

Cole had referred to his car as a babe magnet. That did not bode well. I desperately wanted him to like guys instead of girls. I knew there was small chance of that, but I could hope. He said I was cute. Would a hetero boy say something like that to another boy? Guys knew when other guys were hot, but they didn't say it out loud. Did they?

Our journey was far too short. Cole pulled up in front of my house and I stepped out.

"Thanks for the ride."

"No, thank you for saving my butt."

And what a nice butt it is.

"You're welcome."

"I'll see you at school. Later Daniel."

"Bye Cole."

I turned toward the front door. I could not wait to tell Auddie what had happened!

***

"Are you *serious*?" Auddie asked only minutes later as I lay on my bed with the phone to my ear.

"Yeah. They had Cole shoved up against the wall."

"You're a hero!"

"Hardly."

"Well, you saved Cole."

"He gave me a ride home in his Corvette. That car is so sweet."

"Boys! Forget the car. Tell me about Cole. What did he say? What did you say?"

I recounted the entire tale for Auddie.

"You've got it bad for him."

"Yeah, well that hardly matters. He has girls crawling all over him."

"Apparently including Adam's girlfriend," Auddie said, giggling.

"I'm a little worried about Cole. He doesn't seem to appreciate the danger he's in. Adam and Mike aren't going to let him get away."

"I guess you'll have to protect him."

"Yeah, right. I don't think they'll fall for the same trick again. I'd have no chance against them in a fight. About all I can do is distract them by taking a beating while Cole escapes."

"Well, don't do that!"

"Don't worry. Believe it or not, I try to avoid beatings."

"I always knew you were a smart boy."

Cole wasn't the only one on Adam and Mike's hit list. I walked down the hallway at school the next morning to find them holding Ian up against the wall. Ian was a favorite target of bullies. Being one of the few Goths in school made him stand out. Ian was tall but not physically imposing, so guys like Adam and Mike knew they could intimidate him.

I wondered what I could do. I couldn't tell what was being said at a distance, but the two bullies were leaning on Ian. Ian had his head down, letting his long black hair cover his face. I kept walking forward, still unsure of what to do.

I spotted Cole coming up the hall from the other direction. He slowed when he noticed Adam and Mike. No doubt he feared they would turn on him. He scowled. Our eyes locked. We silently communicated our shared dislike of Adam and Mike. When I looked back at Ian, Adam and Mike had released him and were walking my way. They had failed to spot Cole and didn't give me a second look. We'd all escaped—for the moment, at least. Cole nodded when he passed me. I hurried toward Ian.

"You okay?"

"Yeah, the fuckers couldn't do much to me in the hall during school."

"What did they want?"

"To give me a hard time. The usual. I hate those guys."

"You are not alone, I'm sure."

"I wish I could strike back at them, but they own this place. Life is so unfair."

"You'll get no argument from me. Hey, I need to run. I just wanted to make sure you're okay."

"I'm used to threats and harassment. Thanks, Daniel."

Ian's troubles were over for the moment, but not Cole's. At least Cole's next problem wasn't as severe as Adam and Mike threatening to pound him. Cole somehow managed to get on the wrong side of Mr. Glair, our sociology teacher. No matter how Cole answered a question, Old Lackluster cut him to pieces. Cole didn't seem to care, which only served to infuriate our teacher. The girls in the class were incensed that Glair would dare to harass their golden boy. They glared at him with baleful hatred. I wasn't pleased with Mr. Glair either. Cole hadn't caused any trouble in class. I think Mr. Glair disliked him simply because Cole was so good-looking. I'd noticed he tended to pick on the more attractive boys in class. It was as if he resented them or was jealous of them. Or, perhaps he was attracted to them and had a love-hate thing going. I noted that he never picked on me. Mr. Glair was forty or so and not attractive. I guess I could understand his jealousy, but I thought it was rather unprofessional to give students a hard time because he was envious.

Like most days at B.H.S., this one was uneventful, but time passed quickly. I attended classes, hurried through the halls between periods, and had lunch with my skater buddies. Okay, so it's not much to tell about, but it was fun, and that's what's important.

Cole's presence not only improved the scenery by an incalculable percentage, but added drama to our quiet little school. After lunch I spotted him in a back hallway making out with Josh Lucas' girlfriend. If Josh ever found out... I didn't even want to think about the consequences. Perhaps Cole didn't know he was making out with Josh's girl. I made a mental note to warn him. He did not want to mess with Josh. Cole had plenty of troubles without getting on that boy's shit list.

The sight of Cole lip-locked with a girl did not improve my mood. I didn't like the visual confirmation that Cole liked girls. I was gonna be left out in the cold. My lips would never touch his lips. Even if Cole was gay, I wouldn't have had much chance with him. A boy like Cole could definitely land a much hotter boy than me. Hot! That's a laugh! I was barely lukewarm.

I made it a point to catch Cole after school. I loitered around my locker until he showed up at his. A couple of cute girls were trailing him, of course.

"Cole, can we talk for a sec?" I asked.

"Sure thing Daniel."

The girls looked at me, as if seeing me for the first time. I guess they thought that anyone Cole spoke to was worth noticing.

"I'll see you girls later," Cole said, stuffing his books into his locker. "I need to have a word with my bud here."

The girls walked away disappointed.

"So, what's up?"

"I wanted to warn you. That girl you were making out with after lunch? Sherry? She is Josh Lucas' girlfriend and he's a much bigger badass then either Adam or Mike. He will mess you up if he finds out you touched his girl."

"I live for danger," Cole said, laughing.

"I'm serious!"

"You worry too much Daniel. I can take care of things. Trust me."

"Well, I wanted to warn you."

"Thanks. I do appreciate it. Hey, I've got a half hour to kill. Wanna hang out?"

"Yeah!" I said, far too enthusiastically. "I'm mean, yeah." Cole grinned.

"Let's get some ice cream. My treat," Cole said.

"You don't have to do that."

"Hey, I'm in your debt. I always pay my debts."

A few minutes later, we were sitting in Merton's Ice Cream Parlor. We shared a huge banana split, and I was in heaven. I fantasized that Cole and I were on a date.

"This place is so cool," Cole said, gazing around.

"Oh, yeah. That's right. I keep forgetting you're new to Blackford. Merton's has been here forever." I pointed to the "Established 1901" on the window, which appeared backwards since we were inside.

"I don't think they've changed anything since then," Cole said.

"I don't, either."

"So, does anything exciting ever happen here?" Cole asked.

"Hmm. Not really. We did have this kid from the UK going to our school for a few weeks. He was a nut case, and he was hilarious. The jocks tagged him as queer."

"Oh, so I guess he received a daily beat-down?"

"No. Every time the jocks did something to him, Cedi struck back. He painted Josh Lucas' car pink."

Cole laughed so hard I thought ice cream might come out of his nose.

"Are you serious?"

"Yeah."

"Didn't he get his butt kicked for that?"

"Well, Josh beat him up once, but that didn't stop Cedi. He retaliated. That may have been why he painted Josh's car pink. I can't remember what happened then. Anyway, Cedi made peace with most of the jocks, and he and Chase even became friends. Chase is a football player too. Most of the jocks were plain scared of what Cedi would do if they messed with him."

"I'm sorry I missed out on that."

"Yeah. I miss him. I didn't know him well, but he was entertaining. He sat in your desk in literature."

"Perhaps my desk is haunted by Cedi."

"If it is, I'm sure you'll be hearing crazy laughter."

"I heard someone talking about a school ghost," Cole said. "Is that true?"

"Wow, my friends and I were just talking about the ghost recently. Back when I was in the sixth grade, some of the older kids tried to scare us with stories."

"Yeah?"

"Yeah. The story is that a kid hanged himself in the hallway that leads to the gym. I forget why. For a long time I was scared to walk down that hall, but it's just a story. The seniors probably made it up to scare the middle-school kids."

"I don't know," Cole said. "Now that you mention it, I seem to remember my dad telling me about a kid who hanged himself way back."

"How would he know?"

"My grandparents lived in Blackford. I think Grandfather went to school here when that boy killed himself."

"Really?"

"I think so. It's been a long time since Dad told me."

"Wow. I didn't think there was anything to it."

"I don't know anything about a ghost, but I'm almost sure Dad told me about a hanging. A boy hanged himself in the back hallway that leads to the gym."

"Do you remember why the kid hanged himself?"

"No. I just remember he did. I guess that was the last excitement around here."

"I can do without that kind of excitement."

"Yeah, me too, but it makes you think, doesn't it? A kid actually hanged himself right in our high school."

"Great. Now I'll be freaked out every time I walk down that hallway. It's going to be the sixth grade all over again."

"Sorry."

Cedi

"Thad!"

I ran across the backstage area and jumped into Thad's arms. He had no choice but to catch me. Well, he could've let me fall on my bum. Knowing Thad, he just might have, but he didn't! I resisted the impulse to kiss him, not because we were no longer a couple, but because no one could know what had passed between us. Well, almost no one.

"I see you haven't changed. Get off me, you little monkey."

"Aww, I missed you too Thad."

"When the hell are you leaving? I thought you were going on tour, not hanging around here forever."

"I know you love me," I said. I hugged Thad around the middle.

Thad hugged me back. Yeah, he loved me, even though he didn't like to admit it.

I felt a bit of sadness creeping in, but I refused to let it gain a foothold. Thad and I were about to go our separate ways, but that's how it had to be. Besides, I could still annoy him long distance.

"Thanks for coming to watch me!" I said.

"Watch *you*? I came for cotton candy. I didn't even know you were performing this evening."

"Liar. You know the park is closed."

Thad smiled.

"Good luck, Cedi—not that you need it."

"You know, I have you to thank for this. You're the one who volunteered me to step in for Kieran when he got hurt."

"Don't thank me. It's all just part of my master plan to get rid of you so I can get my work done."

"Sure it is Thad."

"Five minutes guys!" Jordan yelled.

"I guess I've gotta go."

"I'll see you after the show Cedric."

"You can count on it."

An announcer was out front revving up the crowd. Their screams were already deafening. Ross nodded his head in time with a beat only he could hear. Jordan gave Ralph a quick kiss on the lips. This was it; my first time on stage as an official, if temporary, part of *Phantom*. I was so excited I thought I might pee my leather pants.

The crowd chanted *"Phantom, Phantom, Phantom"* and there was even an occasional "Cedi" in there. It was unreal. A little part of me feared it was all one big dream, but no dream went on for days.

The screams of the crowd became deafening—or would have if I hadn't been wearing an earplug in one ear and an earphone in the other. I found myself being pushed through the curtain. We must have been announced, but I didn't hear it. I ran to my guitar as Ross hopped into his seat behind the drums and Jordan grabbed the microphone.

"How are you all this evening?" Jordan asked.

The crowd screamed.

"I see a lot of familiar faces out there."

More screams. The lights partly blinded me, but I spotted a few familiar faces myself. Thad was standing off to one side of the stage, as was Toby. I caught a glimpse of Orlando and Eddie in the crowd. Krista, Chase, and others from school were there too. I also spotted a *really* cute guy. I'd never seen him before, but what a hottie!

I suddenly realized Jordan had spoken my name. I was so lost in my own thoughts I don't know what he said before that, but the crowd screamed for me. I gave a blast on my electric guitar and did an impromptu dance on the stage.

"Now let's get started!"

Ross began a beat by tapping his drumsticks together over his head. I glanced down at the set list taped to the floor, even though I knew good and well we were singing *Jump, Jump, Jump* first.

The three of us began to play, and we were off. *Jump, Jump, Jump* was a crazily fast-paced, intense song that kept my fingers flying. The keyboard sections seemed physically impossible to play, but Jordan did it as if by instinct. Ross was a wild man on the drums, but that shocked no one. The crowd went crazy, and Jordan had the lot of them jumping up and down in time with the music. I sang the words as if I'd known them all my life. The truth was it was a new song I'd heard for the first time only two days before. The guys were impressed I picked it up so quickly.

The song left me breathless at the end. I was glad we were doing the calmer *I Love That Kind of Love* next.

As we played song after song, I forgot about standing on stage with *Phantom*. I forgot that I was replacing my idol. I became lost in the music and the screams of the crowd. As night came on, I could make out fewer and fewer faces. Finally the lights blinded me completely, but I could hear the fans out there, cheering and shrieking and singing. It was a blast!

Kieran came out and sang *Deep in the Darkness*. The crowd went nuts when they spotted him. I shared their enthusiasm. Kieran was bloody awesome.

Deep in the Darkness was a ballad with a slow-paced rhythm. Jordan had often sung it in the past, but Kieran had made it his own. I was in a dream-like state as I listened and played. I almost couldn't believe I was standing so close to Kieran. I couldn't believe I actually knew him! My life had become a fantasy.

The very last song of the concert was *Do You Know That I Love You* with my new violin sections. The crowd went crazy and kept shouting my name. It was such a rush! I seriously felt as if I could fly.

And then it was over. Jordan, Kieran, Ross, and I ran backstage, pulling off our headsets. I was drenched in sweat. The white wife-beater Kieran wore clung to his muscular body so tightly it was as if he wasn't wearing a shirt. I found myself staring. Part of me wanted to run over and rip the shirt right off him, but I controlled myself.

Toby grinned at me when I looked away from Kieran. He'd caught me, no doubt about it. I smiled back and wiggled my eyebrows as I approached. I hesitated to hug him because I was sweaty and likely smelly, but Toby grabbed me and hugged me.

"You were incredible, Cedi!"

"Thanks!"

Ross passed by, slowing down only to give me a thumbs-up and slap Toby on the back.

A few fans were allowed backstage to meet the band. Some girls I sort of recognized from school squealed with delight as I autographed CDs and posed with them for photos. I seemed to remember those same girls hounding me for Jordan's autograph. Now, they were after mine.

It felt truly bizarre standing with Kieran, Jordan, and Ross signing photos and posing for pictures with fans. It was going to take me a good deal of time to get used to being a part of *Phantom*.

When the little group of fans was led away, I looked up and spotted Thad. He looked just as he did the first time I met him—tall, dark, and mysterious. We didn't have time to speak before *Phantom's* bodyguards escorted us across the park to the flat. Soon, we were safely tucked away in the top floor of the Graymoor Mansion. I was alone with Thad, Kieran, Jordan, Ross, Toby, and Ralph. I wondered if I'd ever grow accustomed to being around Kieran, Jordan, and Ross—if I'd ever lose the sense of awe I felt in their presence.

"Great show Cedi," Kieran said.

"Yeah, you were awesome man! Almost as good as me!" Ross yelled.

Kieran rolled his eyes.

"We have someone in once a week to deflate his ego," Kieran said.

"You did a tremendous job tonight Cedi," Jordan said. "You're not only talented. You're a professional."

"If you guys keep it up, you'll need someone in to deflate *my* ego," I said.

"Yes, please don't encourage him," Thad said. "He's full of himself as it is."

"Oh, we're used to handling big egos," Jordan said, giving Ross a meaningful glance.

"What?" Ross asked with a feigned look of innocence.

"Pizza's here," Kieran's bodyguard, Rod, announced as he entered.

"Yes!" Ross and I yelled simultaneously.

"I don't envy you the coming weeks," Thad said to Jordan, never taking his eyes off Ross and me.

Ross and I stuck out our tongues at Thad, then laughed.

"Good lord. They're twins," Kieran said.

"Great minds think alike!" Ross said.

"What minds?" Ralph asked.

"Hey!" Ross said.

"Is that your snappy comeback Ross?" Kieran asked.

"Screw you guys. I'm having pizza," Ross said in a rather good South Park Cartman impersonation. Ross was so cool.

We all sat around the table talking while devouring pizza and drinking sodas. Toby couldn't keep his eyes off Jordan, Kieran, or Ross. He especially had a thing for Jordan. I could read him like a book.

I began to grow extremely tired as we sat there. Nearly two hours on the stage had taken a lot out of me. While I was up there performing, I had felt as if I could go on forever, but now that it was over I felt as though I might doze off and fall face-first into my pizza.

"I think I'm heading to bed," Jordan said after a bit. "Don't forget guys, we leave tomorrow at 9 a.m."

The party broke up. Everyone was tired.

"See you tomorrow Cedi," Ross said.

"Yeah, see you guys."

"I guess this is goodbye for a while," Kieran said. "I'm leaving for Tulsa tomorrow."

"Yeah, he's going to abandon us and spend time with his woman," Ross said.

"When will I see you again?" I asked. I didn't want to part from my idol.

"I might join you guys on the tour, but that largely depends on Natalie's schedule. If you don't see me during the tour, you will after."

"They aren't even married yet and she's already got him whipped," Ross said.

"Go to bed Ross!"

"He likes to order me around," Ross said conspiratorially. "It makes him feel manly, so I play along."

Kieran shook his head.

"I'll give you two a ride," Thad said to Toby and me.

"Thanks," Toby said.

Mike, Jordan's bodyguard, escorted us across the deserted park to Thad's Viper.

"Wow. This is a sweet car," Toby said.

I'd forgotten Toby had never ridden in Thad's sports car.

"You never did let me drive it," I said.

"That's because I never suffered from brain damage. Let you drive this car? Forget it. You'd probably drive it on the wrong side of the road."

"Are you insulting my ethnic background? We British are great drivers!"

"No. I'm saying only an idiot would trust you with a $90,000 car."

"What did I ever see in him?" I asked Toby.

"Oh, I can think of a few things!"

"Have you got your eye on my man?"

"No!"

I giggled. I loved to see Toby flustered.

Thad had the top down, and the wind blew through my hair. I was exhausted but so excited I could hardly contain myself. The moon shone down upon us from above. The whole world looked mystical in the bluish light.

Thad pulled up to Toby's house first.

"Damn, I'm going to miss you!" I said. "You have my cell-phone number, right?"

"Oh yeah."

"Good, don't hesitate to ring me. I may need the sound of a familiar voice when we're on the road."

"I'm sure you'll get along fine, but I'll call."

"Bye Toby. Thanks for everything."

"You too. Bye Cedi. Thanks for the ride Thad."

"Have a good night Toby."

Toby climbed out, closed the door, and walked toward his home. Thad pulled away. It was just the two of us now.

"I guess this is it, huh?" I asked.

"Yes. Tomorrow you begin your great adventure."

"You know I'm still kind of pissed at you for dumping me, but... I'm also grateful."

"You would not have been happy if you had stayed here, Cedi."

"I know. You're right, but I don't like leaving you."

"We'll stay in touch."

"Will we? Isn't that just something couples say without meaning it when they break up?

"It is, but when I say something, I mean it. God help me, but I have become rather fond you Cedi."

"I kind of get into your system, don't I?

"Like a virus."

"Funny!"

Thad pulled up in front of my aunt's house. I slid across the seat and hugged Thad. He hugged me back.

"I love you," I said.

"I love you too, you little punk."

I kissed Thad lightly on the lips, then climbed out of the car. Thad drove away. I stood there and watched until his taillights disappeared. I turned toward home with tears in my eyes.

Toby

I checked out Daniel as he skated up to the school. He looked so sexy and cool with his brown hair flowing out behind him. When he hopped off his board his hair fell down into his eyes. He continually had to flick his hair off his face. He reminded me of C.T. in that respect. C.T. was a boy I'd met while working at Phantom World. He was the most stereotypically gay boy I'd ever met—only he wasn't gay. Anyway, Daniel shared C.T.'s habit of flicking his hair. I wanted to grab him and kiss him.

One step at a time, Toby Riester.

I grinned. I was actually happy. The mere possibility that Daniel might be gay and might be interested in me was enough to bring me back to life. True, I had no evidence to support either of the possibilities, but when you're in the middle of a desert, you don't pass up a chance at water. Even if it turns out to be a mirage, you've gotta try.

"Hey."

I looked up at the sound of the familiar voice. Orlando gazed at me. No doubt he'd caught me checking out Daniel, but that didn't matter. It was the first time Orlando had spoken directly to me since our breakup.

"Hey."

Orlando motioned with his head, and I followed him a short distance so that no one could overhear us.

"Listen, um... I just want to say I'm sorry and..."

"We've been all through this, Orlando. We said everything that needed to be said when you broke up with me. I don't want to talk about it anymore. I'm trying to put our breakup behind me."

"I noticed." Orlando gave Daniel a significant glance and grinned slightly. "Personally, I think you should try for the new boy, Cole."

We stood in silence for a few moments. Words didn't come easily.

"I've missed you Toby. You have every right to be angry, but..."

"I want us to be friends," I said, cutting him off.

"Really?"

"Really. Listen. I'm still angry. I'm definitely still hurt, but I've been thinking. I miss talking to you and confiding in you. I don't like what happened. I don't like what you did. I can't change what has happened, and neither can you. I'm just going to accept it and go on. A part of me wants to forget about you, but most of me remembers the good times. We can never again be as we once were, but we can have... something."

"Something sounds good." Orlando looked as if he might cry.

"Yeah. It does."

"Um, has Krista said anything about me?"

"What do you mean?"

"Well, she once threatened to rip my balls off if I hurt you, and... I hurt you."

"If she hasn't done it already, I think you're safe. I'll tell her to leave your nads alone, just in case."

I smiled sadly. It was too soon to joke with Orlando. There was too much pain in my heart.

"Well, um... I'd better get to class. Thanks Toby. I'll see you later, okay?"

"See ya."

I watched as Orlando walked away. Some might think I was too forgiving. Maybe that was true, but I felt better inside. I'd made the right decision.

Orlando was my past. Daniel was hopefully my future. I wondered how I could get closer to him. I knew he was interested in skating, but I was not talented on a skateboard. There was our shared interest in drama. Daniel was in my eighth-period drama class and had been in the cast of *Peter Pan*. Perhaps I could suggest we practice together for our auditions as I had with Orlando. It was our shared interest in drama that gave me some small hope that Daniel preferred guys. The theatre was supposedly full of gays. It didn't necessarily follow that everyone involved in theatre was gay. That was a stereotype, and I knew how wrong *those* could be. Still, I was willing to grasp at any small bit of hope that came my way.

Cole crossed my path between classes. The sight of him nearly took my breath away. I had terrible trouble concentrating in literature with that hottie sitting beside me. Cole made me drool. I wanted to rip his shirt off and lick him all over. I had the feeling that most of the girls were just as eager to use him as a human lollipop.

Cole had more than looks. He was always ready with a smile. He had not been around long, but he was always kind to me. A guy that good-looking could have easily been stuck up. That's what I'd truly expected when I first laid eyes on him, but Cole had quickly dispelled that notion. As interested as I was in Daniel, I couldn't quite get Cole out of my head.

While it was unlikely that Daniel was interested in me, it was even more doubtful that Cole would go for me. The chances of success with Cole were practically zero, but I saw no reason not to try to get a little closer to him. Just being near Cole was a thrill.

I was hot for two boys. I was on the prowl again. I felt as if I was coming back to life. Sitting and wallowing in self-pity hadn't been good for me. Maybe, just maybe, I'd bag myself a boyfriend. I certainly wouldn't get one if I waited for him to fall out of the sky.

Orlando and I greeted each other in the hallways between classes. That also made my life seem a little more normal. The pain of our breakup wasn't over for me, but it had dulled, and I was ready to go on. At lunch, Orlando and I actually carried on a conversation with each other. Krista and Eddie did not fail to notice.

I was certain that Eddie especially was relieved that Orlando and I were on speaking terms again. Eddie was Orlando's best friend. He had remained my friend too. I'm sure being caught in the middle wasn't easy. Eddie was a rather remarkable guy. Most people didn't give him the credit he deserved. They dismissed him as a stoner, but he wasn't a stoner—not anymore.

I looked over at Daniel. He was deep in conversation with his skater buddies. Auddie sat next to him as always. There were rumors that Daniel and Auddie had something going. I hoped it wasn't true. Somehow I had to enter Daniel's world. I had to get closer to him and test the waters. Krista caught me looking at him and grinned. I was willing to bet she knew exactly what I was thinking.

Daniel

Girls swarmed over Cole as soon as he walked into school, fawning over him and showering him with sympathy. A black eye and a bruise on his cheek marred Cole's handsome face. He walked with a limp. I noted the smirk on Josh Lucas' face as he eyed Cole. There was little doubt that Josh had kicked Cole's butt. Perhaps Adam and Mike had helped. I wished Cole had listened to me.

I got a better look at Cole during Lit. Josh had really done a job on his face. The thing was, Cole was still the hottest boy around. The black eye only served to make him look tough. Cole didn't seem fazed by the beating. If anything, he had a mischievous sparkle in his eye somewhat reminiscent of Cedi.

I looked across Cole toward Toby, who sat on his other side. Toby was also kind of cute. Sometimes I wondered about him...

***

My skater buddies were mysteriously absent during lunch, leaving our table looking lonely and desolate. On a whim, I changed course and sat down next to Toby. Auddie followed me.

"Hey," Toby said.

"Hi."

"Did your friends desert you?" Eddie asked, looking over at the empty skater table.

"Yeah, I think they must be off partying without me."

Toby's friends, Krista and Orlando, smiled to let Auddie and me know we were welcome. I had classes with all of them and they were a generally a pretty cool group.

I gazed down at my tray—a corn dog, applesauce, mashed potatoes, green beans, a no-bake cookie, and chocolate milk—not bad for a school lunch, but then not the best either.

"Hey, does anyone know anything about the ghost?" Toby asked.

"Ghost?" Auddie asked.

I stared at Toby for a few moments. Why was everyone talking about the school ghost all of a sudden?

"I heard some kids talking about it before lunch," Toby said.

"That's nothing but a made-up story," Auddie said. "The seniors are stirring things up to scare the younger kids again."

Krista looked a little lost, but then I remembered she was new this school year.

"This is too weird," I said.

"What is, Daniel?" Toby asked.

"Cole and I were talking about the ghost recently. I kinda thought it was a made-up story, but Cole said his grandfather went to school here way back. Cole's dad told him that a boy did hang himself here—in the hallway that leads to the gym."

"Really?" Toby asked.

"This I've never heard," Auddie said. "Was he serious or pulling your leg?"

"He was serious."

"We have yet another reason to avoid the jock's lair," Eddie said. "Maybe that's why they're all so weird."

"Not half as weird as you, Eddie," Orlando said.

"Thank you."

"Has anyone, like, seen anything weird?" I asked.

"I'm seeing something weird now Daniel!"

I looked up and swallowed hard. Josh Lucas stood over us with his tray, grinning evilly. Butterflies took flight in my stomach. Josh Lucas intimidated the hell out of me. We'd never had a direct confrontation, but he was always on Ian's ass and I was waiting for him to turn on me.

"We were talking about the ghost," Auddie said.

"Ghost?" Josh asked. "You guys are messed up."

"A kid hanged himself near the gym," I said, trying to keep my voice from shaking. "Years ago."

"Yeah, right! I've heard that story before. Why do I even bother with you geeks?"

Josh went on his way. I breathed a sigh of relief. I'd half feared he'd spotted me with Cole and was going to kick my butt too.

I gazed a couple of tables over at my dream boy. Cole was surrounded by his harem. He was banged up, but other than a sneer shot in Josh's direction he seemed his usual cheerful self.

After lunch, I heard other kids talking about the ghost. I guess I shouldn't have been surprised. Rumors spread like wildfire at B.H.S. Even when the news was nothing more than who was breaking up with whom, everyone knew about it in minutes. Suddenly, all the old stories were going around, many of which conflicted. The tale of the school ghost had been circulating for years. During that time, it'd been embellished and altered. Who knew what parts were true and what parts were nothing but fiction?

"Do you think a boy really did hang himself?" I asked Auddie after school as we once again walked home together.

"Maybe, maybe not. Even if that story is true, it doesn't necessarily follow that there's a ghost. My great-grandmother died in our house, and there's no ghost."

"Yeah, but I bet she didn't hang herself."

"No, she didn't. Just because someone dies violently doesn't mean they come back as a ghost. I'm saying that the hanging, even if it did happen, wouldn't automatically result in a ghost."

"Do you believe in ghosts?" I asked.

"I neither believe nor disbelieve. I won't say they don't exist, but I've never seen one."

"I kind of believe in them, but I'm not sure. This whole thing has me curious. I think I'll go to the library and check out the story about the hanging."

"Maybe you can at least get a report out of it for English," Auddie said.

"Hey! That's a great idea!"

"It would give your otherwise-useless endeavor a purpose."

"It won't be useless, even if I don't write a report. It will satisfy my curiosity. It's like... reading a book for fun."

"Well, you'd know all about that, wouldn't you? I hope your books never fall on you. You'll be crushed in the avalanche."

I grinned and shook my head. "I don't suppose you want to come to the library with me?"

"No thanks, but you have fun Daniel."

"I will!"

"Boys," Auddie muttered as I turned and headed back downtown.

I was excited as I walked toward the library. Yeah, I know what you're thinking—I'm a geek, right? If I am a geek, at least I enjoy it. Too few people enjoy their lives so I count myself lucky. I'm the lucky geek! Yay!

I started out with *The History of Blackford, Indiana*. I'd read parts of it before, although I could recall no mention of a hanging. The book was in the reference section and couldn't be checked out, but I wouldn't need it that long. It was published in the 1960s, but surely Cole's grandfather had lived here before then.

The index had no listing for hanging, suicide, or ghost. I can't say I was surprised. I began to skim a chapter called, "Crime and Disaster in Blackford." Predictably, it wasn't a long chapter, but I was surprised to discover that the bank had been robbed three times! The most recent robbery was in 1933, and there was even a shootout on Main Street. How cool is that?

Finally, I found what I was seeking. The chapter mentioned a hanging in 1953, but the details were rather sketchy. According to the book, Martin Wolfe, a student at B.H.S., hanged himself in the high school. A student discovered his body. That was it. That was all the book said.

I was somewhat disappointed, but Cole's story had been verified. The history book said nothing specific about where Wolfe's body had been discovered, but he had hanged himself in the school.

The newspaper!

I hurried to the reference desk and asked the librarian for the 1953 volume of the *Blackford Chronicle*. Our local newspaper was a weekly. The volume was thick, but not impossible to search. I skimmed the front page of each issue. Surely a suicide wouldn't be shoved to the inside columns.

I found what I was seeking on the front page of the January 28th issue. There was a photo of a plain-looking boy. I gazed at him for a moment and an eerie feeling came over me. I was looking at a boy who was now dead. I turned my attention to the article.

Blackford Chronicle—Wednesday, January 28, 1953

LOCAL YOUTH TAKES OWN LIFE

Sixteen-year-old Martin Wolfe, the son of Mr. & Mrs. Frank Wolfe, was found dead in the early morning hours of January 22. Wolfe's death has been deemed a suicide.

Wolfe's body was discovered in a hallway of Blackford High School. Kurt James, a B.H.S. student and baseball player, made the grisly discovery. He arrived before school and found Wolfe's body hanging in a hallway near the gym. "I wasn't sure what to do," James said when interviewed shortly after the discovery. "A few kids were showing up, so I sent one for help while I stayed to keep others back. It's not a sight anyone would want to see. I wish I hadn't." The hallway was roped off and Wolfe's body was removed a short time later.

The official cause of death is believed to be a broken neck. "Wolfe's body was found hanging from the rafters with a noose around his neck," said Town Marshal Bill Sheridan. "A chair lay on its side under the body. There is little doubt this was a suicide."

No one seems to know why 16-year-old Martin Wolfe took his own life. "Martin didn't attract much attention to himself. He rarely volunteered in class, but he was a hard worker," said Mrs. Elma Kendall, B.H.S. literature teacher. "Some of the other boys picked on Wolfe at times, but not much more than they picked on others," Coach Douglas said when interviewed. "He was a quiet kid and not much interested in sports. He mainly kept to himself. I can't claim to have known him well, but he was never any trouble." The citizens of Blackford join the Wolfe family in their grief.

The wake was held at the Wolfe Farm on January 22nd and 23rd. Burial was on January 24th in the Blackford Cemetery, following a short service at the Blackford General Baptist Church.

At last I had hard facts. A boy, Martin Wolfe, had hanged himself in our school, just as Cole had said. Why he might have taken his own life was a mystery. The story behind the ghost was true, but as Auddie pointed out, that didn't prove the existence of a ghost.

***

The next morning I spotted Cole speaking quietly with Ian. It was a peculiar sight. The hottest boy in school was hanging out, however briefly, with the school's scariest Goth. The contrast between the two was striking. Cole looked like a young Abercrombie & Fitch poster boy, while Ian was dressed all in black, wore a spiked collar around his neck, studded leather bracelets on his wrists, earrings, and black makeup around his eyes. I watched the odd couple for a few moments, but even as I did so their conversation ended and they went their separate ways. Cole headed in my direction.

"Guess what?" I said.

"What?"

"I checked out that story your dad told you and it's true! A boy hanged himself here in 1953. It's in the local history book and in the newspaper."

"You actually went to the library and looked it up? You must be interested in ghosts."

"I'm interested in everything! I spend a lot of time in the library."

Cole laughed. A lump rose in my throat. For a moment I thought he was laughing at me. The very thought was torment.

Cole looked at me with a slightly worried expression on his face, but I smiled and managed a small laugh. I was hypersensitive with Cole. I needed to knock that off or he was going to realize just how badly I was crushing on him.

"So... have the jocks been giving you any more trouble?" I asked, changing the subject.

"If looks could kill, I'd be dead." Cole laughed.

"I don't think you're taking this seriously enough. Those guys will hurt you, Cole. When I was in the sixth grade, there was a boy a grade ahead of me, Caleb Fulton. Adam, Mike, and especially Josh made his life miserable. Others guys were in on it too, but those were the main bullies. Caleb was chubby, wasn't into sports, and acted kind of girly. He was a natural-born victim, and those guys were on his butt twenty-four/seven. The things they did to him..."

I stopped and stared at Cole. His lower lip trembled slightly and tears welled up in his eyes. My heart swelled with love for his compassion. He was beautiful on the inside as well as the outside.

"What happened to Caleb?" Cole asked.

"He burned to death in a fire. It was horrible. His whole family was killed. They lived in a trailer. The fire burned so hot it melted the aluminum siding on the house next door. There was almost nothing left of the bodies."

"That's horrible."

"Yeah. I was afraid to go to sleep at night for a long time. We live in a house, but I kept thinking about Caleb burning to death in that trailer. What a horrible way to die."

"I heard that most people who die in fires suffocate from the smoke. Maybe Caleb and his family suffocated in their sleep, and then the fire burned their bodies."

"I hope that's the way it happened. It would be a much better way to go."

"Yeah."

"Anyway. Before he was killed, Caleb's life was a living hell, and all because those jerks were on his butt. You need to make peace with them. You don't want to go through what Caleb did."

"Do you think Josh and the others had anything to do with the fire?"

"No.   They like to beat on kids and make their lives miserable, but I don't think they would stoop to arson.   I remember Mom and Dad saying they figured faulty wiring started the fire.   Caleb's family was really poor.   They lived in a decrepit trailer, so that's probably how the fire started.

"Caleb didn't have much of a life.   Whenever I start feeling sorry for myself, I think of Caleb and realize my life is pretty good."

"Of course your life is good Daniel.   You're awesome!   Damn, we'd better run or we'll be late for class."

Cole took off, but I stood there for a moment.   Cole Fitch said I was awesome!   Was this a dream?   Was I going to wake up soon? If it was a dream, I wanted to make out with Cole before the dream ended.

***

The next couple of days passed in a blur.   As much as I liked school, I enjoyed it a whole lot more with Cole around.   Not only was he totally dreamy to look at, but he was actually nice to me!

I was never one to care much about popularity, but I found that I was becoming more popular by association.   Cole said "hi" to me in the hallways.   He stopped at my locker and chatted with me. Classmates had spotted me in Cole's convertible and with Cole in Merton's Ice Cream Parlor.   People began to notice me and it was odd how much nicer they were than before.   I'd never been a social outcast, but I had been on the fringe.   I was definitely not one of the cool kids.   Now, the cool kids were beginning to say "hi."

Toby paid more and more attention to me, but I don't think it was because of Cole.   Toby and I were slowly getting to know each other better.   The more time I spent with him, the more I liked him.

Cedi

My alarm awakened me at six. Yuck! Only budgie birds should get up so early. I reminded myself that I was up early to spend time with Aunt Liz before I took off. Who knew when I'd be back? Not for months, certainly.

I stumbled down the hall in my wife-beater and boxers. A horrid name for a shirt, isn't it? Anyway, I entered the bathroom, stripped, and took a shower. I didn't truly need one for I'd showered after Thad dropped me off the night before, but I loved to bask in hot water and get all soapy. I thought of the shower as my own private little spa.

I padded back down the hall with a towel wrapped around my waist and then dressed in the clothes I'd set out the night before. I glanced around at my room, taking in my posters of *The Beatles*, *Phantom*, and the Union Jack. It hadn't been my room for long, but I'd miss it.

There was no reason to let myself get sad. Life was too short to waste a moment. As Aunt Liz said, live like your bum is on fire. I've adopted that as my personal motto.

I followed the scent of bacon, fried bread, and beans into the kitchen. I arrived to find scones and crumpets as well. A pot of hot tea already rested on the table. Aunt Liz had gone British for our last breakfast together. We usually had American fare. Well, we usually didn't eat breakfast together at all. Aunt Liz had her life and I had mine.

"Good Morning Aunt Liz."

"Good Morning Cedi. Have a seat. Breakfast is almost ready."

"You've gone all out this morning."

"I thought you might like a taste of home before you depart."

"I think of Blackford as my home now."

"You can have more than one home Cedric."

"I suppose so. Do you miss England Aunt Liz?"

"Sometimes. Whenever I do, I go for a visit."

"Do you see Mum while you're there?"

"Of course."

"I thought you two didn't get along all that well."

"We get along fine Cedi. We're merely different sorts of people, that's all."

"Are you sure I'm not your son? You didn't give me over to Mum and Dad to raise, did you? I'm so much more like you than them."

"I'm afraid not Cedi. I would be proud to have such a son, but I'm just as proud to have such a wonderful nephew."

I smiled.

"You know, I never thought of it before, but I should have spent more time with you," I said as I bit into my fried bread.

"You're a free spirit, like me. True, we haven't spent much time together, but hasn't what time we've had together been fun?"

"Most certainly!"

"Well then, there's no reason for regret, is there?"

"I guess not."

We were silent for a few moments.

"These cranberry scones are excellent," I said. "Everything is, but I like these the best."

"I thought you might like some before you left. I doubt you'll be getting any on your tour."

"I doubt it too. The guys say our tour will be hectic. I think they largely survive on food from Burger Dude."

"Sounds like fun."

"I'm excited."

"I'm sure."

We sat, ate, talked, and sipped hot tea. I was going to miss Aunt Liz, Toby, Chase, Krista, and, of course, Thad. Who would have thought I'd feel so much at home in a foreign town I'd only lived in for a few weeks? I planned to return here after the tour, but who knew what was to come? I certainly couldn't have predicted the events of the last weeks.

"We'd better go if we're going to be on time," Aunt Liz said after we'd lingered over the table for a good long while.

I stood and gave Aunt Liz a hug.

"Thanks for everything."

"Thank you for sharing your life with me."

We walked to the car, and Aunt Liz drove me to Phantom World. A huge bus sat in the parking lot. Luggage was already being loaded in the compartments underneath.

Aunt Liz and I got out. We opened the trunk, but before I could pull a bag out, Mike, Rod, and Shawn, *Phantom's* bodyguards, had grabbed all my stuff and carried it toward the bus. I was left with only my backpack slung across my shoulder.

Aunt Liz and I hugged again.

"Have fun," she said.

"Oh, I will! I'll call."

"Your room will be waiting when you're ready to come back."

I nodded. We hugged again and said our goodbyes. Aunt Liz climbed back in the car and departed. I walked toward the bus where Jordan and Ralph milled around.

"Right on time," Ralph said. "We keep a tight schedule on tour. Our only problem is usually..."

"Ross!" Jordan yelled. "Hurry up!"

"...Ross," Ralph finished, grinning.

Ross came racing toward us in a golf cart so loaded down with luggage I thought the bottom might scrape the pavement. The cart swayed and swerved as if driven by a drunkard.

"Ross, why do you always take so much stuff?" Jordan said. "We almost need another bus just for your junk."

"My own bus! Good idea!"

"Forget it. Now get your stuff loaded."

"He's so bossy," Ross whispered to me loudly. "If we were the Peanuts gang, he'd be Lucy for sure."

Perhaps it was just my imagination, but the bus looked bigger than a normal passenger bus. Perhaps it was because there were so few windows. The bus was a beauty—royal blue on chrome.

"Everybody ready?" Jordan asked.

Ross, Ralph, Mike, Jordan, and I climbed onto the bus. Rod and Shawn got into a big black sedan. The sedan fitted perfectly with their Secret Service look. They wore clothes that allowed them to blend in with the rest of us, but their dark glasses and little earphones made them stand out. I was still getting accustomed to the bodyguards. What was really going to take some getting used to was having my own. Rod had been assigned to me while Kieran was on holiday. Apparently, there had been some argument about the need for a bodyguard for Kieran while he was away from the band, but he won out. I'm sure he didn't want a bodyguard around when he was with his fiancée. Talk about lack of privacy! I wondered how I would get on with Rod. I wasn't accustomed to being shadowed.

"This is Luke. He makes sure we get where we're supposed to be on time," Jordan said, introducing me to the bus driver.

"Hi! I'm Cedi!"

"Nice to meet you Cedi."

We moved on.

"Let me give you the grand tour," Jordan said. "This is the front lounge. We usually hang out here most of the time."

I looked around. The front lounge was part lounge, part kitchen. There was a large built-in booth with enough room for six at least, a sink, fridge, microwave, toaster, and coffee maker. There was also a television with a VCR/DVD player and satellite-dish hookup. The lounge was surprisingly roomy, but then again, the bus was pretty big.

"Here is the bathroom," Jordan said, showing me what looked more like a closet in a corner of the lounge than anything else.

"And this," Jordan said, opening a sliding door at the rear of the lounge "is the sleeping area. There are twelve bunks in all."

At the foot of each bunk was a combination TV/VCR/DVD player, a phone, an iPod, and an alarm clock.

"Ross described his bunk as a coffin when Jordan showed me around," Ralph said.

"Hmm, perhaps with satin sheets... I could lie on my back at night holding lilies!" I said.

Ross grinned.

The bunks weren't very big. I'd say a little over six feet long and two feet wide. I wondered how well I'd sleep in mine.

"And finally," Jordan said, "the back lounge."

The back lounge had a couch, table, wide-screen TV, VCR, DVD player, stereo, Playstation II, Xbox, and all kinds of video games and DVDs.

"It's like a luxury hotel on wheels!" I said.

"I'm glad you like it," Jordan said. "You'll be spending a lot of time here. We spend the night in a hotel whenever possible, but quite often we have to drive through the night to make it to the next venue on time. Well, Luke has to drive. We ride."

I could feel the bus moving. I looked out the window and saw the homes and businesses of Blackford slipping by the windows. A touch of homesickness fell upon me. I'd left Great Britain without the least regret, but a part of me didn't want to leave the dinky little Indiana town I'd come to think of as home.

"So, where are we playing in Indianapolis?" I asked as the lot of us made our way to the front lounge.

"The Murat, which is pronounced moo-ra. It's a really cool venue," Jordan said. "We'll be in the Egyptian room. It's decorated with an ancient-Egyptian motif."

"How long will it take us to get to Indianapolis?" I asked.

"Not long. Two and a half, three hours tops," Ralph said.

"We need to go over the set list for tonight," Jordan said. "Once we hit Indy we'll be busy. We have an interview at one of the local radio stations scheduled at 1:00, followed by a signing at 1:30. After that, we drop by a local TV station to tape an interview. As soon as that's finished, we need to head to the Murat for the sound test. Then, we have a meet and greet at 6:00, and the concert begins at 8:00. Somewhere in there we'll grab a bite and hopefully have time for a little rest, although there's no guarantee we'll manage it."

"Sounds like fun!" I said.

"Just remember that sleep is a luxury on tour," Jordan said. "If you're tired, grab a nap wherever you can because who knows when you'll get to bed."

"I don't need sleep!"

"You will."

"Okay, about the set list. We try to hit our most popular songs at every concert. Those are the songs the fans mainly come to hear. We also try to mix it up as much as possible because a lot of fans will come to more than one concert."

"Yeah!" Ross said. "A few of them will follow us for the entire tour! Mainly because they love *me*!"

"Yeah, sure, Ross," Jordan said.

Ross glared at Jordan with pretend hatred, twitching his left eye as if he had a nervous tick. I might have believed he was really angry had it not been for the slight smile on his lips.

"I think you guys should do the Cedi version of *Do You Know That I Love You* at all the concerts," Ralph said.

"Yeah, I was thinking that too," Jordan said.

"We have been playing that song for *years*," Ross said. "Your additions make for a nice change."

Wow. They were calling it Cedi's version. Who would've thought?

We got down to work on the set list. Even Ross paid attention, although he constantly drummed with pens, pencils, and then his fingers after Jordan took his pens and pencils away. The others took my suggestions seriously. They made me feel like a part of the band.

After we finished the set list, we split up for a little quiet time. Jordan assured me that time to myself was something I'd come to value. There would be precious little of it once the tour began in earnest.

Ross took off for the back lounge. I decided to check out the comfy factor of my bunk. I slipped off my shoes and climbed in. The mattress was surprisingly comfortable, and there was enough room to sit up if I wanted to watch TV. I stretched out and closed my eyes, listening to the gentle whir of tires on pavement. The bus was rather quiet, which was a surprise. Actually, the whole bus was a lot nicer than I expected. I didn't even want to think about what it cost.

I must've drifted off, because some time later Ross shook me awake.

"Come on Cedi! It's time for lunch."

"Where are we?"

"Very near Indy. We're making a rare stop at a real restaurant. Usually we get everything to go. We tend to get mobbed if we go inside."

"So why is this one different?" I asked.

"Ralph says it's an old-people restaurant. It was his suggestion to stop. Mike advised against it of course, but we convinced him it would be okay."

"An old-people restaurant?"

"Yeah. It's called the General Store."

"You do have odd names for things over here," I said.

I followed Ross to the front lounge. The bus was just pulling up near a large wooden building. A porch ran the length of the front. Sitting all along the porch were old-fashioned rocking chairs.

"Stay here," Mike ordered. "I'll check things out."

"He thinks he's a Secret Service man," Ross said when Mike had gone. "Sometimes he's a bit too serious."

"Everyone is too serious for you," Ralph said.

Ross grinned.

Mike was back soon.

"Rod and Shawn are getting us tables next to each other. "You behave yourself," Mike said, pointing to Ross.

"Me?"

Ross put his hand to his chest looking as if he was amazed anyone would think he could cause trouble. I couldn't help but grin.

We exited the bus and entered not a restaurant but a store with all sorts of... I guess you'd call it nostalgic stuff. Ross veered off toward a candy display until Jordan grabbed his shoulder and kept him with the rest of us. Ross looked back at me and mouthed, "Later."

There were two large dining rooms divided by a partial wall. I could see what Ralph meant by this being an old-people restaurant. Customers our age were almost nonexistent. Most were in their forties and up. Most of the diners had probably never heard of *Phantom*. Even if they had, there was precious little chance they'd recognize Jordan or Ross. No wonder it was safe for us here.

We passed by a huge stone fireplace. A fire blazed and popped inside.

"This place is wicked," I said.

Jordan, Ralph, Ross, and I were led to one table, while Mike, Rod, Shawn, and Luke took the one next to it. I opened one of the menus.

"Oh! Breakfast!" Ross said too loudly.

Our waitress arrived for our drink orders. She was a friendly, older lady with black hair. She lacked the southern accent I had grown accustomed to in Blackford. I guessed people spoke differently up north. It was like that in Great Britain. Each region had its distinctive accent. A few had their own language.

I decided on the Grandma's Pancake Breakfast, partly because the name was funny and partly because I could get blackberry topping. The breakfast came with bacon and eggs. I had mine scrambled. Some of the others also ordered breakfast, while some ordered lunch.

"See, I told you," Ralph said to Mike, probably commenting on the fact no one was giving us a second look.

Ralph spoke a bit too soon. A loud squeal caused heads to turn in the direction of a family who was being shown to their table. A girl in her mid-teens was gawking at Jordan and Ross with her mouth hanging open. The girl's family and most of the others in the restaurant stared at her as if afraid she was having a seizure.

"Kara, calm yourself," her father ordered.

Kara stood and gaped at us. Her slightly older brother looked supremely embarrassed.

"Jordan, I told you that you were too ugly to be allowed in public," Ross said. "You've scared that poor girl."

Jordan ignored him. He stood and walked over to the girl and her family.

"Hi. I'm Jordan."

"Oh my God! Oh my God!" Kara said.

"What's going on?" Kara's mother asked.

"That's *Phantom*," the boy said. "Don't you recognize them from the posters plastered on Kara's walls?"

Kara was in the midst of a meltdown. Everyone in the restaurant stared at her.

"I'm your biggest fan!" Kara said, finding her voice at last.

"It's nice to meet you Kara."

Jordan extended his hand and Kara shook it. I had the feeling Jordan had dealt with similar situations lots of times. He was cool and calm.

"I'll be right back," Ralph said and then disappeared.

Ross also went over to talk to Kara. I half expected him to jump at her and yell "boo," but he kept himself under control. Kara was actually crying as she talked to the guys. I'd seen girls screaming over *Phantom* on TV, but this was the first time I'd seen one lose it in person.

I remained seated because I figured Kara didn't know who I was, but I joined the others when Kara spotted me and shouted "Cedi!" Ralph returned carrying a large photo.

Jordan and Ross signed the photo and then it was my turn. I wasn't in the photo as there hadn't been time for a photo session yet, but I signed a huge "Cedi" on one side.

We returned to our seats. A lot of people were looking at us and no doubt talking about us now. Kara's table was several feet away from ours, but she kept looking at us the whole time we were there.

Our food arrived and it was delicious! Jordan, Ross, Ralph, and I laughed and talked. A few people came up to us while we were eating and asked for autographs for grandkids. Ralph had anticipated them. I hadn't noticed when he returned, but he'd come back with a big envelope full of photos. The older people that approached us were far calmer than Kara. I watched carefully as Jordan and Ross spoke with them. I was still learning the ropes.

After our meal, Ross and I hit the candy section. There were all kinds of stuff I'd never seen before. Ross and I loaded up, much to the chagrin of Jordan.

"We should never have had kids," Ralph said, teasing Jordan.

"Hmm. I'm thinking boarding school," Jordan said as he looked at Ross and me.

"No way!" I said. "Been there! Done that! Got booted!"

In minutes, we were back on the bus headed to Indianapolis. In about an hour our bus pulled up outside a radio station.

"Whoa!" I said as I looked out the window. There was a huge queue outside one of the entrances.

Mike, Rod, and Shawn wouldn't let us out until they'd talked with the station's security. Then we were quickly escorted inside as girls screamed at us. It was Kara times a thousand. I wasn't prepared for it.

Once inside, all was calm. We were led to a booth where we met the radio announcer. We were fitted with headphones and mics. We sat for a couple of minutes and then we were on the air.

"Today, we have *Phantom* with us live," said Dirk, the interviewer. "Joining us are Jordan, Ross, and the newest member of *Phantom*, Cedric. We'll get to questions from listeners in just a minute, and remember, *Phantom* will be signing autographs right here at the station after the interview.

"Cedric, what's it like to become a member of such a successful band?"

My voice caught in my throat. I expected my participation in the interview to be minimal. Jordan and Ross were two of the most famous rock stars in the whole world and I was merely the new kid on the block.

"It's a bit overwhelming, especially since it was rather sudden. There's a lot more to being in a band than I ever imagined. I've been a huge *Phantom* fan for as long as I can remember. Jordan, Ross, and especially Kieran inspired me to become a musician. Actually performing with them is wicked!"

"We, on the other hand, have to adjust to Cedi's bizarre language," Ross said. "He claims to speak something called English, but he keeps using words like wicked, ghoulish, and rahther. He also has a disturbing obsession with drinking hot tea, but we've grown to like him."

Ross grinned at me.

"What's been the most difficult aspect for you so far, Cedric?"

"Getting used to the fans. I'm not accustomed to girls screaming at me. As we walked into the station, I couldn't believe how many fans were waiting outside and how excited they were. Of course, I think they were excited to see Jordan and Ross, not me."

"No! They were excited to see just *me*!" Ross yelled. "The babes love me! Who would get excited over Jordan?"

"Jordan, how does the band feel about having Cedric join *Phantom*?"

"We think of him as a pet!" Ross said loudly. Jordan smacked Ross over the head with a roll of papers. I couldn't help but laugh.

"We're very excited to have Cedric join us. As you know, Kieran was injured shortly before the start of our tour. Kieran will be fine, but he won't be able to play for several weeks. Cedric is more than a mere stand-in. He's bringing new life into *Phantom*. Tonight, we'll be playing a new version of *Do You Know That I Love You* that has some unique Cedi additions."

"So, will Cedric be staying with the band after Kieran returns?"

"We haven't discussed that, but it's certainly a possibility. Cedi is a very talented musician. Any band would be lucky to have him."

I smiled.

"Now, let's get to some questions from our listeners. First, we have Kay from right here in Indy. What would you like to ask *Phantom* Kay?"

"This question is for Cedi. Do you have a girlfriend?"

Jordan mouthed, "I told you so."

"No. I'm not dating anyone right now. This probably wouldn't be the best time to date. The guys tell me our tour schedule will be hectic, and from what I've experienced so far, they aren't exaggerating."

"Our next question is from Samantha, who is from Muncie."

"Cedi, your accent is soo sexy. You're from England, right?"

"Well Samantha, I like *your* accent. Until a few months ago, I lived my entire life in Great Britain. I love it here in the States. I've met some great people and made some really close friends."

"Now we have Bethany from Bloomington."

"My question is for Ross."

"It's about time! I thought this was the Cedi Hour!"

"Ross, Jordan is taken, and Kieran just recently announced he's getting married. Will you be following in their footsteps, or do you plan to remain single?"

"I'm staying single! It wouldn't be fair to deprive all those hotties out there of the chance to date me!"

"Do you date fans?" the next caller asked Ross.

"Sometimes, but it's very difficult to make a close personal connection with fans. When we're on tour, we're often running from one event to another. There isn't a lot of time to get to know anyone."

"Now, we have a question for Jordan from Detrick."

"Jordan, are you still dating Ralph? I haven't seen much about the two of you on TV lately. If you're not still dating him, do *you* date fans?"

Jordan grinned.

"Ralph and I are still a couple. We're committed to each other just the same as if we were married. Hopefully, the good and decent people of this country will speak out and demand that couples like us be allowed to legally formalize our relationship. As for dating fans, Ralph was a fan, but he's the only fan I ever dated. Ralph and I met many years ago after a concert in Fort Wayne."

The questions continued. One was about Jordan's hair. He rolled his eyes when he heard it. Other questions were about the tour, when the next CD would be released, and when Kieran would be coming back. The interview seemed to end almost before it started, and we were escorted to a large room where a ton of fans was waiting. They screamed and cheered as we entered.

I took a seat between Jordan and Ross. Ralph immediately took charge and got the line moving. He gathered photos, CDs, and calendars from the fans and passed them to Jordan, who signed, and handed them off to me. I signed and passed them on to Ross. I listened to Jordan and watched him out of the corner of my eye as he interacted with the fans. It didn't take me long to pick up his technique of talking to each fan while signing. I noted that Jordan made sure to look each fan in the eye, if only for a few moments. I tried to make sure I did too, but it took a while to get the hang of it. Each fan had only seconds with each of us, but there was enough time to have a mini-conversation.

I figured most of the fans wouldn't know who I was, but each seemed excited to meet me. Maybe they were worked up over Jordan and Ross or maybe they were excited by the fact I was a part of *Phantom*. Whatever the reason, I was psyched! I could barely remain in my seat, but there wasn't time to leave it even for a moment. I sure hoped I didn't need to pee before the signing was over.

I was amazed at how fast the line moved. That's the way it had to be if we were going to sign for everyone. There were hundreds of fans!

My hand began to ache and my signature grew a bit shaky as we continued. I didn't know how Jordan and Ross did it! I knew I was going to get a cramp, but it was wicked fun! If this was what it was like to be a rock star, I was in!

We actually managed to sign an autograph for every single person before we had to run for our TV interview. When I say run, I mean it. The three of us actually sprinted to the bus and then sped across town. The interview was to be taped, but we had to stay on schedule.

The TV reporter asked us some of the same questions we received in our radio interview, along with others about the future of *Phantom*. The TV interview felt a bit more formal because we were on camera and couldn't goof around as much while we were talking. Of course, Ross jumped from his seat a few times and spent a good deal of his time drumming with his fingers, pencils, and anything else he could reach.

Next, we were driven to the Murat, which looked like no other building I'd seen in Indianapolis. It had an Arabic look that seemed out of place and yet was beautiful. The concert wasn't for hours yet, but there was already a huge queue outside. When the fans spotted our bus, they waved and screamed. Some of them followed us around the back.

Jordan, Ross, and I signed a few autographs as we walked in, but we couldn't stop and sign for everyone. I felt a bit bad about it, but we had work to do. Jordan noticed my frown as we entered the building.

"You won't always be able to give the fans the time they want. If we did, we wouldn't have time to be musicians."

"It just seems... I don't know. It would make them so happy if we could pay some attention to them."

"Their demand is greater than our supply. Just do the best you can Cedi. Sometimes a smile or a quick "hey" is enough. It lets them know we appreciate them and that we care. It would be cool if we could spend time with each fan, but there aren't enough hours in the day. We've got to have some time for ourselves too, or we'll go crazy. Hmm, maybe that's what happened to Ross."

"I heard that!" Ross yelled.

We were escorted to our dressing room first. It was to be our base of operations while we were in the Murat. Getting out to the bus would be too difficult with all those fans around.

"Ohhh, candy!" Ross said and ran straight for a bowl of M&Ms.

"Peanut M&Ms! I love those!" I said.

There was a fridge stocked with Cokes. Ross and I each grabbed one.

"Just what they need," Ralph said. "Sugar."

"Come on kids. Let's see if the crew has everything set up," Jordan said.

"Yes, Daddy!" Ross yelled. I giggled.

Jordan knew his way around the Murat, but then *Phantom* had performed there more than once. The Murat was stunning! I loved the stained-glass windows and all the intricate decorative details. What I saw on the way was nothing to what awaited us in the Egyptian room. Wow! There were ancient looking Egyptian friezes up near the ceiling far above, big stained-glass chandeliers with scarabs, and Egyptian figures and decorations everywhere.

"Dudes!" said a voice I recognized.

"How's it going Chad?" Jordan asked.

"She's all set up. Ready for the test?"

"That's what we're here for."

As we approached the stage, I noticed our instruments were already waiting on us.

"How did the road crew have time to do all this?" I asked.

"They likely got in this morning," Jordan said. "The crew often travels separately from us. It's not unusual for them to arrive hours before we do. When the schedule is tight, as it often is, they'll arrive at a venue when we do. While we're out doing interviews they're doing the real work. It takes a lot of time to set all this up. Luckily, we have Chad. He's a genius with sound equipment."

He's kind of hot too. I checked out Chad's nice bum as he walked away.

We'd done a sound test at Phantom World, so I was clued in to the process. First, we each tested our instruments. My guitars and violin were all in perfect tune. Jordan said Chad tuned the instruments before each concert if he had the time. He also told me Chad had perfect pitch. I believed it.

"Hey, guys!" Jordan yelled.

I looked up and spotted three guys in their early to mid twenties coming up onto the stage. One had long black hair, a lot like that of Ross. The other two had super-short, brown hair.

"Cedric, I'd like you to meet York, Sammy, and Izzy," Jordan said, pointing first to the guy with long hair and then to the others. York plays the keyboard. Sammy and Izzy play electric and bass guitar."

"Nice to meet you Cedric," Sammy said. "I hear you're a kick-ass guitarist."

"I try."

The other guys shook my hand.

Most people barely noticed, but most bands had background musicians playing when they performed. A second keyboardist, drummer, or guitarist could add a depth to music not possible with a single player on each instrument. The presence of York, Sammy, and Izzy explained the great number of instruments on stage. There was a single drum set, but there were two keyboards and nearly a dozen guitars, plus two violins. I was the only violin player, but there was always a backup on hand for each instrument—just in case.

Chad powered up the sound equipment, and each of us took a turn to make sure our instruments checked out. I loved hearing my electric guitar blare over the sound system.

"Okay guys, let's do *Chamber of Secrets*," Jordan said when all of us were ready.

Ross began a beat, and we started to play. At first, something didn't sound quite right. I looked at Chad as he messed with knobs and sliders. Whatever was wrong went away. Sometimes, one instrument became louder than the others, but that was only Chad checking out his boards. The sound test was mostly for him instead of us. Sam was busy as well. She and Chad worked together like a well-oiled machine.

We played through three songs before Chad was satisfied that all was in order.

"What's up next?" I asked as I followed Jordan and Ross from the Egyptian Room.

"We actually have time to eat," Jordan said.

We walked back to the dressing room where Ralph awaited us holding several bags from Burger Dude.

"Yes!" Jordan said. "This is one of the many reasons I love you Ralph."

"I thought it was because he has a tight..."

"Ross!" Jordan warned.

Ross looked at me and grinned.

"The Prince of Rock & Roll is easily upset sometimes," Ross said.

"Shut up Ross," Jordan said, with only a touch of anger in his voice.

Kieran and Ross had told me how they and the crew tormented Jordan with the title of The Prince of Rock & Roll. He hated it, but he couldn't do much about it. I wasn't going to utter the title until I knew Jordan a good deal better.

I didn't possess Jordan's obsession for Burger Dude, but the burgers and fries were bloody good. Perhaps I wouldn't have liked them quite so much if I wasn't famished, but I devoured three.

"I'm going to take a short nap," Jordan announced when we'd finished eating.

"You're getting old Jordan," Ross said. "We'll have to put you in a home soon."

"Yeah, right. If anyone is going to a home, it'll be you checking into a mental ward."

The mischievous gleam in Ross' eyes was intriguing.

"I'll join you," Ralph said.

"Oh!" Ross said, turning to me. "That means they aren't going to nap. They're going to f..."

"Ross!" Jordan warned.

Ross grinned innocently.

"What?"

"Stay out of trouble," Jordan said, pointing at him.

"Me? Get into trouble?"

I laughed. Ross was the very picture of innocence, but I knew what a devil he was supposed to be. It was one of his many attractive features.

"Cedi and I will hang out here. I'll show him around the Murat for a while so you guys can... nap."

Jordan shook his head. He and Ralph departed for the bus, followed closely by Mike.

"Come on Cedi, I'll show you the sights. You guys can stay here if you want. No fans are allowed inside the building. We'll be safe," Ross said to our bodyguards.

"We'll tag along anyway," Rod said.

I wondered if our bodyguards had noticed the wicked gleam in Ross' eyes. He was up to something, or at least so I thought. Ross led me around inside the Murat, pointing out stained-glass windows, paintings, carvings on columns, and other features of interest. The Murat was a warren of large halls and rooms. There was even a full-sized theatre. The Murat could host at least three concerts all at once!

Our bodyguards let their guard down as Ross continued acting like a museum docent. When Rod and Shawn had trailed further behind than ever and were talking between themselves, Ross grabbed my arm and pulled me forward at a quickened pace. We turned a corner, and Ross broke into a sprint. I raced after him. We slid around another corner, down a flight of stairs, and along another hall. Our bodyguards had caught on and taken up the pursuit, but we were younger and faster. I laughed as I ran. I knew Ross would be fun!

Ross made for the New Jersey Avenue entrance, the very one all the fans would be entering later—the very one where hundreds were lined up right now. I laughed even louder. We were about to create chaos.

Ross bolted out the door yelling like a madman. I was a split second behind. We ran right into the astonished crowd and kept on going. The fans waiting were so shocked they parted for us.

"Oh my God! It's *Phantom*!" yelled someone.

"Ross!" yelled others.

There were squeals of delight from girls. Ross and I ran down the line extending our hands to touch those extended by the fans. Shawn and Rod bolted out the entrance and raced after us.

"Gotta go!" Ross yelled.

We raced around the side the building. Several of the girls ran after us. I was momentarily afraid they might catch us, but Ross and I were both excellent sprinters, and we had a head start. We raced around the building to the next entrance. Our plan was to dart inside, but we had to wait while we were buzzed in. We were nearly captured by a small crowd of girls.

Rod and Shawn caught up to us. They were not happy.

"Ross!" Shawn said in warning.

"Come on, man. You know I make your job interesting."

Shawn did his best not to smile. He looked as if he was about to give us a lecture, then decided it was pointless.

Only about a dozen girls had chased us all the way around the building, so Ross opened the door and invited them in. We had a meet and greet coming up soon, so Ross and I made use of the table and stack of *Phantom* photos. We signed photos for each of the girls and talked to them for a good half hour. Jordan and Ralph returned. Jordan signed the photos for the girls, and they were squealing with delight when they departed.

"I hear you guys went for a little run," Jordan said.

"We needed some exercise!" Ross yelled.

"Yeah!"

"You're a bad influence Ross. You're corrupting Cedric," Ralph said.

"I was corrupted when I arrived! Let's go again!"

Rod's hand clamped down on my shoulder, and Shawn closed in on Ross.

"You've got a meet and greet in fifteen minutes," Mike said.

There were about two dozen fans for the meet and greet. It was great fun signing photos for them. I could really get used to this being-famous thing! Running through the crowd outside was such a rush! Talking to excited fans was way wicked. I couldn't wait to get up on the stage.

Ross and I devoured M&Ms back in the dressing room after the meet and greet. While we were loading up on sugar, *Dragonfire,* our opening act arrived. The name made me think of hard rock, but Jordan told me they were a young pop group. He wasn't kidding about the young part. Drew, Daniel, and Drake were thirteen, fourteen, and fifteen. As you might have guessed from their names, they were brothers. Their last name was Dragon, so the name of the group made sense.

All three brothers were little cuties. The girls would go nuts over them for sure. Each was slim and had curly black hair and brown eyes. I'd never heard them sing, never heard of them at all in fact, but they had talent or they wouldn't be opening for *Phantom*.

"I'm so nervous," Drake said.

"You're going to be fine," Jordan said. "It's not as though you haven't performed before."

"It's the first time we've performed in front of over a thousand people," Daniel said. "This isn't like singing at the water park."

"You big babies! Suck it up!" Drew, the youngest, said.

I smiled. I immediately liked Drew.

"Just get out there and do your thing guys," Jordan said. "Don't worry about the crowd. As soon as they hear you, they'll love you. I guarantee it."

"If you get too nervous, just picture the audience in their underwear," Ross said.

"Bad plan," Drew said. "If those two start thinking about half-naked girls, they'll forget the words for sure!"

"There'll be boys in the audience Drew. You might forget some words yourself," Drake said, grinning.

"I'm the family homo!" Drew said, shaking my hand. "Nice to meet you!"

I laughed. I really liked this kid. He was slightly obnoxious, boisterous, and fearless. He was like a little me. A mini-me!

"I like this boy," Ross said.

"I'm not into older men, so just forget it," Drew said totally deadpan as he looked up at Ross. His toothy grin a moment later made him cuter than ever.

There was no more time to talk. We were whisked away backstage. There was a lot more activity right before the concert than there had been at Phantom World, or maybe I was just more aware of it. It took a surprisingly large number of people to run all the lights and sound equipment. Everyone scurried around in what looked like total chaos, but Jordan and Ross seemed completely unconcerned.

The minutes rolled by. *Dragonfire* was introduced to enthusiastic cheers as I paced backstage. They began to play and I immediately understood why they were opening for *Phantom*. Those boys were wicked talented! I loved the way Drew's high-pitched singing voice cut through the others. It created a unique harmony I'd never heard before. I would've sung with those guys any day.

I stepped over and watched from the wings. I was surprised to see Drew at the keyboard. For some reason, I had him figured as a drummer, but Drake pounded away at the drums while Daniel played the electric guitar. Those boys really knew their instruments. They might be young, but they had talent.

Dragonfire played for forty-five minutes, so I had plenty of time to pace. I was eager to get out there and do my thing. I'd played with Jordan and Ross before, but there was something special about the first official concert of the tour.

The crowd went nuts when *Dragonfire* ran off the stage. Drake, Daniel, and Drew gleamed with sweat. All three were grinning.

"I told you guys you'd be great," Jordan said. "Good job!"

"Yeah, you were awesome!" Ross said.

"Wicked!" I said.

There was still some time before we went on. The crew had to take away *Dragonfire's* instruments and bring ours to the front. The waiting was soon over and Jordan, Ross, and I ran out onto the stage to deafening cheers. The next hour and a half was wicked bliss.

My fingers danced over the strings of my electric guitar, seemingly moving by their own free will. I sang into the microphone and listened to Ross, Jordan, and the background musicians through my earphone as our voices and instruments merged together to create a whole greater than the sum of its parts. Creating music was magical.

The bright lights were unbelievably hot, and sweat ran down my forehead and into my eyes. No wonder so many performers wore headbands. I slung my hair around to whip off the sweat and kept right on playing and singing.

I was wearing a wife-beater at Jordan's suggestion, and I was glad I'd taken his advice. I'd noticed Jordan almost always wore one on stage and now I knew why. Standing under those lights, I understood what it must be like for burgers under the heat lamp at Burger Dude. The lights had been hot at Phantom World, but there we performed outside in the cool fall air. I wasn't prepared for the heat bearing down upon me now.

I sweated up a storm and had a blast! I was meant to perform! The hour and a half we performed went by in a flash.

After the concert, I felt as if I could fly. The crowd loved the new version of *Do You Know That I Love You*, but then again, they loved everything.

Our next venue was in Fort Wayne, which I was told was a drive of only a couple of hours or so. We were herded onto the bus right away because we were spending the night in Fort Wayne instead of Indy. For some reason, Jordan and Ralph seemed to have a special attachment to the place.

Drew, Daniel, and Drake joined us on the bus. They would be riding with us for the rest of the tour, and that was fine by me. We guzzled soft drinks and devoured M&Ms and talked excitedly about the concert. I grew tired, but there was little use in going to bed. We'd be in Fort Wayne in less than two hours, and I'd just have to get up again to go to my hotel room. Besides, it was too fun hanging out with the guys. I felt as if I was at summer camp.

I was so sleepy by the time the bus rolled to a stop in Fort Wayne that I could hardly keep my eyes open. I followed the others inside and hardly knew what was going on until the door to my room was being opened. I stumbled inside and fell face down on the bed. I kicked off my shoes and in moments, I was fast asleep.

Toby

I slammed my locker shut. The metal rang loudly, but no one noticed, because everyone else was slamming the doors to their lockers too. It was just after lunch and students reluctantly headed back to class.

I spotted Daniel at his locker. I took a deep breath and approached. I stood there for a moment unable to speak, shifting my weight from one foot to the other.

"Hey, Daniel, um... you want to hang out after school?"

"Um, sure," Daniel said. "What do you want to do?"

Yes!

"Oh, I don't know. We can go to my house and listen to CDs or something."

"Cool."

I smiled. I hoped I wasn't grinning like an idiot.

"I'll catch you after school then."

"Sounds..."

"Get off me!"

Daniel and I both turned at the sound of Ian's voice. Mike Bradley had him pushed up against a locker about halfway down the hallway.

"Uh-oh," I said. "We'd better do something."

"Yeah, but what?"

I shrugged my shoulders, and we both walked toward Ian and Mike. Neither of us had the slightest idea of how we could save Ian from Mike Bradley. Mike was as big as Daniel and me combined.

"You're gonna be sorry you messed with me," Ian said as we neared. "You're gonna be very sorry."

Shocked, Daniel and I jerked to a halt. Ian *never* spoke so boldly. He barely spoke at all. When Mike or another bully picked on him he stared at the floor and didn't utter a word. Daniel and I looked at each other, then back at Ian and Mike.

"And what are you gonna do about it? Huh? Freak?"

Mike slapped Ian's cheeks as he spoke to him. He slapped him hard. I could hear the palms of his hands connecting with Ian's cheeks even from a distance.

Ian stared straight into Mike's eyes.

"You've been warned," Ian said.

Ian's voice was menacing, as was his glare. Daniel and I were frozen in place and unsure of what to do.

"I'm not afraid of you, freak," Mike said. He pulled Ian away from the locker and slammed him back into it again before walking away. Ian stared at his back with hatred.

"Shit, are you okay Ian?" asked Daniel as we closed in.

"Yeah."

There was an awkward silence for a moment. I forced myself to speak.

"Hey, um, we're going to my house after school to hang out and do whatever. Would you like to join us?"

"Thanks, but no thanks. I have something to do." Ian stared down the hallway in the direction Mike had gone.

"Well, we'll see you later," Daniel said.

Ian nodded.

"That dude kind of scares me," I said when Ian was out of earshot.

"Ah, he's cool when you get to know him."

"He's so quiet. He's kind of... strange. I don't mean that as an insult, but I don't know how to act around him. He freaks me out."

"Asking him to hang out with us was very nice of you," Daniel said.

"Well, I know he's your friend, and he's obviously having a rough day..."

"You're a nice guy Toby."

"Shhh, don't spread it around. You'll ruin my reputation as a bad ass."

Daniel laughed out loud, and so did I. The image of me as a bad ass was just too funny.

I became serious once more.

"I heard some kids talking. They say Ian is a witch."

"Don't listen to that. It's stupid. People say that because he dresses in black all the time."

"I guess you're right."

"Of course, I'm right! I'm Daniel Peralta!" he said as if that explained everything.

I laughed again.

"Well, Daniel Peralta, you'd better get your butt in gear or you'll be late."

"Yeah, see you after school Toby."

"I'm looking forward to it."

***

"I'm starving," I said as Daniel and I walked away from the school.

"Want to get something to eat before we go to your house?"

"Yeah!"

"Hmm. A&W or Café Blackford?"

"Since we don't have a car let's go to Café Blackford. Drive-ins aren't nearly as fun without wheels."

"Should I buy a car?" Daniel asked. "I could get one so we can go to the drive-in."

"Um, that won't be necessary."

"Not that funny huh?"

"It was okay."

"I'll work on my material."

I shook my head. I *really* liked Daniel. He had an understated goofy quality to him that I found appealing. He was also rather cute. He wasn't a pretty boy like Cole, and he didn't have the hottest build, but he sure wasn't hard on the eyes. I daydreamed about kissing him as we walked side by side.

"Maybe we should have invited Auddie along," I said.

"Hmm, first you invited Ian, now you mention Auddie. Are you afraid to spend time alone with me Toby?"

The truth was I wanted Daniel all to myself, but I was afraid for him to know that. I wanted him in the worst way, but I had no idea how he felt about me.

"No, it's just that you and Auddie seem really tight. Are the two of you... more than friends?"

"No. It's not like that between us. She's my best girl friend, but not my girlfriend. Actually, she's my best friend period."

"Oh, okay, cool."

"What about you and Krista?" Daniel asked. "The two of you seem close."

Was he asking because he hoped Krista and I weren't a couple? Was Daniel interested in me? *Please, please, God, let him be interested in me.*

"Oh, yeah, we're close. I worked with Krista all last summer at Phantom World."

"But are you... *really* close."

"No. We're just friends, like you and Auddie."

"Cool."

He said cool. *Yes!* It wasn't much, but it was something. I stole a look at Daniel. I wanted to grab him and kiss him. Hmm. I've said that before haven't I?

We stepped into the warm, inviting atmosphere of Café Blackford. I couldn't remember when I first stepped inside, but it hadn't been what I was expecting. It seemed more like someone's living room than a café. In addition to the small tables and comfortable chairs, there were armchairs here and there, lots of books on shelves, and interesting old stuff like tins that tea and coffee came in back in the olden days. The fire in the fireplace was especially appealing in the colder months.

"This place always reminds me of Café Nervosa on *Frasier*," I said.

"Hey, it does, doesn't it? I'd never thought of the *Frasier* connection."

"Do you watch that show?" I asked.

For answer, Daniel took an imaginary handkerchief from his pocket and pretended to dust off the chair before sitting down.

"Niles!" I said.

"That's Dr. Niles Crane, thank-you-very-much," Daniel said. He even sounded like him.

I laughed. "I never thought you'd be into *Frasier*."

"Why not?"

"Well, you're a skater. You guys don't seem to be into *Frasier* kind of stuff."

"Oh, I'm not a skater. I'm a poseur."

"Hey, I've seen you skate. You're awesome!"

"Thanks!

"Hey, do you remember that episode where Frasier and Niles wanted to watch *The Antiques Roadshow*, but Martin told them they couldn't because he wanted to watch his game show?"

"Yeah! It turned out to be the same show! Martin tells Frasier and Niles his game show is one where people bring stuff in and experts tell them if they've won or lost—if their stuff is worth a lot or if it's just junk! That was hilarious!"

Daniel and I were getting along really well. He was smiling and laughing. Maybe this was the start of something.

"I am having French toast with blueberries," I announced after browsing the menu.

"Hmm, there doesn't seem to be any filet mignon or caviar on the menu, so I might have that as well," Daniel said in his not-too-shabby Niles voice.

"That's really good!" I said. "I still can't believe you watch *Frasier*. Almost no one our age is into it."

"I don't know why I can do his voice. I just can. I don't get many opportunities to use it. I tried it once on Ian and the guys, but they didn't get it. They told me I sounded gay."

Both Daniel and I grew quiet and, for my part at least, a bit uncomfortable at the mention of the G-word. *Does he suspect me?*

"I love all the trouble Frasier and Niles get into over the most meaningless things," I said to ease the tension.

"Yeah..."

Our conversation trailed off. I couldn't think of what to say. My mind was still back on the G-word. Daniel was cool, but I wondered if he would still want to sit with me if he knew I had a HUGE crush on him.

The waitress arrived and we ordered. We continued to talk about *Frasier*. We talked about how Adam, Mike, and Josh were jerks. We talked about Ian and the rumor that he was a witch. We talked about all kinds of things.

The French toast was awesome! There was no surprise there. Café Blackford—Café Nervosa, as Daniel and I now called it—was known for excellent food. Perhaps Frasier and Niles would have found the food there too common for their tastes, but we weren't the Crane brothers.

We talked for a good while after we finished eating. I enjoyed chatting. To be honest, I was thrilled just to be near Daniel. The sight of him made my heart race. I hardly dared to hope... but I did hope that there could be something special between us. My hopes had been dashed so often in the past that I was almost afraid to hope again.

Daniel and I walked to my house after we left the café. Unfortunately, my little brother was in the bedroom when Daniel and I entered.

"This is Mackenzie," I said. "Just try to ignore him. I do."

Mackenzie stuck out his tongue. Mackenzie was wearing a blue flannel shirt. The shirt was open, revealing most of his taut, tanned torso. My little brother was far hotter than I was, a fact that was a source of great embarrassment for me. He had a six-pack and muscular pecs. I wasn't sure, but I thought Daniel was checking him out. My heart beat faster. Maybe Daniel was attracted to guys. A horrifying thought entered my head. What if Daniel was gay but was attracted to Mackenzie instead of me? I relaxed almost immediately. Mac was pure hetero. I had nothing to worry about there. I went back to hoping that Daniel was indeed gay.

I began flipping through my CDs while Daniel sat on the edge of my bed.

"Please. No! Not *Phantom* again," Mackenzie said.

"Mackenzie has an aversion to good music."

"Yeah, you just go on believing that," Mackenzie said.

"I'll spare you this time. I want Daniel to hear *Uff*."

"*Uff*? Daniel asked. "Sounds Scandinavian."

"No, they're a Venezuelan boy band. They're awesome. They played at Phantom World."

"Yeah, Toby loves the *boy* bands," Mackenzie said.

I shot my brother a dirty look. I wasn't quite ready to come out to Daniel. I wasn't sure it was safe.

"Most of *Uff*'s songs are in Spanish, but they sound great," I said. "This is their second CD, *Ufforia Latina*."

I handed Daniel the CD cover and popped in the CD. The music began to play.

"Hey, they're good," Daniel said.

"Yeah. I have no idea what most of the songs are about. I'll skip up to *Angel del Mal*. It's one of my favorites. As far as I can figure, the song title translates to *Bad Angel*. Word for word it translates as *Angel of Bad*. I laughed.

I gazed around my room as we listened to the music. I became nervous. I had posters of *Phantom* and other pop groups. What would Daniel think of my shirtless Aaron Carter poster? Was there a more obvious way for a teen boy to say, "I'm gay!"? I looked at Mackenzie's side of the room. His walls were a complete contrast. Posters of more mainstream rock bands and swimsuit models dominated.

Maybe the gayness of my side of the room wasn't such a bad thing. I was interested in Daniel. I could hardly approach him without revealing my sexual orientation. I wasn't ready to say it out loud, but maybe exposing Daniel to my posters of sexy boys would make the eventual moment of coming out easier for me.

"This music is really good," Daniel said.

"Thanks!"

From the tone of his voice, I think Daniel really did like the songs and wasn't just being polite.

"You'll probably like Gil Ofarim too. Ever heard of him?"

"No."

"He's German, and he's got a great voice. Here, I'll put on one of his CDs."

Mackenzie started to say something, but I stared him down.

"So, you like foreign groups?" Daniel asked.

"Some, but I got into *Uff* and Gil Ofarim by way of *Phantom* and *Hanson*."

I handed him the case for Gil's CD while I switched discs.

"Hey, Gil looks kind of like Jordan from *Phantom* and Taylor from *Hanson*."

"Yeah, I've noticed that. I think it's the long, blond hair."

"Hey, this is very good," Daniel said as Gil began to sing a song called *Bandstarter*. "I thought he might sing in German."

"No. He sings in English."

"Cool."

"What other groups do you like that are probably unfamiliar to me?" the cute skater boy sitting on my bed asked.

"Hmm. I love the *Moffatts*. They're really cool. Then there's Billy Gilman. You might have heard of him. I only like his Christmas CD because he sings country. Let's see... *Dreamstreet* is cool. Jesse McCartney and Greg Raposo are both really good. They were in *Dreamstreet* before the band broke up. They're actually better singing alone. I think that's it for bands you're unlikely to know."

I played songs from a lot of my favorite groups. I had an awesome time with Daniel, and we did nothing more than hang out in my bedroom and listen to music. Mackenzie made several smart-ass comments, but he mostly behaved himself. He probably knew I had a crush on Daniel, but he wasn't evil enough to say anything about it.

Daniel yawned. It was beginning to get late. I don't know how many CDs we'd sampled, but I'd played a lot of different songs.

"I should probably be getting home," Daniel said.

"I'll walk you."

"Aww. Yeah Toby, walk your boyfriend home," Mackenzie said, laughing.

"Sometimes he thinks he's funny. He's usually wrong," I said, turning a bit red.

"Yeah, yeah. Get lost!" Mackenzie said. "I need some relief from your wretched music."

"Hey, can I borrow that *Uff* CD?" Daniel asked.

"Sure."

Daniel and I walked downstairs and out the front door.

"Let me apologize for Mackenzie. He's the poster child for contraception."

Daniel laughed.

"He's okay. He's kind of funny."

"Yeah, he is, but I never tell him that. I don't want to encourage him."

As we walked, Daniel and I talked more about the CDs I'd played for him. Daniel was genuinely into my music. It was a good sign. He seemed to like me too, which was even more encouraging. My boy-band posters didn't turn him off either. I was growing increasingly hopeful that Daniel was as interested in me as I was in him. If only I could summon the courage to broach the subject. I tried a few times as we walked along, but each time my voice caught in my throat.

I still hadn't been able to force myself to speak the words as we neared Merton's Ice Cream Parlor on Main Street. I was running out of time. I swallowed hard and made myself do it.

"Listen, Daniel... this is kind of awkward, but..."

"Hey, I thought that was you Daniel."

I looked up. Cole Fitch stood before us.

"Hey Cole. You know Toby, right? We were just at his house listening to CDs."

"Hi Toby."

"Hi."

I frowned. Talk about bad timing. What was happening here? Why was Daniel so chummy with the most gorgeous boy in school?

Cole turned to Daniel and proceeded to ignore me.

"I'd like to talk to you."

"Um, yeah. Sure. Toby was just walking me home."

"Okay. You won't mind then, will you Toby?" Cole asked, turning to me once more.

"Oh... uh... no," I said, trying to keep my voice steady.

To be perfectly honest, I minded very much. It wasn't just that Cole was bringing my time with Daniel to a premature end. Daniel lit up when Cole arrived on the scene. Unless I was very much mistaken, Daniel was hot for Cole.

"Cool," Cole said. He led Daniel off without so much as another word to me.

"Bye Toby!" Daniel called out.

"Bye."

I stood there and watched as my two dream boys walked away—*together*. Tears welled up in my eyes. I couldn't help it. I knew it was totally stupid to get so upset, but I was devastated. I was just starting to open up to Daniel when Cole barged in.

My relationship with Daniel was over even before it started. I'd seen the look in Daniel's eyes as he looked at Cole. He was crushing on him badly. He wanted him. There was very little doubt in my mind now that Daniel was gay, but he wanted Cole Fitch. There was no way I could compete with the hottest boy in school. First Kerry took Orlando away from me. Now Cole walked away with Daniel. When would someone love *me*?

I sat down on the curb and began to cry. I felt like my life was over. Why did I even bother trying? I was cursed. I couldn't remember having ever felt so miserable before.

"Hey Toby. Are you okay?"

"Shit!"

I stumbled to my feet and holding my hand over my heart as I backed away from the dark figure who had silently slipped up on me.

"You scared the crap out of me!"

"Sorry. Are you okay?"

I peered into the darkness and gazed into the concerned eyes of Ian Babcock. I wiped the tears away, but there was no denying I was crying. Tears still flowed from my eyes, even as I fought them back.

"I'm just... I just..."

Another sob broke out. My body shuddered. I wiped the tears from my eyes again. I looked down the street for a moment. Daniel and Cole had disappeared into the darkness. Everything was going so well and then Cole came and took Daniel away from me. I quickly looked back at Ian. I'd always feared meeting him in a dark alley or, in this case, on a dark street. He probably carried a switchblade and maybe other weapons too.

Ian didn't look as if he was about to mug me or work me over. His liquid brown eyes were filled with concern. I bit my trembling lower lip to keep from crying, but I felt so wretched right then I couldn't help it. I hid my face in my hands and began to sob.

"Shh, shh," Ian said.

I flinched when I felt his hands on my shoulders, but Ian drew me in close. He wrapped his arms around me, and I cried into his shoulder.

"I know man. I know. It's going to be okay. I know."

I was confused by Ian's words and his actions, but I was so miserable all I cared about at that moment was his soothing voice and his arms around me. I needed to be held so badly right then. I clung to Ian as I released the pain in my heart.

After I'd quieted, I pulled away and wiped my eyes on my sleeve yet again. I was still fearful. There were all kinds of rumors floating around about Ian. I felt safe enough near him if Daniel was around, but Ian and I were alone. Ian looked dangerous with his spiked collar and that chain that hung from his waist. I tried to calm myself. If Ian intended to hurt me, he wouldn't have hugged me. Ian had shown me a side I'd never seen before. I'd never even guessed it existed.

"You know?"

How could he possibly know anything about what I was going through?

"Yeah, man... Toby. I know."

I swallowed hard and gazed at Ian. My heart pounded with fear. Ian smiled at me. I hadn't realized before that he was cute. Then again, had I ever truly given him a moment's thought? I'd sure never thought of him in *that way*.

"Daniel's my bud, but I think he just made a big mistake. He walked away with the wrong guy."

My eyes widened. Ian *knew*. Somehow he knew how much I wanted to be with Daniel Peralta.

"Don't be afraid Toby. Your secret is safe with me, and so is Daniel's. I've been keeping his secret for a long time, even though he doesn't know it."

"So you know I'm..."

"Gay," Ian finished for me.

I trembled with fear, but Ian smiled at me again. I'd seen him smile more in the last two minutes than I had in all the years we'd gone to school together. Ian gazed at me with hunger in his eyes. He took a step forward. I forced myself not to step back. I had an irrational fear that he was going to bite my neck like a vampire. Instead, Ian reached out and gently grasped my chin. He moved closer, pulled me to him, and kissed me on the lips.

Ian pulled back after that one, brief kiss and gazed into my eyes. I wasn't sure what to feel at just that moment. I stared at him in wonder.

"I'll walk you home," Ian said. "I don't think you should be alone right now."

I nodded. I couldn't speak. We walked side by side down the street, so close our arms touched now and then. The moon above cut through the darkness casting a bluish light. I gazed at Ian once. He was nearly invisible in the night—dressed all in black. I couldn't even think at that moment because I didn't know what to think.

When we reached my home, Ian turned to face me under the shadows of a large oak tree. He leaned in and pressed his lips to mine. He kissed me lightly and stepped away. I gazed at him for a moment in a state of utter confusion. I turned and walked up the sidewalk to my home. I turned again when I reached the porch. Ian was still standing in the darkness under the tree. He was little more than a deeper shadow among the shadows, but his eyes gleamed in the night. I turned and walked inside. Neither of us had spoken a single word on the walk home.

Daniel

"Where are we going?"

"The baseball diamond."

"It's a little late for baseball, Cole."

I needed to be home soon, but there was no way I was turning down Cole Fitch.

"We aren't playing baseball."

Cole grinned at me and I just about melted. His very presence made me breathe a little faster. My mind was reeling. Cole wanted to spend time with me.

Cole had become very popular at B.H.S. in only a few days. He could have his pick of friends, and yet he chose to spend time with me. Cole's popularity isn't what turned my head; it was Cole himself. I knew I'd be as infatuated with him if he was an outcast. His stunning beauty had attracted me, but I'd quickly learned his personality was just as attractive.

Neither of us spoke a word as we walked toward the school. We were equally silent as we crossed the baseball diamond. Cole took my hand and pulled me into the dugout. His touch made my entire body tingle.

"Why are we here?" I asked.

"For this," Cole said, and then he did something that shocked me more than anything in my entire life.

Cole Fitch kissed me.

The kiss lasted only a moment, but that moment stretched into an eternity. Whole universes were born, lived, and died while his lips were pressed against mine. I felt as if I could fly. When Cole pulled his soft, moist lips from mine I stared at him with my mouth open. I fought desperately to tame my wildly beating heart and other parts of my anatomy.

The feelings rushing through my mind and body were so intense they were nearly unbearable. I was so ecstatically happy it was nearly painful. I grabbed Cole and kissed him back. I opened my mouth slightly and Cole slipped his tongue inside. Cole wrapped his strong arms around me and pulled me to him. I nearly cried for joy.

We kissed for several long, slow moments. When our lips parted, we stood gazing into each other's eyes.

"I think you're really hot, Daniel Peralta."

I was... astonished.

"You think *I'm* hot? I'm... ordinary. You're the one who's hot. Damn, you should be on the cover of magazines."

"You must be looking in the wrong mirror," Cole said. "I've wanted to kiss you from the moment I saw you."

My grin widened.

"Wow! Wow! This is... amazing! This is... astounding! I'm going to wake up soon, aren't I? This has to be another one of my dreams."

"You have dreams about me Daniel?"

"Yes. The first time I saw you, I thought... wow. Well actually, I thought *oww* because I wrecked my skateboard because I was checking you out."

Cole laughed, but it was mirth without malice. His eyes sparkled when he gazed at me. I could see that sparkle even in the darkness of the dugout. He truly *liked* me.

"I can't believe this. You *kissed* me."

"I didn't think you'd mind."

"Oh, I didn't! I just... wow! I really, *really* like you Cole. It's hard to believe that you like me too."

"It shouldn't be hard to believe. What's not to like? Just in case you still have doubts, here's a little something to help you believe."

Cole pulled me to him and kissed me again. We made out for the longest time. I'd never made out before. I'd never been kissed before. I was almost overwhelmed. Making out was the hottest thing ever.

I never wanted to stop kissing Cole. I writhed in exquisite agony as our lips and tongues entwined. My entire body was on fire with physical need. We held each other so tightly our torsos melded into one another. My heart raced. Cole and I devoured each other. When our lips parted, Cole and I gazed at each other. Both of us panted as if we'd been running. We laughed.

"This is gonna be fun," Cole said.

My grin could not have been wider.

"Come on," Cole said. "I'll walk you home."

We left the shadows of the dugout and walked under the November moon. There was a chill in the air, but I felt as if my body was giving off waves of heat. Cole and I stepped along, side by side. I felt as if I'd found my soul mate.

"We can't tell anyone about this—not yet. You know that, right?" Cole said.

"Yeah. I don't fancy getting my head kicked in."

"People can be cruel. Some of them love to torment anyone who is different."

"Yeah." I paused for a few moments. "I can't believe you're gay. I never dared dream it. Well, I dreamed it, but I never thought that dream would come true."

"I put on a good act, don't I?"

"Every girl in school wants you."

"Well, none of them can have me. I've got what I want right here," Cole said, staring at me.

"Why me? Cole, you could have any guy you wanted—any guy who was attracted to guys anyway. Hell, I bet there are straight boys who would make out with you. I know finding a gay boy is hard. God, do I know it! But, you can have someone sooooo much better looking than me, Cole."

"Daniel, you can't see your own beauty. Whether you believe it or not, you're hot. There's more to you than your looks. I haven't been around long, but I've seen what kind of guy you are. You never make fun of anyone. You never torment anyone. You stepped in to help me, putting yourself at risk when you had no need to do so. You're the kind of guy who really cares about other people. You feel their pain."

I felt a lump in my throat. How could Cole understand me so well? I did feel the pain of others. I couldn't bear to think of anyone suffering. I couldn't take it when I saw another sad, lonely, or hurting. Memories flooded my mind and tears rimmed my eyes.

"There was a boy, Caleb Fulton. I told you about him before. Sometimes I cried at night because his life was so pitiful. He was chubby. He wasn't athletic. He wore ugly, black-rimmed glasses and what looked like third-hand clothes. The other kids... Some of them were so cruel to him. As if his life wasn't difficult enough, they tormented him. They called him names. They tripped him in the halls. They played nasty tricks on him, like smearing his glasses with Vaseline or peanut butter. I don't know how Caleb managed to get up every morning to come to school. I don't think I could have done it knowing what was waiting on me. I tried to be nice to him. Auddie did too. He sat between us at lunch every day. The other kids used to give us a hard time about it. Poor Caleb. Sometimes he didn't even have money for lunch!"

Tears flowed from my eyes and I began to cry. Cole put his hand on my shoulder. I looked into his eyes and saw tears there.

"I bet you gave him lunch money, didn't you?"

"Yeah. Auddie and I took care of Caleb. We couldn't sit there and let him go hungry. I should have done more for him, but I didn't know how to make the other kids stop bothering him. His life was *so* hard, and then... then he burned to death in a fire. Why did that have to happen?"

I practically shouted the last bit. All the vicarious torment I'd felt when Caleb was alive was coming back to me. My heart ached thinking about how that poor boy suffered.

"At least he had you and Auddie. I'm sure that meant a lot to him."

"Sometimes when we were alone, Caleb would grab me and cry. I'd hold him and he'd cry. I never saw him much outside of school. He disappeared at the end of the day. During those rare times when I did see him, we'd sit and talk, and I'd try to make him laugh. Sometimes I managed it, but he was so sad that it was hard to even get him to smile."

"You're a good person, Daniel Peralta. I knew it that day you saved me."

I smiled through my tears.

"Thanks."

We reached my house all too soon. I didn't want my time with Cole to end.

"This has been an incredible evening," I said.

"This is only the beginning Daniel."

Cole grinned at me. Oh my gosh!

"I'll see you tomorrow."

"You know it. Have a good night Daniel."

"Good night Cole."

I watched Cole walk away. My heart soared. My life was so wonderful at just that moment I felt like it couldn't possibly be real, but it was real! Cole Fitch liked me! Cole Fitch kissed me! I was bursting to share my joy with the world. I wouldn't, of course. What was between Cole and me could not be shared. A part of me wanted the whole school to know we were together; the hottest boy in school and Daniel Peralta! Wow!

I felt ever so slightly shallow because I wanted everyone to know the hottest boy in school was mine. Was that really so bad? I'd been drawn by Cole's looks, but I'd likewise been drawn by his personality. There was way more to Cole than his handsome face. Cole cared about the whole world. Only when Cole was swallowed by the darkness did I turn and walk inside.

***

The morning after Cole Fitch kissed me I walked in a daze. I was all the way to school before I even realized I'd stepped out the door. I found myself with a unique problem. The boy of my dreams liked me back. I'd fantasized about Cole becoming my boyfriend, but now... I don't mean that I was unhappy. No way! It was just that now that I had what I wanted, I wasn't quite sure what to do. Cole and I weren't exactly a couple, but after last night there was little doubt we were headed in that direction.

I spotted Ian digging books out of his locker. With a supreme effort I kept my mouth shut about making out with Cole. I was dying to tell someone, anyone, but I couldn't. Ian somehow managed to find what he was seeking in the tangled mass in the bottom of his locker. He stood and smiled at me. My mouth opened slightly. Ian had seemed more morose than usual lately, but he was smiling. Ian *never* smiled—well, almost never. First, Cole kissed me. Now, Ian was smiling. Had the whole world gone mad?

Mike Bradley hurried down the hallway, looking over his shoulder as if he thought someone might be tailing him. He slowed when he spotted Ian. I feared he'd come after him, but the football player swallowed hard. Mike paled ever so slightly and I could have sworn I read fear in his eyes. I glanced at Ian. His grin broadened, making him look slightly skeletal.

"What's up with Bradley?" I asked when Mike had gone on his way.

Ian turned to me, the smile still on his face. "He's beginning to learn that picking on me may be hazardous to his health."

"Huh?"

"Sorry Daniel. I've got to go to class. Catch ya later." Ian was gone in a flash.

Okay, that was weird.

I didn't have long to ponder the peculiar behavior of Ian or Mike because my attention was drawn by Toby. I thought he'd greet me, but when he spotted me he slowed and then looked away.

"Hi Toby," I said as he passed.

"Oh, hi," he said, as if he hadn't noticed me before.

"What's up?"

"Oh, um, nothing. I'm just on my way to class."

Toby was oddly quiet. He'd been so animated the evening before. I felt guilty when I realized I'd all but forgotten about Toby until I spotted him in the hallway, but then I think that was understandable after what had happened with Cole. My mind was filled with images of making out with the boy of my dreams.

"Hey, I'm sorry about rushing off last night."

"It's okay," Toby said. "I mean... yeah, it's okay."

Why was everyone acting so odd this morning? Was there a full moon last night?

"I had a good time."

"I did too."

"We should hang out again sometime."

"Yeah, I'd like that. Hey, I've gotta run. The bell is about to ring."

"I'll see you later Toby."

The residents of B.H.S. were behaving strangely this morning, but it didn't matter. I was happier than I'd ever been in my entire life.

Cedi

My eyes popped open. I sat up. I was in a large, rather luxurious hotel room. I was still dressed. I vaguely remembered stumbling into the room and falling face down on the bed the night before. The memories came rushing back; the concert, the bus ride to Fort Wayne, and our late-night arrival.

I got up, stretched, and walked to the window. My room was fairly high up, probably about the eighth or ninth floor. The city spread out in the distance. I could make out a few church steeples, lots of houses, a Rally's, a Taco Bell, and a McDonald's. To the far left was a big old hotel. I stepped over to the desk. Lying there was a folder with my room key in it. The outside of the folder read "Hilton." I guess that solved the mystery of the name of the hotel. I walked toward the toilet. I spotted a piece of paper lying on the floor near the door. I bent down, picked it up, and read "Cedric, Ralph and I and some of the others are meeting for breakfast in Desoto's downstairs at 9:30. If you're up by then, join us. If not, make sure you're back in your room by one p.m. We'll be leaving soon after that for a radio interview and another signing. Don't leave the hotel without Rod. Here's a list of the room numbers for our group. If you need anything, call my cell. Jordan."

I walked back toward the bed and looked at the clock. It was a bit past nine. I stripped off my clothes and climbed into the shower. I showered in record time, then dashed out. As I was drying off, I realized I'd left all my stuff on the bus. I had no clean clothes.

There was a knock on my door. I wrapped the towel around my waist and looked through the peephole. Rod stood on the other side.

"Hey," I said as I opened the door. "Here to make sure I don't escape?"

"Something like that."

Rod didn't smile, but I could detect a trace of humor nonetheless.

"Have you had breakfast? I'm getting ready to go down and join Jordan."

"No. Will you be wearing anything else besides that towel?"

"Yeah, yesterday's clothes. My bags are still on the bus."

Rod stepped to the mirrored doors of the closet and opened them. There were all my bags, neatly stacked.

"Oh! Let me get dressed, and we can go down."

Rod walked over to the window to give me some unnecessary privacy. I was not shy, and I looked pretty good naked! It took me only a few moments. I was a fast dresser.

"Ready?" I asked.

I grabbed up my key card and stuck it in my pocket. I took note of the room number, 834, as I closed the door.

Rod led the way.

"I'm surprised you, Mike, and Shawn are letting us eat in a public restaurant," I said as we rode the elevator down to the ground floor.

"It's early. The fans don't expect you to arrive until this afternoon. Jordan tends to do what he wants regardless, although he is very good about listening to our advice."

"He probably especially listens after those religious nuts almost killed him."

"That made him more cautious, but he's always been rather attentive to our instructions—most of the time. I think it's more out of consideration and a desire to make our jobs easier than fear for his own safety, but he is *very* concerned about the safety of those around him."

"Yeah, Ross almost died when that bomb went off, didn't he?"

"As you probably know, he went into a coma. No one expected him to come out of it. He should be a vegetable, but instead he's merely insane. That's just Ross, of course; perfectly normal for him."

Rod grinned ever so slightly.

"I'll try not to make your job difficult. I know you're used to Kieran. I'm sure he didn't give you any trouble."

"Very little. Just remember Cedric, my job is to protect you. There are those who will hurt you if they get the chance, but the biggest danger is from your own fans. They won't intentionally harm you, but a crowd of overzealous fans can be far more dangerous than a gunman."

I nodded. We were on the first floor and walking toward Desoto's by then. The Hilton was a very nice hotel—posh without being stuffy. Rod and I entered the restaurant and spotted the guys. Several tables had been shoved together to form one long table. Desoto's wasn't all that large, so the table took up most of the main room. Seated at one end were Jordan, Ralph, Chad, Sam, and Mike. Seated at the other were Shawn, Drew, Daniel, and Drake, along with a woman I didn't recognize. Various members of the crew were seated in the middle. It looked as though most of our company was present. Ross was conspicuous by his absence.

"You're up," Ralph said. "I figured you'd be a late riser like Ross. He won't get up before noon if someone doesn't go in and poke him."

"I just got up."

"Have a seat dudes," Chad said.

Rod and I sat down. Everyone else had ordered. I decided on strawberry pancakes and bacon.

"Who's the lady down by Drew?" I asked Jordan.

"His mom. She'll pop in now and then during the tour to check on her boys and make sure they're not letting their schoolwork slip. That reminds me; your tutor will be joining us later today."

"There's no escape from school," Ralph said. "I finished up my senior year with a tutor."

I secretly wondered how I would find time for everything. I knew I'd manage, somehow. I could do anything!

Breakfast was delicious, and it was wicked fun hanging out with the crowd I decided to name the Phantom Company. Everyone got on well with everyone else. We were like a family.

"Today is the easiest day we'll have for a long time so enjoy it," Jordan said. "We're free until noon or so. Then we should have some free time between three and six. You can hang out in your room and rest if you want. There's also a hot tub and pool on the second floor."

"Ohhh, I like the sound of that!"

"You might want to hit the hot tub and pool early," Mike said. "Later this place will be surrounded by fans."

"All right! Streaking around the Hilton after lunch! Count me in!" Ross announced as he entered Desoto's.

"Sit down, shut up, and eat," Jordan said.

"Do you see how he treats me?" Ross whined. "I'm so glad you're here Cedi. Jordan and Kieran used to gang up on me all the time. My life was hell!"

I grinned. Ross was wicked!

After breakfast, the company broke up. I headed toward Ross.

"I'm going to hit the hot tub. You want to come?"

"Hot tub?" asked Drew. "Where?"

"Jordan said it's on the second floor."

"Can I come?"

"Sure. Why not?"

"Cool!"

Before we were out of Desoto's, Ross, *Dragonfire*, and I all agreed to meet in the pool area as soon as we changed into swimsuits. I could almost feel the soothing hot, bubbly water already.

Minutes later, I'd found my way into the fitness area. A room key was required for entrance, so we'd be safe from any fans unless they were staying at the Hilton. I walked past the treadmills and passed through a glass door into the pool/hot-tub area. Drew, Daniel, and Drake were already in the hot tub.

"Come on Cedi!" Drew said.

Dragonfire's mum was seated in a deck chair nearby. I walked over to her and shook her hand.

"Hi, I'm Cedric."

"It's nice to meet you. You're British, right?"

"I guess my accent gave me away."

"Instantly."

I laughed.

"It's nice to meet you, Mrs. Dragon."

"Cecilia."

"You can call me Cedric or Cedi."

I pulled off my shirt, shoes, and socks and then eased myself into the hot tub. The water was almost too hot, but I quickly grew accustomed to it.

Ross arrived a couple of minutes later. He sniffed the air upon entering.

"What's that I smell? Smells like... boy soup!"

I rolled my eyes. Ross stripped to his swimsuit and pretended he was going to do a cannonball into the hot tub. The boys rushed to make way for him, and Ross ended up sitting directly across from me.

Ross looked wicked sexy shirtless. I'd guessed he had a nice build, but bloody hell he was hot! He was perfectly smooth, tanned, and defined. His handsome face and long black hair made him all the more appealing. I gazed at him for several moments thankful my midsection was submersed and hidden from view by all the bubbles.

I looked away for a bit and then back at Ross. He had a devilish gleam in his eye. Did he guess what I was thinking? Drake gave me a look, and I wondered if I'd been obvious.

According to the warning on the wall, it was unsafe to remain in the hot tub for more than fifteen minutes. As we neared our time limit, I began to get a bit dizzy, so I climbed out. The others followed soon after.

"All right, boys. Dry off, then go back upstairs and change. I'm taking you to the botanical gardens across the street," said Cecilia.

"Plants? Who wants to look at plants?" asked Drew. "Booorrrrinnnng."

"Humor your mother. I'll be out of your hair soon. Besides, you might like it."

"Isn't there a paint-drying exhibition at the art museum?" asked Drake. "Maybe we could go there next."

"Good one Drake," Drew said, giving him a high five.

"If only I'd had daughters," Cecilia said, shaking her head.

Soon, Ross and I were alone. I had a mad desire to kiss him.

"Let's swim," Ross said.

I suddenly had more than the usual amount of excess energy to burn. Ross did a cannonball for real this time, and I followed suit. We swam and cavorted around in the pool for several minutes. I couldn't keep my eyes off Ross. He was unbelievably sexy.

I felt a bit guilty for letting such thoughts enter my mind, but my guilt made no sense. I hoped Thad and I would someday get back together, but we weren't together now, nor would we be for months. We'd likely never be a couple again. Even if we did get back together someday, there was nothing wrong with the thoughts running through my head.

Ross and I wrestled around in the water. I had absolutely no chance against him. After all, Ross was about 6'1" and 180 compared to my 5' 9" and 125. Ross took it easy on me. Touching him made me mad horny. I found myself breathing harder.

We swam to the shallow end and stood in water chest high. We gazed into each other's eyes for several moments. We were absolutely silent. The only sound came from the waves gently hitting the sides of the poor and the empty hot tub bubbling. Ross leaned in. Our lips met. We kissed only briefly, but the sensation sent a ripple of desire racing through my entire body.

We pulled away from each other as we heard the glass door open.

"You're actually where you said you'd be," Shawn said. "I'm impressed."

"You know how trustworthy I am," Ross said to his bodyguard.

I wondered how much Shawn had seen. The wall that separated the pool and hot tub from the fitness equipment was glass. Our kiss ended just as Shawn had opened the door. I guess it didn't matter. I wasn't worried about it, merely curious. Ross and I were adults. If we wanted to kiss that was our business. Shawn gave no indication he'd seen anything, but who knew?

"It's getting close to one," Shawn said. "Everyone needs to be on the bus in a few minutes. Leave your stuff in your rooms. You're spending the night here after the concert."

Ross and I climbed out of the pool and dried off. My mind raced with possibilities as we followed Shawn to the elevators and back up to our rooms on the eighth floor. The kiss Ross and I shared made our already exciting tour a lot more interesting.

Our radio interview in Fort Wayne was much like the one in Indianapolis. It was a blast, but if you've heard about one, you've heard about them all, and I don't want to bore you with the details. If there is one thing I refuse to be, it's boring!

The signing was mad fun. More of the fans recognized me than in Indianapolis. At our first venue I was the "new guy performing with the band." Now I was Cedi, the "wild British boy who adds a new dimension to *Phantom*." That last bit was a quote from a music review in one of the Indianapolis papers. Ralph showed it to me just before the signing.

Some girls even screamed when they neared me. The first time it happened, I jumped. Ross laughed, but then Ross would. Some of the girls who passed through the line were sexy birds. I guess it didn't matter. There was no time to get involved with anyone on the road. Still, they were rather fine to look at. It was all Ross' fault that I was thinking about sex. Swimming with him, then kissing him had me all worked up!

Okay, you might be confused, since both Ross and some of the girls at the autograph signing excited me. I go for both girls and guys. People call that bisexual, but I don't go in for labels. I just go after whomever I fancy. If it's a girl, fine. If it's a boy, that's just as fine. We're all human, so what does it matter?

There were some hot boys in line, real cuties. Most of *Phantom's* fans were girls, but based on the number of males coming through the autograph line, I'd say at least a third were guys, maybe more.

I couldn't get my mind off Ross. Things between us were left hanging. What would have happened if Shawn hadn't walked into the pool area? Would Ross and I have really gotten into making out, would we have gone further, or would we pulled away and decided the kiss was a mistake? I felt as if I was stuck in one of those old-time cliffhangers my aunt once told me about. They used to show these short movies where something huge happened right at the end, and everyone had to wait a whole week to find out what happened next. It was way worse to be in the story than watching it, but then again it was extremely exciting.

The next installment of the Cedi-Ross adventure was not to come soon. After the signing, we were driven back to the Hilton. A crowd of fans awaited us. We shook hands with several of the fans and signed a few autographs, taking more time than usual. As I'd already learned, there often wasn't more than a minute to spare. We had a bit of all-too-rare free time so we were more than willing to share it with our fans. Our bodyguards ushered us inside after a few minutes and we found ourselves in the comfortable carpeted world of the Hilton.

I thought I might have some time to discover where things were going with Ross and me, but Jordan informed me that my tutor was waiting to meet me in my room. I wasn't eager to think about schoolwork, but I did need to finish school. Even if my music career took off, I didn't want to be a dropout.

"Hi," I said, entering my room.

"Hello. You must be Cedric. I'm John."

John was a bookish, older man in his early forties. His studious manner reminded me a bit of Thad, but that was the only similarity. Where Thad was tall and handsome, John was of average height and rather ordinary looking. He was totally lacking in sex appeal—at least in my opinion. That was just as well. I didn't think I could learn from a guy who turned me on. I could just imagine how little I would have learned if Thad had been my tutor. My mind would have constantly turned to thoughts of seduction. That was not going to be a problem with John.

My tutor outlined my course of study and gave me a list of assignments to complete. He explained what to expect in the sessions. It didn't sound as bad as I'd expected, but it was still going to be difficult to do my assignments while on tour. Ralph had managed it, so I guess I could too.

By the time John departed, most of my free time was gone. I was quite tempted to seek out Ross, but I thought it wiser to rest a bit. I wanted to be at my best for the concert. Besides, I'd have weeks to spend with Ross.

I made myself a mug of hot tea and gazed out the window as I sipped it. During the ride to the radio station, I'd learned that the old hotel off to the left was connected to the Embassy Theatre, where we'd be playing tonight. Jordan said it was even more impressive than the Murat.

I had to fight the urge to run wild. Being part of a band came with a lot of responsibility. My time wasn't my own anymore. My life was scheduled for me and it was a hectic schedule indeed. Still, there were plenty of opportunities to liven things up, and Ross was the perfect partner in crime. He lived for mischief. That trait was one of the things that attracted me to him—that, and his sense of humor, his handsome face, his long black hair, and wickedly sexy body. I couldn't get the image of him in the swimming pool out of my mind. I could still picture the rivulets of water cascading down his nicely muscled chest and sexy abs. Yum.

We walked from the Hilton to the Embassy when the time came for the sound test. There was a sky bridge that connected the hotel to the theatre. Despite the number of fans hanging around outside the theatre, we could come and go with little chance of being noticed.

"You weren't kidding," I said to Jordan as we entered the mezzanine of the Embassy. "It's like Buckingham Palace."

"You've been there?" Ralph asked.

"Yes. It's magnificent. A lot of people think it's a huge waste of money, but it's already there and much of it is like a museum."

"Been having tea with the Queen, have we?" Ross said in a British accent that made me laugh.

"No."

The Embassy was magnificent. It's one of those places you just have to see for yourself to truly appreciate. The chandeliers, the sconces, mirrors, and intricate decorative work were like something one would find in a grand mansion. Jordan had told me it was an old movie palace, but I didn't know he meant the "palace" part literally.

We turned to the right to enter the auditorium, which was equally impressive. It reminded me of some of the fine old theatres in London. It was going to be a pleasure to perform in such a beautiful place.

***

The Embassy was packed for the concert. Some girls were even holding signs that read, "We love you, Cedi!" and "Cedi Rocks!" There also were signs for Jordan and Ross, of course, but it was the signs for me that took me by surprise. I felt as if I was becoming more famous by the moment. I smiled when I thought of how I told Toby I was going to be a famous rock star. I needed to call him soon and tell him he should've let me autograph his bum. No telling what his backside would be worth now if I had!

We played a long set list of *Phantom* songs: *'Til I See You Again; Jump Back; You Don't Know; Rock It Down Deep; I'll Keep You Up All Night; I Love That Kind of Love; Jump, Jump, Jump,* and, of course, the new version of *Do You Know That I Love You.* Sweat poured off me by the end, but I loved every second of the concert! I didn't want it to end! Being a rock star rocks!

Performing is a tremendous energy drain. Anyone who hasn't been up on stage playing and singing for an hour and a half can't begin to understand the physical strain. Performing is like running flat out until you drop. By the end of the concert, I felt as if I didn't have the energy to walk off the stage. I bet Toby, Chase, and all the other guys back in Blackford would never believe it.

I hit the shower as soon as I made it back to my room. From the shower, I climbed straight into bed.

I put my hands behind my head and stared at the ceiling. My life had changed so much in the past few months. First, I was kicked out of the detestable Danforth Academy in Great Britain, the last in a long line of British prep schools that quickly tired of my presence. Then, I was booted across the pond to the little Indiana town of Blackford. I'd made some good friends there, actually enjoyed school for the first time in my life, and I'd met Thad. Finally, I'd been at the right place at the right time to temporarily step in for Kieran. That single concert was a dream come true, but the dream didn't end there. I was actually touring with *Phantom*. For the next few months, I was a part of the band!

***

We were up and on our way far too early for my liking the next morning. Still, I had time for a shower and a nice breakfast right in my room. By nine, Jordan, Ross, Ralph, Drake, Daniel, Drew, Mike, and I were all on our way to Detroit for our next concert. The crew was a good two hours ahead of us. Shawn and Rod followed us in the sedan. *Dragonfire's* mum had departed for home, no doubt confident that her boys were well supervised. They even had their own bodyguard.

I was relieved that John, my tutor, was not riding on the bus with us. I had unpleasant visions of being stuck doing lessons while the others had fun. John was traveling by himself. No doubt he'd ambush me when we reached Detroit. I learned he was also tutoring *Dragonfire* so I didn't have to suffer by being his sole pupil.

I didn't mind the idea of lessons so much as I minded what I might miss while I was studying. I was sure lessons with John wouldn't be as fun as classes back in Blackford High School, but I was equally certain they would be far more enjoyable that classes in a stuffy prep school back in Britain. I wasn't about to complain. I was living *THE* life!

As Jordan had warned, the tour was hectic. After Detroit, we hit one town after another in rapid succession. Between the concerts, interviews, meet and greets, autograph signings, sound tests, and tutorial sessions with John, I barely had time to breathe. Spending the night in a hotel was a treat. More often than not, we slept on the tour bus as it sped to our next venue. Quite often I had to ask where we were and I lost all track of time. I usually didn't know what day it was. Sometimes, I had to think hard to puzzle out the month! It was a blast, of course! Hard work to be sure, but I'd never had so much fun!

I kept in touch with Toby. I called him and told him all about my first concert and about others as well. He called and told me about the new hottie in school. What really blew me away was when he told me about Ian Babcock. I remembered him well. He was kind of scary looking, but I instinctively liked him. It was hard to picture Toby and Ian together, but if he made Toby happy, then I was all for it. I hoped Toby would finally be able to get over Orlando.

You're wondering about Ross and me, aren't you? I know you are! I've half a mind not to tell you, just to watch you squirm. Chad says I have half a mind, period, but that's beside the point and he was kidding—I think. Anyway, it was days before Ross and I had so much as a moment alone together. We were whisked from one location to another, constantly surrounded by others. The tour bus was always crowded, so we could just forget about any alone time there.

Ross and I were finally alone for a few moments nearly a week after we kissed in the pool in Fort Wayne. It was in Philadelphia after yet another sound test. Ross and I were in the dressing room. Our sudden privacy took us both by surprise. We stood there gazing at each other for a few moments. I had the feeling both of us were waiting to see what was going to happen.

Such inactivity and indecision was quite uncharacteristic of us both. What happened next wasn't. We ran at each other. I jumped up on Ross, wrapped my legs around his middle, and passionately kissed him. His tongue was in my mouth in a flash.

We stayed right there making out like nobody's business until Ralph knocked on the door two minutes later and announced it was time for our photo shoot.

Ross grinned at me as we followed Ralph. From the look in his eyes, I knew he wanted more. I'd grown to know Ross and Jordan far better since the Fort Wayne concert, but I couldn't keep from being overwhelmed by the fact I'd just made out with Ross from *Phantom*! Unless I was much mistaken, we'd be making out a good deal more.

"This is your first photo shoot?" Ross asked as we climbed in the back of a limo.

"Yeah."

"It's quite an experience. Some of the photographers are real characters. You'll probably hear the word 'fabulous' more in the next three hours than you have in your entire life."

"Three hours? Just to take some pictures!"

"We've done far-longer sessions, haven't we, Jordan?"

"No kidding. Remember the one in New York? We were stuck in there for at least eight hours. Some of them last days."

"Bloody hell!" I said.

"Don't worry," Jordan said. "Three hours is the limit today. This is for some event posters, new 8x10s for signings, and publicity shots. It should have been done weeks before the tour, but there wasn't time. We weren't expecting a new band member."

"And now you're stuck with me!" I said.

"With us!" Ross said.

"The terrible twins," Ralph said. "What did we do to deserve this, Jordan?"

"Maybe you were very naughty in a past life," I said.

"No one could be that naughty," Jordan said.

"Hey!" Ross shouted so loud it made my ears ring.

The photo session was, as Ross had said, quite an experience. I was told to look natural while holding the most unnatural poses.

In one shot, the photographer had Ross and me on either side of Jordan, looking at him and standing so close we were almost touching him. When the photographer said, "Just look at Jordan as you would if you were talking to him," I giggled.

"But I don't usually stare into his ear from two inches away while I'm talking to him."

I giggled some more, Ross giggled, Jordan grinned, and then we all lost it. Ross laughed so hard he got down on the floor and rolled around. It took us a good deal of time to calm ourselves. After that, one or another of us would snort or laugh when we tried the pose. On our fourth attempt, I willed myself to be serious. I filled my mind with unpleasant thoughts. Despite my best effort, I grinned, and my whole body began to tremble as I fought to suppress a laugh. Jordan snorted, and we all lost it again. The poor photographer had to give up on the pose. He tried another with Ross and me a bit further from Jordan, and we succeeded, barely, without losing it.

The photo session was actually a great deal of fun. I got to wear a lot of cool clothes, including a pair of leather pants that were so tight two assistants had to help me into them. I could barely walk! Then, there was a spandex bodysuit that made me feel like Spiderman. I had no idea what the photographer planned to do with that shot.

The lights were hot, but nothing compared to the electric suns that glared down upon us during a concert. If Jordan, Ross, or I showed the slightest trace of perspiration, an assistant darted in, dabbed our faces, and applied makeup when necessary. I wasn't accustomed to so many people paying so much attention to me, but it was rather cool.

I yearned to be with Ross again. There was definitely mutual attraction there. I had no idea what kind of a relationship we might have, but I was eager to find out. It wasn't just Ross' fame or incredible good looks that attracted me to him. He was a kindred soul; wild, fun loving, unpredictable, and intense. We were partners in mayhem and mischief. If we could be more, so much the better, but who knew when I'd be able to find out where our relationship was going? We didn't have a moment alone!

Toby

Mike Bradley passed our table at lunch, flanked by Adam Henshaw and Josh Lucas.

"It looks as though Mike is still out of it," Eddie said. "Did you guys hear what happened yesterday evening after football practice?"

"Sure Eddie. You know how obsessed I am with football," I said sarcastically.

"Read between the lines Riester," Eddie said, holding his three middle fingers toward me. It took me a few moments to realize he was flipping me off.

"Mike freaked out after practice yesterday," Eddie said.

"Aww, bad day on the field?" Orlando asked. "The poor guy. I feel for him."

"No, he freaked out—big time. I heard he was screaming and talking shit about a ghost. They had to hold him down."

"Seriously?" Orlando asked.

"Yeah."

"It was probably some freak steroid/alcohol interaction," Orlando said.

"Hey Chase!" I called out as he left the lunch line with his tray.

Chase was a football player. I wanted to get an eyewitness report. I liked Eddie, but I didn't trust second-hand rumors. Chase altered course and walked to our table. Chase was fairly cool for a jock. He had been as bad as the rest, but he and Cedi had become friends and I guess Cedi rubbed off on him. Chase was still friendly with those of us who weren't popular.

"Yeah?"

"What happened with Mike Bradley?"

"Oh, that was some freaky shit. I was out in the parking lot, bullshitting with some of the guys…"

"Swapping steroid stories?" Eddie asked.

"Fuck you Eddie. As I was saying, I was out in the parking lot with some of the guys, waiting on Mike to get his ass out to the truck, when Mike comes fucking flying out. He was screaming,

'Keep him away from me!' and 'Don't let him get me!' as if he was a fuckin' madman. We thought he was kidding around at first. Then, we realized he was freaked out for real and we ran to him.

"Josh got to him first. Mike took one look at him and fuckin' lost it. You would've thought Josh had pulled a knife on him. Mike went fucking nuts. He was hysterical. He kept pointing at Josh and screaming, 'Martin Wolfe! He's dead! Don't let him get me!'"

"Martin Wolfe?" I asked.

"Yeah."

Before Chase could continue, Daniel hurried over to our table.

"What about Martin Wolfe?" Daniel asked.

"Do you know him?" Chase asked.

"No, but I know who he is... or rather was. Martin Wolfe is the boy who hanged himself here about fifty years ago."

"The school ghost," Orlando said, slightly creeped out.

"Weird," Chase said. "Anyway, Mike looked right at me then. He told me how Martin Wolfe appeared to him as he was walking down the hallway coming out of the gym. He said Martin tried to grab him and was gonna kill him. A couple of the guys ran inside and checked things out, but the hallway was empty.

"We got Mike in my truck and Adam and I took him home. Mike wasn't screaming anymore, but he was edgy and jumpy. He kept looking around as though he thought Martin was still coming for him. Mike's brother was home, so we left Mike with him. Mike is still shaken up. Anyway, that's the story."

"Thanks Chase," I said.

"This is such a setup," Orlando said when Chase had departed.

"Setup?" asked Daniel, who was still standing there.

"Yeah. The jocks obviously have some major hazing planned. This whole thing with Mike was set up to freak everyone out. Just watch. The jocks will scare the crap out of the little sixth graders soon."

"I don't know," Eddie said, slowly.

"Think about it. Stories about the school ghost are used to scare the new kids, right? What better way to frighten them even more by pretending a guy like Mike freaked out because the ghost attacked him?"

"Martin Wolfe did hang himself in that hallway," Daniel said. "I did a little research in the library. The story about the hanging is true—the main events anyway."

"Maybe so," Orlando said, "but the jocks are up to something. Mark my word."

"How would they know the name Martin Wolfe?" I asked.

"They could have researched it like Daniel," Orlando said.

"Jocks in the library? Is that possible?" Eddie asked.

Everyone laughed.

"Do you think Chase would be a part of a big scam?" I asked. "He's pretty cool with us."

"If they're up to something, it's probably not directed at us," Eddie said. "We're a little old for ghost stories."

"True," Orlando said.

"Hey Toby, didn't you say Mike was pushing Ian around yesterday?" Eddie asked.

"Yeah, so?"

"Well, didn't Ian tell Mike he was going to be very sorry for picking on him?"

"Yeah."

"Well, I saw Ian walk towards Mike before lunch, and Mike turned and scurried away like he was scared to death."

"Okay, but what has that got to do with what happened with Mike last evening?"

"I'm just saying that Mike picked on Ian. Ian threatened Mike. Something bad happened to Mike. And now Mike is afraid of Ian. I don't see how Ian can be connected with what happened, either, but Mike Bradley should not be afraid of Ian Babcock. Ian has been a punching bag for Mike and his buddies for as long as I can remember. And, they say Ian is a witch."

"I've heard that before. But come on..."

"Who is *they*?" asked Daniel, obviously angry. His anger was understandable. Ian was his friend.

"You know... people," Eddie said. "He's supposed to do weird ceremonies and shit."

"I've known Ian for a long time," Daniel said. "He's never mentioned anything like that to me."

"He probably wouldn't, would he?" Eddie asked.

"Come on, you can't believe in that witch stuff," I said.

"Well, it doesn't matter if I believe or not. What if Mike believes? He's scared of Ian. He's never been scared of him before. He's sure not afraid Ian will beat him up so why is he afraid?"

"Yeah, but still... A ghost? It's interesting to think about and all, but that's a little far out there."

"It's coincidence," Krista said. "Mike pushed Ian around. Ian told Mike he'd make him sorry. Mike probably got high before practice. He started seeing things that weren't there. He knows Ian is supposed to be a witch, so he thinks Ian cursed him. Mike is simply gullible, and Ian is taking advantage of the situation."

"That does make more sense than any other explanation so far," I said.

"I used to get high a lot," Eddie said. "I mean *a lot*. I never saw a ghost."

"Maybe Mike saw one because he's got a guilty conscience," Orlando said. "Or maybe he was playing with something a lot stronger than pot."

"Well, let's not worry about what happened," Eddie said. "Let's look at the bright side. If this whole thing isn't a big fake, something scared the crap out of Mike Bradley. I for one, think he had it coming. If you're out there Martin Wolfe, good job!"

Most of the table laughed. Maybe Krista was right. Maybe it was just a coincidence. Maybe the whole thing was a big setup. I wasn't sure. I didn't believe Ian was a witch, but something in my gut told me there was more here than met the eye.

I called Cedi after school and told him about the latest gossip. He laughed so hard I thought he'd choke when I told him about Mike freaking out. I told him about Ian kissing me. We talked a lot about that. Cedi likewise had some news for me. I couldn't believe he kissed Ross! How lucky can you get?

Cedi and I talked until he had to go. He was living the busy life of a rock star. I envied him, yet I didn't know if I would trade places. I still almost couldn't believe Ian Babcock had kissed me. I was beginning to have warm, fuzzy thoughts about Ian that a few days before I wouldn't have thought possible.

Daniel

Cole took me to the A&W after school and insisted on paying. It was a little chilly, but we sat eating cheeseburgers and fries with the top down. We kept grinning at each other. I felt giddy.

"I want to make out with you so bad," Cole said quietly so no one could overhear.

"I want to..." I was about to say "tear your clothes off," but I stopped myself. "I want to be with you too."

"I wish it was dark," Cole said. "How about your house? Could we fool around there?"

"Not a chance. *Both* my parents will be home all evening."

"Damn. I *need* you."

I grinned. I loved the yearning tone of Cole's voice.

"What about your house?"

"Hmm, well, maybe. Let me think." Cole was silent for several moments. "Yeah okay. I don't think Dad will be around."

We could hardly wait until we finished our cheeseburgers and fries. I couldn't wait to get my hands—and lips—on Cole.

Cole drove back toward downtown. I was eager to see where he lived. I was interested in everything to do with Cole Fitch.

"Uh-oh, trouble," Cole said as we drove by the park.

I looked to the side. There was Ian. Facing him were Adam Henshaw and Josh Lucas. The jocks didn't look friendly. Cole quickly pulled his Corvette to the curb, and we got out.

"You guys are next," Ian said as we approached. He wasn't talking to us. He was speaking to Adam and Josh. "You'd better be damned nice to me or you'll be very sorry."

"I don't know how you made Mike *think* you had something to do with what happened to him, but we're not afraid of you, freak."

"If you were smart, you would be."

"Yeah? Is that so, freak?" said Adam, poking Ian in the chest.

Ian stared into Adam's eyes with hatred.

"You are so dead."

Adam shoved Ian to the ground.

"Come on, fucker. Do whatever you're gonna do now. Hurt me!"

Adam laughed.

"Hey guys!" Cole said loudly and cheerfully as if he was greeting friends. "What's up?"

"Stay out of this Fitch, or you're next. I haven't forgotten you were sniffing around my girl!"

"Whoa, insecure, aren't we? You must not keep her very happy in bed."

Oh, shit.

Adam forgot about Ian for the time being and stomped toward Cole. He stopped when he was only a few inches from Cole's face.

"What did you say to me pretty boy? Huh?"

Josh pushed in between Adam and Cole and stared into Cole's eyes.

"I found out something interesting about you Fitch," Josh said.

"And I care about this for what reason?"

"You told Cindy Erickson you went to Ben Davis High School in Indianapolis before you moved here. I have a couple of cousins there. They've never heard of you. I told them what you look like and what car you drive. They said they've never seen you."

Cole swallowed. I could detect a trace of fear in his eyes that he was trying very hard to hide. I didn't understand.

"It's a big school."

"Not big enough for a guy like you to go unnoticed."

"You must think I'm pretty special."

"I think you're a fake."

"Come again?"

"You heard me. One of my cousins has a girlfriend who has a friend who works in the office at Ben Davis in lieu of a study hall. She did some checking. There never has been a Cole Fitch at Ben Davis."

"Hey, so your cousin's girlfriend's friend is incompetent. What's that got to do with me?"

"You lied Fitch. You never attended Ben Davis. That makes me wonder what else you've lied about. I intend to find out."

"You're walking on thin ice Josh."

"You seem upset Fitch. What's wrong? Am I onto something?"

"You wish."

"Let's just beat the shit outta him," Adam said. "Who cares if he lied?"

"Leave him alone," Ian said.

Trembling, I stepped up beside Cole. Ian moved over to join us.

"Come on," Josh said, tugging at Adam's shoulder. "He's not worth the trouble of bruising your fist."

Adam glared. For a few moments I thought he was going to ignore Josh and jump on Cole.

"I'm keeping my eye on you!" Adam said.

Adam and Josh departed. I heaved a sigh of relief. I was surprised Cole, Ian, and I didn't all get our asses kicked. Ian glared at the jocks' backs as they strutted away. Cole grinned.

"Can we give you a ride?" Cole asked Ian.

"No, that's okay man, but thanks for stopping by."

Cole and Ian gazed into each other's eyes. For a moment, I was jealous, but I was being ridiculous. Cole and Ian? No way!

Ian nodded to me. Cole and I walked back to the Corvette, hopped in, and drove away.

"I was just thinking about something," I asked. "If you like guys, why were you making out with Adam's girl?"

"I like to make out—with girls and guys."

"Are you bisexual?"

"Maybe. Girls are okay to make out with, but I much prefer guys. Who needs labels? I'm going to do who and what I want when I want." Cole looked at me and raised an eyebrow. "Right now, I want you."

"Just right now?"

"Oh no. Now and again and again and again and..."

"I think I get the picture."

Cole pulled into the drive of an impressive, two-story brick house. He pushed the garage-door opener on his sun visor, and the garage door opened.

"This is the cleanest garage I've ever seen in my entire life," I said as the Corvette rolled to a stop and we got out.

It was true. The garage was completely empty. There were no tools, no boxes of junk, no clutter.

"My dad is a neatness freak," Cole said. "He's also a minimalist."

"Minimalist?"

"It means he believes less is more. Like... well, wait until you get inside and you'll see."

A door in the side of the garage led directly into the house. A short hallway passed a closed door and led us to the kitchen.

"Wow, this is nice!"

Everything in the kitchen looked brand new, almost as if it was never used. The place was spotless. Cole led me on into the living room. It was sparse but beautifully furnished. There was an expensive-looking leather couch, two armchairs, a couple of small side tables, an entertainment center, and that was it. The walls were empty except for a single painting of a stormy sky.

"This is minimalist," Cole said.

"I think I get it now."

Cole took my hand and led me upstairs. The hardwood floors echoed with our footsteps. Cole's touch made my whole body tingle. I yearned to press my lips to his.

Cole's room was a complete contrast to the rest of the house. It looked lived in. The queen-sized bed was made, but there were boxers, socks, and CD cases strewn on the floor. The desk was cluttered with a laptop, books, papers, and more CD cases. The computer had been left on. Screen-saver photos of mushrooms flashed on the screen. There was a wide-screen TV on the wall across from the bed and shelves of DVDs, CDs, and books. The room was so huge it almost seemed empty. Cole's bedroom had to be three or four times the size of mine.

Cole took both of my hands in his and stared into my eyes. I forgot about his room. Cole pulled me to him and kissed me.

"I've been waiting for this all day," he said.

I started to speak but Cole pressed his lips to mine once more and we began to make out as we stood in the middle of his bedroom. Cole kissed me hungrily and I once again found myself wondering why such a beautiful boy was interested in me. I didn't think about it long because Cole's lips and tongue were the ultimate distraction.

Cole tugged at my shirt as our tongues entwined. I lifted my arms and he pulled my shirt over my head. My breath came hard and fast. My inhibitions sailed out the window. I clawed at Cole's shirt and practically ripped it off his sexy body.

I stood and gazed at him for a few moments. He was beautiful. He wasn't heavily muscled like the jocks at school, but he was smooth, firm, and defined. His pecs were taut and beautifully shaped. I wanted to lick his small, brown nipples. His abdomen was flat, and I could easily make out his six-pack. I reached out and brushed my fingers across Cole's chest as he watched me. I looked into his eyes for a moment and then back at his body. I ran my hand over his pecs and then down over his abdomen. Cole reached out and began to feel me too.

Cole kissed me again and led me to his bed. We climbed up onto it. The bed was so massive we became lost upon it. We lay back and our lips met once more. We made out as our hands roamed everywhere over our torsos. I wondered if I dared to touch him *there*.

Still kissing me, Cole rolled over on top of me. I could feel his bare chest on mine. It was the sexiest thing ever. His smooth, soft skin rubbed against my own as we made out. Cole was every bit as excited as I was and I thought I'd go mad with pleasure.

Making out to our hearts' content, we rolled around on the bed. My heart was racing; pounding so hard I thought it might explode. Cole pulled his lips from mine and licked my jaw-line. I shivered with delight. Cole began to chew on my ear. Oh, my gosh!

"You're driving me crazy!" I gasped.

Cole kept right on chewing on my earlobe. His tongue darted into my ear and I squirmed with pleasure. I'd heard the guys at school talk about making out, but I'd never heard them mention ears. Was it a gay thing? I didn't know. Anyone who hadn't experienced it was sure missing out.

I rolled over on top of Cole and mimicked his movements. He gasped as I began to chew his earlobes. I was a virgin, but I learned fast.

I was so worked up I couldn't stand it. I didn't protest when Cole went for my pants. Soon, my jeans were on the floor. I leaned up on my elbows and watched as Cole removed his own jeans and then climbed back onto the bed with me. He was wearing sexy, white Calvin Klein boxers. The sight of Cole in nothing but boxers drove me mad with desire.

More making out, feeling, and rubbing against each other followed. Cole slid my boxers off. I was naked with another guy for the first time in my life. Sure, I'd been naked around other guys in the locker room plenty of times, but this was totally different.

I was completely at ease with Cole. I slid his boxers off. I'd checked out other guys at school. Fleeting glances. Mental snapshots. Now, I didn't have to steal a quick look. I could gaze upon Cole's naked body to my heart's content. I could see why so many artists chose nudes as their subject. Cole was beautiful.

I looked up at Cole and he smiled at me.

"Come here," he said.

Cole pressed his lips to mine again, and we lost ourselves in kissing. Cole ran his hand over my chest, down over my stomach, and lower still. I mimicked his movements. We made out as our hands roamed, but soon I was too curious to keep my mind on kissing. Cole and I leaned back on the pillows while our hands worked their magic. I began to breathe harder and harder. My body trembled. I cried out. I thought I might actually black out from the intense pleasure that ripped through my body.

I focused my attention solely on Cole after that. Soon, Cole began to breathe harder. He moaned and arched his back. I watched in fascination as his body convulsed with pleasure. I was mesmerized.

Cole turned his head to me when he'd finished. He was still panting. His brow was sweaty, and he was smiling.

"I'll be right back," he said.

He got up and padded into his private bathroom. I watched as he walked away. He had the cutest little butt! Cole returned soon with two wet, warm washcloths. We cleaned ourselves off.

After another trip to the bathroom to get rid of the washcloths, Cole climbed into bed with me again and held me close.

"Wow, my first time."

"Was it good?" Cole asked.

"You have to ask? You were there! It was incredible!"

"I'm glad." Cole held me closer.

"You make me feel so wonderful. I don't just mean the way you touch me. I mean the way you make me feel inside."

Cole hugged me and kissed my forehead. He gazed into my eyes and smiled.

"You make me happy," he said.

We lay entwined on his bed. I reveled in the closeness and the warmth of Cole's body. I snuggled up against him. Cole and I fell asleep and didn't awaken until it was nearly dark.

***

"Martin Wolfe!" Adam Henshaw screamed as he bolted into the cafeteria during lunch hour. "Martin Wolfe!"

Kids scurried out of the way. Everyone stared. Adam glanced frantically around the cafeteria. His chest heaved. His eyes were wide, wild, and panic-stricken. Mike Bradshaw jumped to his feet—his face chalk-white. Josh Lucas rushed to Adam. The whole gang at our table watched with rapt attention as Adam lost it.

"He was back there! Hanging there dead! He looked at me! He pointed at me and said he was coming for me!"

"Adam, calm down," Josh said.

Adam jerked his head in one direction and then another, as if fearful someone, or something, would slip up on him. He grew more frantic as he stood there, panting like an animal. Josh moved closer, and Adam freaked. He screamed and bolted away from Josh, crashing into a table. Josh closed in on him, trying to calm him, but Adam scrambled away.

"Stay away from me, demon!"

"Adam! It's me! Josh!"

"Stay away!"

Adam grabbed a fork and swung it in an arch, as if he was swinging a knife.

"Dude, chill!" Josh said.

"Adam, put the fork down," Mrs. Corlett, my literature teacher said. She was on cafeteria duty. Lucky her.

Adam turned toward her and held the fork out as if to ward her off. She didn't dare approach.

Josh motioned to some of his football buddies with his head. While Josh made sure Adam kept focused on him, the others crept around behind him. Kids scurried to get out of the way. Some cried. More teachers arrived and soon the principal. Adam's football buddies darted in from behind and grabbed him. Adam went nuts fighting and thrashing. The fork clinked as it hit the floor. Adam shrieked and fought like a wild man, but he couldn't break free.

"Take him to the office," Principal Duckworth said to the jocks. "No, take him to the nurse."

Principal Duckworth followed the football players and the struggling Adam. Mrs. Corlett and the teachers attracted by the disturbance tried to quiet the cafeteria and restore order. I glanced over to see Ian watching the jocks cart Adam away. The grin on his face disturbed me.

Mike Bradshaw watched as his friends manhandled Adam out of the cafeteria. When they disappeared from sight, Mike nervously looked over at our table. Ian's grin widened and he raised his eyebrows. Mike grabbed Chase's elbow, said something to him I couldn't hear, and then both of them looked back toward us. Chase pulled Mike back toward jock territory.

I said nothing about the incident until at the end of the lunch period. When Ian stood and went to dump his tray, I followed. I fell into step beside him.

"Ian, what's up with Mike and Adam? They act like they're scared of you."

"They are."

"But why?"

"Don't worry about it Daniel."

"Ian, come on!"

"Let's just say we have a new ally and that things are gonna change around here."

"Who are you talking about? What do you mean?"

"Martin Wolfe."

"Martin Wolfe? I don't get it."

"Haven't you heard the rumors yet Daniel? Haven't you heard that I'm a witch and control the ghost of Martin Wolfe?"

"Dude, that's crazy!"

"Is it?"

"Come on, tell me what's going on."

"I just did. There's nothing to worry about Daniel. Guys like us aren't going to have to live in fear anymore. There's not gonna be any more bullying. There's not gonna be any more abuse. I'm ending it."

"Ian..."

"I've got to get to class, man. Stop worrying. I've got your back. Martin Wolfe has us covered. If anyone gives you shit, tell me and I'll take care of them or rather *he* will."

Ian left me standing in the hallway. The chain at his waist clinked as he walked away. He seriously wanted me to believe he'd called up the ghost of Martin Wolfe? He wanted me to believe that the school ghost did his bidding? I didn't know what was up with Mike and Adam, but I seriously doubted a ghost attacked them.

Cedi

My life on the road settled into a routine, although that's probably not the best way to say it. The word "routine" carries with it a suggestion of dullness and my life was anything but! My routine consisted of waking up in a new place each morning, speeding in the back of a limo from one interview or signing to another, performing on stage, and meeting screaming fans. Each day was long but passed as if it lasted minutes instead of hours. Almost without exception, I fell asleep as soon as my head hit the pillow.

Ross and I made out at every opportunity, but those opportunities were few and far between and they rarely lasted for long. If we had ten minutes, we counted ourselves lucky. Something about the whole situation made our relationship more intense. There was something terribly exciting about stealing a kiss when others might discover us. It became a game with us. We stole even a few seconds together whenever we could. Our unpredictable, fleeting physical contact made me want Ross all the more.

An unexpected break came in our hectic schedule between our St. Petersburg and Orlando appearances. Well, it was unexpected to me. Everyone else knew about it and had doubtless looked forward to it. A good many of the crew planned to spend their time sleeping. Others intended to get out and enjoy the Florida sun.

Ross called my room at 11 a.m. on our first free day. I'd slept in until 10:30. I had just finished my shower and was giving some thought to breakfast or lunch when the phone rang.

"Wanna go out to eat and then walk on the beach?" Ross asked.

"Sure."

"I'll be right over."

My heart pounded wildly in my chest. We had the entire day free, and the next day too! The possibilities were limitless.

I quickly changed into cargo shorts, leather sandals, and a chocolate-brown t-shirt. I was reaching for my baseball cap and sunglasses when Ross knocked on the door. I opened the door to find Ross standing there dressed much the same as me, only wearing a red t-shirt that accented his tanned face and dark hair.

"There's a little place on the beach I thought we might try; it's called Tropic Delights," Ross said.

"Sounds good."

I half hoped Ross would push me into my room and take advantage of me, but I was equally excited to hang out with him. I'll admit I had a bit of a crush on him. Well, more than a bit. Ross was incredible! I was still somewhat star-struck, but don't get the idea that I was into Ross because he was famous. His fame added an extra touch of excitement, but I liked Ross for Ross. What was not to like?

Ross and I wore our baseball caps and sunglasses in an attempt to disguise ourselves, but isn't that the disguise all celebrities use? It's like wearing a sign that says, "Look at me! I'm famous!" It was a fine, hot Florida morning, and lots of people were walking along the beach sporting caps and glasses. Ross' long hair was a definite giveaway. Not many guys had hair *that* long, except for Jordan, of course.

Ross and I made it to our destination unmolested. Tropic Delights was well named, as it definitely had a tropical feel to it. It was an open-air restaurant with only a large thatched roof of palm fronds protecting customers from the sun. It gave one the feeling of sitting in a large grass hut. The sandy beach just beyond the wooden floor and the view of the Gulf of Mexico completed the effect.

I ordered a Hawaiian Dog, which was a foot long hot dog served with pineapple relish, mango, and coconut. Ross ordered skewered shrimp, which was grilled with tropical fruits.

A few people looked at us now and then, but Ross and I were still wearing our sunglasses and no one was quite sure who we were.

"I'm surprised Rod and Shawn aren't trailing us," I said in a low voice.

"I gave them my solemn word we'd remain within walking distance of the hotel and wouldn't create any mayhem."

"And they believed you?"

Ross grinned.

"They know how I love the beach. This area isn't one of the big tourist spots, so I think they figured we'd be safe enough. Besides, they probably have binoculars trained on us even now."

We admired the view and enjoyed the warmth of the moist, salt sea air as it drifted through the restaurant.

"This is a great place for a break," I said.

"Jordan and I insisted on it. Everyone is usually getting a bit worn down by this point in a tour, the crew especially. A little break works wonders."

"The crew works hard."

"Yeah. They have a lot more free time than we do, but they often have to work in a rush. It can be stressful, I'm sure. Jordan negotiates with the management company to make things as easy on them as possible, but even with a few perks, it's still a tough job."

Our food arrived. I had some reservations about the unique toppings and sides for my hot dog, but it was rather good. Ross pronounced his skewered shrimp "smashing" in his steadily improving British accent. He never failed to make me laugh.

Halfway through our meal, we were approached by two young girls. They couldn't have been more than thirteen.

"You're them, aren't you?" one of them asked.

"What 'them' do you mean?" asked Ross, grinning.

"*Phantom.*"

Ross took off his sunglasses. The girls squealed and caused everyone in the restaurant to look in our direction. It was largely an older crowd, so we weren't mobbed.

"I hope they're not bothering you," a middle-aged woman said as she approached. "Girls, you really shouldn't..."

"It's okay," Ross said. "We don't mind."

The girls were so excited they could hardly contain themselves. We autographed paper napkins for them since we didn't have anything else. Their mother had a digital camera, so we posed with the girls for a few photos. They left smiling and happy.

"I still can't get used to that," I said.

"Used to what?"

"How excited the fans get when they meet us. I mean... I'm just me."

"Hey! I'm just me too!" Ross said. "What an amazing coincidence!"

"You know what I mean."

"Well, get used to it Cedi. Your life will never be the same again. There's no going back. Even if you never sing again after this tour and spend the rest of your life working in a bookstore or diner, people will still recognize you."

"I don't know. I think of other people as famous. You're famous. Jordan's famous, but not me."

"I guess you haven't seen the most recent issue of *Teen Pop Stars*."

"What do you mean?"

"I'll show you in a bit."

Ross and I enjoyed a long, leisurely lunch. We were interrupted only once more by a grandmother who wanted our autographs for her grandkids.

"They'll be so thrilled!" she said after she thanked us. It was rather cool making someone happy just by signing a piece of paper.

After we paid our check, Ross and I stepped onto a boardwalk and walked further away from our hotel. Soon, we came to a news/souvenir stand, and Ross pointed to a copy of *Teen Pop Stars*. My eyes grew wide. I was on the cover! A title under my photo read, "The New British Invasion."

"I feel as though I'm in a dream world," I said as we walked away from the stand and headed for the beach.

"I know what you mean. I can remember the first time I saw myself staring back from the cover of a magazine... and the first time I saw myself on TV... and the first time I heard myself on the radio... and the first time I was mobbed by girls. It seems unreal in the beginning, but I got used to it. So will you."

"It's still fun, right?"

"Are you kidding? It's a blast! If I wasn't having fun, I'd be outta here so fast it'd make your head spin."

Ross pulled off his shirt. The sight of his bare, tanned chest made my breath catch in my throat. I pulled off my shirt too. I knew this would be one of my few chances to get some sun.

"You tan easily, don't you?" I asked.

"Yeah. It's the advantage of having a dark complexion. I have Native American ancestors."

"Mine are mainly British."

"You think?" Ross teased. "What is your full name again? I can never remember."

"Cedric William Arthur George Oliver Forbes-Hamilton, the Fourth."

"Only the British could come up with a name like that."

"I wish I had Native American ancestors. I don't tan easily."

"Just think of poor Jordan. He burns more easily than he tans. It must be all those Scandinavian genes."

"I might trade with him if I could be that good looking."

"You're cute just as you are, Cedi."

I could feel myself redden slightly. Why could Ross make me blush when almost no one else could?

"I'd rather be hot than cute."

"The two aren't mutually exclusive Cedi. You're cute *and* hot."

I began to breathe a bit faster. I stole a look at Ross' taut, muscular body. I wanted to lick him like a lollipop.

"Do you miss Kieran?" I asked to pull my mind from Ross' sexy, sexy body.

"Yeah. He can be rather a pain. He's a bit too serious, you know. Jordan, Kieran, and I are like brothers. We argue and get ticked off with each other, but we're there for each other when it counts."

"Do you think things will change when he gets married?"

"They almost have to change."

"Are you afraid he'll leave the band?"

"Kind of, but I'm not too worried. Even if Kieran leaves *Phantom*, we'll still be friends. We'll still keep in touch. We've been through too much to drift apart. We knew *Phantom* wouldn't last forever when we started. Of course, back then we didn't expect to last more than a couple of years, even if we did make it big. Most bands are like that; a flash in the pan. One day they're on every TV show and on the cover of every teen magazine and the next day they're gone."

"I kind of have a thing for Kieran," I admitted.

"Kind of? Dude, you've got it bad for him. It's so obvious."

"It is?"

"Yes."

"Do you think Kieran knows?"

"Probably."

"This is embarrassing."

"Don't worry about it. Kieran won't think anything about it. You do realize that he's not into dudes."

"His upcoming marriage to Natalie clued me into that."

"Well, getting married doesn't necessarily mean a guy isn't into guys, but in Kieran's case, he's about as hetero as one can get. Jordan, Kieran, and I are very honest about such things with each other. Jordan's gay and has virtually no interest in girls. Kieran is just the opposite. I like both."

"Me too. I like both, I mean. To be honest, I don't quite understand how anyone can be attracted to only males or only females. We're all humans. There isn't any difference between us."

"Well, there are physical differences, Cedi. Males and females do have different parts."

"I know, but mostly we're the same, you know? I'd hate to think I had to pick one or the other. Of course, if I fell in love with someone I could choose."

I thought of Thad, but I didn't want to discuss him with Ross just then.

"I'm embarrassed that Kieran knows I like him, like *that*."

"Cedi. Do you know how many girls have told me they love me? How many guys? A lot. The thing is, they don't love me; they love an image of me. They love the Ross they've created in their minds. They don't know me well enough to love me. I'm quite sure if they knew me better they wouldn't love me at all."

"I don't know about that Ross."

"What I'm saying is that you love a version of Kieran. What you love is a fantasy. It's not real. I'm not saying Kieran isn't worth loving, because he is. I love him as a friend and as a brother. Kieran is your idol. You told me yourself he's the reason you got into music. You've got a larger-than-life image of him. You don't know the real Kieran, at least not well. You're in love with that larger-than-life image, and Kieran knows it. So don't worry. It's cool. I'm sure he takes it as a compliment. The two of you could never be lovers, but you can be friends."

Ross looked thoughtful.

"Have you ever had feelings for Kieran?" I asked. "You know, romantic feelings?"

Ross didn't answer right away.

"No, I haven't. I've never had romantic feelings for Kieran..."

Ross seemed lost in thought and also a bit sad.

"I'm sorry. I'm asking about things that are none of my business."

"It's okay, but don't worry about Kieran. I'm sure he's cool with how you feel about him."

We walked on along the beach, our distance from others giving us privacy to talk. No one paid us any special attention. We were just two guys walking and talking, like so many others. After all the concerts and all the autograph signings, it felt good to just be me.

I felt as if I'd known Ross forever. I liked his easygoing, fun-loving manner. Like me, Ross never took anything too seriously. He looked for what was good in life and enjoyed what he found.

We pulled off our sandals and waded in the surf. The sand and warm water rushed between my toes. It might have been the most enjoyable day of my life.

Ross paused and gazed into my eyes.

"Cedi, would you like to come to my room?"

My heart beat faster. I felt as if I could breathe fire.

"Yes!" I said, trying to calm my breath.

The two of us walked onto the sand, slipping on our sandals as we left the water. Moving faster now, Ross and I walked along the beach toward our hotel. Anticipation filled the air. I was consumed by need and want. I resisted the urge to break into a run. My body actually trembled with desire.

We stepped into Ross' room. Ross closed and locked the door. He turned to me, leaned down, took me in his arms, and pressed his lips against mine. I melted into Ross, clinging to his strong, lean torso as our lips met and caressed. At that moment, nothing mattered but him.

Our kiss was long and deep, an act of intimate sharing that went far beyond the physical act. It created a bond, a connection, between us more emotional than physical. It was meant to be. People weren't drawn together to mate. We were drawn together to share ourselves, to become as close as humanly possible. I knew the exquisite pleasure of sex, but sex was more a byproduct of whatever it was that drew two people together. Sex was merely the physical expression of something far more important. I could feel that indefinable something surrounding us, penetrating us, as Ross and I stood kissing and holding each other close.

After several long, slow minutes of making out, Ross and I drew back from each other slightly. I ran my hand over Ross' bare chest, feeling his hard muscles and soft skin. I pushed his cap off and ran my fingers through his long, black hair. I caressed his face and explored his torso with my fingertips.

When Ross touched me, his caress was electric. I was more intently aware of the sensation of his fingertips on my torso than I'd been aware of anything in my life. My breath came hard and fast; my heart raced. I trembled with excitement, desire, and emotions I cannot even begin to describe.

Our fingertips and lips began to roam. Ross chewed on my ear lobes and bit at my neck and shoulders. He explored my torso and teased me by drawing ever closer but never quite reaching what was stirring in my shorts. Soon, it was my turn. I caressed Ross' beautiful body with my lips and fingers, coming to know him intimately. I hovered in a state of intense arousal, yet I hesitated to move on to what I knew could satisfy my desire. This time with Ross, this intimacy, was too precious to rush.

Ross was an incredible lover. He was forceful, yet gentle; intense, yet tender. His touch was so exquisite it was nearly unbearable, yet I never wanted him to stop touching me.

We sank onto his bed and made slow, passionate love. It was an hour before we even pulled off our shorts. Even when we were naked, we spent another hour exploring, caressing, and kissing each other without performing a single act that most would consider sex. When Ross finally leaned down and engulfed me, the pleasure was nearly more than I could bear. I couldn't control myself for a moment longer and climaxed almost before he got started.

I would have been embarrassed by my lack of control, but Ross and I had been making love for over two hours. Ross quickly lost control too when I swallowed him. His cries of ecstasy filled me with joy.

Our sexual needs met; we lay on the bed holding each other close. Neither of us wanted the moment to end. We fell asleep in each other's arms, completely content.

We were awakened by a knock at the door. Startled, Ross jumped up and pulled on his shorts, leaving his boxers lying on the floor. I arose more slowly and slipped on my boxers as Ross peered through the keyhole. He opened the door.

Jordan took in the scene at a glance. There was no mistaking it; the rumpled bed, our near nudity, Ross' boxers on the floor. I was glad Ross had opened the door for Jordan. Had we hidden from him, it would have cheapened what we'd shared. It would have made it seem wrong. Ross and I were both adults and could sleep with each other if we chose.

Jordan gave no hint of disapproval. I couldn't read his expression at all. The only indication that he was surprised by what he witnessed was the too long moment of silence before he spoke.

I don't even remember what he said to Ross. My mind raced. Jordan had caught me in bed with Ross! What would he think of me now?

I almost laughed at myself. I'd never cared what anyone thought before, but this was Jordan. I'd come to know him, but still... he was Jordan from *Phantom*! I grinned at the absurdity of my fear. I was in a tizzy because Jordan of *Phantom* had discovered us. I was completely overlooking the fact I'd made love with Ross, *Phantom's* drummer, and that I was a member of *Phantom* myself. When would my life begin to feel real?

Jordan departed and Ross closed the door.

"Want to get something to eat? I'm hungry again."

"Hmm. I wonder why?" I asked, grinning.

Ross didn't kick me to the curb now that he'd had me. I didn't expect that and yet it was reassuring. I didn't know where our relationship was going, but it was obviously about more than sex. Ross wasn't one of those guys who showed his partner the door as soon as he got off. We'd lingered in bed after our needs were satisfied, we'd slept together, and now we were going out to spend yet more time with each other. I smiled.

Ross and I dressed and headed out. The sun was low and gilded the Gulf with an orange/golden hue. Ross and I walked along the beach in no particular hurry.

"Do you think Jordan will be okay with... us?" I asked as we walked upon the sand and listened to the surf.

"Does it matter?" Ross asked.

"I guess not, but... If he was anyone else, it wouldn't matter to me, but... I don't know. It's weird, but I feel like I need his approval. I know it doesn't make sense, but that's how I feel."

"Maybe it's because you're new to the band. Jordan does run things. Jordan, Kieran, and I have always had an equal say in what goes on with *Phantom*, but Jordan has an incredible talent for organization and a very good business sense. If he wasn't a musician, he could probably be a C.E.O. of a major corporation. Kieran and I have always let him make most of the decisions because he always makes the right choices. Jordan has this... presence. I think that's probably why you feel like you do."

"Do you think he'll disapprove?" I asked.

"If his opinion about us matters to you, you'll have to ask him not me."

"I'm not making you angry, am I?"

"Why would I be angered by honesty?"

Ross smiled at me. We walked onto the boardwalk and checked out the little restaurants and shops as we passed. We found one called simply "The Gulf" that served gourmet hamburgers and stepped inside.

The restaurant was more upscale than Tropical Delights where we'd eaten lunch. It was closed off from the beach, although the sunset was visible through large windows that faced the Gulf. The interior was dark, lit by candles and lamps, rather romantic for a burger place.

Ross and I took a seat in a booth. We placed our orders and then chatted while an oil lamp lit our faces with a golden glow. We talked and laughed and made fun of Jordan and the way he got ticked off when someone called him the Prince of Rock & Roll. Even I dared say it to him now.

Our burgers arrived and they were delicious! Mine had bacon, cheddar, Swiss, and Colby cheese, lettuce, red onion, tomato, and barbeque sauce. Ross had one with Portobello mushrooms, honey Dijon, lettuce, red onion, and Swiss cheese. Each burger came with a mound of spicy fries. I hadn't realized how famished I was until my food arrived. I pounced on it.

We weren't quite so lucky as we had been earlier in the day as far as privacy was concerned. A few college kids spotted us and swarmed around our booth. Some high-school kids soon joined them. Before long, our presence had created quite a disturbance. While Ross and I talked with the fans and signed autographs for them, he whipped out his cell phone and made a call. I didn't know whom he'd called until Rod and Shawn showed up a few minutes later.

With the help of our bodyguards, we extricated ourselves from the restaurant. We shook hands with fans, signed autographs for them, and even posed for photos while we slowly maneuvered toward the doors. Once outside we moved a little more quickly, but not so fast as to be rude. Most of the fans who had discovered us followed us along, which was fine. The presence of Rod and Shawn kept everything under control.

When we reached our hotel, we bid our fans goodbye. Rod and Shawn made sure they stayed put while we made our graceful getaway. Soon, Ross and I were alone again.

"That should make me some brownie points with Shawn," Ross said. "He'll think I was very mature and responsible for giving him a call." Ross grinned mischievously.

"I'm glad you did. I don't know how we would've gotten out of there without them."

Ross looked as tired as I felt. It wasn't all that late, but it had been quite a day. We stopped in front of his room.

"I'll see you tomorrow?" I asked.

"Wanna do breakfast? I'm whacked, but I know I'll be up early after going to bed this soon."

"Yeah!"

"I'll call you when I get up."

"Cool. Nite, Ross."

"Goodnight, Cedi."

I felt like kissing him, but we were standing in public view. Sure, no one was around for now, but that could change at any moment.

Replaying the events of the day in my mind, I walked on toward my room. As I passed the room Jordan shared with Ralph, the door opened and Jordan stepped out.

"Hey," I said.

"Hi Cedi," Jordan paused. "Do you have a minute?"

"Sure. I was just on my way to bed."

"This won't take long. Come in."

I felt an impending sense of doom as I entered Jordan's room. Ralph was out so it was just the two of us.

"Listen Cedi, what you and Ross do is your business. It's not my place to say anything, but be careful, okay?"

"Careful? You mean like... safe sex? I wouldn't do anything..."

"No. I mean... well... I feel like I shouldn't be sticking my nose in, but I don't want to see you get hurt. Don't expect too much from Ross, okay?"

"What do you mean?"

"I don't know what you two have going and I'm not asking you to tell me, but be careful if you feel yourself getting too serious with Ross. He's a great guy and he would never hurt you on purpose, but he doesn't always think things through. He's not the relationship type of guy, either—at least, he never has been. I hope that changes, but Ross is... Ross."

"He sure is," I said, a sense of admiration slipping into my voice. Jordan smiled.

"I'm not putting Ross down, but he can be a bit immature. He's twenty-two going on twelve. He's very sweet, even innocent in some ways, but he's also capable of hurting someone without even realizing it. Ross would never hurt you, or anyone, intentionally, but he might hurt you without meaning to."

"I don't know what Ross and I have, Jordan. Today, well, that was the first time we've ever been together. I don't know where we're going from here. I don't even know what I want. My life is so crazy right now. I like Ross. We've become good friends. I care about him and I know he cares about me. What we shared today... well, I don't know what it means. I don't even know what I want it to mean."

"Like I said, it's none of my business, but I don't want to see you get hurt. I'm sticking my nose in way further than I should, but sometimes I can't help myself. I'm sure Ross can tell you all about that." Jordan grinned.

"I appreciate that you care. It's okay. And don't worry. I'll be careful."

"Have a good night Cedi."

"Good night Jordan."

I continued my journey to my room. Once there, I shut myself in. I stripped down to my boxers and then put on the wife-beater I usually wore to bed. I slipped under the covers and gazed at the ceiling. Where were things going with Ross and me? Where did I want them to go? Did I want a boyfriend or just a friend I could get intimate with at times? Perhaps not knowing was a good thing. Jordan had warned me not to expect too much from Ross. If I was in love with him, I might be in for a disappointment. Things were likely much better as they were. I loved Ross, but I wasn't in love with him. Those are two different things. For the time being I was going to be happy with what I had. All things considered that was an easy task.

Toby

"Wanna freak everyone out?" Ian asked as we talked quietly between seventh and eighth period.

"What do you mean?" I asked nervously.

"Kiss me. Right here. Right now."

"Are you crazy?"

Ian laughed. Once more, I got a glimpse of his veiled cuteness.

"Just think of how they would react."

"That's what scares me."

"The time of fear is coming to an end," Ian said confidently.

"Well, I'm not quite ready for everyone to know about me."

Ian nodded.

"Meet me tonight then."

"Where?"

"At the edge of town, by the old church."

"The abandoned church? By the old graveyard?"

"Yeah."

"It's creepy out there."

"Which is why no one else will be there. It'll be just you and me." Ian grinned. I began to breathe a little faster. I remembered the taste of his lips.

"Okay. What time?"

"Eight p.m. Meet me in front of the old church."

Nervous anticipation flowed through me as I walked toward eighth-period drama. The idea of setting foot in the old cemetery at night frightened me, but the idea of being alone with Ian excited me even more. I was beginning to see a side to Ian that I never suspected was there. Underneath the scary Goth façade was a sweet and caring boy. I wanted to know that boy better.

***

Visions of ghosts and goblins flowed through my mind as I walked toward the old church on the north edge of town. I tried to be brave, but I was skittish and fearful. I thought about the boy I was meeting. I was intrigued by Ian to say the least. Before the night he kissed me, I'd never once considered him romantically. I'd never fantasized about him, ogled him, or even casually checked him out. Ian was so different from everyone else that I'd never thought about him like that at all. My dream boy was someone like Orlando, Cole, or Daniel. A Goth? What was I thinking?

I replayed our first kiss in my mind. I relived the moments when he walked by my side. I remembered the feel of his arms around me as he sought to comfort me. My fear began to ebb and was replaced by warm and fuzzy thoughts of Ian. He was far more than a scary Goth.

The houses grew fewer as I walked north, until there were none. Gnarled trees leaned over the street, as if seeking to block out the moonlight. I could just make out the old church in the distance. Its weathered clapboard siding was the only thing standing out in the gathering darkness. I felt a shiver travel up my spine as I stepped closer.

Tall dead grass surrounded the old church. It had been an abandoned relic for my entire lifetime. I didn't know why it had closed. Perhaps the parishioners had died off one by one until none was left. Maybe the church had merged with another. Maybe a newer church had been built in town to replace it. Who knew? Not me.

The weatherworn paint of the clapboards glowed blue in the moonlight. The stained-glass windows were dark, revealing nothing of their brilliance. I trembled slightly. I reminded myself that nothing was present in the darkness that was not there in the bright light of day. All the talk at school of ghosts had me spooked. I couldn't help but gaze into the forsaken cemetery to make sure it was empty.

I drew in a sharp breath as Ian hopped down out of a tree with his overcoat flying like a cloak. He seemed to appear out of the air. Standing before me, he was a darker shadow among shadows. My heart raced with anticipation and fear.

"I don't know anyone else who would have come," Ian said. "You're brave."

"I'm not that brave."

"Brave enough. Come on. I want to show you something."

Ian took my hand and led me toward the graveyard. My heart raced with fear, but the touch of Ian's hand calmed me. We stepped through the old iron gates, permanently rusted open long before I was born. It was like entering a haunted world.

Ian and I waded through a sea of dry, waist-high grass. Many of the old grave markers were almost completely hidden. I wondered how many of them we could not see at all. It was hard to make anything out by the moonlight except shadows and shapeless forms. I drew closer to Ian. I was comforted by his presence.

We stepped under ancient cedars. The old boughs were so thick the moonlight did not penetrate, but Ian moved confidently forward as if he had the eyes of a cat. *Or a vampire.*

A small flicker of light appeared ahead. As we drew closer, I spotted another and another. Soon, Ian and I stood before a tombstone, illuminated by half a dozen votive candles. The flickering flames only intensified the spookiness of the scene. The candlelight made our surroundings theatrical. My journey into the darkness had an unreal quality and I felt as if I was in a play.

"I found it," Ian said. "The grave of Martin Wolfe."

His name was carved deep in the stone, along with the dates of birth and death—August 4, 1938 to January 21, 1953. A chill went up my spine. There had been so much talk in school of Martin Wolfe that standing before his actual grave was a bit too freaky. I turned and looked into Ian's eyes.

"Ian, what's going on—at school? Why are the football jocks afraid of you?"

"Not me." Ian pointed to the grave. "They're afraid of Martin Wolfe. He was one of us, you know; an outsider. He was tormented when he went to school too. Guys like Mike and Adam drove him to suicide."

"They're afraid of you too. Krista thinks you're taking advantage of coincidence. Eddie thinks it's all a plot by the jocks to freak out the sixth graders. Most people think you've summoned the ghost of Martin Wolfe and that he attacks whomever you curse. So I'm asking; what's going on?"

"I'm not ready to tell you yet, Toby, but don't be afraid. I promise you that no harm will come to you. You're one of the few who has always been kind to me."

"I barely knew you until recently."

"True, but you never tormented me. You smiled at me. You said 'hi' in the halls. You always treated me with kindness and respect, as you do everyone. I remember who treats me with kindness—and who doesn't."

Ian was freaking me out. He spoke as if he actually controlled the ghost. He didn't say so in words, but his confidence spoke volumes. It was as if he had no doubt he could handle guys like Mike Bradley and Adam Henshaw—guys who had, until recently, preyed upon Ian without fear.

"Do you trust me Toby?" Ian asked, stepping closer.

"Yes."

I didn't know why I trusted him, but I did. I trembled slightly with fear, but it wasn't fear of Ian. His presence comforted me.

Ian closed in on me slowly, as one might approach a fawn in the forest. He leaned down and gently kissed me on the lips. Just like the first time, the kiss was fleeting but wondrous. Ian was so gentle, so tender, that I could feel the sweet boy inside of him. Had anyone known the Ian that I sensed within? I had the feeling the answer was "no." Not even his Goth and skater buddies knew this Ian.

Holding me as he kissed me, Ian pressed his lips to mine again, taking my face in his hands. His touch was delicate. He barely moved his lips, but something about the way he kissed me held me in the moment. I was more aware of Ian, more aware of the kiss, than I'd ever been aware of anyone or anything in my life. Ian's kiss was pure magic. Maybe he *was* a witch. Maybe he'd cast his spell upon me.

I grasped Ian's slim abdomen, running my hands up and down his sides under his coat. He was firm and sexy. I wrapped my arms around him as he pulled me close. His overcoat engulfed me, closing us off from the world. It was warm inside with Ian. I felt the same cozy feeling I did when walking in a downpour safe under an umbrella.

Ian and I stood holding each other and kissing while time passed without meaning. Not once did our mouths open. Not once did our tongues entwine. We moved ever so slowly, but I'd never experienced such an intensely sensual sensation in my entire life.

Ian didn't pressure me for more than a closed-mouth kiss. His hands didn't wander beyond my back. Part of me wanted to tear at clothes, but Ian held me spellbound. His presence and manner calmed me. I knew Ian was content to kiss me and hold me close. He made me feel special. I felt my wounded heart begin to heal.

When our lips parted—ten minutes, twenty minutes, an hour, a day later?—Ian grinned at me. He even laughed, a warm joyous laugh such as I'd never heard from him before. I had the feeling no one had ever heard it. Ian caressed my face.

"You're beautiful Toby."

I shyly looked down for a moment, but I did not disagree with him. At that moment, I felt beautiful. I looked back up into his eyes. How had I missed seeing this wonderful boy? How had I looked at him day after day without seeing the sweet, beautiful boy inside? I was seeing him now. Orlando, Daniel, and Cole no longer mattered.

"I'd better take you home Toby. It's getting late."

I looked at the tombstone. The candles had burned low. Two had already gone out, and the others were near their end. Ian took my hand and we walked away from the grave, leaving the remaining candles to burn themselves out. I no longer feared the old cemetery or church. I felt safe with Ian as I had with no one else. Most of my classmates said Ian was a witch. I didn't believe that for a moment, but he possessed magic without a doubt. It came from inside him, from his beautiful soul.

I sighed and leaned my head on Ian's shoulder. He wrapped an arm around my waist. He leaned in and kissed the top of my head. I felt loved as I never had before.

"I'm so happy," I said quietly.

"So am I."

"When can I see you again?" I asked.

I couldn't see his face, but I was certain Ian smiled.

"Whenever you wish."

"Would you like to... I don't know... go out... like on a real date? We could... I dunno... eat supper together."

"That sounds wonderful."

Ian's words nearly made me swoon. I was crushing on him big time.

Ian walked me all the way home. We kissed again under the shadow of the oak, and then Ian stood on the sidewalk and watched as I went inside. I could feel his eyes on me, watching over me. I turned as I opened the door and waved to him. Once inside, I leaned up against the door with a smile on my face. It had been a truly wonderful night.

"You're out a little late," said my mom, who was sitting in the living room. I hadn't even noticed her when I came in.

"Not too late I hope. I lost track of time."

"You're well within curfew. What were you doing that made you lose track of time?"

"I was with a boy, a wonderful boy."

Few gay sons could say that to their mother, but my family knew about me. I could talk to them about anything. I was lucky.

"Orlando? Are the two of you back together?"

"No, not Orlando. Someone new."

"From the smile on your face, I gather you like him."

"He's incredible!"

"It's nice to see you smile again."

I walked over to my mom. I gave her a hug and a kiss. I bade her "good night" and walked up the stairs. I felt as though I could dance my way to my room, as if I was in a musical.

Mackenzie sat on his bed listening to his iPod. He looked up when I entered and ripped his earphones off.

"You were making out with Daniel, weren't you?"

"Wrong."

"Ah, come on. I saw you checking him out when he was here. You want him bad. You have a big, dopey grin on your face. That either means you were making out with Daniel or that you and Orlando are back together."

"Orlando and Daniel are history."

"So, what's his name?"

"I'm not ready to tell you."

"So, I am right, aren't I?"

"You're quite a little psycho," I said.

"Don't you mean psychic?"

"No." I laughed.

"You are so not funny."

I quickly stepped over to Mackenzie, leaned down, and kissed his forehead.

"I love you, little brother."

"Oh my God. You've got it way bad!"

"I think I do," I said sighing.

"Tell me who it is!"

"No."

"You know I'll find out."

"I know. I'll tell you soon but not just yet."

"You're impossible! You're in one of your sickeningly happy moods."

"Yes!"

"Toby?"

"Yeah?"

"I'm glad."

"Thanks, little bro."

I realized as I sat down at my desk that I'd completely forgotten about the play auditions the following afternoon. Ian had shoved *A Christmas Carol* right out of my head. Nothing and no one had ever done that before. I had chosen to try out for the role of Scrooge's nephew and had planned to spend the entire evening and night practicing. I already had the lines down, but I'd done virtually no work on getting into character. I looked at the clock. There was no time now. I had homework and then I had to get to bed. I would have to wing it. That would normally have put me in a panic, but the play didn't seem to matter anymore. Yeah, Mackenzie was right. I had it way bad for Ian.

Daniel

Auditions for *A Christmas Carol* were after school. I tried out for the Ghost of Christmas Past, but I didn't think I did all that well. I'd probably get stuck with a non-speaking role again. Maybe, if I got lucky, I'd get cast as the Ghost of Christmas Yet to Come. It was a non-speaking role, but it was totally cool. I wanted to try out for it, but I didn't know how. I wasn't going to worry about the outcome of my audition. It wasn't as if I was planning to be an actor when I grew up.

After my audition, Cole took me out to eat and then to his house for the third evening in a row. I had yet to meet his dad, but his absence meant Cole and I had plenty of private time. You're probably thinking Cole and I went at it like rabbits. I'd be lying if I said a part of me didn't want to do just that, but we were taking things slowly. I was a virgin and it was Cole's suggestion that we take things one-step at a time. He said that's how a meaningful relationship had to start. I was so thrilled Cole was *that* interested in me, that I didn't mind keeping my raging hormones in check. Besides, my pent-up passions had now found a release that didn't involve my own hand. To be honest, I would have done anything Cole wanted. I would've been his sex toy! What he was offering me was so much more than sex. I felt as if I could walk on air!

We entered Cole's empty, echoing house and made our way directly to his bedroom. We made out, clothed, for the longest time. Then, the clothes began to slowly come off—my shirt, Cole's shirt, Cole's jeans, my jeans, and so forth—until we were both naked. We rolled around on the bed as we made out, and it was a wonder I didn't lose control from that alone. Cole's beautiful body aroused me to such a fever pitch I felt I could reach orgasm just by looking at him.

I yearned for oral sex so powerfully I nearly went for it. I controlled myself. I let Cole set the pace. My patience was rewarded. Cole introduced me to something new. As we made out, Cole licked my chest. He slid his tongue over my right nipple, and I moaned. He began to suck it and ever so gently bite at it. I squirmed with pleasure and moaned yet more. When Cole had introduced me to the delights of having my ear lobes chewed upon, I thought nothing could feel more erotic and pleasurable. I was wrong.

Cole worked on my nipples, moving from one to the other until I thought I'd die from the pleasure of it. When he lifted his face from my chest to kiss me once more, I grabbed his head and darted my tongue into his mouth. I was all over that boy. In no time at all, I had him on his back and licked my way down his chest. I licked, sucked, and bit on his nipples as he moaned. Could making love get any hotter than this?

We finished off with hand action again. I was more than content. Cole's hand upon my penis felt a hundred times better than mine ever had. Touching him *there*, in his most intimate spot, was so sexy, so intimate I almost couldn't believe he allowed it. I shared things with Cole I'd never shared with another.

When we finished and wiped ourselves off with damp, warm washcloths, we lay on the bed again and cuddled. Cole drifted off to sleep, but I lay awake. I gazed down at his naked body as he slept, thinking how beautiful the human body can be. Cole's body was so perfect it was as though he wasn't real, yet he was completely real. I guess some wouldn't have thought him perfect. Some would've thought his muscles weren't big enough or shoulders weren't broad enough. In my eyes no one in the entire world was more beautiful than Cole Fitch.

I became aroused again as I lay gazing at Cole's smooth, sculpted body. I knew that if I didn't get up I'd never be able to keep my hands off him. I slipped out of bed and pulled on my boxers. I slipped into my jeans and hung my shirt from my belt, just in case Cole's dad returned home. I didn't want him finding a strange and nearly naked boy wandering around his house.

I gazed back at Cole as he lay sleeping. His chest rose and fell with each breath. He looked like an angel. I stole out of the room and down the hall. I didn't think Cole would mind me looking around a bit, so I turned a doorknob and opened a door. I walked into a large bedroom. At least, I guessed it was a bedroom, for it was completely empty. There was not a stick of furniture, not so much as a picture on the wall. It was a large house so perhaps Cole and his dad had no need of this room.

I closed the door behind me and walked down the hall. I entered another room to find it was also empty. Cole had told me his father was a minimalist, but this was crazy. I tried yet another door with the same result. What was going on?

I began to feel like a snoop as I wandered through the house, but I was intrigued by the mystery of the empty rooms. I didn't want to stay away from Cole's bedroom too long for fear he would awaken and find me gone. I didn't check out all the rooms, but those I did were empty. I knew Cole and his dad had moved in recently, so perhaps most of their stuff hadn't arrived yet. It seemed to me that it would've all come at once in a big truck, but maybe not.

I thought about Cole's dad. I hadn't seen him once. Cole said he was a very busy guy, but Cole and I were hanging out more and more, quite often at Cole's house. It seemed odd that his dad was never home.

I was being foolish. I guess I was skittish because my relationship with Cole was too good to be true. The mere fact that Cole Fitch was interested in me was, in itself, nearly impossible. We're talking about a boy who could have easily been on a magazine cover. Pile on top of that his feelings for me and our relationship became unbelievable. It was truly a million-in-one shot. As unlikely as it seemed, it wasn't a fantasy. Cole cared about me. Our relationship was real. Those were the facts. I was so deliriously happy I feared someone or something would come along and ruin it all.

I crept back to Cole's room, undressed, and slipped into bed. The sight of Cole lying there naked turned me on like mad. I couldn't help myself. I leaned over and kissed him. Cole slowly awakened and began to kiss me back. Before long, we were making out like nobody's business.

Later, our passion spent once more, I lay in Cole's arms as we gazed at the ceiling.

"When do I get to meet your dad?" I asked.

"Do you think we're to the meeting the parents stage?" Cole teased.

"I just feel weird being here without ever having met him. What if I go down to the kitchen sometime and he's there? He'll see this strange boy and wonder what's up."

"First of all, you're not strange."

"You know what I mean!"

"Yeah. Second, I think he would assume you're one of my friends."

"I guess you're right, but I'd still like to meet him."

"You will. Soon. I'm not sure when, but soon. When do I get to meet your parents?"

"Any time you want."

"Can I introduce myself as your boyfriend?"

"Don't you dare! My parents don't know about me."

"I'm just teasing you Daniel. You're so cute when you get upset."

"You're cute all the time."

"Would you like me if I wasn't cute?" Cole asked.

"Well, I was drawn by your looks. I'm still rather fond of your sizzling hotness. I've spent enough time with you now that I have a sense of what you're like—inside. You are the best-looking guy I've ever met in my life, but you're not conceited. You're kind. You care about others. You're sweet and loving. I can honestly say I would like you if you weren't cute. I know that's easy to say, but it's the truth."

"I believe you Daniel," Cole said, giving me a little squeeze. "I'd also like you if you weren't cute. You're beautiful on the inside."

"That's the only place I'm beautiful."

"Grrrr. You are so wrong. You're hot Daniel. Why do you think I can't keep my hands off you?"

"Mmm. I love to hear you say that."

"I'm not only saying it. I mean it."

"That makes it even better."

***

I noticed the football jocks began to give Cole a wide berth at school. I didn't know what was up, but I was relieved. I had very much feared that Adam, Mike, and Josh would beat Cole senseless. He was hot enough to be a threat to them, and those guys got off on being at the top of the food chain.

The real shocker, in more ways than one, came after school when I discovered Cole making out with Cindy Erickson, Adam's girlfriend. I burned with jealousy and anger, but I didn't have time to wallow in my feelings. At almost the same time as I spotted Cole and Cindy, Adam came around the corner and spotted them too. I hurried forward. I was prepared to jump in and help Cole. Despite what was going on, I cared for him deeply. I'd do anything to protect him.

Adam didn't charge toward the pair as I expected. His muscles tensed and flexed as if he wanted to tear Cole to pieces, but he didn't grab Cole and punch him in the face. He didn't do anything except glare. Cole pulled away from Cindy just long enough to give Adam a smirk. I watched, astonished, as Adam didn't do shit. He looked away and headed right on down the hallway.

I was too amazed to be angry for a few moments, but then anger consumed me. Cole was mine! I'd known all along that what we had was too good to be true and the proof was before me. Cole was cheating on me—with a girl no less!

"Thanks Cindy. I have to get going."

"See you later Cole."

Adam's girlfriend departed. Cole turned. Only then did he spot me.

"Hey Daniel."

"Don't "Hey Daniel" me! Why were you kissing her? I thought you and I had something special."

"We do."

"So why were you making out with Cindy?"

"To rub salt in Adam's wounds."

My lower lip began to tremble, but I willed myself not to cry.

"Damn, Daniel. I'm sorry. Listen, making out with Cindy is nothing. I did it to get at Adam. I'm sorry. I should have talked to you about it first."

"Do you plan on doing anything else with her to get at Adam?"

"Nothing beyond kissing. I don't feel that way about her. I don't want to hurt you. I just want to make Adam suffer for the pain he's caused others. He deserves a taste of his own medicine."

"Let's forget about us for a minute. What about Cindy? How can you use here like that Cole?"

"I'm not using her Daniel. I already told her I'm not interested in her as a girlfriend. I told her we weren't going beyond making out."

"She's willing to do that with you and risk her relationship with Adam?"

"Yes. I'm getting back at Adam, and she's making him jealous. Cindy told me Adam takes her for granted. He won't now. Cindy will have that boy on a leash soon and it will serve him right. Everybody wins."

"I don't know..."

"About us Daniel? I'm truly sorry if I've upset you. I swear there is nothing more to Cindy and me than I've just told you. You're the one I care about. You're the one I want to be with."

I looked into Cole's puppy-dog eyes and melted.

"I can't even stay angry with you!" I said.

Cole smiled.

"I'll see you later Daniel."

Cole looked around to make sure the coast was clear and quickly kissed me on the lips. He smiled at me and walked away. He looked as sexy from behind as he did from the front. Mmm. What a nice butt.

Maybe I was naïve, but I believed him. I knew in my heart that Cole Fitch cared about me.

The Cole/Cindy/Adam drama wasn't the only shock of the day. I also witnessed a bizarre scene between Ian and Josh Lucas. Josh stomped over to our table during lunch period and glared at Ian. Once again, I thought I was going to have to rush to the aid of someone I cared about. But, once again, it was unnecessary.

"Call your ghost off Ian. I'm warning you."

"And what are you going to do about it if I don't, Josh?"

I was amazed at Ian's bravery—or his stupidity—depending on how one looked at it. Ian didn't do confrontations. Usually, he lowered his head and took whatever abuse the jocks hurled at him. He had little choice. He was tall but not strong. He wouldn't have stood a chance against one of the jocks, and those guys stuck together. Ian had been more defiant of late but never to such an extreme.

"I oughta beat the shit outta you right now," snarled Josh.

"Go for it," Ian said dispassionately. He stared straight into Josh's eyes.

My jaw dropped open. Andy and Jake stared at Ian, amazed.

"Ian..." Auddie said in warning, but he ignored her.

"Yeah, that's what I thought," Ian said.

Josh sneered. He would've obviously liked nothing better than to beat Ian senseless, but he stood motionless.

"Now, why don't you go back and sit with your little jock buddies and pretend everyone is impressed with the way you strut around?" Ian said.

It was more than Josh could take. He leaned over the table, grabbed Ian by the front of the shirt, and jerked him out of his seat. Andy, Jake, Auddie, and I all stood.

"You're going to be very, very sorry you did that," Ian said, glaring into Josh's eyes.

Miraculously, Josh didn't punch Ian in the face. An expression of anger mixed with fear contorted his features. Something held Josh back. Josh released him.

"This isn't over, Babcock!" Josh said. He turned and walked back to the jock table.

"He's going to kill you," Auddie warned.

"The only thing he's going to do is apologize," Ian said, grinning at Josh's back.

Jake and Andy looked upon Ian with awe. The Goths had the same expression on their faces. I was afraid for Ian and confused. He was acting completely out of character. He'd grown bolder by the day, but now he was suicidal.

After school, Cole came home with me for a change. I yearned for some naked time with Cole, but one of the things I loved about our relationship is that it wasn't just about sex. By some definitions, we hadn't had sex yet. We hadn't even gone as far as oral. We'd had sex by my definition. More importantly, we'd made love.

I hadn't forgotten about Cole making out with Cindy, but he was so attentive and kind to me that I believed he was making out with her solely to mess with Adam. Perhaps I was naïve, but in my heart I knew he was telling me the truth.

I was nervous as Cole followed me through the front door. My family was fairly large, which meant more chances for someone to say something stupid or embarrassing in front of Cole. My fifteen-year-old brother Joey was sprawled on the couch watching TV as we entered. His only reaction to our presence was a quick, "Hey." So far, so good.

Cole and I raided the 'fridge, grabbing up Diet Cokes. Christopher, my eighteen-year-old brother, was leaning up against the counter eating Count Chocula straight from the box.

"Hey, I'm Christopher," said my big brother. "I've seen you at school. Aren't you *way* too popular to be hanging out with dufus here?"

"Hell no. I'm lucky he lets *me* hang out with *him*."

Christopher laughed. I pulled Cole out of the kitchen before my big bro thought of something else witty to say.

"Let me apologize now for my family," I said.

"Ah, they're cool."

"Even Christopher? Oh, by the way, never call him Chris. He'll freak."

"Touchy about his name, huh?"

"Yeah, it's a big thing with him. I think he fears that someone will think he has a girl's name if he goes by Chris."

"Hmm, closet case?" asked Cole as we entered my bedroom.

"Not from what I've seen."

"Too bad. He's kind of cute."

"Eww. Eww."

Cole laughed.

"I already have my very own Peralta. I obviously picked out the best."

"For once, I won't argue with you."

"So you have two brothers or are there more?"

"There are two and that's more than enough. I also have a sister, Ashley. She's seventeen. You might have seen her at school. She's way cooler than Christopher or Joey."

"Nice room. I like it," Cole said, looking around.

"It's my sanctuary from my siblings," I said, looking at all the skating posters plastered on the walls.

"You're really into skating, aren't you?"

"Yeah."

"Skaters are hot," Cole whispered in my ear. My body immediately reacted.

"Don't get me started."

"I promise to behave myself while I'm here."

"And the next time we're at your house?"

"I'll be a very, very bad boy."

"Ohhh," I said, fanning myself. "We'd better talk about something else."

Cole laughed.

We played CDs and my Xbox for the next couple of hours. Cole was pretty good at my Tony Hawk game. I was rather good at it, but not as good as I was at actual skating. In some ways, the game was harder than actual skating.

Mom stuck her head in and invited Cole to stay for supper. Cole was polite and charming. I was sure Mom would express her approval of my new friend after he departed. I wondered what she would think if she knew just how close I was to Cole. I spent a lot of time wondering how my family would react when I someday came out to them.

During supper, Ashley checked out Cole. Who could blame her, right? Cole pretended not to notice. He was good at that, probably because he got so much practice. Even people who weren't hot for him often looked him over because he was so good-looking. Of course, I guess I didn't know who was hot for him and who was merely admiring his beauty.

Joey noted Ashley's interest in Cole but mercifully kept his mouth shut. He didn't do it for Ashley's sake, I'm sure. He loved to torment her—and everyone else. I think Cole overwhelmed my little brother. Even he wasn't immune to Cole's charm or good looks. I don't mean that Joey was hot for him. Anything was possible, but as far as I knew, my little brother was as hetero as my big bro. Cole was already extremely popular at school, so I think Joey didn't quite know how to act around him. I'm sure all my siblings wondered what the likes of Cole was doing hanging out with me.

I heaved a sigh of relief when the fried chicken, mashed potatoes, corn, and yeast rolls had been consumed. No one embarrassed me or did anything stupid. I believe I even went up a notch in my family's eyes for having such a cool friend. It was sad and pathetic that popularity was such a big deal, even in my own home.

After supper, Cole and I played air hockey with my brothers in the basement. Ashley came down to watch Cole and me take on Christopher and Joey. She had zero interest in air hockey, so I knew what, or rather who, she'd really come to watch.

It was a rather pleasant evening. When it was over, I wanted to walk Cole home, but that was completely unnecessary since his Corvette was parked outside. My brothers drooled over his car when they spotted it at the end of the evening. Cole was gracious enough to promise them a ride sometime. I looked forward to gloating about all the times I'd already been in Cole's awesome car.

I yearned to kiss Cole goodnight, but it was quite impossible with Christopher and Joey loitering nearby. Instead, Cole and I just said goodbye. I contented myself with the knowledge that we would be able to express our affection for one another soon enough.

Cedi

I was awakened by the sound of the phone ringing. I looked at the clock by the side of my bed. It was just after nine. I answered.

"Hey Cedi. Up for some breakfast?"

"Sure Ross. I just need to shower."

"Come over when you're finished."

I stumbled toward the shower. I couldn't believe I'd slept so long. Ross had worn me out the day before. I grinned when I remembered how.

In less than half an hour, I knocked on Ross' door. He was dressed and ready to go. We headed out onto the beach once again, but this time we left the sandy shore and after a few minutes headed across the street to the Pancake Palace, a restaurant that looked like it had sat there for decades.

When we entered, I noticed Ross and I were the only customers under fifty. That meant we wouldn't have to call in Shawn and Rod to rescue us as we had the night before. Even if there were *Phantom* fans about, the older ones weren't quite so intense. I was kind of surprised at the number of fans in their 30s, 40s, 50s, and even older. They were always among the most polite and commented on my musical talent rather than squealing or telling me how awesome I was—not that I minded that!

We took a seat in a booth by a window. Palms trees swayed in the breeze outside. The sunlight made the surface of the ocean sparkle.

"How did you sleep last night?" Ross asked.

"Like the dead. I was worn out."

"Maybe it was all that sun."

"Maybe it was you."

Ross grinned.

"Want to hang out on the beach today?"

"Wicked idea," I said.

"We'd better enjoy it. We leave tonight for Atlanta."

"It doesn't seem like winter down here. I'm not at all used to tanning in December."

"I bet not. Winters are cold in England, right?"

"Chilly and wet. It was getting rather chilly in Blackford when we left. For all we know, it could be snowing there."

"I'm glad we're here."

"Me too! Couldn't we tour around Florida for the winter? Or maybe do some concerts in the Caribbean?"

"You're filled with good ideas Cedi."

"Banana-walnut pancakes and bacon sounds like a good idea right now."

"I'm thinking caramel-pecan pancakes."

"I think I'll steer clear of the pineapple-and-orange pancakes."

"I don't know Cedi. They might be good."

"Perhaps, but it's banana-walnut for me."

We ordered, then talked while we waited. Neither of us mentioned our lovemaking of the day before. I very much wanted to do it with Ross again, but I was also looking forward to hanging out on the beach. There are lots of ways to have fun that don't involve nudity. Before Ross and I made love, everything had been building and leading up to it. Now that I'd been naked with Ross, I felt as though I could relax and let events carry me along. I yearned to feel his taut body against mine, but just being with him was almost as good.

Our orders arrived and the pancakes were delicious! Ross and I traded plates for a bit, and his caramel-pecan pancakes might have been even tastier than my banana-walnut. We lingered over breakfast. We had the whole day before us. We ordered hot tea, naturally. We talked about the upcoming tour and whatever came to mind.

"So what did Jordan say about me?" asked Ross as we walked back to the beach after breakfast.

"Jordan?"

"Yeah, after what he saw yesterday, I'm sure he felt the need to share his words of wisdom." I was reassured by Ross' smile. He obviously wasn't angered by the thought of Jordan having a talk with me.

"He said not to expect too much from you. He was worried about me getting hurt."

"I'd never hurt you on purpose Cedi."

"He said that too."

"He knows me well."

That was all we said on the topic. We didn't discuss what our time together meant. Perhaps, like me, Ross wasn't sure.

Ross and I were feeling a bit lazy, so we returned to our rooms momentarily to grab towels and sunscreen. We spent most of the morning lying in the sun, talking, dozing, and listening to the waves and the sea gulls. The sunscreen was a capital idea. Without it, I would've been baked red as a lobster. Ross, of course, was in no such danger.

"I don't think I've seen Jordan on the beach once," I observed late in the morning. "Maybe he's afraid of sunburn."

"More likely he and Ralph are going at it like rabbits."

"Really? Jordan strikes me as quiet and mild-mannered."

"That type is the wildest of all. I met this girl once... mmm. She looked like a librarian, but when I got her back to the room— wow! And there was this NYU boy on our last tour. He looked like a young professor, but once we were alone... Damn that boy liked it rough."

"I think you're a lot more experienced than I am."

"Well, I am older. That, and Jordan says I'm a slut."

"He said that?"

"Just as joke, but he does think I get with too many girls and guys. I am selective. It's not as if I do it with just anyone. I have a thing for hotties—male or female."

"So you think I'm a hottie, huh?"

"What happened yesterday should have already answered that question, but if you need reassurance..."

"Yeah?"

"We can go back to my room..."

"Let's go!"

My experience with Ross in his room was much like the day before. That is to say, mind-blowing, erotic, and intensely enjoyable. We made love at an unhurried pace and then went at it like wild boys. When we were finished, we showered together, then climbed back on the bed. We lay there naked, side-by-side, and fell asleep.

When we awakened, we went to Tropical Delights for lunch again and then hit the beach. Jordan and Ralph finally came out of seclusion and joined us, as did Chad, Sam, and some of the crew. Drake, Daniel, and Drew joined us as well. It turned into a big beach party, and we had a blast!

We didn't have to board the bus until eight p.m. All of us made good use of our time. Ross and I considered making love again while we had the chance, but we were having too much fun on the beach. Hard to believe we'd pass up sex for sun and surf, right? Like I said before, there are lots of ways to have fun, and not all of them involve being naked.

What a wicked break! I didn't want to leave! I considered wrapping myself around a palm tree and refusing to leave, but I feared they might go on without me. I reluctantly climbed on the bus when the time came. Ross and I huddled close together in the front lounge. Jordan, Ralph, and the *Dragonfire* boys joined us as the tour bus pulled out for Atlanta. All of us grabbed soft drinks and talked about how we'd spent our Florida vacation. If my tutor asked me to write an essay about it, I was ready!

Ross put his arm around me, and I settled into his side. Jordan noticed but didn't comment. I got the sense he was still a bit worried, but I was a big boy. I knew what I was doing. Drew grinned at us wickedly. I liked the kid. He reminded me of myself at his age.

"You guys fucked, didn't you?" Drew asked, grinning across the booth at Ross and me.

"Drew, I don't think your mother would appreciate you using that word," Jordan said.

"Okay, you guys screwed, didn't you?"

I would have laughed, but I wasn't quite ready for such a question coming from a thirteen-year-old. I knew plenty about sex when I was his age, but still...

"That's none of your business," Ross said.

"Yeah, you guys did it!" Drew said, laughing. Ross and I couldn't help but grin, which make it obvious we were guilty as charged.

"Man, you're lucky. I wish I was older!"

"Don't get yourself worked up, Drew," Drake said.

"Yeah, or you'll be tying up the bathroom, if you know what I mean," Daniel said.

"Explain it to me," Drew said. He had a mischievous look in his eye that reminded me of Ross.

"Okay squirt. I mean you'll be in there whacking it, and none of the rest of us will be able to get in."

"Why? You need to whack it? I know you do it *all* the time, Daniel. Or did you mean you wanted to help me? That's incest, bro."

"Shut up Drew," Daniel and Drake said together.

"Drake does it lots too!" Drew said.

The boy was incorrigible, an admirable trait in my book. I liked him. His older brothers didn't seem to share my opinion. They locked eyes for a moment.

"Swirly," Daniel said.

"Definitely," Drake said.

They grabbed their little brother and pulled him toward the bathroom. He laughed and squealed.

"I take it back! I take it back!"

His brothers relented.

"I'm going to the back lounge," Drake said. "I need some time away from the squirt."

"Yeah, me too," Daniel said. "You guys can deal with him."

Drew started to follow.

"Stay!" Drake said.

Drew curled his hands up like paws and panted. He sat back down.

"They really do whack it all the time," Drew said in a low voice. "Straight boys!" Drew rolled his eyes.

"Thanks for sharing," Jordan said. "Let's talk about something else."

"Ross and I have a great idea for a Florida and Caribbean tour," I said.

"I wish," Jordan said.

"Wouldn't that be awesome?" Ross said. "Just imagine touring around the Caribbean all winter!"

"Well, South America is a possibility," Jordan said. "The tour is going extremely well, so our management company is thinking of adding some more foreign venues. I'm afraid winter will be over by then. We're booked for the next several weeks, except for a bit of scheduled down time."

"They're actually thinking of adding venues this late?" Ross asked.

"I said they're thinking about it. They smell money." Jordan grinned.

Our conversation roamed into other areas and thankfully farther away from what Daniel and Drake did while they were alone in the bathroom. I could tell Jordan was especially relieved to get away from that topic, probably due to the young age of *Dragonfire*. Sure, boys that age did it, but something seemed wrong with listening to Drew talk about it. He wasn't afraid of any topic. Yeah, he reminded me of a younger me!

The minutes as well as the miles rolled by, and I grew sleepy. All that frolicking in the sun—and with Ross—had worn me out. Even so, I felt rested in a way. Our time in Florida had been a break from the tour that I hadn't even realized I needed. It broke up the routine and allowed me to step back a bit so I could appreciate what I had. Ross and I had finally gotten together, and that relaxed me in another way. There's nothing like good sex to release tension.

We all retired to our little bunks and slept peacefully while the bus drew us ever nearer to our next venue. I couldn't wait to get up on the stage and do my thing.

***

Atlanta was a blast! We did two shows, as we occasionally did in the bigger cities. Both were sold out. I claimed the crowds had packed in just to see me. Jordan and Ross pelted me with popcorn for the remark. I knew I'd truly become one of the guys.

One venue followed another, and Ross and I had precious little time alone. It was frustrating but not unexpected. We did work in a quick make-out session now and then, but I yearned to get naked with Ross again.

An unpleasant surprise awaited me in Phoenix. We arrived back at the hotel about 10 p.m. We didn't have to depart the next day until four. For the first time since Florida, I had hours to spare. You can bet my mind went straight to Ross.

I took a quick shower, dressed, then walked the short distance to Ross' room and knocked on the door. He answered wearing only a towel, a sight both enticing and filled with possibilities.

"Uh, hi Cedi."

It wasn't quite the enthusiastic reaction I'd been hoping for.

"Hey, we can sleep in late tomorrow so..."

My voice trailed off as I caught a glimpse of a naked female walking from the bathroom into the bedroom. The color drained from my face. Ross glanced over his shoulder, then looked back at me.

"Hey, uh... we can have breakfast or something in the morning, okay?" Ross said. "I'll call you."

"Um, yeah. Okay, I guess."

Ross looked uncomfortable as he shut the door. I couldn't help but think he was shutting it in my face. It wasn't like that, but I still didn't feel so good.

I walked back to my room feeling almost as if I'd like to cry—almost. Ross and I had said nothing about being a couple. We hadn't mentioned being exclusive or even that we were dating. Still, I couldn't help but feel disappointed and likewise a bit rejected. Ross was in his room with a girl. He was with her in the way I wanted to be. While they were making love, I was sitting in my room all alone.

I didn't cry. I *really* liked Ross, but I wasn't in love with him. We were friends, and what had just happened didn't change that. Jordan had warned me not to expect too much from Ross. Jordan probably thought I hadn't listened, but I had. It was a good thing too, or finding Ross with a girl would have been far harder.

An odd emotion mingled with the disappointment; relief. It was a feeling I hadn't anticipated. A small part of me was actually relieved that Ross was with a girl, but why did I feel that way? The answer wasn't long in coming—Thad. I missed him. Our relationship had been a good one, mostly, but the sting of our breakup was still with me. I didn't know if I was ready to get involved with someone else. I didn't know if I was ready to take the risk. That's why I was both relieved and disappointed to find Ross with a girl. It meant I didn't have to worry about the two of us becoming too serious, at least not yet—maybe never. I also felt a sense of relief because I knew where I stood with Ross. There was no more wondering.

The sense of relief didn't make up for the disappointment. I'd looked forward to being with Ross again. All the stolen kisses, all the quick make-out sessions since Florida had been leading up to another intense bout of lovemaking, or so I'd thought. Now that we had the time, Ross had chosen a girl instead.

I didn't want to think about it anymore. I considered climbing into bed and losing myself in the oblivion of sleep, but I was too keyed up. I was restless and agitated. I opened my door and peeked out into the hallway. Rod was patrolling. Shawn and Mike also might well be prowling around. There seemed to always be at least one of them on guard. I waited until Rod disappeared around a corner, quickly slipped out of my room, and sneaked down the hallway in the opposite direction. I felt a sense of apprehension as I crept toward the lift. The risk of getting caught added a touch of excitement to my escape attempt. I smiled. Now, this was fun!

I made it to the lift and slipped inside. I pressed L for lobby and the lift began to descend. If one of the bodyguards wasn't standing there when the doors opened or prowling in the lobby, I might make good my escape. The lift deposited me safely on the ground floor. There were no bodyguards in sight, but there were girls about—likely *Phantom* fans. I ducked behind a large plant and then slipped down a side hallway. The girls never knew I was there. I felt like a spy escaping an enemy stronghold.

I made it outside. I was free! Now that I'd escaped, I wasn't quite sure where I wanted to go or what I wanted to do. I spied an IHOP in the near distance. Food was always good there. There was the risk of being spotted by fans, but who would expect to find me in IHOP at this time of night?

I wished I'd thought to put on my cap and dark glasses. Then again, I'd probably be more conspicuous wearing sunglasses at night than I was without them. I could've used a cap, but it's not like my hair was bright pink or green. It was coal black now. I didn't miss my wild hair colors as much as I thought I would. Black was a novel color for me. Besides, I'd be back to purple or blue soon enough.

I walked into IHOP. The hostess looked as if she recognized me, but if so she didn't mention it. She gave me a seat in a booth, and I browsed the menu. The Rooty Tooty Fresh `N Fruity Pancakes sounded good—for the name if nothing else. How could one go wrong with pancakes topped with strawberry, blueberry, or cinnamon-apple? The Harvest Grain N' Nut Pancakes likewise appealed to me. Then, I spotted the Chocolate Chip Pancakes. Yes! Pancakes with chocolate chips. How wicked is that?

I ordered my pancakes, some bacon, ice water, and hot tea. That's one thing I liked about the States. Ice! In Great Britain, ice in drinks was the exception and not the rule. Putting ice in tea was practically a crime there.

There were several other diners, but we were spread out enough that I could only hear mumbled voices. Where and who I was suddenly dawned on me. That happened now and then. Mostly, I went through my life without giving it much thought. Sometimes, like now, self-awareness hit, and I felt almost a stranger to myself. Here I was sitting in an IHOP in Arizona in the middle of the night, just hours after performing on stage with *Phantom*. Not that long ago I'd attended high school in a little town in southern Indiana. Not long before that, I was stuck in a boring British prep school. How did I get from there to here? Well, I knew. It was my life after all, but it was still a bizarre and unexpected journey.

My pancakes arrived. I experimented with the different syrups on the table—blueberry, strawberry, boysenberry, and butter-pecan. Hot maple syrup mixed with my chocolate-chip pancakes was the best combination. They were wicked delicious!

I tried not to think of Ross in bed with that girl, but Ross kept slipping into my mind. I remembered his smooth skin and hard muscles. I remembered the way he kissed me, the way he held me, and the way he made me squirm with delight. I pushed the thoughts from my mind and concentrated on the chocolaty goodness of my pancakes. Mmm.

A loud squeal pulled my mind from my meal. Two teenage girls halted and gawked at me. The other customers looked in our direction momentarily but soon lost interest.

"You're... you're..." began one of the girls.

"Shhhh," I said, putting my finger to my lips. I nodded to the seat across from me in the booth. "Have a seat."

It seemed the best way to quiet them down and keep from drawing attention to myself. The girls were also a welcome distraction. As much as I loved chocolate, it couldn't keep my mind off what Ross was probably doing in his room.

"We were just at your concert!" one of the girls said a bit too loudly. I motioned with my hand for her to tone it down. "Sorry. You were awesome!"

"Thanks."

"What are you doing here?" the other girl asked.

"Eating pancakes." I laughed.

"Are we bothering you?" one of the girls asked.

"No. I'm glad to have someone to talk to."

"I would think you'd always have someone to talk to."

"Well, I do, but I'm usually in such a rush I barely get to say 'hi.'"

"Are you really eighteen?" asked one of the girls. "You look younger in person."

"Yeah. I'm eighteen. How old are you?"

"Eighteen."

"Nineteen."

"I love your accent," the blond eighteen-year-old said.

"I love yours," I said, grinning.

"Wow. You're really cute."

"You're going to make me blush."

"I can't believe we met you! I can't believe you're talking to us!"

"Why not? I'm just me."

"You're famous!"

"I'm not that famous."

"We saw you on MTV, and you're in a bunch of magazines. That's famous."

A bunch of magazines? That was news to me. I only knew of the one Ross pointed out.

"Well, I'm not as famous as the guys."

"What are they like? Jordan is sooooooo hot. It's too bad he doesn't like girls. Ross is hot too. Well, so are you Cedi! It's okay if I call you Cedi, isn't it?"

"Sure it is, since it's my name. Jordan and Ross are really great guys. Kieran is also, although I haven't spent as much time with him. They're a lot of fun, and Ross is crazy."

"Ross is really like that in real life? He's really that wild?"

"Oh, he's exactly like that in real life."

"You're pretty wild too Cedi. I laughed when you climbed up that lighting tower during the concert and again when you jumped into the audience. I wished you would jump on me."

The blond was definitely flirting. I didn't mind. She was hot; attractive features, nice body. Her friend wasn't bad either; brown hair and eyes, big breasts. Any guy would've gone for her.

"Do you have a girlfriend Cedi?" the girl with dark hair asked.

"No."

"You must get really lonely sometimes."

The dark-haired girl was more than flirting. That was definitely a come-on.

"Sometimes."

"Any girl would be lucky to date you," the blond said.

"How do you know I like girls?" I asked mischievously.

"You mean you're gay, like Jordan? Why are all the hotties gay?"

"I didn't say I was gay."

"Are you?"

"I'm neither gay nor not-gay. I am what I am."

"Does that mean you're bisexual?"

"I don't like labels, but that one would fit me best. I go with whomever I want. If it's a girl, cool. If it's a guy, also cool."

"Bisexual boys are soo hot!" the blond said.

Most people would think that someone in the public eye wouldn't dare to give out such personal information, but I had no reason to keep my sexual orientation a secret. I wasn't about to lie and say I was one thing or another. I was me, and that's how it was going to be.

"A couple of bi boys go to our school. Well, there may be more, but there are two everyone knows about. They are such hotties."

"But not nearly as hot as you Cedi," her friend added.

Both girls were checking me out and flirting with me like crazy. It was more in their gestures and facial expressions than anything else. They were hot birds, and I was seriously considering asking them back to my hotel room. What would be the harm in it? I was a big boy, and they were both legal. They were obviously interested, so why not? I could imagine myself with the two of them. Mmm. Ross would certainly have no reservations about inviting them to his room.

My thoughts ground to a halt. No. This wasn't right. If I took them to my room, it would be for the wrong reason. Earlier in the tour, I'd made out with a couple of girls and went a bit further with another, but this was different. The real reason I wanted to have sex with those girls was because Ross was with a girl. I'd almost tricked myself into ignoring that fact, but it was true.

I continued talking with the girls, but I deflected their attempts to flirt. I'd seen Jordan do that with guys who came onto him. He had a way of pushing aside advances without upsetting or angering his pursuer so I tried to copy his moves.

I signed autographs for the girls and then told them I had to get back. They were disappointed and made a last attempt to get into my pants, but I feigned exhaustion and an early wake-up the next morning. Neither was quite true, but the ploys did the trick. I accepted the girls' offer to walk me back to my hotel. My cell phone rang as we walked the short distance. I looked at the caller id.

"Uh-oh, busted," I said.

"Who is it?"

"My bodyguard."

I answered.

"Hi Rod."

"Where are you Cedi?"

"I'm just outside the hotel. I'm heading back now."

"I'll meet you at the front doors."

"Okay, bye."

Rod didn't sound pleased.

Two minutes later I stood in front of the hotel. Rod stared down on the girls and me from the top of the steps. I gave both the girls a hug and a kiss on the cheek. They seemed content.

"Bye Cedi. Thanks for talking to us."

"It was fun. Good night."

I turned to face the music. Rod didn't say much, but he escorted me to my room. I had little doubt he'd be watching my door all night to make sure I didn't escape again.

I undressed and slipped into bed. I wondered if I'd made a mistake. Perhaps I should have brought the girls back to my room. Where would the harm have been in that? Yeah, part of my desire to be with them was connected to Ross, but not all. I wanted to be with them. We could've had a fun time, but a part of me would've thought I was taking advantage. *That* was the problem. I would have felt like I was using those girls, and I wasn't a user. Still, I didn't feel entirely sure if I'd made the right decision. The girls had walked away a bit disappointed. I hoped I hadn't led them on.

I shook my head and laughed to myself. When did I become such a prize? The idea of girls I didn't even know wanting to have sex with me was ridiculous but true. Was this what it was like to be famous?

I stretched and yawned. It had been a long day. I closed my eyes and fell asleep.

Toby

I think most everyone was surprised that I didn't audition for the role of Scrooge. When I announced I'd be trying out for Scrooge's nephew, there were gasps of surprise. There was even a muffled cry of dismay, likely from someone who had his eye on the role. I had landed the lead role in the last three plays, but I wasn't interested in playing Scrooge. It was a great part, but it didn't appeal to me.

My audition went off without a hitch. I don't mean to sound overconfident, but I had the feeling I landed the role. There wasn't that much competition and Mrs. Jelen knew what I could do upon the stage. I had the feeling she would give me the role for no other reason than I'd stepped aside to let someone else have the spotlight. I know those who were trying out for Scrooge and Tiny Tim were relieved when I didn't read for the parts.

I hoped someday to be auditioning for roles on Broadway or maybe for major motion pictures. Even TV would be cool. I was more likely to end up as a high-school drama teacher, performing with local theatre groups, but that was okay too. I loved acting and planned to dedicate my life to the stage.

After the auditions, I went home and spent an exciting evening catching up on all the homework I'd been neglecting. Ah, yes, Toby Riester knows how to have fun on a Friday night. I could have put my homework off until Saturday or Sunday, but I had procrastinated more than usual lately, and I didn't want it to become a habit. Besides, who knew when some real excitement might come my way? If it did, I wanted to enjoy it without homework hanging over my head. As it turned out, it was fortunate that I was in geek mode, for excitement came my way not long after I'd finished my last assignment.

Krista, of all people, dragged me to a party at Chase Simmons' house. Krista wasn't what I'd consider a party animal, but she insisted I go with her. I think she thought I was still down in the dumps over my breakup with Orlando, but she should've known just by looking at me that I'd all but forgotten about him. I was dying to tell her about Ian, but I wasn't sure how she would react. I knew Krista wanted me to be happy, but Ian was definitely on the fringe. He had always been considered more than a little strange, and recent events had actually made some of my classmates fear him. We were an odd couple to be sure, but I *really* liked him.

I would rather have been with Ian on this Friday night, but he did have a life. I hoped things would get more serious between us, but I didn't want to push. I really needed to take things slowly. I wasn't ready to be hurt again.

I was anxious as Krista and I walked up Chase's sidewalk. I could hear music vibrating the windows.

"Are you sure you want to do this?" I asked.

"Yes. Chase invited me. I thought it might be interesting to see how the other half lives."

"I dunno… I've never gone to a jock party."

"A jock party?"

"You know what I mean. All of Chase's buddies will be here; probably the entire football team. I don't exactly run with that crowd."

"That's all the more reason to check it out. Consider it a new experience."

"I've been to the zoo before."

Krista opened the door and pulled me inside. I was right. Every jock at B.H.S. was squeezed into Chase's house. I felt as if I'd walked into the lion's den. It was too loud. Some kids were dancing, and everyone was shouting to be heard over the music. The living room was dim, lit only by lamps covered with scarves. There were couples on each end of the couch making out. Another couple was going at it on the loveseat. Josh and his girlfriend were in a dark corner pawing at each other. There were heteros everywhere. Scary.

Krista pulled me toward the dancers. I tried to escape, but she wasn't letting me get away. Krista began to dance to the too-loud music, and soon I gave in and joined her. I was a bit self-conscious at first, but it's not as though all eyes were on me. I was probably invisible to most of the other kids there.

I actually had fun. I'm a rather good dancer, if I do say so myself. I'm gay, and everyone knows all gay boys can dance.

A few boys eyed Krista. I hoped one of them would cut in and dance with her. I enjoyed dancing, but I was more than willing to step aside. I had Ian, and I wanted Krista to have someone too.

No one cut in. Krista and I danced and danced. I laughed and acted crazy, even though I didn't drink any of the spiked beverages that were readily available.

All those bodies squeezed into a small space created a lot of heat. The exertion of dancing soon made me hot and sweaty. Some of the guys pulled off their shirts so they could show off their gleaming muscular bodies. Those guys thought they were hot stuff. I had to admit that, physically at least, they were. It almost seemed unfair that some guys were blessed with hard, sculpted bodies while the rest of us remained mere mortals.

"I'm glad you forced me to come."

"See. You should learn to trust me."

Soon, I was glad I'd come for another reason. I had a ringside seat for a scene that was sure to be the talk of the school on Monday. All heads turned toward the French doors as a loud scream tore through the air, drowning out all conversation and even the music.

Pulling his girlfriend along with him, Josh Lucas bolted through the door. Sherry was hysterical. There was no doubt it was she who screamed. Josh was even more panic-stricken than his girlfriend and looked from face to face as if he thought the crowd might attack and tear him to pieces.

Someone cut the music, and everyone stared at Josh. His eyes were wild. He panted like an animal.

"Get away from me! Get away from me!" Josh screamed to no one and everyone. He twisted and turned in one direction, then another, as if fearing an attack from every side. "Martin Wolfe! NOOOO!"

In his frenzy, Josh even pushed his girlfriend away. He stared at her as if he didn't recognize her. I don't think he recognized anyone. He looked straight into my eyes, and I read sheer terror there.

"Martin Wolfe! Martin Wolfe!"

Some of Josh's football buddies tried to approach, but he bolted. Josh would have jumped right through one of the front windows if Chase hadn't tackled him. Josh shoved him off with almost superhuman strength, but the jocks jumped in and helped hold him down.

"Don't let him get me! Don't let him get me!" Josh screamed.

Adam and Mike stood to the side—horrified. Adam trembled, and Mike looked as if he was about to wet his pants. Chase dropped down beside Josh.

"Josh! It's me! Chase! You're okay! No one is going to hurt you!" Chase shouted to make himself heard over Josh's ravings.

Josh seemed to recognize Chase at last.

"Don't let him get me! He was out there! He's in here! NOOO!"

The guys had to hold him down again as he thrashed about. The rest of us were shocked into silence. We stood in a circle around Josh, watching the unreal scene.

A couple of guys ran out into the yard but soon returned.

"There's no one out there."

"There was," Sherry said. "I saw him."

All eyes turned to Josh's girlfriend.

"Who?" Chase asked.

"Martin Wolfe."

Unlike her boyfriend, Sherry seemed in her right mind. She was shaken and no doubt frightened, but she wasn't frantic or paranoid. While the football jock freaked out, his girl kept her cool.

"What exactly did you see?" I asked, my curiosity getting the best of me.

"A boy, fifteen or sixteen, with a noose around his neck. He was pale, even whitish, except around his eyes, which were dark. He came out of nowhere. He called Josh's name. He said he was coming for him."

"You actually saw the ghost?" someone asked.

I heard others mutter, "the ghost." I also heard Ian's name whispered in more than one place in the room.

"Yes. I saw it. I didn't get a good look because it was dark. As soon as Josh saw the ghost, he freaked out. It was as though he lost his mind."

"Freaky," said one of the football players.

Josh was still squirming and raving. The jocks struggled to hold him down.

"What should we do with Josh?" Chase asked. He was looking at Mike and Adam, both of whom had freaked out when they had their own encounter with Martin Wolfe.

"There's nothing you can do," Mike said. "Just hold him down so he doesn't hurt himself or anyone else." Mike looked as if he was on the verge of freaking out again himself. "He'll be okay in three, four hours or so."

"What's happening to him, Mike?" Chase asked.

"His heart is racing. He's seeing and hearing weird shit, mostly Martin Wolfe. He can't focus his thoughts. He's restless, unable to hold still. That's what it was like for me. I felt as if... as if I was somewhere that wasn't real. Everything and everyone shifted and changed. I was frantic. Paranoid. It was like a bad dream. No. A nightmare."

Adam stared down at Josh as Mike finished speaking.

"When it happened to me, Martin Wolfe was everywhere I looked," Adam said. "He was after me. Everyone turned into him. No matter which way I turned, I couldn't escape him. I thought I'd go insane. I thought maybe I had."

Mike and Adam looked as if they were reliving their own terror as they described what Josh was seeing and feeling. The hunky blond football player lay on the floor with wild terror in his eyes. He strained against those holding him down. He panted like an animal. His eyes were unfocused. He looked more than anything like an escapee from an insane asylum.

The party broke up. No one felt like dancing or hanging out anymore. Chase and some of the other football players carried Josh upstairs. Later, I heard they had to hold him down on the bed for hours as he raved.

"What do you think about that little scene?" I asked Krista as we walked away.

"If Josh was faking, he's a brilliant actor. Did you see Mike and Adam? I thought they were both going to cry. I don't know what's going on, but I don't think this is a scam."

"I agree. Do you think they're doing drugs?"

"No. Adam and Mike were upset and scared. If they got high on something and freaked out, they would know why. The drug would mess with them while they were high but wouldn't make them so frightened later. Those guys were scared in there. They're dealing with something beyond their control."

"Why do you think Sherry didn't freak out? She said she also saw the ghost."

"I don't know Toby. Maybe she didn't see it. Maybe she lied to get attention."

"Even if that's true, why does seeing Martin Wolfe cause those guys to go nuts? If I saw a ghost, it would probably scare the crap out of me. I might scream. I might wet my pants, for all I know, but I don't think I'd act like those guys. Did you see Josh's eyes? He looked insane. I can't imagine anything scaring Josh Lucas *that* bad."

"I don't know Toby. None of this makes sense. It's getting scary."

I didn't mention the Ian connection. I didn't want to talk about it. Rumor was that Ian controlled the ghost, but that was crazy. Wasn't it? Even if I was willing to accept the existence of a ghost, how would Ian, or anyone, control it? I didn't believe there was any connection between Ian and Martin Wolfe. True, the guys who were attacked had given Ian a hard time not long before the ghost came after them, but I was willing to chalk that up to coincidence.

***

I won't bore you with my Saturday. Most of it was too uneventful to be interesting. Not everything can be a thrill, right? When the light began to fail, I pulled on a sweater and a windbreaker and stepped outside for a walk. November was getting on, and it was colder than it had been. There was no danger of snow, but the pleasant fall weather was nothing more than a memory. Still, I enjoyed walking in the growing darkness, until my thoughts turned to Martin Wolfe, that is. The whole thing with Mike, Adam, and Josh freaking out over the ghost was unsettling.

I let out a cry when a dark form swept down from above. All I glimpsed was a mass of flying blackness, as if Dracula had swooped down upon me with his cape streaming out behind him. My racing heart calmed when Ian smiled at me.

"Sorry to scare you, but I thought I'd drop in."

I looked at the limb above.

"Do you often hang out in the trees?"

"Only sometimes," Ian said, his dark eyes gleaming. "It's a good place to think."

Ian was wearing his massive black overcoat. No doubt that's what I'd mistaken for a cape.

"I'm glad you dropped in."

"I've been looking for you."

"Have you?"

"Yes."

"You could have called me, you know."

"Your parents might have answered. Most parents don't like me."

"Mine are reasonably cool."

"Do they know about you, that you like making out with boys?" Ian asked mischievously.

"Yes."

"Really? I'm surprised."

"My mom saw me making out with... a boy."

"Ah, the gay boy's nightmare. Are your parents okay with it?"

"Actually, they are. They're worried about me, but they're okay with it. Do your parents know about you?"

"No, but then I have no idea where my parents are. Well, that's not entirely true. My old man is in prison for dealing meth. Mom? She split a few weeks after Dad was locked up."

"Oh, damn. I'm sorry."

"Things are better this way, believe me. Dad isn't here to knock me around, and Mom... well, let's just say she liked to sample the old man's inventory too much. Things got ugly after Dad was taken away. He was no longer around to cook meth, so Mom had to buy it on the street. There wasn't much money, and... well, let's just say I don't miss the guys she brought home to earn money for her addiction."

"Oh, my God," I said before I could stop myself. "Sorry."

I wondered how Ian survived. Where did he live? Who did he live with? I decided this was not the time to pry.

"So? Still want to hang out with me or has my family history scared you away?"

"You're not your parents."

"Most people judge me by them."

"They shouldn't."

"Yeah, well... I'm not like them. I never touched that stuff. I don't do drugs, period."

"I never thought you did."

"Most people do."

"I'm not most people."

"No, you're not," Ian said, gazing at me. "That's one of the things I like about you. So, do you want to go to a movie?"

"Are you asking me on a date?"

"Yes."

"Good. I accept."

Ian smiled.

"You should smile more," I said.

"I usually don't have that much reason to smile."

"Maybe I can change that."

"What are you suggesting?"

"You'll see."

"I like this boy," Ian said. He pulled me close and kissed me on the lips. His long hair flowed around us hiding us in a shadow among shadows.

"Hey," Ian said. "We'd better get a move on. The show starts in just a few minutes."

We walked toward the newly restored Delphi Theatre. I almost couldn't believe how fast the old theatre had been whipped into shape. It seemed like only yesterday that Orlando and I had rushed to check it out when we heard the news it had been sold and was going to be restored.

The lights on the marquee filled the night with flashing light as we drew close. *Darkness Falls* was written in big bold letters, while a sea of blue, red, and green neon surrounded it. Not once had I considered what movie was playing. As long as I was with Ian, I didn't care.

Ian and I bought our tickets and went inside. The lobby was breathtaking. I remembered what it looked like all dusty and empty. The transformation was amazing. Every time I walked into the lobby it was as if I was seeing it for the first time. I simply couldn't believe it. The lobby was the 1920s come to life; art deco lighting, mirrors, and designs. Gilded cherubs looked down from above, and the massive chandelier looked as if it had just been polished. It was nearly worth the price of admission to stand in the lobby and gape. There was crimson and gold everywhere.

I could tell by the expression on his face that Ian likewise appreciated the beauty of the old theatre. Ian revealed a side of himself to me that no one else was allowed to see.

"Wanna get popcorn, or maybe we can eat out later?" I asked.

"Let's eat after the movie."

We stepped into the auditorium. The ceiling above was painted with a cloudy sky so realistic it looked as if the theatre had no roof but was open to the heavens. Ian and I selected seats near the back. I noted some kids from school eyeing us.

"I bet they wonder what we're doing together," Ian said. He'd obviously noticed our classmates staring at us.

"Let them wonder."

"You want to make out and really freak them out?" Ian asked.

"You're serious, aren't you? You would really do it."

"Hell, yeah. I'm serious."

"You're braver than I am. I'm not ready for that."

"You sure?" Ian asked. I loved the mischievous sparkle in his eyes.

"I'm sure."

The house lights dimmed, and Ian took my hand. My instinct was to pull away in fear that someone would see us, but I fought my instinct. No one was likely to notice our hands in the dark, and the touch of Ian's hand filled me with joy. How could just holding his hand make me feel so good?

I'd never been a big horror fan, but like I said, the movie didn't matter as long as I was with Ian. *Darkness Falls* was about "the tooth fairy," a woman who was unjustly accused of a horrible crime. For a hundred and fifty years she terrorized the town of Darkness Falls, waiting to pounce on anyone unlucky enough to see her in the dark.

I actually screamed at one point (although luckily not like a girl) and nearly climbed into Ian's lap. Ian laughed at my frightened reaction to the movie, but his laugh was neither cruel nor demeaning. I ended up laughing about it too, and we got the giggles.

I could see Ian's bright, white teeth in the dark as he grinned. His teeth were such a contrast to his clothes, his hair, and the darkness that surrounded us. Ian was so freaking sexy it was unbelievable. Before I knew what I'd done, I leaned over and kissed him. We made out for several moments before I realized we were in a public theatre with classmates only feet away. I pulled my lips from Ian's reluctantly and looked around to see if anyone had noticed us. I heaved a sigh of relief. Our potential audience was oblivious.

"Oh, my gosh! That was so scary," I said as we left the theatre.

"You must not watch many horror films."

"I can count the scary movies I've seen on one hand. That includes *Scary Movie*, which wasn't all that scary."

"Oh, that one is so funny! I'll have to take you to another horror film so you'll jump on me again."

"I'll jump on you anytime you like, Ian. Oh! Did I say that out loud?"

I buried my face in my hands. I was sure I'd just turned completely red. Ian laughed.

"Please do."

Ian and I grinned at each other.

"You smile a lot when we're together."

"That's because I like you."

"Don't you like Daniel and your other friends?"

"I like them, but I don't *like* like them. We're skating buddies. We eat lunch together. We hang out, although I'm mostly a loner."

"Doesn't that get lonely?"

"Yeah, but no one truly understands me. I'm an outsider even among outsiders. The guys don't give me crap about the way I dress or the fact that I wear an earring, but I'm still not like them. I'm not even like the other Goths."

"I think your earring is sexy and your collar... mmm."

"I like the sound of that 'mmm.'"

"Damn, why didn't I notice you before? You were right in front of me and I barely noticed you."

"You didn't see Ian. You saw *the Goth*. You saw the black clothes, the leather bracelets, and the chain. You didn't see me, because you couldn't get past what I was."

"I guess you're right. I feel... I dunno. I guess I was judging the book by the cover without even thinking about it."

"Well, the cover isn't completely misleading. This isn't a costume I'm wearing. This is me. This is how I want to be."

"This is how I want you to be too." I wanted to kiss Ian so badly I couldn't stand it.

Ian smiled.

"We are very different," I said. "I listen to *Phantom,* and I have a poster of Aaron Carter in my room. You probably think I'm girly and lame."

"No. I listen to hard rock, not pop. I also listen to other types of music. To be honest, I'd just as soon beat the crap out of Aaron Carter as listen to him. I think everyone should go their own way and do their own thing. If that's what you like, then it's cool for you. Just as what I like is cool for me."

"You're kinda deep," I said.

Ian laughed. "No one has *ever* said that to me before."

We had been slowly walking toward Café Blackford. Without discussing it, we walked inside and took a table near the bookshelves in one corner. A fire crackled merrily in the fireplace not far away. I caught the faint scent of wood smoke in the air. The waitress fearfully eyed Ian's spiked collar when she brought us our menus, but said nothing.

I gazed at Ian across the table. It was almost as if he was from another world. The black makeup around his eyes made him mysterious. Ian was more than a Goth. He was a real, live boy with thoughts, feelings, hopes, and desires. I especially liked the desires.

We both ordered cheeseburgers, fries, and Diet Cokes.

"Don't tell me you have to watch your weight. You're so tall and thin!" I said.

"Nah, I just like Diet Cokes. The regular kind tastes all syrupy to me. Yuck."

We looked at each other across the table. I was so happy to be with Ian.

"So, Toby Riester likes listening to *Phantom* and has the hots for Aaron Carter. What else can you tell me about him?"

"Hmm, well... I worked at Phantom World this summer. It was a blast. I love theatre, but you probably know that already."

"Yeah, I saw you in *Peter Pan*. You were great. You looked hot in those tights."

I smiled shyly.

"I'm pretty boring for the most part."

"That I could never believe."

"Thanks! Hmm, I don't know. I like to read. I love movies. I love watching plays even more. I like taking long walks and looking up at the stars. I'm starting to sound like a bad personals ad, aren't I?"

"I'd answer your ad."

"So, what about Ian Babcock? He's a Goth. He likes hard rock. He loves horror films. He wants to beat up Aaron Carter. What else?"

"Well. I'm a huge music fan. You've probably never heard most of the stuff I'm into, but I have a massive CD collection. I like to read; horror novels, philosophy, and true-crime stories. I also like taking long walks and looking at the stars. I'm into preppy boys who listen to *Phantom* and lust over teen pop stars."

"You think I'm preppy?"

"Preppy-ish. It's not an insult. True, I do sometimes want to punch someone in the face simply because they're wearing a polo shirt, but you have your own style. I'm probably wrong in calling you preppy, but that's as close as I can come to describing your look. You don't try to copy others. I like that."

"I never thought you would go for a boy like me. Well, I never thought you would go for boys, period."

"Too scary to be queer, huh?"

"Something like that. To be honest, I could picture you beating up a boy like me before I could picture you dating one. I don't mean that I think you're violent, but you look intimidating."

"It's too bad the jocks weren't intimidated by the way I look."

"No kidding. I haven't made you mad, have I?"

"Why would I be angered by honesty? Besides, I understand what you mean. I do hope you aren't intimidated by me now."

"Honestly? I'm a little scared of you. You're an unknown. People are always talking about you as if they think you might keep human hearts in your freezer. I don't believe that, of course; I wouldn't be here if I did. Mostly what frightens me about you is that I *really* like you. I've been hurt before. I'm afraid of getting too close, because I might get hurt again. Wow, I'm amazed I'm talking about these things. I'm saying too much, aren't I?"

"No. That is something else I like about you. You're honest. You express your feelings. I can't predict how things will work out between us Toby. I can promise that I'd never hurt you on purpose. I know you don't know me all that well. I haven't earned your trust. Believe me when I say that I've been looking for someone like you for a long time Toby. I'm not about to hurt you."

I smiled. I felt like I'd found the perfect boy.

Daniel

I jumped up and down with delight when I read the cast list. Thankfully, I stopped short of squealing like a girl. Mrs. Jelen gave me the role of the Ghost of Christmas Yet to Come! Yes! Not only did I have no lines to memorize, I also had the coolest costume. I would be dressed like the Grim Reaper. It would have been a good role for Ian—dark and brooding.

Ian had been a good deal less brooding in recent days. I wasn't quite sure why. He'd been hanging out with Toby Riester quite a bit, so maybe having a new friend had improved his mood. Perhaps he was happier because the jocks were giving him less trouble. Maybe he enjoyed his increased notoriety. Perhaps it was a combination of all three.

On Monday morning, rumors about Ian reached my ears before I even hit the front steps of the school. Everyone was talking about Ian and Josh Lucas. Josh had freaked out at a party on Friday night. Most of my classmates were now convinced that Ian controlled the ghost of Martin Wolfe.

There had been rumors floating around about Ian and his parents for as long as I could remember. His all-black wardrobe, black makeup, collar, and chains gave him an almost sinister appearance. He didn't dress like everyone else, so some people were frightened of him. The fear had now intensified and spread. Whenever Ian walked down the hallway, kids got out of his way.

I thought back to the scene in the cafeteria on Friday. Josh had stomped to our table and ordered Ian to call his ghost off—or else. Ian was defiant, and Josh ended up jerking Ian out of his seat. Ian's words rang in my ears. "You're going to be very, very sorry you did that." Hours later, the ghost had come for Josh Lucas. Coincidence? It seemed unlikely.

I spotted Josh in the hallway before first period. Everyone stared at him as though he was a freak show. According to some, Josh had cried like a baby after the attack. According to others, he'd gone insane. Josh had a haunted look, as if he feared Martin Wolfe would come after him right there in school. Most kids were keeping their distance from him. Perhaps they feared he was cursed and if they got too close, the curse would rub off on them.

I spotted both Mike Bradley and Adam Henshaw later in the day. They had dark circles under their eyes as if they hadn't slept well. The ghost had attacked both of them. I didn't know exactly what had gone down, but Mike, Adam, and Josh weren't the same cocky jocks they had been.

Not all the bullies in our school were cowed, not even close. Right before lunch, I witnessed an ugly scene between Billy Kelly and Julian Curtis. Billy knocked Julian's books out of his hands and then knocked Julian over when he bent down to retrieve his stuff.

"You should skip lunch, wide load," Billy said, laughing. He thought he was funny. He was wrong.

I didn't know Julian well. He was about my age and seriously overweight. A lot of kids made fun of him. I thought it was cruel. I knew Billy Kelly by reputation. He was a bad ass and a jerk. I walked toward Julian to help him pick up his books.

"Let him do it!" Billy said in a threatening tone. "He needs the exercise. Don't you, fat ass?"

"That's enough, Billy," I said.

"Are you talking to *me*?" Billy asked, glaring at me.

I trembled slightly. Billy Kelly could and would kick my ass, but how could I stand by and let him torment Julian? The kid never hurt anyone.

Billy stepped toward me and poked me in the chest.

"If you know what's good for you, you'll mind your own business!"

I spotted Ian coming up behind Billy. He heard Billy's threat. Kids parted for Ian as he made his way through the crowd. Ian grabbed Billy's shoulder and jerked him around. They stared into each other's eyes. Billy did his best to live up to his bad ass reputation, but his eyes were wide with fear.

"Don't mess with me, freak," Billy said finally. His attempt at an intimidating tone wasn't successful. His voice shook.

"You're next, Billy," Ian said, poking him in the chest.

Whispers filled the hallway. Ian had just cursed Billy.

The color drained from Billy's face. He licked his lips and swallowed hard. All pretense of being a bad ass was gone. He turned and hurried away.

Billy's name spread through the hallway like wildfire. I knew everyone would be waiting to see if Martin Wolfe paid him a visit.

Ian and I helped Julian gather his books.

"Thanks guys," he said.

The poor boy had tears in his eyes.

"If anyone bothers you, come see me," Ian said. "I'll take care of them. We're not putting up with this anymore."

"Thanks," Julian said. He seemed slightly fearful, but even more in awe of Ian.

Ian and I watched Julian depart.

"Ian, what's going on?"

"I'm making the world a better place."

"But how? Are you seriously telling me there's a ghost? Are you really saying you control him?"

"You've seen the results, haven't you? Mike, Adam, Josh..." Ian counted the victims on his fingers. "Billy's next."

"Ian, we're friends. Tell me. This is getting serious. A lot of kids are afraid of you."

"There are some things you're better off not knowing Daniel. Only the bullies need fear me. I'm going to protect the rest of us from *them*."

Ian said the last bit loud enough for all those near to hear as if he was making a public-service announcement.

I was not satisfied with Ian's explanation, but I couldn't force him to talk. I didn't know what was going on or how Ian was involved. At least it was the bullies who were suffering. There was a certain justice to it. I did feel a little safer as I walked down the halls.

I was determined to see this ghost for myself. Only when I saw it with my own eyes would I believe that Martin Wolfe had risen from the dead.

I stalked Billy Kelly through the hallways all day long. I wanted to witness whatever was going to happen to him, if anything. Nothing out of the ordinary occurred all day, except kids staring at Billy and whispering. It pissed him off so much that he turned and shouted for the whisperers to shut up. I chuckled to myself. Ian's curse was getting to Billy Kelly.

I had play practice after school, so I had to give up on tailing Billy for a while. Practice was largely a waste of time for me. My part was small, and I didn't come in until the very end. I was relieved when Mrs. Jelen told me I wouldn't have to attend all the practices. She would tell me when my frightening presence was needed.

Cole was waiting for me in the parking lot when practice ended. He was sitting in his Corvette, listening to a CD. Cole confused me. I still didn't know why such a hottie wanted me.

"How was practice?" Cole asked.

"Oh, I've got my part down. Want to hear my lines?"

"Sure."

I sat there in silence for a moment. "How was that?"

"That was awesome Daniel. You are the best at saying nothing."

"Mrs. Jelen says I don't have to attend most of the practices. My part is sooo easy. Ian would have been perfect for it. He would've loved the costume, but drama isn't his thing."

"Your buddy is becoming notorious."

"He's always been notorious. He's just more so now."

"I like him. He's an original."

"Yeah, he is. I've seen you talking to him."

"Yeah."

"What do you think of this whole ghost thing?"

"Strange things happen."

"Yeah, but a ghost attacking people? Ian controlling the ghost?"

"I've seen plenty of stuff in my life I can't explain. It sure looks as if Ian can turn the ghost on whomever he wishes."

"Billy Kelly was giving a kid and me trouble today. Ian told him he was next. I followed Billy around in case something went down, but nothing happened."

"Maybe Ian hasn't sicced the ghost on him yet."

"I want to see this ghost for myself."

"Well, I hear Billy spends a lot of time in the Grove."

"Making out with a girl no doubt. Pervert."

Cole laughed.

"I'm saying that might be a good place to check for him once it begins to get dark. That's prime make-out time in the Grove from what I hear. Unless, of course, he's too scared to go out."

"Hmm, good idea. What do you propose we do until then?"

"I'm afraid I can't go with you. I've already promised Dad I'd set aside some time for him tonight. He wants to have a father/son talk."

"Uh-oh. That doesn't sound good."

"Perhaps it's a safe-sex lecture."

"Ohhh, safe sex. I like the sound of that."

Cole reached over and ran his hand up my leg.

"If you keep that up, you're gonna make me have an accident."

"We wouldn't want that now, would we?" Cole said.

I couldn't wait until we reached Cole's house. That short drive seemed to take hours. Why were the speed limits in town so low?

Cole pulled his Corvette into the garage. We walked into the echoing house and went straight to his room. I remembered all the empty rooms I'd peeked into on my previous visit, but I didn't have much time to think about them. As soon as we were in his bedroom, Cole pulled me to him and kissed me. After that, my mind wasn't on empty rooms anymore.

***

As the shadows deepened into night, Cole dropped me off at the entrance to the Grove. I wished I could have met his dad, but now was not the time. I made my way along the narrow road that led into the Grove. Once I was under the trees, I could barely see. I cursed myself for not thinking to bring a flashlight. Then again, a flashlight would have given me away. If I was going to get close to Billy and keep him under surveillance, he couldn't know I was there. I just hoped he was in the Grove. With my luck, he was miles away.

It was rather spooky under the trees. The leaves had fallen, so it wasn't as shadowy as it would have been in summer, but it was still plenty dark on the old road. The Grove was a large, dense forest on the edge of town. Its sole appeal was solitude appropriate for making out. There were likely to be several couples there, even though it was cold. The problem was going to be finding Billy and his girl.

My task was far more difficult than I anticipated. Once I was deep into the Grove, I wandered about looking and listening for signs of life. An owl hooted close by and scared the crap out of me. That sort of thing doesn't seem all the scary when you read about it in a book or see it in a movie, but in real life, it's a whole other experience.

I stealthily crept up on three separate couples wrapped up in blankets and sleeping bags only to find they weren't Billy and his girl. I recognized the voice of Chase Simmons when I got close to the last couple. I didn't recognize the girl's voice, but those two were up to more than making out. I heard the girl say, "Harder Chase." It didn't take a genius to figure out what they were doing.

I was slightly tempted to watch, but I didn't want to be a pervert. I crept away again. I resumed my search for Billy and his babe.

I was entirely unsuccessful in my efforts. All I'd received for my trouble were some cheap voyeuristic thrills that didn't do that much for me. Let's face it, hetero couples are only half-hot—the guy half of course. Just when I was ready to give up the evening as a lost cause I heard a scream, a male scream. The scream was loud and not far distant. I rushed forward through the dark, heedless of the limbs whipping my arms and face.

Billy screamed again. I was close enough now that there was no doubt it was Billy. I could see him standing in the moonlight, a girl beside him, staring into the darkness. I followed his line of sight and peered through the trees. I thought I could just make out a dark form, a shadow among the shadows.

I wasn't the only one drawn by the screams. The three couples I'd briefly spied on, and another couple who had escaped my notice, rushed toward Billy. Chase Simmons ran up beside me, followed closely by his girl.

"Look!" Chase said pointing.

The ghost of Martin Wolfe emerged from the shadows. His face was pale, his eyes dark, and a noose hung around his neck. I could not believe my eyes.

The ghost was real.

Billy stumbled over his own legs and fell backwards as the phantom approached.

"NO! NO! Leave me alone! NO!"

I shook with terror but forced myself to edge closer. I had to get a better look.

Billy went berserk as the apparition closed in on him. He scrambled to his feet, turned, and bolted, screaming "Martin Wolfe." Unfortunately, he ran right at me. He was on top of me before I knew it. Before I could jump out of the way, he knocked me flat on my ass. Billy didn't even slow down. He kept on running.

By the time Chase helped me to my feet, Billy was gone, and so was the ghost of Martin Wolfe.

"Did you see that?" asked one of the guys, yet another football player, I think.

"Shit!" Chase said. "I didn't think this thing was real, but... damn!"

Billy's abandoned girl walked toward us, shaky and clearly frightened.

"Are you okay?" Chase asked.

"I think so," she said.

I didn't recognize her. She was younger than I was—too young to be in the Grove with Billy Kelly.

"What a coward," Chase said, looking in the direction Billy had run.

I was thinking the same thing. The phantom had scared the crap out of me, but I hoped I wouldn't abandon my girl if I was in Billy's shoes. Of course, I had no interest in girls, but still...

"We'll give you a ride home," Chase said.

"Um, could I get a ride too?"

I hated to ask, but I was still shaking with fear myself. I felt as though I'd awakened from a nightmare. I didn't want to walk home in the dark.

"Sure," Chase said, eying me. "You're out here alone?"

"Yeah."

"What are you doing out here alone dude?" Trevor Duncan asked.

"Ghost hunting, to be honest. I heard Ian tell Billy that he was next. I wanted to see the ghost for myself. I had a hunch Billy would be out here."

"Well, you've seen it now," Chase said. "I thought the whole thing was bullshit. I didn't believe in the ghost, despite Mike, Adam, and Josh freaking out. I guess they weren't putting on after all."

"You thought they were faking?" Trevor asked. "No way, man! I was at your party Friday night. I saw Josh lose it. How could you think he faked that?"

"I don't know. It was too far out there to be real."

"Could we please go?" the girl at Chase's side asked.

"Sure baby," Chase said. He leaned down, kissed her on the lips, wrapped his strong arm around her, and walked toward his car. I followed, along with Billy's abandoned companion.

Chase was right. I'd seen the ghost for myself now. It was a sight I'd never forget.

***

I *finally* met Cole's father. I was relieved. An unreasonable suspicion had grown in my mind that he didn't even exist. That was ridiculous, of course. Cole sure wasn't living all alone in that big house. He didn't even have a job. There was no way he could've paid the bills. Unfortunately, attending high school doesn't pay well.

Cole's father was nothing like I expected. He looked nothing like Cole and seemed... I dunno... off. I don't mean off in the head or anything like that. Cole's dad just didn't seem right. He was out of place in his own home. Of course, I'd never seen him there before, so it was probably just me. At least I could put my irrational fears to rest. Cole did have a father.

I followed Cole upstairs after the introductions were made. My eyes were glued to Cole's cute little ass. I wanted to reach out and grab it, but the presence of Cole's dad in the house made me fearful.

Cole closed and locked his door, then pulled me close and kissed me. We began to make out, but I pulled away.

"What about your dad?"

"I'm not willing to share. I doubt you're his type anyway."

"That's not what I mean!"

"He won't come in here."

"How can you be sure?"

"He never comes in my room. He respects my privacy, and I respect his. I seriously don't think he'd come in even if I had a girl in here. He definitely won't suspect we're up to anything."

"Um, okay."

"Don't worry Daniel. The door is locked, and I guarantee Dad will not so much as knock."

Cole kissed me again, and I forgot my fears. We tugged at each other's clothing, and before long we were naked and making out on the bed. I'd dreamed all day about being with Cole. I daydreamed about him a little too much a couple of times. I had to force my thoughts in another direction before I could stand up, if you know what I mean.

Our lovemaking was passionate and intense. I'm not going to say much more about it than that. I've already said more than I feel like sharing. Making love is something special between two guys. You know? To describe it in detail would somehow cheapen it. It would make it seem like nothing more than sex. Making love is so much more than sex that I don't even know how to explain it. I just hope you get the chance to make love if you haven't already.

We lingered in bed for over an hour, making slow, passionate love. Much of time we did nothing more hold each other close. I'd never experienced such happiness.

"I really, really like you Daniel." Cole hugged me closely, and I nuzzled up against him.

"What did I ever do without you?" I asked. I meant it. I couldn't imagine life without Cole.

Cedi

I was coming out of the shower when a knock at my door startled me. It was likely Rod, checking to see if I was still in my room. I peered through the 'spy hole.' Ross stood outside. I paused for a few moments to calm myself, then opened the door.

"Hey."

"Hey. Can I come in?"

"Sure."

The events of the night before rushed through my mind; knocking on Ross' door hoping we could make love again, finding him with a girl instead. The disappointment, jealousy, and rejection hit me again.

"I hope you aren't angry about last night. I met Gabriel after the concert. One thing led to another and... well, you know."

"Yeah. I know."

"You look sexy in that towel Cedi."

Ross walked over to me, pulled me close, and kissed me. His kiss and embrace made me mad horny, but I pulled away from him. The effort required to resist Ross was tremendous. He was the most seductive guy I'd ever met.

"You are upset, aren't you?"

"I'm upset. I'm a little disappointed, a little jealous, and kind of relieved. I'm a lot of things right now."

"Let's talk about it. Why don't I call up room service and order us breakfast? We'll eat and talk. I really like you Cedi. I want us to be friends—remain friends."

I nodded. Ross ordered breakfast while I dressed. I was a tad uncomfortable, but Ross' reassurance that he wanted us to remain friends set me more at ease. The mention of the word "friend" did indicate he wasn't considering a serious relationship, but hadn't I decided last night that I wasn't looking for anything serious just yet?

Ross had breakfast ordered by the time I finished dressing. We took seats around a small round table near the window.

"I'm really sorry I upset you," Ross said.

"Well, I'm only a little upset, not a lot upset. I have mixed emotions about us. I guess I don't really know what I want."

"I think we should get everything out in the open Cedi. I think we should be honest with each other about how we feel and what we want. If we leave things unsaid, it will create problems, either now or later. I don't want it to be like that with us Cedi. I don't want our life to be like a drawn-out soap opera plot."

"You just want to skip to the climax, huh?"

"Oh, you know me better than that Cedi. I like to prolong pleasure, but we're not talking about sex. Well, not *just* sex." Ross grinned.

"Who goes first?"

"I will if it will make it easier for you, but promise me you'll tell me how you feel, no matter how you feel, and especially if you feel differently."

I nodded.

"Okay, total truth, with no sugar coating. I *really* like you Cedi. I like you as a friend and more than a friend, but not as a boyfriend. I have feelings for you. You've already become special to me. I even love you, but it's not quite romantic love. Well, maybe it is a bit, and yet. I want us to be friends, and more than friends."

"Meaning, friends with benefits?"

"I'm talking about more than sex. Yes, I want to make love with you. You're cute, sexy, wild, and damn good in bed. I also want us to be close. Those two times we were in bed with each other in Florida, do you know what I liked best?"

I shook my head.

"Holding you close after we'd had sex and sleeping beside you. It made me feel so comfortable and secure. A lot of guys and girls are more than willing to have sex with me but not sleep with me. They want to do it with me because I'm famous. They aren't even really having sex with me but with whatever fantasy they have of me."

"I'm sure there's more to it than that Ross. You're wicked hot!"

"Thanks! The same to you, big boy. The thing is that I wake up alone the next morning. There's so much more when I'm with you. I know you'll be there in the morning. You'll be there the next day, and the next. We share more than our bodies. We share our thoughts, our feelings, our hopes, and dreams. Like now, never in my life have I sat down and talked to anyone about my feelings like this. You're a part of my life now."

Room service interrupted us. A handsome waiter draped a white linen tablecloth over the table. He set out silverware, linen napkins, and a single red rose in a vase. He set out a silver teapot, blue & white porcelain cups, and a cut-glass bowl with sugar, sweeteners, honey, and creamer. Next, came plates with silver covers. It all looked so fancy.

"Will there be anything else sirs?"

"No thank you," Ross said.

Ross tipped the waiter with a fifty! I was sure room service wasn't cheap, but it was still an incredibly large tip. The waiter seemed to think so too.

"If there is anything I can do for you, ask for Benjamin."

Benjamin departed.

"Did you get the impression Benjamin was flirting?" Ross asked.

"Yeah, or maybe he just liked the big tip."

"I always give big tips. I have plenty of money and waiters work hard for theirs."

"You speak like someone who has been a waiter."

"Oh yeah. Before Jordan, Kieran, and I got *Phantom* going, I had a part-time job in a diner back home. I was just a kid then. Even after we started performing, I waited tables now and then. Some of the customers were nice; others were real jerks. I was paid practically nothing, so tips meant a lot. I've got more money than I know what to do with now and I remember how much a big tip meant to me back in my table waiting days."

"I bet no one ever tipped you a fifty!"

"I think twenty was the most and I was thrilled."

We sat down and pulled the silver lids off our plates.

"Pecan pancakes, scrambled eggs, toast, and bacon. Good choice," I said.

"I thought you'd like it."

"So, where were we?" I asked. Part of me wanted to avoid our conversation, but I knew things would be much better if everything was brought into the open.

"I was saying that I don't want us to be boyfriends. I don't want to be exclusive, but I do want us to be close friends. How do you feel about that? Be honest. I want to know what you really think. I don't want you to tell me what you think I want to hear."

Ross looked more serious at that moment than I'd ever seen him. He wasn't even tapping his fingers.

"Well, my feelings are mixed. I could really fall for you Ross. You're sweet and sexy and kind. You're wild and yet compassionate. You're a wicked drummer. You're damned good in bed, and you have a romantic side I find very appealing. You have a bad-boy thing going that excites me. I like all the mischief we get into. If you told me you wanted to date me, I'd seriously consider it, yet I'm relieved you don't want to date. I don't think I'm ready to get serious with someone again. I don't want to get hurt. I'm not saying I think you would intentionally hurt me, but I might get hurt anyway. Understand?"

"Yes. That's one of my reasons for not wanting to get too serious, but it's not the biggest reason. I'm not ready to limit myself to one person, no matter how wonderful he or she might be. There are *so* many guys out there, and girls. I like to be with different people. The girl last night; she was the same as a lot of other girls, but she was different too. Everyone is unique. I feel like I'd be depriving myself if I stuck with one person. I know Jordan thinks I'm a slut. His opinion is important to me, but I've got to live my life as I see fit."

I couldn't help but laugh. Ross grinned.

"There's also the fact I'm bisexual. If I date a guy, there are things I can't do with him simply because he's a guy. The opposite is also true.

"The big reason I don't want to get serious with you or anyone else Cedi, is... well, there's someone... there's someone I'm not over. That's not quite the way to put it, because we were never together, but there's someone I truly care about. I try not to think about him too much because I can't have him. I can deal with it most of the time, but sometimes it's rough."

Ross looked at me. "I'm telling you something I haven't told anyone. Even... he doesn't really know how much I care, how much I want him. I pretend I'm over him, but I'm really not. We were together just once—in bed, I mean. We made love, and it was the most wonderful, intense experience of my life. I'm not saying it's not great with you Cedi, but there's something about him. I love him. I'm in love with him. I can't have him, but I can't change the way I feel. It would be unfair to date you or anyone else because a part of me would be thinking about him."

Ross' lower lip trembled. He looked sadder than I'd ever seen him. I stood, walked around the table, and hugged him. His body shuddered and Ross began to cry. I held his head against my chest. I could hear the pain in those sobs. I never guessed for a moment that Ross carried such pain within him.

Ross grew quiet, leaned back, and wiped his tears away with his napkin.

"Thanks Cedi."

I took my seat once more.

"I can't claim to truly understand, but I understand a little. There's someone I care about too. Thad. Things aren't nearly so serious for me because Thad and I might get back together some day. We probably won't, but the possibility is there. If I were dating someone, I'd think of Thad at times. I know that's not much compared with what you've told me, but it helps me to understand."

"I'm okay most of the time. Well, you know me. When I act crazy, that's the real me. I don't put on an act, except around Jor..."

Ross halted in mid-sentence. His eyes widened and his face paled.

"Jordan? You're in love with Jordan?"

Ross swallowed hard then took a deep breath.

"I did say total truth, didn't I? And I know I can trust you to keep this to yourself."

"Of course, you can."

"Yes. Jordan. Now, before you start thinking he was unfaithful to Ralph, let me explain something."

"You don't have to. I'd never think that of Jordan. Besides, you could have slept with Jordan before Ralph entered the picture."

"I hadn't thought of that. I wish I had said something to Jordan before he met Ralph, but I couldn't. I didn't know Jordan was gay then. I wasn't sure about my feelings. Anyway, few people know this, but Jordan and Ralph broke up for a while. There was a big misunderstanding between them. We were in California and Ralph was still living at home. A tabloid printed a photo of Jordan kissing Corey Thomas. It was a fake, but Ralph saw it and thought Jordan cheated on him. Things got nasty, the way they can when something bad happens between two people who love each other. Jordan was hurt. It messed him up badly. I tried to comfort him and things went farther than either of us planned. I'll be honest; there was a part of me that wondered if I was taking advantage of the situation, but at the time Jordan and Ralph had broken up. Well, Ralph dumped Jordan. Still, Jordan was vulnerable and a part of me felt like a predator. He needed someone so badly and I wanted to be that someone. I guess part of me saw it as a chance to have what I'd always wanted, but most of me wanted to be there for him."

"So the two of you made love?"

"Yes. Just once. Just that one wonderful night. The misunderstanding was cleared up right after that and Jordan and Ralph patched things up, but at the time, both Jordan and I thought things were over between them."

"It must have been hard for you when Jordan and Ralph got back together."

"Yes, but at the same time, it's what I wanted. Okay, to be honest, I would have liked it if Jordan had remained single. Then, I would've had a chance. The thing is, I knew how much Jordan loved Ralph and I also knew how much Ralph loved Jordan. I knew how good they were for each other. I want Jordan to be happy, even if that means he's with someone else. I don't think Jordan was interested in me as a boyfriend. The next morning... well, I don't want to get into all of it, but it was obvious that making love was a one-time thing between us. I even convinced myself for a while that one night was enough for me. I wasn't even sure I was into guys then. I know that sounds ridiculous, but I was so obsessed with Jordan he was the only guy I desired. It took me a while to work it all out in my head."

I reached across the table and took Ross' hand. He seemed very much a little boy just then—a little boy who wanted nothing more than to be loved.

"You're really wonderful, you know that?"

"That's what I keep telling everyone, but they won't listen!"

I grinned.

"Seriously, you are."

"Thanks. So are you."

"Not like you."

Ross smiled.

"Oh, I don't know about that. Listen Cedi, I know you've already promised and I trust you, but you can't tell Jordan how I feel about him. Not now. Not ever. He doesn't need this to deal with. He's happy with Ralph, happier than I've ever seen him. I don't want to do anything to mess that up."

"I'll never breathe a word."

"Good. I want it to be my problem. I don't want Jordan to even suspect I'm still hung up on him."

"It can be *our* problem. Whenever you want to talk to me, I'm here. Whenever you need a hug, or more, I'm here."

"Thanks, Cedi. So... us. I want us to be close. I want us to be intimate friends. And, I want in your pants."

I grinned.

"I like the sound of all that."

"Good. What are you doing after breakfast?"

"I'm making love with you."

"Mmm."

Despite our sudden and intense need for sex, Ross and I didn't hurry our breakfast. We enjoyed the remainder of our pancakes, eggs, toast, and bacon. When we finished, we sipped hot tea, talked, joked, and laughed. That was something I liked about Ross; he looked for fun in every situation. He wanted to enjoy everything. He didn't rush on to whatever was next. He enjoyed every moment of life.

I set my teacup down, stood, and walked to the door. I put out the "Do Not Disturb" sign. I walked to where Ross sat at the small table. He looked up at me. I leaned over and kissed him. I pulled him to his feet. Ross leaned down, pressed his lips to mine, and pulled me close. We stood there and made out for the next several minutes.

Ross tugged at my shirt. I raised my hands over my head as he pulled my shirt off. We undressed each other ever so slowly, spending lots of time making out between each article of clothing. Ross pulled me to the bed. We lay down. Our hands and lips began to roam. Ross moved with deliberate slowness. His every caress set me on fire with need and lust. How he could so completely turn me on by doing nothing more than caressing my jaw line I'll never know. Ross had to be the most talented lover ever. When he touched me in more intimate places, well, I can't even begin to describe it.

Ross and I made love all morning. Lunchtime came and went, and still we went at it. We held off our orgasms for as long as humanly possible. When one of us couldn't hold out a moment longer, we both cut loose. As soon as we experienced the intense sensation of release, we went right back to making love.

Ross and I varied our pace. Sometimes we went at it like wild animals, sometimes we giggled and covered each other with kisses. Being with Ross made me never want to leave the bed again, even to sing with *Phantom*! I'd never had such an enjoyable experience in my life. Our time together in Arizona was even better than our vacation in Florida! I think it was because we'd cleared the air and said everything that needed to be said. There were no unanswered questions, no uncertainties; just two intimate friends making each other feel exquisite pleasure.

Hours later we lay side by side, looking up at the ceiling, smiling and gasping for breath. We couldn't keep it up a moment more. Ross sat up. His long black hair flowed over his beautiful body.

"I'm starving. Room service again?"

"Yes!"

While Ross made the call, asking specifically for Benjamin, I padded into the bathroom and showered. When I finished, I walked naked into the room. Ross took his turn in the shower while I dressed.

We were both dressed once more when Benjamin knocked on the door. I opened it, and Benjamin pushed a cart into our room. Ross had ordered quite a feast. Good thing too. I was famished! Making love with Ross took more energy than performing a whole concert!

Benjamin smiled knowingly. Did he somehow sense how we'd spent our morning and afternoon? Ross tipped him another fifty, and Benjamin seemed even more pleased than before.

The table was laid with fresh linen and a fresh red rose. Ross had ordered lasagna, garlic toast, soft drinks and more. Everything was delicious. We finished off our meal with chocolate cake that had frosting so creamy and delicious it was orgasmic.

After our late lunch, Ross departed for his room. I changed into a swimsuit and met Ross at the lift. Rod appeared out of nowhere as soon as I stepped out my door. Shawn stuck close to Ross.

"You'd think they didn't trust us," Ross said as if insulted.

Shawn raised an eyebrow.

"You know, going to the pool isn't the best idea," Rod said.

"Come on, cut us some slack," Ross said. "We've been good boys all day. This is the first time we've left Cedi's room."

I wondered if Rod and Shawn had any idea about what Ross and I had been doing in my room. I had the feeling they wouldn't care one way or another.

The four of us stepped into the lift and descended to the third floor where the pool, spa, and gym were to be found. The pool was practically empty except for a family with three small kids and a mom with her two teenage boys. The little kids paid us no attention at all, but the boys looked at us and whispered together when we entered. They didn't miss our bodyguards, either.

Rod and Shawn took up positions among the potted palms and other plants. What a life they must lead. I guess they liked it or they wouldn't keep doing it. It likely paid well at any rate.

Ross yelled and did a cannonball, attempting no doubt to douse Shawn. Shawn was all too aware of Ross' wicked side and had positioned himself far enough away from the pool to keep dry. He shot Ross a look that said, "Nice try."

I dived in. Ross and I swam, splashed water at each other, and generally had a great time. The boys, who were about fourteen and fifteen, cautiously began to play with us by splashing us with water. As soon as they discovered we weren't going to eat them, they let loose a barrage of flying water. It was then that *Dragonfire* arrived, accompanied by their bodyguard.

"Picking on kids again, I see!" Drew yelled as he stared down at us with his arms crossed over his chest. "Never fear! Drew is here!"

Drew did a cannonball right in front of Ross and me, practically drowning us. Drake joined our side, but Daniel allied himself with his little brother and the two boys. *Dragonfire* had come armed with super-soakers. Apparently, they'd planned to have a battle of their own. Now, they used their weapons in the fight, which put us at a bit of a disadvantage, considering they had two to our one. We were outnumbered four to three as well, but our larger size made up for that.

Drake was the mature one on our side, even though he was fifteen and Ross and I were twenty-two and eighteen. What can I say? Ross and I are little boys at heart. Drew was a wild boy. I wondered if he'd spent the morning eating sugar. He was even more hyped up than Ross and I, and that's saying something! Daniel was calmer, but still into the fight.

Our battle ended in a draw. Our opposition was fierce, but there was no way Ross, Drake, and I were going to let the kids defeat us. It was wicked fun.

"This is so awesome!" said one of the boys who'd been in the pool when we arrived. "I can't believe you guys are here!"

"Hey. I'm Cedi."

"I know! I'm Tobbias. This is my brother Andrei. Wow, *Phantom* and *Dragonfire*. This is so cool!"

Tobbias' mom looked confused.

"Do you know who these guys are?" Andrei asked his mum. "They're rock stars!"

A flurry of questions followed. We swam and talked to the boys and generally had a good time. Tobbias was a huge fan of Jordan, so when Ross asked Shawn to run up and get some photos for us to sign for the boys, he also quietly asked him to see if Jordan could come down for a minute.

Shawn came back with the photos, but no Jordan. I figured Jordan and Ralph were probably out and about. I'd seen no sign of them or Mike all day. Of course, Ross and I had remained secluded in my room until we decided to go for a swim. I was glad Tobbias didn't know he'd missed out on meeting his idol.

Jordan arrived just a few minutes later, escorted by Mike. Tobbias spotted him before I did.

"Oh my God!" he said and stared for several moments. I looked around to see Jordan, looking like an angel with his long blond hair.

Tobbias climbed out of the pool and slowly approached Jordan, as if irresistibly drawn to him and fearful of him at the same time. I'd seen it happen before. Jordan had a tremendous presence. When he was around, fans paid much less attention to Ross and me. Jordan was something special.

"Hey," Jordan said.

"Hey."

"What's your name?"

"Jordan... I mean Tobbias!" The kid turned completely red. Jordan smiled.

"It's nice to meet you Tobbias." Jordan reached out and shook Tobbias' hand. I thought the boy was going to pass out.

Andrei approached Jordan far more calmly than his brother, but it was clear he too was star-struck. Jordan talked with the boys a few minutes, signed the photos for them, and then went back upstairs.

The rest of us played around in the pool a while longer, but our free time was disappearing fast. Soon, we had to climb out, dry off, and prepare to return to our rooms to pack.

Ross, *Dragonfire*, and I all signed the photos for the Tobbias and Andrei. *Dragonfire* had their own group photos, of course. We bid the boys goodbye and then were on our way.

Phoenix had been incredible. Performing was a blast. We actually got to swim in a pool. And, best of all, Ross and I had worked everything out and were the best of friends—more than friends. I couldn't wait to see what adventures awaited us next.

Toby

"Okay," Krista said. "Spill it. What's his name?"

We were walking away from the school after play practice. It was the end of an uneventful but rather pleasant school day.

"What do you mean?"

"You know what I mean. I haven't seen you this happy or content since you were dating Orlando. So, I repeat, what's his name?"

"Am I that obvious?"

"Yes."

We walked along in silence for several moments.

"So..." said Krista.

I still said nothing.

"Why are you holding out on me? Don't we tell each other everything?"

"Yes, but this is different. I'm not sure you'll approve."

"What's the big deal? Is it an older man? A much older man? Is he married?"

"Nothing like that."

"Well, tell me. Toby, if he makes you happy, then I'm happy for you."

"Okay, but... Well, here goes. I'm dating Ian Babcock."

Krista stopped and stared at me for several moments.

"You're serious, aren't you?"

"Yes, I'm serious. Why would I make something like that up?"

"Ian Babcock?"

"I know we're not a likely couple. We appear as different as night and day, but we have a lot more in common that I ever dreamed."

We began walking down the sidewalk again.

"Ian Babcock?"

"Would you stop repeating his name already? Yes! I'm dating Ian Babcock!"

"I'm sorry. It's... I'm shocked. Are you sure that's wise? There are a lot of rumors going around about Ian. There's also that whole thing with the ghost."

"Since when do you listen to rumors? I seem to remember you saying you thought the whole thing with the ghost was a scam."

"I'm sorry. You're right. It's just... whoa. So how did this happen?"

I told Krista about my "date" with Daniel Peralta and how he went off with Cole Fitch, abandoning me without so much as a backward glance. I told her how Ian was there for me. How he'd been so kind and caring. I told her about the sweet and gentle Ian hidden beneath the black clothes and makeup.

"He's wonderful," I said in a dreamy tone.

"Oh, you do have it bad. I am happy for you Toby. I guess I never thought of Ian as anything more than a Goth."

"That's how most people see him. No one can look past the chains and his vampire-like attire. He's wonderful Krista. He makes me so happy. He's also a great kisser."

"So the two of you have been making out, huh? What else have you been doing?"

"Nothing... yet. We're going slow."

"Hmm, I never thought of Ian Babcock as an old-fashioned boy."

"Ian is an original. He's interested in a lot more than what's in my pants."

"Then I approve."

"Thanks Krista. This is a huge relief. I didn't know how you would react."

"It's going to take me a little while to get used to the idea, but I'll manage."

Krista and I talked all the way to her home. I'd been dying to tell someone about Ian, and at last I had my chance. I was so excited I blabbed a mile a minute. Krista smiled at my over-enthusiasm. Ian made me so happy I felt as if I could fly.

I dropped Krista off and headed on my way. I was so lost in thought I didn't even notice the footsteps behind me for several moments. I turned.

"Oh, it's you," I said without enthusiasm.

"Aww. Why don't you like me Toby?" Kerry asked.

Kerry must have spotted me from the house and then rushed out to harass me. The only bad thing about Krista was her evil twin brother. Krista and Kerry looked a good deal alike, but the similarity ended there.

"I'm sorry, but I don't have time to give you the entire list. It will be dark in a few hours."

"Ouch! Such hostility can only mean you're suffering from intense sexual frustration. I can help you with that Toby."

"You never give up, do you? Why are you so obsessed with me?"

"Don't flatter yourself. I've had guys way hotter than you. I'm curious about you, nothing more. I bet you're a screamer."

"Shut up Kerry."

"If you had any idea how good I can make you feel, you'd beg me to fuck you."

"What an ego!"

"Hey, it comes with the body—and the big dick."

"I'm not interested in your body—or your little dick."

"Liar."

I tried not to look Kerry in the eyes. Kerry was a complete and total jerk. I despised him, but he was incredibly hot. He had a gorgeous body and I couldn't keep mine from reacting to it. I felt as though my own body betrayed me. Kerry grinned at me. He knew the sight of him aroused me.

"Come on. I'll sneak you inside. Sis will never know."

"In your dreams."

"No Toby. In your fantasies."

"Leave me alone! You've got Orlando. He should be more than enough for you."

"Oh, still bitter about Orlando, I see. You know, Orlando would never have left you if you kept him happy in bed."

"I hate you. I've never said that to anyone before and meant it, but in your case it's true. I hate you."

"And still you want me," Kerry said with a smirk.

"Goodbye Kerry."

I turned and started to walk away. Kerry grabbed my arm and swung me around.

"Get off me!"

I pushed him away.

"It's only a matter of time, you know. Sooner or later, you'll want me so bad you'll come begging for it."

"Stay away from me," I said through clenched teeth.

"Do you know why I make you so angry Toby? Because you know it's true. You know how bad you want me. You just won't admit it."

"Shut... the... fuck.... up!"

I turned and rushed away, trembling with anger. I could hear him laughing at me as I hurried down the sidewalk.

Just thinking about Kerry made me mad enough to breathe fire. He was a user. He didn't care who he hurt. All that mattered to him was his sick little game of conquest. I shuddered to think of how many innocents had fallen into his web. Kerry still had his claws in Orlando too. It saddened me to even think about it. Orlando and I were over as a couple, but he was still my friend. I had gotten over the anger I'd felt toward Orlando, mostly, and I was worried about him. Kerry was no good for him. Sooner or later, Kerry would hurt him and hurt him badly. I remembered what Krista told me, that I had to let Orlando make his own mistakes. I couldn't talk to him about Kerry without angering him and making him feel guilty. No. I had to keep my nose out of it. As much as I hated it, I had to stand back and let Orlando take a fall, but I despised Kerry for what he was doing to my ex-boyfriend.

I pushed all thoughts of Kerry and Orlando out of my mind. I simply could not think about them without boiling with anger. There was nothing I could do about the situation, so it was no good worrying about it. I turned my thoughts to the one thing, or rather the one person, who could banish Kerry and Orlando from my mind—Ian.

Who would have thought that the scary Goth boy would turn out to be my boyfriend? Certainly not Krista. Not even me. If I'd had more sense and had my eyes open, perhaps I could have dated Ian instead of Orlando. I could have spared myself a good deal of pain. Then again, even if I had known Ian was gay, I would never have had the nerve to approach him. Perhaps things worked out as they did because they couldn't have worked out any other way. I didn't want to give up the good times with Orlando either, and there had been good times. Just because things got messy at the end didn't mean I should throw away what had been special between us. I was glad we were still friends.

My life was turning out quite nicely. I guess that should have put me on guard. The biggest shake-ups always came when my life was in order and going smoothly. It was as if I was allowed a time of peace before a major upheaval—the quiet before the storm.

The storm broke the next day at school. It came without the least warning (other than my currently awesome life). I had no idea when I awakened that morning that my life was about to change—permanently.

I'm not sure why Ian and I threw caution to the wind. I'm not sure what possessed us to kiss in the hallway at school. Perhaps we momentarily forgot that we lived in a prejudiced and cruel world. We did it without thinking. Had I stopped to think about my actions, even for a moment, I would never have dared, but my mind was on vacation and a few moments changed my future. It was as if it was meant to be. I smiled at Ian's approach, and he grinned back at me. We both leaned in, our lips met, and we shared a brief but passionate kiss. Just like that we outed ourselves.

"Whoa!"

Chase Simmons slammed to a halt and gawked at us. It was very likely the first time he'd ever seen two guys kiss. Chase's sudden stop caused a mini pile-up. Kerry plowed into him from behind. Cindy Erickson, Christopher Peralta, and Trevor Duncan all nearly ran over Chase and Kerry as they stopped to stare. The whole lot of them got an eyeful. Kerry smiled evilly.

Ian and I pulled away from each other, but it was too late. There was no taking back what we'd done. The color drained from my face.

The whispering began instantly and spread down the hallway in both directions. I had the feeling the news reached the most remote corners of B.H.S. in under a minute. I stood in a daze. I could not believe I'd just outed myself.

Kerry gazed at Ian and me. He looked Ian over, sizing him up and probably making plans for his seduction. I wasn't going to let it happen. I was going to warn Ian about Kerry's sick little games. Kerry was *not* going to take another boyfriend away from me.

Our classmates weren't the only ones who witnessed the kiss. Mr. Glair headed straight for us. Soon his hand was fastened on my shoulder like a vise, and Mr. Glair led Ian and me toward the office. I could hear Kerry laughing at us as we were escorted away.

Two minutes later, Ian and I were seated in Principal Duckworth's office. I was mortified. Mr. Duckworth wasn't there yet. Ian and I sat in front of his empty desk.

"I can't believe this is happening," I said.

"I guess we've given everyone something to talk about," Ian said.

"What are we going to do?"

"Um, hold hands as we walk down the hall from now on?"

"This isn't funny Ian."

"It will be okay Toby. You'll see."

Ian didn't show a trace of fear. He even smiled.

"How can you be so calm?"

Ian didn't have time to answer. Principal Duckworth entered, carrying two folders. He sat at his desk and gazed at the contents of the folders for a few moments before looking at us. The silence was unbearable.

"You boys know why you're here," Mr. Duckworth said.

"Because the school is prejudiced?" Ian said.

"No, because the school has a policy against public displays of affection. That includes kissing."

"If one of us was a girl, we wouldn't have been hauled in," Ian said.

"Mr. Babcock," the principal said as he gazed at Ian's folder, "you've been involved in several altercations."

"If you call being the victim of bullies 'involved,' then yes."

"I see."

The principal turned his gaze on me next. I trembled slightly.

"Mr. Riester, this is your first visit to my office. Hopefully, it will be your last."

"So, um... what happens now?" I asked.

"Are you going to give us detention for being gay?" Ian asked. I couldn't believe Ian had the balls to say that. "That's why we're here, isn't it?"

"No. I'm not giving you detention. Your sexual orientation has nothing to do with the situation. You're here because you violated the school's policy on P.D.A."

"Yeah? What's the difference between us and all the boy/girl couples that don't get hauled in for kissing?"

"The answer to that is very simple. You got caught."

I wasn't sure I believed him. A lot of kissing went on in the halls. Now that I thought about it, teachers were rarely around to witness it. Maybe he was telling the truth.

"I'm sure you boys can understand why P.D.A. isn't allowed. Kissing may be a fairly innocent act, but it's connected to not-so-innocent activities. The line must be drawn somewhere. The two of you have crossed it."

"So, if you're not giving us detention, what are you going to do?" Ian asked.

"I'm giving you a warning. P.D.A. will not be tolerated here. The next time I will give you detention. That's all. You may go."

Ian and I stood up and left. I could hear Principal Duckworth scribbling in our folders as we departed. I could imagine what he was writing. The principal's secretary gave us both passes to get into class, as we were now late. I knew everyone would stare at me when I walked in.

Ian and I hadn't landed ourselves in serious trouble, but our problems were far from over. We were going to be very lucky if we made it through the rest of the day without getting our asses kicked. I looked at Ian. I was worried about him. The jocks had backed off, but what would they do now that our secret was out?

The witnesses to our mini make-out session were long gone when Ian and I made it back to my locker. They were no doubt giving their first-hand account to all who would listen. I was not looking forward to the rest of the day.

All eyes were on me as I entered class. At least, I felt as if everyone was looking at me. A few guys definitely eyed me during class, but I tried to lose myself in the lecture and ignore the sense of panic that clutched at me.

When class ended, I stepped out into the hallway to find Ian waiting.

"I thought you could use some company," he said. "Come on, I'll walk you to your next class."

Ian was so confident, so strong and caring. He was my knight in shining armor—or in Ian's case, my knight in leather and silver chains.

Our journey was uneventful, but I felt as though I was squirming under a microscope. Whispers surrounded us. Eyes stared at us. I wanted to hide in my locker. I wasn't the least ashamed of being gay, but I didn't like everyone knowing my personal business. I didn't like the scrutiny. I felt naked.

Josh Lucas crossed our path. One look at him told me he knew, but he didn't swoop in to torment us. Instead, he veered off to avoid us. Perhaps my boyfriend's notorious reputation would protect us. Josh feared Ian that much was certain, but I sensed he was circling, waiting for his chance to attack. Josh was dangerous, and I was uneasy whenever he was near.

People gawked at me all morning. I felt like a sideshow freak. Ian and I were the only out gay boys in the entire school. Everywhere I went, heads turned in my direction, but no one offered to hit me. No one tripped me. No one gave me a hard time. The very worst of it was a muttered "faggot" here and there.

"I hear you're officially a homo," Mackenzie said when he spotted me between classes. "Everyone is talking about you. Ian Babcock? Whoa, big bro. I never would have guessed you'd get it on with him. You like the bad boys, don't you?"

Mackenzie laughed and rushed on before I could reply. Our encounter actually made me feel a good deal better. Mackenzie had accepted my sexual orientation some time ago. He'd been a little shit about it at first, but he'd grown to be downright supportive. He loved to give me a hard time, but he loved me. I couldn't wait until he started dating. I was going to make his life hell.

Krista pulled me to the side right before lunch.

"Everyone is talking about you Toby."

"Duh!"

"Are you okay?"

"I'm... good. I'm uncomfortable and I feel like I'm walking around naked, but it's not so bad."

"I'm relieved, but be careful Toby."

Ian spotted me. He joined Krista and me. Krista smiled at him.

"So, you're Toby's new boyfriend."

"Yeah," Ian said shyly.

I loved Krista. She was shocked when I told her I was going out with Ian, but she was accepting and obviously happy for me.

Krista leaned over and whispered something in Ian's ear. Ian swallowed hard. I wondered if she'd just given him the same warning she'd given Orlando when we were dating. Krista had threatened to rip Orlando's balls off if he hurt me. Luckily for Orlando, she hadn't made good on her threat.

The three of us went through the line together. Ian and I drew plenty of stares. Of course, Ian was stared at a great deal because of his rumored connection to the school ghost. Now, everyone gawked at both of us. We had become the school queers.

"Would you like to sit with us?" Krista asked Ian.

"Thanks, but I'd better stick with the guys. They'll be ticked off if I dump them. I'll see you later Toby."

I wanted to hug him so badly I couldn't stand it, but I thought it best not to push it. I didn't want to find myself in the principal's office twice in the same day.

I sat down in my usual spot. Eddie immediately coughed, "homo." I grinned at him. Like my brother, Eddie knew I was gay and didn't care.

Orlando's eyes met mine. There was a touch of sadness in them and also maybe a bit of jealousy. Now that I was dating someone else, was he experiencing a bit of remorse for dumping me? Who knew?

"You're the talk of the school dude," Eddie said. "You've come out with a bang. Cedi would have been proud."

"Cedi would have done it in the middle of the gym floor during a pep rally," I said.

"No kidding," Orlando said. "That boy was crazy."

"I miss him," I said.

"We have been hard up for entertainment since he left," Eddie said. "You and Goth boy should provide some much-needed drama."

"His name is Ian."

"I didn't mean anything by it. I've always liked Ian, witch or no witch."

The jocks eyed me during lunch, some of them angrily. I prayed I could make it through the day without one of them punching me in the face. Josh Lucas particularly looked as if he would like nothing more than to kick my ass. He didn't so much as utter a slur, so I hoped his fear of Ian would keep him from pummeling me.

"Hey Toby, wait up," Orlando said when I stood up and grabbed my tray near the end of lunch period.

Orlando walked with me. We dumped our trays together.

"Listen, if anyone gives you any trouble, let me know, okay? I'm not sure how much I can do to help, but I don't want anyone to hurt you."

"Thanks Orlando."

"I still care about you, you know."

"Yeah, I know."

I couldn't quite bring myself to tell him I cared about him too. I did, but my feelings were so mixed up where Orlando was concerned I didn't know what I was feeling most of the time.

"So... you and Ian, huh?"

"Surprised?"

"I'm shocked right down to my toes, but if he makes you happy, then I'm happy for you."

"Thanks Orlando."

"I'm sorry I couldn't make you happy. I'm sorry about everything."

"Well, let's not get into that, okay? Let's just be friends."

"Yeah, you're right, but I am sorry. Let me walk you to class. I'll be your weak and pathetic bodyguard."

I laughed.

No one gave me any real trouble until after play practice. By that time, I had developed a false sense of security. The expected beat down had not come all day. My first day as an out gay boy had been almost anticlimactic. I was glad to leave the whispers and prying eyes behind, but my day hadn't been that bad—considering.

The attack took me completely by surprise. As I exited the back doors of the school, Eric Michaels jumped out of nowhere and slugged me in the stomach.

"Faggot!"

I doubled over in pain and waited for the next punch. None was forthcoming. Chase Simmons jumped between us and shoved Eric away.

"This is no concern of yours Simmons."

The two muscular boys faced off. Chase was a football player and Eric was a bad ass. They stood glaring at each other, only inches apart.

"I'm making it my concern. Lay off Toby."

Eric made a disgusted noise and turned away. "He's not worth the trouble."

"Thanks Chase," I said as Eric walked away.

"It's the least I can do for one of Cedi's friends. I miss the little jerk."

I grinned.

"Thanks anyway. My stomach and I appreciate it."

"Are you okay?"

"Yeah."

"If he gives me any more trouble, let me know. I need an excuse to kick his ass."

I nodded.

"See ya later Toby."

"Bye."

I was surprised Chase came to my rescue. I guess being exposed to Cedi had increased his understanding of gay boys considerably. Of course, Cedi could be more accurately described as bi, but it was the same difference.

No one else tried to molest me on my walk home. I wondered about guys like Eric. Why did they attack boys like me? Did they feel threatened or was my sexual orientation merely an excuse? I had the feeling it was the latter. There was no way Eric Michaels could see me as a threat. He was more than capable of breaking me in half. Why did people have to be like that? What pleasure was there in bringing pain to another?

I was edgy and a little afraid, but I felt a huge sense of relief. My secret was out so I didn't have to worry about it anymore. I didn't like the way so many of my classmates stared at me, but I hoped they would get bored soon and go back to ignoring me.

Daniel

I couldn't believe it when I heard the news. Ian was caught making out with Toby Riester by Mr. Glair! It was no mere rumor. My brother Christopher had seen it with his own eyes. It wasn't the getting-caught part that shocked me. Never, in my wildest dreams, had I considered the possibility that Ian might be gay. We had been friends for years, but I'd never once suspected him. Toby was another story. I had wondered about him for several months.

Visiting Toby's bedroom had increased my suspicions exponentially. Toby had posters of boy bands on his walls. If that wasn't enough of a tipoff, his shirtless Aaron Carter poster was a sure sign Toby liked guys. I seriously doubted a hetero boy would have that kind of poster hanging by his bed. If his little brother wasn't in the room with us, I might have summoned the courage to ask Toby if he was gay. I'd even given some thought to Toby as a potential boyfriend, but then Cole came along and pushed Toby right out of my mind. There was no doubt about it anymore; Toby was gay and so was Ian.

I watched as Ian, Toby, and Toby's friend, Krista, walked across the cafeteria to get into line. They were the center of attention. That was no surprise. I was willing to bet everyone was as shocked as I was to find out Ian was gay. I feared someone might pelt them with food or call them nasty names, but nothing happened. Ian and Toby made it safely to the line without incident.

I wondered if Ian would still sit with us, or if he would join Toby instead. He might be rather uncertain about his reception at our table. I wasn't sure how he'd be received, either. When Ian left the lunch line, he headed in our direction. I nervously waited to see how Andy and Jake would react. I'd long wondered if my friends would accept me if they knew I was gay. I was about to find out. If they jumped on Ian, they would jump on me the same.

"Hi Ian," Auddie said, smiling.

"Hey."

I knew Auddie would be there for Ian. I did my part to make him feel welcome. I smiled even before he was close enough to notice. Ian showed no sign of fear as he walked toward us, but Ian had always been talented at hiding his feelings. I couldn't remember seeing him cry even once in all the years I'd known him and he had plenty to cry about.

"Hey Ian," I said.

"Hey."

I watched Andy and Jake for their reaction.

"Wanna skate after school today?" Jake asked.

"Yeah, that would be cool," Ian said.

I heaved a sigh of relief.

"I'm in," I said.

"So. Is it true? Are you a fag?" Andy asked.

Uh-oh.

"Lay off him Andy," Jake said. "What do we care? He's still Ian."

"Because that's some sick shit," Andy said. "Doing it with another guy—yuck."

"Thank you, Pat Robertson," Jake said. "Don't be so judgmental. Two guys having sex is no grosser than a guy and a girl. Just think about eating a girl out. Hell, I don't even wanna think about it while I'm eating."

"So, are you a fag too?"

"The term is gay Andy. No. I like girls. I'm just saying there's no big difference."

"The hell there's not!"

"Andy, if you think your opinion matters to me, then you're seriously mistaken," Ian said, speaking for the first time. "You can either accept who and what I am or you can fuck off."

"Making out with a guy is sick, man," Andy said. "I bet Daniel here would never do something like that. Tell them you're with me Daniel."

I froze. I did not want this to happen. I considered lying through my teeth, but I was already feeling like a traitor for sitting in silence. Jake was defending Ian, and he wasn't even gay.

"You're completely wrong Andy," I said, fighting to keep my voice from trembling.

"What? You don't think it's sick?"

"No."

"Are you seriously telling me you would make out with another guy?"

I hesitated for only a moment.

"I have."

"*What?*"

"I have made out with a guy—several times in fact."

I had not meant to out myself on that day, but I wasn't going to let Ian down. Auddie took my hand and we interlaced our fingers.

"*What?*" Andy repeated.

"Let me spell it out for you; I'm gay."

"You are not gay."

"Oh, I'm pretty sure I am."

"You've *really* made out with another guy?"

"That, and more," I said.

Andy sat in a state of shock. Jake looked just as stunned. Ian didn't look surprised at all. He was actually grinning slightly.

"Fuck," Andy said. "I thought I knew you guys."

"You do Andy. You know pretty much everything about us, except that we're gay. Why does it have to be a big deal?" I asked.

"I don't know."

"Come on Andy," Jake said. "This is Ian and Daniel we're talking about. You can't even believe Daniel is gay. I bet you never suspected Ian for a second. It's not as though they're pansies afraid to get their clothes dirty. You know these guys. They're skaters. They're cool. How bad can it be? So they suck dick—big fucking deal. It doesn't bother me in the least."

I almost laughed at Jake's little speech. He was usually so quiet and here he was talking about sucking dick.

"You have nothing to worry about Andy," I said. "It's not as if Ian or I are going to put the moves on you. We never have before, and we're not going to now. Besides, we're both taken."

"You're taken?" Jake asked. "By whom?"

"I'm not ready to tell you that. I'll have to ask him if it's okay. Even if I told you, you'd never believe me."

That was as much as I dared say. I feared my mouth would run off with me and I'd give Cole away.

"So come on Andy, be a man," Jake said. "Don't fall for all the bullshit that some of those religious freaks put out. Do you really want to ally yourself with a cult like Focus on the Family? Are you going to let Pat Robertson tell you what to think? Come on! Don't be a Republican dupe. We skaters have to stick together."

"Yeah, okay."

"Perhaps with a little enthusiasm," Jake teased.

"Yeah! Okay!" Andy said loud enough to draw the attention of others. "Listen guys," he said more quietly. "I'm sorry, okay? This is just weirding me out. Give me a little time to get used to it?"

"Sure Andy," Ian said. "It's not every day you find out two of your friends are homos. We'll cut you some slack." I nodded.

"Jake if you EVER call me a fucking Republican again I will kick your ass," Andy growled.

"I did not call you a Republican. I would never say anything that nasty to a friend. I called you a Republican dupe."

Jake should be a diplomat. I had the feeling things would have worked out very differently if Jake hadn't stepped in. I admired him for what he'd done. I was also very grateful.

I turned and gave Auddie a wide-eyed look. I couldn't believe I'd told the guys I was gay! I had to do it. I had to be there for Ian. Butterflies were still flying around inside my stomach, but I was proud of myself.

"Guys, I would appreciate it if you keep what you know about me to yourself," I said. "I'm not ready for everyone to know."

"Your secret is safe with us," Jake said. Ian and Andy nodded.

"My secret, however, is out," Ian said.

"Are you scared?" Andy asked.

"Not in the least."

"You're braver than I am," I said.

"No one is going to mess with me," Ian said. "Or if they do, I'll make them very, very sorry."

Jake, Andy, Auddie, and I looked at each other.

"Ian, isn't about time you told us the truth about the ghost?" Jake asked. "How are you pulling it off? I mean, a ghost can't *really* attack people."

"Can't it?" Ian said.

"I saw it," I said. "I saw the ghost. I was there the night it came for Billy Kelly."

"What did you see?" Andy asked.

I gave the guys my eyewitness account.

"You're not jerking us around, are you?" Jake asked. "This isn't a homos-sticking-together thing, is it?"

I laughed.

"I swear to God I'm telling the truth. I wasn't the only one who saw it. Ask Billy. Ask Trevor Duncan or his girl. They were there too. Ask Chase Simmons."

Andy and Jake looked at Ian a bit fearfully.

"Guys, you know I would *never* hurt you," Ian said. Martin Wolfe is one of our kind. He was driven to suicide by jerks like Josh Lucas. He's got our back. You don't have to be afraid anymore."

There was silence at our table for several moments. I think Andy, Jake, Auddie, and I were all reeling from Ian's words. I'd seen the ghost with my own eyes. I knew it existed. I couldn't quite make myself believe Ian was controlling it, but Martin Wolfe went after anyone who gave Ian trouble. Could he really communicate with the other side? Could he really control the ghost of Martin Wolfe? I would have thought it impossible, but how could I doubt my own senses?

Near the end of lunch, Ian motioned with his head for me to follow him outside. It was too damned cold to be out in a short-sleeved shirt, so I hoped he didn't want to talk long.

"So, is Cole good in bed?" Ian asked.

My jaw dropped open.

"How do you know I'm dating Cole?"

"You haven't been able to take your eyes off that boy from day one. I was also there the night you dumped Toby and went off with Cole."

"You were there?"

Ian nodded.

"I didn't dump Toby. He was walking me home and then we met Cole."

"Yes. Then you went off with Cole, leaving Toby behind with barely a thought about him. I know you didn't mean to hurt him Daniel, but you did."

"Oh shit! I had no idea."

"Toby really liked you."

"Damn. I feel like such a jerk."

"It's okay. Toby and I have you to thank for getting us together. I think maybe it was meant to happen that way. I came along just as you were leaving Toby for Cole. I was there for Toby, and that's what started our relationship."

"He's not pissed at me, is he? He doesn't act like he's mad."

"No. He understands. You hurt him, but he's over it."

"Good."

I gazed at my old friend for a few moments in silence.

"I never guessed about you Ian. Never once did I suspect you were like me, but you knew about me. Didn't you?"

"Yeah. I've known for a long time. I've seen the way you look at other boys. You get a look of longing and then you get sad. The first time I saw that, I knew you wanted someone to love you."

"I've never seen *you* look at a guy like that."

"I'm better at hiding my feelings. I've done it so long it's automatic."

"If you knew about me, why didn't you say something?"

"I figured you would tell me when you were ready. Thank you for what you did in there, by the way. I know that took guts. I know you weren't ready for anyone to know your secret. Thanks for sticking up for me."

"What are friends for?"

"Let's go back in. I'm freezing my nuts off out here."

***

Cole joined the guys and me after school. The guys included Auddie, of course. I was well aware she was a girl, but she was still one of the guys. I invited Cole skating before the news about Ian broke and before I outed myself. I wondered about the wisdom of the timing. My friends weren't stupid, and they might well put two and two together. I guess I was worrying for nothing. If the guys realized Cole and I were more than friends they would keep it to themselves.

The wind rushed through my hair as I sailed down the sidewalk on my board. It was too damned cold to be skating, but soon there would be snow, so it was now or never. I'd taught Cole a few things about skating, so he wasn't a complete novice. I think the fact that Cole wasn't a kick-ass skater made the guys like him more. My boyfriend seemed almost too perfect at times and that intimidated some people. Cole also made points with the guys by admiring their talent and asking for pointers.

Cole and Ian's eyes met now and then. I got the impression they knew each other better than they let on. I wondered if I should ask them about it later.

I had the feeling Andy and Jake suspected Cole was the boy I was dating. I was sure Auddie had figured it out. I wanted to talk to Cole the next time we were alone and see if he would be okay if I told my friends about us.

We had a blast, but the cold got to us. Before long, everyone except Cole and me went their separate ways. We headed to Café Blackford for hot cocoa. In hindsight, we should have taken Cole's car, but the café wasn't far and it seemed silly to drive. I wasn't so sure as we strolled down the sidewalk. I couldn't even feel my cheeks, and my fingers were getting numb. Still, I couldn't have been happier. Merely walking by Cole's side filled me with contentment. Cole was the boy of my dreams—and fantasies.

Warm air and the scent of hot coffee greeted us as we stepped inside. The fire crackled merrily in the fireplace, and I caught a faint scent of wood smoke. The café was crowded, so we had to settle for a table well away from the fire. It didn't matter. It was much warmer inside the café than out.

I felt a touch of guilt as I took my seat. I remembered the way Toby and I had talked about how the café reminded us of Café Nervosa on *Frasier*. I had no idea he had a crush on me. I thought we were just getting along well. I was so stupid.

"What's wrong?" Cole asked.

"You know Toby, the guy that got caught making out with Ian?"

"Sure."

I told Cole about Toby's crush and how I'd hurt him.

"I didn't realize he felt that way about me," I said when I'd finished.

"Don't be so hard on yourself. You didn't know how he felt. You didn't mean to hurt him. He's got Ian now anyway."

"Yeah, I guess you're right, but I don't like hurting anyone."

"That's one of the things I love about you Daniel."

"Knowing I hurt him and didn't even know it scares me. What if I've hurt someone else without realizing it?"

"What an ego. You think everyone wants you, huh?" Cole teased.

"You know what I mean!"

"I know, but you can't worry about things like that Daniel."

A couple took the table right next to ours. That was the end of our privacy. Cole and I talked about skating and the small events of our lives while we drank our cocoa. Cole was so handsome everyone kept looking at him. His lack of conceit enhanced his looks even more. I wondered how it would feel to be that good-looking.

Toby and Ian entered the café just as Cole and I were leaving. If Ian hadn't already known I was dating Cole, I'm sure seeing us together would've given him a major clue. The four of us said "hi" and then went our separate ways.

***

Our visit to Café Blackford had been most pleasant, but Cole and I had a nasty surprise waiting for us outside. We were walking back to Cole's Corvette when Josh Lucas and Adam Henshaw crossed the street and blocked our path.

"It's time we had a talk Cole. If that's your real name," Josh said.

"I don't know what you're talking about," Cole said.

I detected a trace of fear, even panic, in Cole's voice, and I didn't know why.

"Oh, I think you do."

"Didn't you learn your lesson Josh? You know bad things will happen to you if you step over the line."

My suspicion that Cole and Ian knew each other better than they let on flared.

"You're just a little too perfect to be true, pretty boy," Josh said. "A guy like you can't be real."

"I told you before that you were skating on thin ice Josh. Be careful you don't fall through."

"Ohhh, he's getting scared," Josh said to Adam. "I found out some interesting things about you Cole. For one thing, there's no Fitch listed in the phone book or with directory assistance."

"Unlisted number," Cole said.

"Your name is on the deed to the house you live in."

"I'm Cole Fitch the second, dumb ass. How did you get a look at the deed anyway?"

"The property transfer was in the paper. I also checked at the county courthouse."

"You have an unhealthy obsession with me, don't you? What is it Josh? Are you hot for me?"

"I'm no fag, but when a guy like you comes to town, I get suspicious."

"Don't you mean envious?"

"Let's talk about your dad. Where does he work Cole? Why has no one ever seen him?"

"I've seen him," I said.

"Yeah? You sure?" Josh asked. "What did he look like?"

I described the man I'd met in Cole's home.

"Hmm, you know that does sound like the man I saw you with last week Cole, so maybe I'm wrong. The funny thing is, that was in Evansville, and the two of you were going into the Executive Inn."

Cole was silent for just a moment too long. Josh smiled.

"You followed me?" he said at last.

"Yes. It's not hard to keep track of that sweet car of yours."

"All that establishes is that you're obsessed with me."

A point for Cole!

"Hmm, what were you doing in that hotel room Cole?"

"Dad had a... conference in town." I noted the slightest hesitation on Cole's part—again.

"Blackford isn't that far from Evansville. There was no reason to stay the night."

"You know, none of this is any of your business. I stayed the night in Evansville with my dad. Why don't you call the cops and have me arrested?"

"The funny thing is, Cole, you left with him two hours later and dropped him off at a home in Evansville. I can give you the address if you like."

"And your point would be?"

"I went back the next day. Guess what? Your 'dad' was still there. He lives there. Isn't that interesting? I told him I was a friend of his son and asked to see him. He let me in. I met his son. You know what, Cole? It wasn't you. Why are you lying, Cole?"

"Because my life is none of you fucking business, perhaps?"

"So, you admit you're lying. That's good. It will save us time. That's not all, after you dropped off your 'dad,' you drove to Biaggi's and had supper. Good choice, by the way. It's a little pricey, but then you have plenty of money, don't you? Anyway, you drove from Biaggi's to the airport. There you picked up another older man and took him back to the Holiday Inn. This is getting interesting, isn't it?"

"Only to you Josh. Come on Daniel. Let's go."

"Just how many daddies do you have Cole?"

Cole tried to get around Josh, but Josh and Adam blocked him.

"Now you are getting scared, aren't you? What are you hiding Cole. Huh?"

"Fuck off!"

Cole shoved his way past Josh and Adam.

The two football players didn't try to stop Cole this time. I hurried to catch up to him. I wanted to ask him what the scene with Josh was all about, but I was afraid. I'd never seen Cole so angry or scared before. He was doing his best to hide his fear, but something Josh said had scared him.

Josh had scared me too. Pieces of the puzzle were beginning to fall into place, and I didn't like the picture that was emerging. The virtually empty house, the nearly always absent father, and Josh's accusations all fit together too well. I began to wonder if Cole had been lying to me, and if so, why. I looked at the boy walking beside me. What did I really know about him? Did I know him at all?

Cedi

"We're going *where*?" I asked, my voice rising in pitch.

"England," Ralph said.

"You know," Ross said. "It's a big island in the North Atlantic. You used to live there? Hello?"

"When was this decided? Why did no one tell me before?"

"It was decided months ago Cedric. You did read the tour itinerary I gave you, right?" Jordan asked.

"Well I, uh... I skimmed it. There were so many papers, so much to do, and so little time... I never thought... I figured we'd only be touring in the States."

"Duh! Even I knew we were going to England!" Drew said. "I can't wait! Those British boys are so cute!"

"Still hot for Harry Potter, huh?" Daniel asked. "Still fantasizing about his long, hard wand?"

"Shall we talk about *your* obsession?" asked Drew. "What's her name?"

"Shut up, you two. Sorry guys," Drake said, turning to the rest of us as we sat in the front lounge on the bus, "I tried to convince my parents of the advantages of contraception, but they didn't listen. Such a pity."

Drew stuck out his tongue. Daniel flipped Drake off.

"Most of the tour is in the U.S.," Ralph said, as if there hadn't been an interruption. "We were able to book the Royal Albert Hall and a handful of other venues in England and Scotland, so we scheduled a short tour in Great Britain in the middle of our U.S. tour. Won't you be excited to go back for a visit?"

"Well, I..."

"You can be among your own kind," Ross said, grinning. "You know, people who think drinking tea is a sport, who drive on the wrong side of the road, and use words like crumpet and scone. You know; freaks."

"Look who's talking," Ralph said.

Ross did his fake facial tick, twitching his left eye while he glared at Ralph. Ralph snorted and then giggled. The *Dragonfire* boys cracked up.

I stared at the floor for a few moments, then looked back up.

"I just didn't think I'd be going back so soon."

I stood up and walked to the back of the bus, leaving the others in the front lounge. I wasn't alone for more than a moment. Ross followed me.

"Are you okay Cedi?"

"I... yeah, I guess."

"What's wrong? Are you a wanted man in England? Do you have a wife and kids there that you abandoned? A pregnant girlfriend? You're not a pirate are you?"

I grinned. Ross was such a goof.

"I'm surprised is all. I don't know how I feel about it. It's as though I'm going back to a previous life. Things were different for me in England. My life was dominated by boarding schools and people trying to get me to be someone I wasn't. There were all these expectations from the time I was born. It was as if my whole life had been mapped out for me before I even existed. It was as if... I dunno how to say it... as if I was playing a role. I felt as if I didn't matter. The role was important, not me. Anyone could have been me, you know? Anyone could have filled the role."

"Yeah, but you didn't stick to the script, did you?" Ross asked, smiling. He already knew the answer.

"No! I began rewriting the script before I was out of diapers."

"So, that was when, last year?"

"Funny! Not! The more they tried to force me to be what they wanted, the more determined I became to be me."

"*They* being your parents?"

"My parents, professors, the headmasters of various schools, relatives—everyone but my friends."

"You must've had a blast wreaking havoc! I can imagine you in a British prep school. I know what I'd do..."

I grinned.

"Okay, it was fun, but the fun always led to trouble. Those stuck-up prigs have no sense of humor! I was kicked out of more prep schools than you'd believe. Each time I got the lecture—'We're so disappointed in you Cedric. Your family expects more of you Cedric. How can you expect to take your place if you keep pulling these stunts Cedric? You have responsibilities Cedric.' Grrr!"

"What are you? The Prince of Wales?"

"Thank God, no. Can you imagine what a hell that would be? I'd rather die."

"Ah, and here I thought you had your eye on the throne."

"That would be anarchy! There's little chance I will become King, unless a freak accident happens to take out the right couple of hundred people or so."

"You mean you're actually in the succession for the throne?"

"Technically, yes. It was pointed out to me during one of the post-booting lectures—after I was tossed out of Harrow, I believe. I lasted less than a week there! Anyway, Mum had a genealogist or historian or someone figure it out. I think it was meant as a guilt trip. It hardly matters. In reality, it would never happen. I'm so far down the line that it would take such a major catastrophe to place me on the throne that there probably wouldn't even be a Great Britain anymore."

"Hmm, so we could take over if we eliminated the right people," Ross said, rubbing his chin. "King Cedric the First. I'd be your advisor of course."

"Don't you think that would look just a wee bit suspicious? Two hundred people who stand between me and the throne just happen to bite it?"

Ross laughed. I looked at him and smiled.

"Thanks Ross."

"For what? I'm trying to think of a way to take over the world! First, Great Britain, then um, all those other countries."

"You're a geography whiz."

Ross pulled me down onto the couch with him and wrapped his arm around me.

"Visiting the UK will be fun Cedi. You can show me around London. We can check out hot British boys."

"I've been surrounded by British boys most of my life."

"Mmm, nice. I wouldn't have mind being in one of those all-male prep schools; communal showers, a hot roommate..."

"Ross, have you been reading trashy novels about boys in prep schools? Reality is quite different."

"That's why I don't like reality!"

"You're so weird."

"Which is why we get along so very well."

Ross leaned in and kissed me. In moments, we were making out, and I forgot all about England.

"Get a room or make room for me!"

Ross and I pulled our lips apart and looked at Drew. He was standing in the doorway. Ross and I had been making out for ten minutes. I wondered how long Drew had been watching.

"Dream on squirt," Ross said. "You aren't ready for the big league yet. You're still in the peewee league."

"I was kidding. You think I'd wanna make out with *old* dudes like you? No way!"

"It's a good thing you feel that way, because it ain't gonna happen," Ross said.

"Hey, I just came back to see if Cedi was still whining."

"I wasn't whining."

"Was too!"

"Was not!"

"Wow!" Ross said.

"What?" Drew and I asked at the same time.

"This is amazing. I've never been the most mature person in a room before."

"You're not now!" Ralph yelled from somewhere up front.

"Screw you Ralph!"

The sound of a laugh came back at us.

"Okay, well, if Cedi is done *whining* maybe we can play the Xbox," Drew said.

"You're on," Ross said.

"Okay, Ross and I will play. Then, when I beat Ross, you can be my next victim Cedi."

"You are so going down punk!" Ross said. "What game do you wanna play?"

"It doesn't matter. I can beat you in anything."

"What an attitude," Ross said, looking at me. "I really like this kid."

"Just keep your hands to yourself. I told you I'm not into older men."

"Shut up and pick out a game, you little freak."

Drew giggled and began sorting through games. Yeah, traveling with *Phantom* was an interesting experience.

***

The next few concerts went by in a flash. At this rate the whole tour would be finished in the blink of an eye. Before I knew it, I found myself on a jet heading for Great Britain. The initial shock of discovering I'd be heading back to the land of my birth was gone. Now I was eager. We would be landing in Gatwick in a few hours. From there, a car would take us to Claridge's. I'd have some free time, so I hoped to visit a few old haunts, such as Harrods; one can find practically anything there. I'd made a few calls. Sam and Nibs were coming to our concert at the Royal Albert Hall. Ralph had already FedExed them front-row tickets and backstage passes. I couldn't wait to introduce my old band mates to my new ones. Sam, Nibs, and I kept in touch through e-mails and chats online, but it would be good to see them again in person.

During the flight, I was seated between Ross and Sam. Everyone liked Sam. She was witty, funny, and oh-so-sexy. She had the most beautiful strawberry-blonde hair. Ross had the nerve to ask her if she wanted to join the Mile High Club. Her response was, "In your wet dreams Ross." I lost it and nearly shot Diet Coke out of my nose. Sam was about three years older than I was, and she was hot. I wouldn't have minded joining the Mile High Club with her, but after she shot down Ross, I wasn't about to try!

Mike, Shawn, and Rod helped expedite us through customs, and soon we were in a limo headed for our hotel. The *Dragonfire* boys gawked out the windows, but Jordan and Ross had been to London before. I gazed at the passing scenery, realizing that I had really missed home. It felt good to see a few familiar sights. I wished we could've taken the train. I hadn't ridden on a train in ages, but it was out of the question. We would have been mobbed. That was the downside of fame. The upside more than made up for it!

It was about an hour and a half from Gatwick to the hotel, but I didn't mind. I was tired from the long flight, but it felt good to be home.

"You'll be rooming with Ross, if that's okay," Jordan said.

I realized I'd been paying no attention whatsoever to the conversation in the back of the limo.

"Huh? Oh. That's great!"

Ralph grinned at my enthusiasm. Ross and I had been frequently caught making out. Well, caught isn't the right word, since we weren't trying to hide it. I guess 'seen' or 'noticed' would fit better. Jordan didn't look quite as pleased as Ralph. No doubt Jordan still feared Ross would hurt me.

"We've booked suites, so you'll have plenty of room. Drake, Daniel, and Drew will be sharing a suite. We didn't see any reason for everyone to have their own room. Claridge's is rather pricey," Jordan said.

"Ross and Cedi would be in the same room anyway," Drew said mischievously.

"I think you two are corrupting Drew," Ralph said.

"He was born corrupted," Drake said. "Don't worry about it."

Hearing all the British "accents" on the flight and after landing gave me a sense of comfort. I loved American accents, but I had spent most of my eighteen years hearing various British dialects. I grinned when I noticed that Jordan, Ross, and the others had a bit of trouble understanding the Brits. I acted as translator now and then, translating the Queen's English into American English.

Claridge's was far more posh than anything I was accustomed to—before I went on tour with Phantom, that is. We'd stayed in some rather luxurious hotels. It was an odd sensation sleeping in my little bunk on the bus one night and finding myself in the lap of luxury the next. The suite I shared with Ross had a bedroom, bath, and a living room.

"This looks like the inside of a palace," Ross said after we were left alone.

"Or a museum."

"We've never shared a room before," Ross said, wiggling his eyebrows.

"Yeah. Are you thinking what I'm thinking?" I asked.

"Yes. Let's take a nap!"

Ross and I giggled. He was obviously as exhausted as I was from our long flight and the drive into London. We stripped down to our boxers and climbed into bed. I snuggled up against Ross. He put his arm around me, and we were soon fast asleep.

I awakened before Ross and hit the shower. I was still a bit jet-lagged and thought it might wake me up. The bathroom was mostly marble, and about the fanciest bathroom I'd ever seen. I needed to remember to tell the guys that if they were looking for a place to pee, they needed to ask for a toilet instead of a bathroom. Otherwise, they might be given directions to a room containing nothing but a bath. Bathroom didn't mean quite the same thing in the U.K. as it did in the U.S.

I entered the shower and worked citrus shampoo into my hair. I soaped up my body and let the hot water relax me. Feeling warm usually tends to make me sleepy, but the hot water helped banish the last of my drowsiness.

Ross entered the bathroom as I rinsed my hair. I was aware of his presence but little more. I couldn't open my eyes for fear of getting soap in them. Just as I finished I felt his hands slide around my waist. I turned, grinned at him, and ran my eyes down his sculpted, taut body.

"Well hello," I said.

Ross leaned down and pressed his lips to mine.

"I'm all rested up now. We have the whole evening free. What do you say we don't go out and see the sights?"

"Sounds good. All the sights I want to see are right here."

Ross leaned under the showerhead and wet his hair. I took the shampoo and worked it in. Ross' long hair turned me on like mad. I took my soapy washcloth and ran it over Ross' chest. Soon, our hands wandered all over our soapy bodies as we made out in the shower.

We caressed, kissed, and stroked each other to our hearts' content. It was a good thing Claridge's had plenty of hot water, because we were using hundreds of gallons of it. I slid to my knees on the floor and looked up at Ross. He looked like a god standing there with water cascading off his beautiful body. I leaned in and made him moan.

We kept going at it right in the shower. We made slow, unhurried love. Ross was incredible in so many ways. It seemed almost unfair that one person should have his musical talent, his looks, and his incredible lovemaking abilities. Ross took me to the heights of passion right there in the shower.

When we turned off the hot water at last, the room was so filled with steam we could barely find our way. We dried off, slipped into robes provided by the hotel, and then realized we were both famished.

"Room service?" Ross asked.

"I'm actually in the mood for some fish and chips, not fancy hotel food."

"Hmm, Shawn and Rod will have a fit if we sneak out here in London. It probably wouldn't be the wisest idea either. The chances of getting mobbed are extreme."

"What's this? Caution from you Ross? Jordan will never believe it."

"To be perfectly honest, I'm feeling too relaxed and lazy to go anywhere, let alone pull off a daring escape attempt."

"Well, we can order room service."

"I've got a better idea."

Ross picked up the phone and dialed. I could only hear half of the conversation, but he was talking to Shawn about escorting us to a restaurant. At first I didn't know what was up, since Ross had said he was feeling too lazy to go out, but then I began to suspect he was being devious. My suspicions were confirmed when Ross hung up the phone.

"Shawn's getting us fish and chips. He'll be back as soon as he can."

"Don't you feel guilty turning your bodyguard into a delivery boy?"

Ross grinned. "Not too guilty. Shawn would MUCH rather pick up fish and chips for us than to have us sneaking out and running all over London by ourselves."

"So you're actually doing him a favor, huh?"

"I like the way you think."

"Poor Shawn and Rod. Can you imagine having to put up with us?"

"Hey! We make their lives interesting!"

"Don't you mean miserable?"

"They could be stuck guarding a boring old politician. Instead they have fun and excitement!"

"Hmm. I wonder if they share your opinion."

It was nearly an hour before Shawn arrived carrying bags of fish and chips and a cardboard tray with drinks. I was truly famished by then.

"Thanks Shawn," Ross said. "As an expression of gratitude, Cedi and I promise not to set foot outside of our room until you come and get us in the morning."

"Why don't I trust you?" Shawn asked.

"Um, because I'm not trustworthy?"

"Yeah. That's it."

"I'm telling the truth this time. Cedi and I have plenty to keep us busy right here."

Ross and I were still in our robes. It was no secret among the inner circle that we had something going. Shawn probably had a good idea of just how we'd keep busy.

"I actually believe you—this time."

"Have a good night Shawn, and thanks," Ross said.

"Good night guys."

Ross shut and locked the door.

"You know it's too bad we don't want to sneak out. This would be the perfect opportunity." Ross wiggled his eyebrows.

"You're devious. That's one of the things I like about you, as I believe I've said before. There will be no sneaking out tonight. I have plans for you."

"Ohhh. Tell me."

"No. I'll show you later. Right now I'm hungry enough to eat fish and chips, bag and all."

"Exactly what are fish and chips anyway?"

"Open your bag and see."

Ross did so and pulled out the paper container.

"Oh! Fish and French fries!"

"Close enough. We call them chips. Maybe it has something to do with all those wars with France in the past."

Ross took a bite.

"We've been to the UK touring before, but I missed out on fish and chips. This is a lot like Long John Silver's, but better."

"Definitely better, although Long John Silver's is a good substitute when I'm in the U.S."

"Cedi, do you think you're going to stay in the U.S., or do you plan to move back here some day?"

"I don't know. It depends on what happens. I love it in the U.S., but I love it here too. I couldn't wait to leave England, but that was when I was stuck in those bloody prep schools. I'll be finished with school soon, unless I want to go on to university. Thanks to the money I'm making on this tour, I'll be free to do what I want."

"I'd miss you if you moved back."

"I'd miss you too."

"We do make a good team, don't we? It's nice to be able to gang up on Jordan! Kieran was always so sensible."

"We can really gang up on Jordan now, with Drew."

"I like that kid, but he's a little scary. He's hot for you. You know that, don't you?"

"For *me*?" I asked.

"Yeah. Haven't you noticed? The boy has a crush on you."

"I thought he had one on you. You should see the yearning expression on his face when he looks at you when you aren't looking."

"Uh-oh. Here I thought he was *your* problem."

"It's just a crush. He also has a thing for Jordan. He probably doesn't know many gay boys his own age."

"Yeah. He's a crazy kid. That's why I like him!"

"Me too. Too bad I didn't have a little brother like Drew. That would have driven my parents insane. I nearly did the job myself," I said.

"What if I'd been your older brother? Then, there would have been three of us," Ross said.

"Mum and Dad probably have nightmares like that."

"Are you going to visit your parents while you're here?"

"Oh, I don't know. I doubt it. There won't be much time. They don't live in London. Their place is up in Lincolnshire. We won't be performing anywhere nearby."

Ross and I talked and laughed while we finished our fish and chips. We always had a good time together. I was so glad we'd been honest with each other about our feelings. I liked knowing exactly where I stood. I have a feeling there would be a lot fewer problems in the world if people were more honest.

After our meal, Ross and I cleaned ourselves up. Fish and chips are delicious but a bit greasy. We washed our faces and then lay back on the bed together. Of course, it wasn't long before we were making out. I untied the belt on Ross' robe and revealed his smooth, hard body. Our robes lay on the floor moments later. Ross and I were all over one another once again in that slow but intense and focused way we had of making love.

Ross drove me out of my mind with need and desire. He was addictive. I couldn't get enough. The mere sight of him was enough to drive anyone insane with lust, but his technique in bed was mind-blowing. Technique sounds so mechanical. Ross was anything but that. He was very much alive; strong, virile, confident, and oh-so-talented.

Most people wouldn't think so when looking at me, but I tend to be dominant in bed. Perhaps it was my small size that throws people off. And, no, I don't mean small there! I'm quite happy with the size of my penis, thank you very much! I'm only 5'9" and weigh about 125 pounds, so I guess it is a bit hard to think of me as aggressive.

It was different with Ross. When he rolled on top of me, I liked it. When he held my hands above my head by the wrists while he kissed me and explored my torso it made me mad horny. So, when it came time to take things a step further, Ross was the top.

We were safe, of course. Ross and I were wild and crazy, but we weren't stupid. Anyone who does it bare is just plain ignorant. You just never know, no matter whom you're with. I think of unsafe sex the way I do an "unloaded" gun. Play around with it long enough and it will blow your head off.

I was nervous as I lay on my stomach and Ross climbed on top of me. Ross is rather well endowed, but bigger isn't always better and I wasn't experienced in my role. I craved it with Ross or I would've never had the nerve to try it. I trembled slightly as Ross caressed my back.

"It's okay Cedi. I'll take it nice and slow. It's going to hurt a little, but then it will feel more incredible that you can imagine. Trust me."

"I trust you."

I experienced a unique mixture of pain and pleasure as Ross penetrated me. It did hurt quite a lot, but Ross kept his word and went slowly. Whenever I tensed or cried out even a little, he held perfectly still to allow me to grow accustomed to the new sensation. There was pain, yes, but there was also something incredibly sensual about sharing such an intimate act with Ross. The very idea of it was an incredible turn-on. Somehow the pain and pleasure mixed until they became one. Then, the pain lessened and there was only pleasure—intense, mind-blowing pleasure such as I'd never experienced before.

I don't want to get into too many details. I'm not shy, but some things are private, you know? I'll just say that soon there was no need for Ross to take it slow and easy. I asked for it faster and harder, and together Ross and I reached new heights of ecstasy. When we were finished, we lay side by side upon the bed, sweating and gasping for breath.

"How did you like it?" Ross asked.

"When can you go again?"

Ross grinned. "Give me five minutes. I have to catch my breath!"

Shawn had no need to worry. There wasn't a snowball's chance in hell that Ross or I would leave our room.

Toby

Daniel and Cole were leaving Café Blackford as Ian and I entered. I felt a momentary tinge of jealousy, but it disappeared the moment I glanced at Ian. Daniel Peralta had been a mere possibility. Cole Fitch was even less than that. Ian Babcock was my boyfriend.

We were given a seat right next to the fire. The warmth of the flames was delicious. I'd gone home after play practice to change, then walked to meet up with Ian. My cheeks were rosy and my ears numb by the time I made it downtown. I reveled in the warmth of Café Blackford.

Ian's cheeks were rosy. He'd been skating with his buddies while I was in practice. I couldn't imagine skating in the cold for so very long. I would've been a human Popsicle after an hour or so of racing through the frigid air. Ian was obviously a good deal tougher than me.

"How did your day go?" I asked.

"You mean after our kiss?"

"Yeah," I said, grinning. "After we outed ourselves to the entire school."

"Uneventful. There were lots of stares, but that's nothing new. I would have to rate my coming out as anticlimactic."

I laughed.

"Same here, mostly. I'm not accustomed to that much attention. I'm usually ignored, so the stares make me uncomfortable."

"They'll quit staring soon."

"I hope so."

"So, how was your day?"

"Not a tenth as bad as I imagined. The low point was when Eric Michaels attacked me after school."

"He attacked you?" Ian's eyes narrowed.

"Yeah."

I told Ian my tale of Eric's single punch to my gut and Chase's intervention on my behalf.

"I've always liked Chase," Ian said.

"Yeah, he's cool."

Our waitress interrupted our conversation. I ordered a bowl of Italian chili, while Ian went for Irish Potato soup. The candle on our table flickered and released the delicate scent of jasmine and sandalwood. I smiled at Ian and clasped his hand across the table.

We talked of music as we sat by the fire. We then turned to philosophy and religion as we waited on our order. I laughed as Ian gave me his take on the teachings of Plato.

"What's so funny?"

"I was thinking how no one would believe we were sitting here discussing Greek philosophers and obscure ancient religions."

"Yeah, I'm sure everyone at school thinks I only know about Satanic worship."

I giggled. "Maybe it's the heavy-metal-band t-shirts you sometimes wear."

"That music isn't Satanic; it's like Mozart or Bach, only louder."

I laughed again.

"I almost can't believe that you listen to Mozart," I said.

"It depends on my mood. Sometimes I want to hear heavy metal, sometimes I'm in the mood for classical. Music is all about feeling."

My soup was delicious as were the buttery rosemary rolls that Ian and I shared. I was comfortable and content. Happiness flowed through my body as I sat with Ian. I loved being with him. This is what I'd sought all my life.

***

The whole school was buzzing. Martin Wolfe had stuck again. The latest victim was Eric Michaels. The ghost had turned the school bad ass into a quivering crybaby. When Eric's eyes met mine between third and fourth period, he looked away in fear.

Was it a coincidence that Eric was attacked only hours after I'd told Ian about my run-in with him after school? It seemed unlikely. The whole situation was too weird. If Eric had merely been worked over, it would've been one thing, but a ghost attacked him. I had to find out what was going on!

Ian's name came to me in whispers wherever I went. Everyone knew Martin Wolfe came for those who pushed others around. It was widely believed that Ian directed the ghost to his victims. My boyfriend was becoming legendary.

I figured getting my butt kicked would be a daily event, but Eric Michaels was the only guy who slugged me. I thought I'd had it when he started in on me. Eric was tough. He was the kind of guy who got into fights for fun. Thank God, Chase stepped in. I wasn't sure who would come out on top when Chase and Eric faced off. Luckily, Eric decided that beating on me wasn't worth the pain of fighting his way through Chase.

If the look in Eric's eyes was any indication, I wouldn't need Chase's protection again. I wondered what could scare a bad ass like Eric so severely he would actually cry. Seeing a ghost with my own eyes would freak me out, I'm sure. I would probably quake with fear. I might even pee my pants, but I don't think the experience would turn me into a crybaby. Eric and the other victims of Martin Wolfe were so traumatized by their encounter it was almost unreal. Of course, never having been attacked by a ghost, perhaps I just didn't understand the terror involved.

The attacks would have preyed on my mind even if my boyfriend wasn't involved, but Ian was wrapped up in the mystery and hadn't been forthcoming with details. I didn't believe all the bullshit about Ian being involved with witchcraft and Satan worship. A boy that sweet and kind could not be into that stuff, but there was a connection between Ian and the ghostly attacks; that fact could not be denied. There were too many coincidences to explain away. Anyone who messed with Ian or Cole paid the price. I thought about that for a moment. I hadn't considered the Cole connection before. How did he fit into all this?

Ian had changed since the Martin Wolfe thing had begun. He walked confidently down the hallways as if he owned the place. I don't mean he strutted or acted like a jerk, but he acted as if he was invincible. Most of our classmates shared his opinion. Everyone had feared Ian at first, but they were slowly figuring out that only the bullies had reason for fear. Without exception, Martin Wolfe had come for those who liked to push others around. A lot of kids were even beginning to look up to Ian and seek his protection. They really believed he controlled the ghost.

I still didn't know what I believed. As impossible as it seemed, it appeared that Martin Wolfe had risen from the dead and attacked whomever Ian cursed. I also had to admit that B.H.S. had become a much nicer place. Bullies like Billy Kelly were afraid to push other kids around. Guys like him feared Martin Wolfe would come for them if they caused trouble.

I know Ian's reputation protected me too. Maybe my coming out was so anticlimactic because the guys who would've given me trouble were too afraid to do so. Eric Michaels had come after me, and look what happened to him. I was thankful for the protection and for guys like Chase who weren't afraid to step in. The world needed more people like Chase.

***

"Come on," Ian said. "I want to show you something."

Play practice had just ended. I was pleased to see Ian waiting on me. He met me after practice more often than not and I was always delighted. Play practice was going well. I wasn't accustomed to such a small part, but Scrooge's nephew was a cool role. Not being the lead was a relief in a way. I didn't feel as if the success of the entire show rested on my shoulders.

Thoughts of *A Christmas Carol* flew from my mind as Ian and I walked away from the school. Ian's immense black overcoat flapped in the wind, making him look mysterious and larger than life. Ian seemed almost like a character from a play himself, although from what play I had no idea.

I followed Ian to the edge of town. We waded through tall, dead grass past an old house so dilapidated it leaned to one side. Beyond it was one of the largest oak trees I'd even seen in my life. The dead brown leaves on the tree rustled in the wind and partly obscured an old tree house.

Ian stepped onto a board nailed to the tree and began to climb. I was a bit apprehensive, but the boards seemed sturdy enough. Ian disappeared into a hole in the bottom of the tree house. Seconds later his hand reached down to help me up. The tree house was in much better repair than the house that stood near it. Someone had obviously maintained it—perhaps Ian. Large windows looked out in four directions and the view was incredible.

"I sleep up here sometimes when it's warm enough," Ian said. "When the wind blows, like now, I can lie here and feel the whole tree sway. It's awesome when it's raining. I love to hear the raindrops patter on the tin roof."

"This is incredible," I said.

"It's a little cold to be of much use at this time of year, but I spend a lot of time here in the summer. It's my own little hideaway. When the leaves are full and green, the tree house is almost completely hidden."

Ian paused and gazed at me. He leaned in and pressed his lips to mine. We began to kiss, and our surroundings disappeared. Nothing else existed in the entire universe except for Ian and me. Once again I was struck by how sweet, loving, and tender Ian could be. His outward appearance was such a contrast to what was inside.

We made out for the longest time. We went no further. We never had. I knew that some day we would go beyond kissing, but I felt as if we had all the time in the world. Feeling Ian's soft lips brush against mine filled me with such contentment that I needed nothing more. It was as if nothing could possibly be better than what we already had.

I couldn't bring myself to ask Ian about the ghost. I didn't want to ruin the moment. Our world was too wonderful to disturb. Besides, no one was getting hurt, and whatever was going on made B.H.S. a far more pleasant place.

Daniel

"Someone's here to see you, bro," Joey said.

I looked up from my skating magazine and immediately stood. Josh Lucas stood in the doorway to my bedroom.

"We need to talk. In private," Josh said. There was a wicked gleam in his eye I didn't like. There was no way I was going anywhere with him.

Josh gave my little brother a stare and Joey scurried away. Josh stepped in, then closed and locked the door behind him.

"I found out something interesting about your boyfriend. He is your boyfriend, isn't he Daniel?"

I didn't say a word. There was no way I was going to answer *that* question.

Josh moved toward me, and I had to fight to keep myself from backing away. Having Josh Lucas in my very own bedroom unnerved me.

"Wanna see what I found on the Internet?" Josh pulled a few sheets of paper out of a large envelope. He handed me the top sheet.

"Does this guy look familiar?"

It was a photo of Cole—shirtless. There was no doubt about it; it was him. It looked like a professional modeling photo.

"It's a photo of Cole. So what?"

"That's the enlarged version. Here is how it looks on the web page."

Josh handed me another sheet of paper. There was the same photo again, only smaller. Below it was Cole's age, which was given as eighteen, his height, weight, and...

"This isn't funny," I said.

"No. It's not."

I looked at the page again. I read the title at the top. I read the short biography. The more I read, the more disturbed I became.

"Cole isn't who he says he is. Your boyfriend is an escort, a whore."

"You're pathetic," I said. "You made this, didn't you? You took this off the Internet and put Cole's photo on it."

"No. I didn't. Take a look at these."

Josh handed me more sheets of paper. I wanted to refuse them, but curiosity forced my hand. Each page showed a photo of Cole. In one he was in a football uniform. In another he was dressed as a soccer player. He was done up as a Goth in yet another. On one of the pages he was shirtless, with leather straps running across his chest. In the final one he was completely naked.

"Do you think I faked those too? The web address is at the top. You can look for yourself if you like."

All the color had drained from my face. I looked up at Josh in fear.

"Your boyfriend is finished here. I'm going to show him these, and then he's either going to get the fuck out of town or I'll destroy him. Where is he?"

"I, uh, don't know. I'm supposed to meet him in about half an hour, but..."

"Then we'll meet him together," Josh said, grinning. I wanted to smack that grin off his face, but I didn't dare.

I looked through the pages again. I began to cry. Something hadn't been quite right all along. I'd pushed aside Josh's previous accusations because I couldn't believe them. There was no denying them now. I didn't know my boyfriend at all. Was the man Cole had introduced as his father a... customer? If that wasn't his dad, where was Cole's father? The big empty house, the fancy car—it all started to make sense.

Cole pulled up in his Corvette half an hour later. His face paled when he spotted Josh approaching the car with me. Josh hopped in the front and I was forced to get in the back.

"What the fuck are you doing here?" Cole asked Josh.

"How's the escort business, Cole?"

"Shut the..."

Josh shoved the papers in Cole's face. Cole turned white.

"Let's go to your house. We need to talk."

We drove in silence. I couldn't see the faces of Cole or Josh face from the back seat so I couldn't read their expressions. I was worried and upset. I kept thinking that what was happening couldn't be real. Then again, my entire relationship with Cole seemed too good to be true. Maybe it was.

We went straight to the living room upon arriving at Cole's house. Josh looked around appreciatively at the widescreen TV and sound equipment.

"Whoring pays well. Doesn't it?"

"Just tell me what you want," Cole said.

Cole's voice trembled when he spoke. He looked at me nervously. My boyfriend didn't deny anything, but how could it be true?

"Aren't you afraid your dad will walk in? Oh, that's right..." Josh said with a smirk on his face.

"What do you want?"

"I'm glad to see you aren't playing innocent. That will save us a lot of time. What I want is simple. I want you to get the fuck out of Blackford."

"You think I can pack up and leave? Just like that?"

"Please, drop the rich-boy-living-with-his-daddy bullshit. You know you're on your own. You can leave anytime you want. I'm sure you can pay someone to be your dad in another town just like you did here. That's what you did, isn't it? You either gave him cash or... something else," Josh said, running his eyes up and down Cole's body suggestively.

Cole denied nothing. My lower lip began to tremble.

"If I refuse?" Cole said.

"I'll make copies of these and spread them all over the school. I'll post the web address for the escort site everywhere."

I had an irrational impulse to grab the papers from Josh and tear them to bits, but they were nothing more than printouts. Josh could churn out more any time he wanted.

"Who else knows about this?" Cole asked.

This couldn't be happening. It just couldn't.

"No one. It's our little secret—as long as you do as you're told and get the fuck out of town."

"I must have really upset your little world. You can't stand not being the big man on campus, can you? You live for that shit."

"I don't have to listen to your bullshit. If you're not out of here in two days, everyone will know what you are."

Josh threw the papers to the floor, turned, and walked out the front door with an insufferable smirk on his face.

I stood looking at Cole for a few moments. He gazed back at me fearfully.

"You lied to me."

"I had to Daniel," Cole said, tears filling his eyes. "I had to lie to you. Don't you see? I'm so sorry."

I shook my head, turned, and walked out.

"Daniel! Daniel!"

Cole called after me, but I didn't turn. I didn't even slow down. I had to get away from him. My whole world was coming apart at the seams.

I walked through the cold winter air, shivering slightly. I didn't know if it was the cold that made me shiver or the knowledge that the boy I'd come to love wasn't real. Who was Cole Fitch? Was that his real name? Unlikely. Who were his parents, and where were they? Where had he come from, and what was he doing here? Had anything between us been real? That's what hurt the most; not knowing if Cole truly cared for me or if it had been a part of his act.

I'd felt like Cole was too good to be true from the beginning. I feared that somewhere along the way he'd tire of me, or I'd find out he had a girlfriend, or he would turn out to be a jerk. None of my fears even came close to the truth. Cole wasn't what he appeared to be at all.

My body shuddered. I began to cry. I hurt so badly on the inside I wanted to die.

Cedi

Ross and I joined Jordan, Ralph, *Dragonfire*, Chad, Sam, and a few others for a catered breakfast in a private dining room in Claridge's. I noted with some amusement that many of the others didn't quite know what to make of the fried bread or beans on the table. Some, like Ross, were adventurous enough to try something new. Others stuck with more familiar cuisine.

Our breakfast was a leisurely beginning to a busy day. After our breakfast we—*Phantom* and *Dragonfire,* that is—dashed off to the Marriott Grosvenor Square for a press conference, which was to be followed by a signing.

The press conference was about our UK appearances, and as I soon discovered, me. I hadn't realized it, but I was big news in the UK. I suppose it made sense. *Phantom* was the most popular band in the whole bloody world, and I was a "local" boy who was now a part of it. It was a story that was so unlikely it bordered on fantasy, yet it was true. I was living the dream of thousands of wannabe rock stars. Yay!

We had just enough time for a cup of tea before our signing. I'd wondered why the event wasn't held in one of the larger music stores in London, but as soon as I peeked into the huge conference room set aside for the signing I understood. There were hundreds and hundreds of fans lined up!

"How can we possibly sign for all of them?" I asked Jordan.

"By signing fast and waiting until the last possible second to leave. We've scheduled four hours for this signing, and we might squeeze in another half hour. A car will be waiting to take us to the Royal Albert Hall."

"Four hours?"

"Yeah, we knew this would be a big one, and we hate to leave anyone out."

I gulped. I hoped my hand wouldn't cramp from signing all those photos and CDs.

We got right into it. We entered the room to the cheers of the fans. We waved, took our seats, and starting signing photos, CDs, shirts, and an unbelievable array of other items as if our bums were on fire. I'd already mastered the talent of talking to each fan while I signed for them. I made it a point to look each of them in the eye and smile. As Jordan had told me long ago, our fans made our life possible.

I felt as though the previous signings were only a practice for this one. I knew *Phantom* had loads of fans. We'd already performed in front of audiences that numbered well over a thousand and, in some cases, several thousand. The sheer number of people who were willing to stand in line for hours to meet us was mind-boggling.

I smiled. I was finally thinking of *Phantom* as "us." I felt as if I belonged. I knew I might not be asked to remain with *Phantom* when Kieran returned. I had mixed feelings about that. I knew that no matter what happened I was part of *Phantom* now. I'd always have that.

Signing for all those fans was a jolly good time. I talked, laughed, and joked with them. Sometimes I got up, ran around or over the table, and gave one of them a hug. Ross overheard a girl say she'd die for a lock of my hair. He took it upon himself to jerk several strands out of my head for her. I grabbed him and returned the favor. Ross and I got into a short mock fight, slapping at each other. No doubt we looked like something out of an old-time Three Stooges film. I couldn't keep from laughing.

We had to keep such antics to a minimum or we wouldn't have had time to sign for everyone, but we had a blast.

"What a stuck-up prig! Look at him, giving out autographs as if he is someone!"

I knew that voice. I looked up.

"Nibs!"

"Hiya Cedi! Come back home just to show off, huh?"

"That, and do some concerts."

"He always was a showoff," said another voice I also immediately recognized.

I turned and looked at my other old band mate.

"Sam! I've missed you guys!"

"Well, at least he remembers our names," Sam said. "Fame hasn't gone completely to his head."

There wasn't time to talk just then, but it was great to see Sam and Nibs. They were part of most of my good memories of home.

"Hey, I'll see you guys tonight after the concert, right?" I asked.

"Sure. We'll be giving you our review of your performance," Nibs said.

Others in line gazed at Sam and Nibs with interest. As they departed, I heard a girl ask them, "Do you know Cedi?" Sam put his arm around her, "Let me tell you about Cedi, babe." I shook my head and continued signing.

I was seated right between Jordan and Ross. A lot of the fans were so excited, I feared they'd pee their pants. A lot of the girls actually cried when we talked to them. It was unreal.

Jordan was especially popular. You'd think girls wouldn't go crazy over an openly gay boy, but you'd be wrong. Of course, Jordan was extremely good-looking and sexy. He was so handsome he went beyond good-looking into a whole other realm. Ross was extremely handsome and sexy as well. Both the guys and girls drooled over him. I grinned when I thought of the things we'd done the night before.

I felt a bit inferior sitting between those two young gods. Sure, I'm cute and sexy, but I was more like a cuddly puppy than a hunk. The girls didn't pay quite as much attention to me, but many still squealed and giggled when I talked to them. Some of the boys flirted with me, although they too were more interested in my band mates. I didn't mind. Jordan and Ross were already famous when I was a kid stuck in boarding school.

My hand cramped after an hour and a half. Ross showed me how to massage and relax it back into working order. His touch turned me on like mad, as did his knowing smile. The massage and relaxation technique did the trick, and I was able to get right back to signing.

It took the extra half hour, but we actually managed to sign for everyone who'd been let in. Of course, there were plenty of fans who couldn't get in at all, but we did our best to meet as many of them as possible.

Our bodyguards ran us to a waiting limo, and we sped to the Royal Albert Hall with a police escort.

"Usually only royalty gets this treatment," I said to Jordan. "Perhaps your title of the Prince of Rock & Roll confused the authorities."

Jordan groaned.

"Make way for his Royal Highness, Jordan the First," Ross yelled.

Dragonfire, who was riding with us, extended their arms and began bowing to Jordan. Ralph tried not to laugh but couldn't help it.

"Screw you guys!" Jordan said, but he took the teasing with good humor.

There were only the usual minor problems during the sound test, but our tight schedule still meant there was little time to spare. As soon as we vacated the stage, the fans were let in for the concert.

I headed backstage with the guys to change. Since we were in the UK and I was a British citizen, I wore a sleeveless Union Jack muscle shirt. My black leather pants toned down the otherwise-bold outfit. Jordan wore a wife-beater under an open long-sleeved shirt as usual. Ross wore a tight muscle shirt that made him look wickedly delicious.

I listened to *Dragonfire* as Jordan, Ross, and I prepared ourselves backstage. Drake, Daniel, and Drew were bloody awesome. I had little doubt they would go far. The crowd had come to see *Phantom*, but if the screams from the audience were any sign, *Dragonfire* was going to be a smashing success.

The *Dragonfire* boys dripped with sweat when they ran off the stage. Performing might not look that strenuous, but it was like running a marathon, or so I guessed since I'd never run one. Anyway, it took a great deal of stamina and endurance. I wondered how my old buddy Chase from B.H.S. would stand up to the test.

Jordan, Ross, and I sprinted onto the stage to deafening screams and cheers. I was shocked to see so many Cedi signs held up by the fans. I grinned and looked back at Ross. He gave me a thumbs up. We broke into *You Don't Know,* and the crowd went wild. Once again I felt as if I was living in a dream, but if a dream I was taking me a long time to wake up.

There was something extra cool about performing in the UK. London wasn't my hometown, but it felt like it. I'd associated England with stuffiness and conformity most of my life, but I knew that wasn't a true picture of Great Britain. I was certain my parents had chosen stuffy schools in an effort to rein me in. That was my experience and it left me feeling as if England was a land of boredom and automatons. Now, I was back, seeing a side of England that had largely been hidden away from me. This was the true Great Britain, and it was good to be home!

We performed song after song with barely a break. It was a good thing we mixed in slower ballads with fast paced songs. Too many songs in a row like *New York Nights* and *Jump, Jump, Jump* and I might've collapsed upon the stage.

The cheers deafened me when we finally left the stage. I couldn't hear anything but a loud buzzing for a bit. We wore earphones during the performance so we could hear each other play, but I'd made the mistake of taking mine out a bit too soon. Oww!

I had only a couple of minutes for a breather before the meet and greet. Sam and Nibs would be there. I planned on inviting them back to the hotel room. It was a good thing they already knew I went for both girls and guys or the single king-sized bed in the room I shared with Ross might've been hard to explain.

I peeled off my sweat-soaked shirt in the dressing room and slipped on a neon-green shirt. It was time for a bit of bright color. I also dumped the leather pants for loose jeans. I made it back just as the fifteen invited guests, plus my two mates, were being led backstage by Ralph.

"Sam! Nibs!" I yelled.

I ran at them and hugged them both.

"I'm so glad you guys could make it."

"Hey, free tickets and backstage passes to meet *Phantom*? Of course we're here," Sam said. "Getting to meet Jordan and Ross is almost worth having to listen to you sing."

"I like these guys," Ross said as he walked toward us.

"Oh, no. You three are not ganging up on me. No way!"

Sam and Nibs gazed at Ross with a look of awe. I wondered what they'd think if they knew Ross and I were lovers. Perhaps I'd tell them and find out.

"So you're Cedi's old band mates, as he puts it? He's told me a lot about you."

Sam and Nibs looked a bit overwhelmed. It was as if they couldn't believe Ross was speaking to them and had actually heard of them.

"We taught him everything he knows," Sam said, after a pause.

"He was bloody horrible when we found him," Nibs said. "Couldn't play a chord. And his singing! It could make your ears bleed."

"As if!" I said.

"Ready, guys?" called Ralph. He was waiting with the rest of the meet-and-greet group.

"Sorry, I have to go be famous now. Stick around, and we'll talk after I'm done," I said.

Nibs rolled his eyes. Sam just shook his head.

"Yeah, you guys can come back to the hotel with us and tell me all about Cedi," Ross said. "I want to know all the good stuff."

"Really?" Sam asked.

"Sure."

My old mates were completely star struck. Ross had that effect on people.

Ross and I joined Jordan. We signed photos, posed for photos with the small group of fans, and stood around talking. I liked spending time with a handful of fans far more than I enjoyed big signings. There was time to really talk with them.

When we were finished, Jordan, Ross, Ralph, *Dragonfire*, our bodyguards, Sam, Nibs, and I headed for the limo. Mike rode up front with the driver. Shawn and *Dragonfire's* bodyguard followed in a sedan. Sam and Nibs seemed a bit intimidated by the bodyguards. My old mates looked as if they'd stepped into another world.

"Hey, I'm Jordan," Jordan said as if he needed an introduction.

My mates introduced themselves.

"Oh, yeah, Cedi's friends. This is Ralph, my boyfriend."

Sam and Nibs weren't fazed in the least. Sam was solely into girls, but he'd been exposed to me long enough not to be uptight around guys who liked guys. I knew meeting a gay boy wouldn't bother Nibs. Nibs was mostly into girls, but we had made out a few times.

Drake, Daniel, and Drew introduced themselves too. I noticed Drew checking out Sam and Nibs. I grinned.

Nibs looked over at me as if he couldn't believe who he was with or that I knew them. I nearly laughed out loud but controlled myself. I remembered how I'd been blown away when I first met Jordan and Ross.

"You know, when Cedi first told us he was going to be touring with *Phantom*, we thought he was pulling one on us," Sam said. "We kept waiting for the joke."

"Then we saw you on MTV," Nibs said. "We couldn't believe it."

"Have I ever lied to you guys?" I asked.

"Hmm, let's see," Sam said. "There was the time you told us terrorists forced you to order a Happy Meal at McDonalds."

"Then there was the time..." began Nibs, but I cut him off.

"Those weren't lies, merely stories for your entertainment. A story is not a lie if it's so outrageous it can't possibly be true."

"Like you touring with *Phantom*?" Sam asked.

"Well, that one was true."

"But you see why we didn't believe you. We thought it was another crazy made-up story."

"Well, now you have proof!"

"You guys were awesome!" Sam said.

"Yeah, it's just a shame Kieran couldn't be here. Cedi is a rather poor substitute," Nibs said.

"Remind me why I missed you?" I asked.

Nibs laughed.

We talked until we arrived at Claridge's. Jordan, Ralph, and *Dragonfire* said their goodbyes. Ross and I led Sam and Nibs to our suite. Shawn and Rod followed to make sure we didn't slip off.

"Do those guys follow you everywhere?" Sam asked when we were in our suite.

"Pretty much," Ross said, "unless we give them the slip, which isn't easy. They're good."

"Things can get scary without them," I said. "The fans can be a bit intense."

"It must feel bizarre to have fans," Nibs said.

"I've had a hard time adjusting."

"The girls go crazy over Cedi 'cause he's so cute," Ross said, mussing my hair.

Sam and Nibs gawked. Maybe I wouldn't have to tell them Ross and I were lovers. I think they were on their way to figuring it out for themselves.

"Guys! Have a seat," Ross said.

Sam and Nibs looked at each other, then sat down. I nearly laughed out loud again. I'd never seen Sam and Nibs intimidated by anyone before, but they couldn't quite get over their awe of Ross. Who could blame them?

"How's school?" I asked, hoping to put my mates at ease.

"Same old bore!" Sam said.

"Be glad you escaped!" Nibs said.

"Well, it wasn't truly an escape. I was tossed out, if you remember."

"I'd get myself tossed out if I thought I wouldn't be sent somewhere worse," Sam said.

"There is no place worse," Nibs said.

"The only thing I miss about school is you two. Hey, I just got a capital idea for a song title! How 'bout *Danforth Academy, Kiss My Bum*?"

Ross, Sam, and Nibs all laughed.

I sat by Ross, facing Sam and Nibs in a matching loveseat. Sam, Nibs, and I began to talk about old times. Ross and I told my mates about our adventures on the tour. Sam and Nibs began to relax around Ross after a while.

As we talked, I became aware of Ross' arm around my shoulder. I was so accustomed to it being there, I had no idea when he'd wrapped his arm around me. Nor was I aware when I'd scooted closer to him. I might not have noticed at all had it not been for the look of understanding my old mates gave me. Ross picked up on it as well, but he only smiled. When he left to take a shower, the guys wasted no time in asking about Ross and me.

"You've got something going with Ross, haven't you?" Nibs asked. "The rumors are true, aren't they? He's bi."

"This is just between us, but yes and yes."

"Is he the older man you e-mailed us about?" Sam asked.

"No, Ross isn't... well, I guess he is an older man, but only four years older. I went with Thad before I met Ross."

I didn't tell them Thad was Thad T. Thomas, the famous novelist. I figured my old mates had enough to absorb the way it was.

"So, what happen to Thad?"

"He dumped me."

I told the guys the whole story, which surprisingly didn't take long. They were far more interested in my current lover.

"Wow, I can't believe you're dating Ross," Nibs said. "That's incredible!"

"We aren't dating. We're friends—and more than friends."

"You're not dating?" Sam asked. "Come on, you guys are obviously a couple."

"No. It's not like that. We're mates. We're band mates. We have incredible sex, but we're not boyfriends. We see other people if we want."

"Been banging the groupies, huh?" Sam asked.

"Actually, I've been way too busy. You wouldn't believe how much work this is!"

"Oh, boo hoo," Nibs said. "Poor little famous boy. Let's cry for you!"

"I'm not saying I don't like it—just that it's a lot of work, and I'm almost always busy. Ross finds time for a few groupies."

"Damn, I'd just about do it with Ross," Sam said.

Nibs and I looked at him in surprise.

"You?" I asked.

"Since when are you into guys?" Nibs asked.

"I'm not, but he is hot, and he's Ross. I also said I'd *just about* do it with him. I didn't say I would."

"Closet case," Nibs said.

"Definitely," I said.

"Screw you guys!"

"See, there's proof. He wants to screw us."

"Shut up, you poof!" Sam said.

Nibs laughed.

"You know we're each only half-poof," I said. "Well, I am. Nibs is more like a quarter-poof."

"Yeah, well, that quarter of me would do it with Ross any time."

"Back off, he's mine!"

Ross chose just that moment to reenter, wearing only a towel. Nibs turned completely red. Sam laughed his bum off. I controlled myself and merely grinned.

Nibs checked Ross out as Ross dressed. I knew the moment Nibs got an eyeful of Ross' penis, because his eyes went wide. Sam checked out Ross too, but not with the obvious interest of Nibs.

We talked until it grew late. Ross and I had to be up early, so we called it a night.

"I'll have Shawn call up the car to take you home," Ross said.

"You don't have to do that," Sam said.

"It's no problem." Ross picked up the phone and dialed Shawn.

"Hey, how did you guys get away from the Academy?" I asked.

"We're on leave, sort of," Nibs said.

"Who'd you pay to pose as a relative this time?" I asked, smiling.

"Our usual, of course. 'Uncle' Simon is only too happy to sign us out for a few pounds."

"Oh, yes. Say hi for me."

I well remembered the old guy in the village next to Danforth Academy who had posed as Nib's uncle on several occasions. Thanks to him, we had some freedom, at least.

"I'd say it is about time for Uncle to return us to the Academy. It was great to see you again Cedi."

"You too."

Sam, Nibs, and I hugged each other. Nibs about went crazy when Ross also gave them a hug. Shawn knocked on the door and announced that the limo was waiting.

"E-mail me sometime," I said. "Or call."

"We will," Sam said.

We bid each other goodbye, and then Ross and I were once again alone.

"Nibs definitely has the hots for you," I said.

"I noticed."

"And you didn't invite him to stay for a three-way?" I teased.

"I figured that would be a bit awkward for you."

"You're right. That's okay. Nib's loss is my gain."

"Just not tonight. I'm ready to crash."

"I'm right behind you."

Ross and I climbed into bed, wrapped our arms around each other, and were soon fast asleep.

Toby

"Martin Wolfe! Stay away from me!" a voice wailed, hysterical and terror-ridden.

Play practice was just letting out. Krista, I, and half the cast of *A Christmas Carol* were coming out of the auditorium when we heard the distant voice. Only moments later, there was a scream, followed soon by the doors to the gym bursting open and slamming against the walls. Josh Lucas tore through the doors as if the hounds of hell pursued him. His eyes were wide and crazed. He didn't even seem to notice the throng coming out of the auditorium.

Ian rounded the corner from the other direction. Josh spotted him and screeched to a halt.

"No!" Josh screamed. "I'm sorry! I won't tell anyone! Call him off! Call your ghost off! For God's sake! Please!"

Ian grinned.

Josh gasped, toppled over backward, and hit his head hard on the floor. He lay motionless. His eyes were closed. The crowd gaped at his still form. Krista ran to him. She raised his wrist and checked his pulse.

"He's dead." She looked directly into my eyes. "Oh, my God. He's dead!"

Ian's grin faded, and the color drained from his face. He stared down at the dead football player in horror.

I couldn't believe it. Josh Lucas was dead. Just like that. The ghost had attacked others. He had come after Josh before. No one had ever died from an attack—until now. I looked at Josh's still body lying on the floor. I had no love for him, but I didn't want him dead.

I looked up at Ian. He was staring at the lifeless corpse on the floor with tears in his eyes. I walked toward my boyfriend, took him by the arm, and led him away. We walked in silence until we were out of earshot.

"He wasn't supposed to die!" Ian wailed. "I swear Toby! He wasn't supposed to die!"

"Ian, this has gone way, way too far. Josh is dead and you have something to do with it. I want answers. I want to know exactly what has been going on."

"I've got to... I just need to..." Ian buried his face in his hands and rubbed his temples as if he had a headache. "Can we go to the park and sit for a bit?"

"Ian."

"Please," he said, looking up again. "I just need to think."

We walked to the park without saying another word. My mind reeled. What had Ian done? Would he end up in prison or on the run? What had gone wrong this time? Why had Josh died?

We sat on a bench as a cold breeze whipped around us. Ian wrapped his arms around himself and rocked back and forth. Tears flooded his eyes. We must have sat there for half an hour in the cold. I felt for Ian, but I was losing patience.

"Ian, what happened? Tell me."

Ian looked up at me as if he'd forgotten I was there. He nodded.

"Come with me. I'll tell you everything."

We walked in silence for a good long time. After several minutes, Ian turned. We walked to the front door of an expensive-looking house. Ian knocked. I wasn't entirely surprised when Cole Fitch opened the door, but he was quite surprised to see me. He ushered us both inside.

"What's wrong?" Cole asked. Tears still streamed from Ian's eyes.

"Josh Lucas. He's dead!"

"*What?*"

"He's dead."

"He can't be dead."

"He's dead! I saw him lying there. You think I'd lie about something like this?"

Ian was upset, scared, and angry.

"Oh my God," Cole said, sinking down on the couch, one of the only pieces of furniture in a mostly empty room. "How could this have happened?"

"What's going on?" I asked.

"This doesn't concern you," Cole said.

"The hell it doesn't! Ian is mixed up in something that caused a boy to die. I want to know what's going on right now!"

"Tell him," Ian said. "Or I will."

Cole looked at me for a few moments before speaking.

"No one was supposed to die. No one was supposed to get hurt. You've got to understand that right off. We only meant to give the bullies a good scare so they would back off. I hate bullies. I know how miserable they make guys like Ian."

"How do you scare them? What about the ghost? There can't really be a ghost."

"No. There is no ghost. Or rather, I'm the ghost. The story of Martin Wolfe is true. He was driven to suicide fifty years ago by jerks like Adam and... Josh. I used Martin as a starting point. I raised him from the dead—sort of."

"You're the ghost?"

"Some old clothes, a little face paint, a noose—that's all it takes to transform me into Martin Wolfe."

"That can't be enough to scare a guy like Josh Lucas to death. Hell, none of those who were attacked would fall for a kid's Halloween trick like that."

"No. The fear is amplified by 'shrooms."

"'Shrooms?"

"Hallucinogenic mushrooms," Cole said. "Specifically *Psilocybe cubensis*. They're the easiest to grow. Mycology is one of my hobbies."

"Mycology?" I asked.

"The science of mushrooms."

"Where do you get them?"

"They grow wild in the southern U.S., among other places. I grow my own. They aren't native to southern Indiana."

"Grow them? Where?"

"In the basement. It's really quite easy. I started out with a kit I bought through the mail."

"Isn't that illegal?"

"The mushrooms I grow are illegal. The kits for growing mushrooms are not. Lots of people grow edible mushrooms. I've done it myself."

"What do these... 'shrooms have to do with the ghost?" I asked.

"One of the main effects of *Psilocybe cubensis* is hallucinations. I dry the mushrooms, grind them into a powder, and then slip the powder into the victim's food or drink. Thirty to sixty minutes later the hallucinations begin. I made sure to get everyone talking about Martin Wolfe well before the first attack. That way, when I appear as the ghost, the victim's mind is set to believe that Martin Wolfe has come for him. Seeing Martin is merely the trigger for a terrifying experience. Under the influence of 'shrooms, the victim sees wild shit, probably comparable to the best special effects you can imagine."

"That's why the victims don't even recognize their friends?"

"Who knows what they see when they look at someone they know? Most likely they see Martin Wolfe everywhere. The mind can play nasty tricks. I help it along. It's exactly what those bastards deserve."

It all made sense now. I'd never truly believed in the ghost, but so many swore they had seen it that it was hard not to believe.

"Did Josh deserve to die?" I asked.

Cole looked guilty. Ian gazed at him, hoping for an explanation.

"I don't understand it," Cole said. "Those mushrooms are not poisonous. I used *Psilocybe cubensis* because they're safe. *Amanita muscaria* would have given better results, but it's far too easy to get it and *Amanita verna* or *Amanita phalloides* confused. Those types are deadly. Even they wouldn't have killed Josh that fast. It would take hours for him to even get sick and far longer to die from the resulting liver and kidney damage."

"Are you sure you grew the right kind of mushrooms?" I asked.

"Positive. Mycology has been one of my hobbies since I was a kid. I could identify *Psilocybe cubensis* when I was eight."

"And these *Psilocybe cubensis* mushrooms aren't poisonous at all?"

"No. They can make the victim yawn. They increase the heart rate and make it difficult to concentrate. They make the victim restless, and, of course, there are the hallucinations. There's nothing life-threatening about any of that."

"Well, Josh Lucas is dead. How do you explain that?"

"I can't."

"Maybe he was allergic?" suggested Ian.

"It's possible..." Cole said. "If that's true, why did he survive the first time?"

There was a loud knock at the door. Everyone froze. Ian turned white and even Cole looked frightened. I half expected it to be the cops. Cole crossed to the door and looked through the peephole. He opened the door. Daniel Peralta entered.

A look of surprise animated Daniel's face when he spotted Ian and me.

"What's going on?"

"I'm in big trouble," Cole said.

"Yeah. I know that. You lied to me. I..."

"I'm not talking about that. Josh Lucas is dead."

"He's not dead," Daniel said.

"He's dead. Toby and Ian just told me."

"No. He's not dead."

"He wasn't breathing!" I said. "Krista checked his pulse."

"Yeah, well. Krista wouldn't make much of a paramedic. After you and Ian took off, Mrs. Jelen rushed out of the auditorium. She checked Josh's pulse on his neck. He was alive. He was standing by the time I left."

Cole let out a huge breath and fell back on the couch. Ian looked relieved enough to start crying again.

"So, we didn't kill him?" Ian asked.

"What? *We*?" Daniel asked.

I wasn't quite sure how Daniel fit into this. I thought Daniel and Cole had something going, but I was certain of nothing. Cole brought Daniel up to speed.

"So, Ian wasn't cursing people and summoning the ghost to attack them?" Daniel asked. "I was starting to believe, especially after I saw the ghost myself."

"You saw it?" I asked.

"Daniel was snooping around a little too much, so we arranged for him to see the ghost the night it came for Billy Kelly," Cole said.

"It was damned convincing, even though I wasn't under the influence of your mushrooms."

"This must come to an end, guys," I said. "Josh isn't dead, but someone could die. What if a future victim is allergic to the mushrooms? What if Josh had hit his head on the floor hard enough to kill him? What if someone seriously harms themselves or others when they are under the influence of the 'shrooms? What you're doing is irresponsible."

"Martin Wolfe has made his last appearance," Cole said, looking nearly as distressed as relieved. "I thought I had everything under control, but... I guess I didn't. I'm probably lucky to get off with nothing more than a good scare."

Cole gazed into my eyes. "Are you going to turn me in, Toby?"

I stood there for a few moments wondering if I should. Cole had been stupid. He'd been irresponsible. He'd taken risks with the lives of others. Was what he'd done criminal? Perhaps. The mushrooms themselves were illegal, and drugging others with them probably was too. Still...

I glanced at Ian. If I turned Cole in, Ian would likely be in serious trouble. I didn't know how he was mixed up in this, but the last thing I wanted to do was to hurt Ian. That, more than anything, made up my mind for me.

"No. I'm not going to turn you in. Nobody got hurt. I can understand why you did what you did. I'll go so far as to admit I enjoyed seeing those jerks get what they had coming. If you end this now and destroy your mushrooms, I'll forget everything you told me."

"Deal. Listen Toby. I truly never meant to harm anyone. This whole plan was about making things safer and getting the bullies to back off."

"He's telling the truth, Toby" Ian said. "After Cole saw Adam and Mike picking on me, he recruited me into his scheme. I pretended to control the ghost. Cole made it happen."

"Ian was perfect," Cole said. "Half the school already believed he was a witch. Who better to throw curses and summon spirits?"

"I feel a little as if we're at the end of a Scooby Doo mystery," I said. "Shouldn't someone say, 'We would've gotten away with it too, if it hadn't been for those damned meddling kids'?"

There were a few half-hearted laughs, but we all knew that disaster had been narrowly avoided.

"Yeah, well. It has to end," Cole said. "I couldn't live with myself if someone died because of this. That's not what I'm about."

"Me either," Ian said.

Everything that needed said had been.

"Well, I, uh, guess we should get going," I said.

Ian and I departed. We walked silently away from Cole's home.

"Do you hate me?" Ian asked after we'd walked a few blocks.

"Why would I hate you?"

"Because of... everything. The ghost... not telling you what was going on... what almost happened to Josh."

"I don't like what you did, but I understand why you did it. I know how those guys treated you and how they tormented others. They deserved payback, but what you and Cole did was too dangerous."

"Yeah. I realize that now. I hadn't considered the possibility that someone could get hurt. Maybe I was a little too eager for revenge. Cole told me he'd make me the most dangerous and feared guy in all of B.H.S. Part of me liked that idea because it meant I wouldn't have to be afraid anymore."

I nodded.

"So, you really don't hate me?"

"I love you. How could I hate you?"

Ian gazed at and smiled. Tears welled up in his eyes.

"I love you too Toby."

Daniel

When Toby and Ian departed, I glared at Cole. I'd fallen head over heels for him; that magnified by a power of ten the pain of discovering he was not what he seemed.

"I'm glad you came back," Cole said.

"I returned for one reason only. I never thought I'd say this to you Cole, but we're over."

"You're breaking up with me?"

"You can't possibly be surprised. Our whole relationship was based on lies. There's no future for us. How could there be? I don't even know who you are now! Do you have any idea how that makes me feel? Do you?"

Tears streamed down my face. I felt as though Cole had ripped out my heart and stomped on it. I'd barely been able to force myself to come to him, but I wasn't going to end things like a coward. I had to tell Cole to his face that we were over.

"I know I haven't been honest with you and I'm sorry. I would have told you everything eventually, but it was so hard. You mean sooo much to me Daniel."

"If I mean so much to you, then why did you lie to me?"

"It's a very long story."

"You know, it doesn't matter. Just forget it. I said what I came to say. Goodbye Cole."

I turned and walked toward the door. It was the hardest thing I'd ever done in my entire life. Cole ran after me and grabbed my arm.

"Please Daniel. You've got to listen. You, of all people, have to listen."

"Why? Why do I have to listen to you? I thought we had something special, but then I found out it was nothing but a lie."

"No. Daniel. Please listen to me! What we had was special. I can't even begin to express how special it was, and is, to me. I've waited for this, for you, since I was thirteen-years old."

"Cole, you aren't even trying to make your lies believable! You moved here only a few weeks ago! You didn't know me when you were thirteen-years old!"

"But I did."

"That's not possible."

"I did know you, Daniel. You were the only one who was nice to me. You were the only one who cared about me at all. Even my parents didn't..." Cole took a shuddering breath and tears flowed from his eyes.

"You're talking crazy Cole. Have you been sampling your own 'shrooms?"

He shook his head.

"My name isn't Cole. That's the name I took when I... started over."

"Why am I not surprised? What is your name then?"

"Caleb," he said, gazing into my eyes. "Caleb Fulton."

"No. No, it isn't! How dare you!" I said trembling, tears welling up in my eyes again. "I told you what happened to Caleb! I told you what his life was like! How dare you show him such disrespect! It's bad enough he had to die in a fire, but you...!"

I couldn't even finish. I was so enraged I thought my head was going to explode. When I thought of how that poor boy had suffered...

"I am Caleb Fulton."

"NO! I'm not listening to any more of your lies!"

I turned and headed for the door again. Cole grabbed me. I jerked away from him, but he seized my arm once more. I fought to get away from him, but he gripped both my arms and wouldn't let me go.

"You've got to listen to me! I know what Caleb went through! Believe me, I know! I am Caleb!"

I kept struggling to escape, but Cole was stronger than I was. My breath was coming hard and fast. No matter how I pulled against him or how I twisted and turned I couldn't break his hold on me. I surrendered and glared at him.

"Let me explain."

I said nothing. I had no choice but to listen.

"I didn't die in the fire that killed my parents. I awakened to a crash when part of the trailer collapsed. Smoke poured into my room through the cracks around the door and even through the walls. I jumped out of bed and ran to my door. I grabbed the doorknob but jerked my hand back in pain. I remembered what they taught us in school about fire safety, about how not to open a door if it was hot. I took my chair and smashed my way through the window. I climbed out. I stumbled around to the front door, but by the time I made it to the front of the trailer it was engulfed in flames. The siding was melting. I ran toward my parents' bedroom window and that's when the trailer exploded. I guess the fire got to the propane tanks. I had to throw myself to the ground to miss being engulfed in the ball of flame. When I looked up, all that was left of the trailer was a mass of flames."

Cole cried as he spoke. I began to wonder, just a little, if he was telling the truth.

"My parents were never very good to me, but they were my parents."

Cole took a shuddering breath and sobbed. Soon, he had himself back under control.

"I stumbled away. I guess I was in shock. The sirens were coming by then. I wandered off into the darkness. I don't remember where I went that night, just that I wandered out into the woods. I fell asleep at some point, for when I awakened it was light.

"I knew my parents were dead. I was afraid to go back. I thought someone might blame me for the fire. I know that was silly, but I was so used to my parents blaming me for things I didn't do that had become a habit. I hid out, sleeping in the old church by day and stealing food by night. It wasn't long before I read about the fire in the paper. I found out everyone thought I was dead.

"I realized I had a chance to start over. I didn't have to be Caleb Fulton anymore. Caleb Fulton, fat boy. Caleb Fulton, trailer trash. Caleb Fulton, the pitied, the hated, the bullied, the abused. I hated my life. I saw my chance, and I took it. I left Blackford behind and headed for Indy."

I frowned at Cole.

"You don't believe me, do you?" he asked.

"Why should I?"

"I know you have no reason to believe me, but I'm not lying now. The mushrooms should tell you something. Remember how we used to go mushroom hunting Daniel? Remember how we hunted them in your grandfather's woods? You even showed me his secret mushroom patch. I could take you there right now."

I peered at Cole more closely. No one but Caleb could possibly know that I'd shown him grandfather's secret mushroom patch. I'd never told anyone about that. I'd never shown anyone else.

Cole laughed for moment. "It always amazed me that I could be so fat when we had so little to eat. Then again, I was addicted to donuts. The nice lady who ran Whitman's Bakery used to give me all the day-old donuts. I pigged out on those. You know, sometimes that's all I had to eat?"

I remembered Caleb and his donuts. I also remembered wondering how he could be so chubby when his family was on food stamps. Cole could have done his research and learned a lot of things about Caleb. Maybe he'd even asked around about him and found out about things like Caleb's donut addiction, but what about grandfather's mushroom patch? Only Caleb and I knew about that.

I peered closely at Cole's face.

"Caleb's hair was blond and his eyes blue."

"I know. Hold on."

Cole ran up the stairs. I considering making a break for it, but I was curious to see what he had to show me. It's not as though I was in any real danger. Or was I? By the time the possibility occurred to me, Cole had returned with a small bottle in one hand and a contact lens case in another.

Cole sat down, leaned over, and removed contact lenses that I hadn't realized he'd been wearing. He put them in the case, stood, and walked to me.

"Take a look."

I gasped. His eyes were blue.

"My hair is dyed," Cole said. "If you look very, very closely, you can see my blond roots."

Cole leaned over, and I examined his hair carefully. The barest hint of blond was visible next to his scalp.

"You were the only one who was ever nice to me, Daniel. It didn't matter to you that I was poor and chubby. The other kids made fun of me because of my weight and the clothes I had to wear, but not you. You protected me when you could and comforted me when you couldn't. You even gave me some of Christopher's clothes to wear. You tried to give me yours, but they wouldn't fit, remember?"

"Caleb?" I said, tears welling in my eyes. It was him. It was really him. "But, how? You look—"

"I look completely different. I know. When I walked away from my old life, I was determined to reinvent myself. Being on the road and away from Mrs. Whitman's donuts helped. Food was scarce. I began to lose weight. Those first days were a lot easier because I was determined to slim down. I'm not saying those were good times, but I was headed in the right direction."

"You walked all the way to Indianapolis?"

"I walked a good deal of the way. I hitchhiked my way along as best I could."

"What happened when you got there?" I was almost afraid to hear the answer.

"It was rough at first, but then I was lucky enough to catch the eye of Bennie."

"Bennie?"

"The owner of *the* most prestigious escort service in Indianapolis. I thought he was just another customer, but he took me to a nice restaurant instead of a motel room. There he made me an offer I couldn't refuse. I went from living on the streets to residing in Bennie's penthouse just like that."

"So you were his... boy toy?" I could barely stand to say it. It was so... disgusting.

"No. In the restaurant, I told Bennie about my hopes and dreams. I guess it was silly to tell a stranger all that. Then again, maybe it wasn't, because it increased Bennie's interest in me. He offered to help make my dreams come true."

"At the cost of selling your body?"

"I was already doing that Daniel. I'm not ashamed of it. Please don't judge me. It's what I had to do to survive. Bennie took me away from that. You wouldn't believe his penthouse! I had my own room with my own bathroom and everything! I thought I'd died and gone to Heaven. Bennie bought me expensive clothes and gave me access to his private gym and his personal trainer."

"So how many guys did you have to do it with every week for all that?"

"None. It wasn't like that. I didn't have a client for almost three years. Bennie said I wasn't ready and that I was too young."

"So, you were what, fifteen when he sent you out to..."

"Sixteen. Bennie won't send a boy under sixteen to a client. And in case you're wondering, no, I never had sex with Bennie."

"Never?"

"No."

"So he let you live in his penthouse and bought you all those clothes for... nothing?"

"No. Bennie made it quite clear he was making an investment. When his investment paid off, he'd get back all the money he spent and more. Bennie was always very up front about that. I profited even more. You wouldn't believe the money I made as an escort.

"You wouldn't have recognized me by the time Bennie decided I was ready to meet clients. I was still blond, but I'd dropped the extra weight and was in great shape."

"Why didn't you tell me you survived, Caleb? Why didn't you write me? Do you know how much pain your death caused me?"

"I'm sorry Daniel. I should have told you. I almost came to you the night after the fire, but I was afraid. I knew you might turn me in for my own good. I feared you would think that was better than letting me run off. I couldn't take that chance. I promised myself that someday I'd come back and make it up to you."

"It might have been better if I had turned you in Caleb. Maybe you could have been adopted by a nice family."

"Maybe I would have been moved from foster home to foster home. Maybe someone who would beat me or molest me would have adopted me. I wasn't willing to take that chance Daniel. My own parents never cared about me. My dad and even my mom sometimes knocked me around. I thought I deserved better than that."

"You did, Caleb. You did deserve better. I guess I can understand why you couldn't tell me. It was just so hard Caleb. Your life was so rough and then for it to end like that..."

"I'm sorry you suffered Daniel. Really, I am. I'm going to do everything I can to make it up to you—if you'll let me."

I turned away from him for a moment and then turned back.

"I've been dating a fantasy. Cole Fitch isn't real."

"But most of what we had together was real Daniel. I'm real."

"I don't know where Caleb ends and Cole begins."

"You will Daniel. I'll tell you everything. No more lies from now on. I swear I will never lie to you again. Please believe me when I say that I only lied to you because I had to. Please believe also that I intended to tell you everything when the time was right."

I nodded.

"I love you Daniel. I always have. Caleb could never tell you that, but I can. My attraction to you is real. The love I feel for you is real. When I laughed at your jokes and smiled just because you were near—all that was real too. All the important stuff was real."

"I don't know Cole... Caleb. I love you, but I don't think I can date you knowing you have sex with other guys for money. It would cheapen our relationship. It would take a very special, intimate part of it and taint it."

"I don't do that anymore Daniel. Those two guys Josh saw me with were the last. One I owed for posing as my dad. The other was a commitment made before I moved here. I'm not an escort anymore Daniel. That was a means to an end. I have more than enough money in the bank for college now—and more besides. Bennie taught me how to save my money and how to invest it. I'm set for life Daniel, and I'll never do that again."

"Escorts make *that* much?" I asked.

"Most don't. When I was on the street before Bennie found me, I was lucky if I got fifty bucks for having sex with someone who disgusted me. Sometimes, I had to turn a trick for a meal. Bennie's boys get a minimum of a thousand dollars a session. The average is two or three thousand. I was paid as much as five thousand."

"Are you *serious*?"

"Yes, but you've got to understand that Bennie has connections. If I told you the names of some of my clients, you would be shocked. I had sex with a governor Daniel. I've had sex with CEOs of companies you would recognize. I've even had sex with music, television, and movie stars."

"Couldn't a movie star get any guy he wanted?"

"Not if he wants to keep his secret. Not if he doesn't want the story sold to a tabloid. My clients paid for discretion most of all. They know that each of Bennie's boys is carefully selected. None of us met a client without living in Bennie's penthouse for a minimum of a year. While I was there, some were asked to leave because they did drugs, sold their bodies on the side, or proved they couldn't be trusted. I didn't know it when Bennie was buying me clothes, getting me in shape, and teaching me what he called 'social graces,' but I was being tested. Very few of the boys Bennie selects actually get hired. Most are sent on their way.

"Not all the clients required such discretion. Some use Bennie's service because they know he has only the best. I was lucky to make it. All the boys working for him are gorgeous."

"In case you haven't looked in the mirror recently Caleb, you're really gorgeous."

Caleb grinned shyly.

"Well, I'm no longer the chubby, pathetic physical specimen I was when I was thirteen."

"You were kind of cute even then," I said.

"Thanks."

I think Caleb could tell I meant it.

"I know you probably think I'm nasty for being an escort. I would be lying if I said some of it wasn't unpleasant. Mostly, it was okay. Sometimes I enjoyed it. Most of the guys I was with were really quite attractive. They were the kind of guy you wouldn't imagine having to pay for sex. Of course, it was different when I was on the streets, but I don't want to talk about that."

"I don't think you're nasty. I'm sorry you had to do that, but I know you did what you had to do."

"Exactly. I would much rather not have lived that life, but I was lucky that Bennie spotted me and took me in. He saw something in me when we met. God knows it wasn't my looks that attracted him. Bennie told me that he seeks out inner beauty. He said he can make any boy beautiful on the outside, but it takes God to make him beautiful on the inside; that always made me feel special. Being one of Bennie's boys was a world away from selling myself on the streets

"Sometimes, the guys who hired me didn't want sex. Some of them merely wanted to talk about things they couldn't discuss with others. There was this one guy, a CEO, who asked for me every time he was in Indy on business. We never once had sex. He always ordered us a wonderful supper from room service, and we sat in his room, ate, and talked. He paid a thousand bucks to spend a few hours with me. At the end, we always hugged, but that was it."

"Really?"

"Yeah. I think I was like a therapist for him."

"What did you talk about?"

"A lot of what we discussed had to do with being gay. He told me what it was like for him growing up. He liked to hear about my experiences too—not the gory details, but what it was like being young, attractive, and sexually active."

"I always thought escorting was just about sex, although I can't claim to know much about it."

"It's about a lot more than that. I was taken to a lot of fancy restaurants. I went to concerts and plays. Even when the evening ended in sex, I was more of a companion than anything else.

"One guy paid five thousand bucks to have me for a whole weekend. You know what we did? We flew to Florida and spent the whole weekend at Disney World. The guy told me he picked me because I looked so much like his son. His son was killed in an auto accident when he was sixteen. The boy had always wanted his dad to take him to Disney World, but his dad was too busy with business. He kept putting it off, and then it was too late.

"That whole weekend I was Tommy.

"The whole trip was about me having a good time. We did anything and everything I wanted to do. I felt guilty at first, but that's exactly what he wanted. On the last night, he tucked me in, then held me and cried. I felt so sorry for him. I don't know what made me do it, but I said, "I forgive you, Dad, and I love you." It was freaky. I had the weirdest sense that it was Tommy speaking through me."

"Whoa, that's kind of scary."

"Scary, but cool. We flew home the next day, and the guy gave me a thousand-buck tip. He told me I'd never know what that trip had meant to him or how much it had helped him. I felt really good about it."

"I'm envious in a way. You've truly lived life."

"Well, don't envy me. I'm telling you some of the highlights. I'm leaving out most of the bad stuff. Even when my time with clients was enjoyable, in the back of my mind I knew I was a whore. I'm glad to leave it behind."

"I'm sorry I judged you so harshly. When I found out you sold your body for cash, it seemed so... nasty."

"Sometimes it was."

"I'm sorry you had to go through that. I don't think any less of you for it now. I guess anyone could find themselves in that situation. It hurt so much when Josh told me. I felt as if you were cheating on me."

"I was only with two guys after we met, Daniel. I wouldn't have done anything with them if it wasn't absolutely necessary. My life as an escort is over. I'll never go back. I want to live a normal life. I want to be with you."

Tears welled up in my eyes again. I hugged Caleb closely.

"I want to be with you too."

We hugged for several moments and then released each other.

"Can we be together?" I asked. "What about Josh?"

Cedi

The last stop in the UK tour was Edinburgh. It had been an amazing few days. I was overwhelmed by my reception everywhere I went. Most of the fans actually paid more attention to me than Jordan or Ross! I wasn't expecting that. I think the UK *Phantom* fans felt as if I represented them. I was a UK boy who had actually become a part of *Phantom*. It was the dream of many. I think many of the fans vicariously lived out their fantasy through me. I felt as though I was living in a fantasy myself—but it was real.

We had an entire day free after our last concert. I woke up beside Ross, sat up, and gazed at him as he slept. He was lying on his back, the covers pulled up almost to his navel. His long black hair fanned out around him. I would have taken him for an angel had I not known how much devil was inside him. Then again, despite Ross' mischievous side he was one of the kindest people I knew. During the tour, I'd seen him go out of his way time and again to make others happy. He stopped and talked to the fans, signed autographs, and posed for photos with them whenever he could. He knew what it meant to a fan to have even a few moments with him and he gave what happiness he could.

Ross awakened as I gazed at him. He smiled mischievously.

"Don't tell me you want to do it again. You wore me out after the concert."

I giggled.

"What's wrong old man? Can't keep up?"

Ross smacked me with his pillow.

"I'm hungry," Ross said. "I need breakfast."

"Better make that lunch. It's past eleven."

"It's that late? I must have been tired."

"After last night, I don't doubt it."

Ross smiled and sat up.

"Okay, shower first, then lunch."

"You go first."

I admired Ross' backside as he walked to the bathroom. I lay there for a bit, looking around at the room. We were staying in a little bed & breakfast hidden away on the outskirts of Edinburgh. It was an ancient, two-story stone structure that had long ago been an inn, then a private residence, and was now a B&B. I was sorry we'd missed breakfast, but we'd have another chance the next morning. I needed sleep more than food. Our hectic schedule and making love with Ross drained my energy away. Thad would never believe my energy could be depleted, but it was true.

Our room was small, but beautiful—all creamy yellows and hunter green. There were antique prints of Edinburgh Castle and other sites of local historic interest. The furniture was old, looking as if it could've come out of a castle, but the room didn't leave me feeling as if I was living in a museum. It was comfortable and cozy.

Ross was soon finished, and I took my turn in the shower. Soon, I rejoined him in the room and dressed.

"I know this awesome little pub where we can eat," I said. "It's actually not that far away. We can walk there if you'd like."

"It's cold out, but I would like to stretch my legs. A walk sounds excellent."

"Should we tell Shawn and Rod or try to give them the slip?"

"Sneak out of this little place without them knowing? Not likely. Besides, they need a rest, and they might enjoy the pub too."

"I guess we do have to be good now and then," I said.

"You were good last night—very, very good."

I gave Ross a quick peck on the lips.

Shawn and Rod were both sitting in the hallway when we stepped out of the room. They didn't seem too distressed when we announced we were walking to a pub. Edinburgh was a large city, but we were in a quiet little section. It was unlikely we'd run into many fans.

"Should we ask Jordan and Ralph?" I asked Ross.

"They're out sightseeing," Shawn said. "They left with Mike a couple of hours ago."

I didn't mention inviting *Dragonfire*. As much as I liked them, being around Drew sometimes gave me the feeling I was babysitting. Besides, they were probably out and about driving their bodyguard insane.

Confident we weren't going to make a break for it, Shawn and Rod trailed us at a discreet distance. If they stuck too close, they'd draw attention to us. There was almost no one about as we began our walk. There were more people as we left the residential area for the business district, but still no large crowds. Ross and I were bundled up against the cold. Our long coats, wool caps, and scarves helped to disguise us. There was no hiding Ross' long hair, of course, but he did look rather different wearing a bright-red wool cap.

"This place looks really old," Ross said as we neared The Lion's Mane.

"Fairly old, ancient by American standards. I believe it dates to the Twelfth Century."

"The Twelfth Century?" asked Ross incredulously. "You mean this pub is nine-hundred-years old?"

"Yeah, give or take a few decades. So?"

"That is ancient!"

I laughed. "Americans."

Ross and I walked under the large wooden sign of a roaring lion, his mane fanned out somewhat like Ross' hair that morning. The interior was a bit dark, but not too dark. There were small tables along the walls and in the center of the pub. Those along the walls had benches with high backs on either side instead of chairs. Ross and I took one of these. Shawn and Rod took a table half way across the pub.

"Whoa! This is like stepping into the Middle Ages," Ross said. "It's the pub that time forgot."

"The food is great."

"We don't have to order haggis or anything strange like that, do we?"

"Not unless you want to. I'm thinking of ordering a burger and potato soup—an odd combination I guess, but it just sounds good right now."

Ross browsed the menu while I gazed over at the fire in the hearth. We'd pulled off our caps and scarves upon entering. Now, we slipped off our coats.

"It feels nice in here," Ross said. "I like warmth."

Ross ordered vegetable soup and toast, while I ordered my burger and potato soup. We ordered hot cider and Cokes to drink.

"So you've been here before?" Ross asked.

"Only once. I can't remember who told me about it, but I rather liked it.

"It beats Burger Dude any day, but don't tell Jordan."

"He does have rather an obsession with Burger Dude, doesn't he?"

"It's an addiction, I think. We should probably send him off to a clinic somewhere. I wonder if Betty Ford treats Burger Dude addicts."

I suddenly stiffened.

"What's wrong?"

I remained silent for a few moments, listening.

"That voice is familiar."

"Which voice? I hear several, and that's not counting those in my head."

"Shhh."

I turned my head toward the center of the room. The voice was coming from behind me, a few tables away.

"It can't be."

"What?" Ross asked.

I stood up and walked toward the voice. I spotted him almost immediately. He looked up at almost the same moment.

"Cedric?"

"Thad? What are you doing here?"

Thad stood up. I thought I'd imagined his voice, but there he was.

"What are *you* doing here?" Thad said.

"We just finished our UK tour," I said, walking closer.

That's when I spotted *him,* sitting across from table from where Thad had been seated moments before. I frowned. I wasn't at all happy, and that's putting it mildly.

"You know Josiah," Thad said.

Josiah stood and began to extend his hand, but I turned quickly to Thad.

"What are you doing here?" I asked again. I had to fight to keep from adding "with *him*."

"Research for a book. Josiah was good enough to come along as my guide."

I looked back at Josiah and narrowed my eyes. What kind of guide could he be? Josiah couldn't be more than fifteen! Thad had assured me before that Josiah was older than he looked, but even if he was older, he was still a kid. What was Thad doing with him—*again*?

"Hey Thad," Ross said as he walked up behind me.

"Hi Ross. Let me introduce my friend and guide through the UK, Josiah Huntington."

"Hi Josiah."

"It's an honor to meet you. I've been a fan of your music since the beginning. I saw your concert at the Indiana State Fair."

"Wow, you must have been in grade school. That's way back. It was our first 'big' appearance. Before that, we were playing at festivals and water parks. So you're from England like Cedi? I love the accent."

"Yes. I am. Thank you."

I just couldn't help hating that kid. He was so bloody polite it was hard to hate him, but I managed. He was flirting with Ross. I just knew it. *Isn't Thad enough for you, kid?*

"Why don't you join us?" Ross asked. "We just ordered."

"Well, sure," Thad said, somewhat reluctantly. He was probably ill at ease because I'd caught him with his boy toy. When we were dating, Thad had assured me there was nothing between Josiah and him beyond friendship. He'd even told me Josiah had a boyfriend. Had he been lying? That wasn't like Thad, but maybe that was why he was so quick to dump me when he found out about the tour with *Phantom*. Josiah was just a kid. It was obscene.

Josiah was ever so polite and charmed Ross completely. If Josiah hadn't been obviously underage, I think he could have charmed his way into Ross' pants. That was probably his plan, but Ross was no pedo. I was no longer so sure about Thad. What thirty-year-old had a fifteen-year-old friend and took him to the

UK? Didn't Josiah have parents? How could they let him run around with a man practically old enough to be his father?

"I've been reading your last novel," Ross said as we waited on our orders. "It all seems so very real. I love the way you write. You pull me right in. I've read your other books, and I miss the characters when I'm finished. I think that's the mark of a great novel."

I bet few would suspect that Ross read books. He was as wild and crazy as he appeared on stage, but he was also rather intelligent. He was immature, perhaps, but still smart.

"I think the background research makes the difference," Thad said. "I write fiction, but I like to stick with reality as much as possible."

"So you're researching your next book now?" Ross asked.

"Well, I'm doing research for a few books. Josiah here has an interest in Dark Age and Medieval Britain. He's quite knowledgeable, and he's been taking me to some obscure sites."

"Wow, I'm impressed," Ross said looking at Josiah. "That's incredible that you know all that stuff. When I was your age, I was stupid."

Thad and Josiah exchanged a look I didn't understand. *Yeah,* I thought, *they're getting it on.*

"I doubt that," Josiah said.

"I've been keeping up with you as much as possible Cedi," Thad said. "You've been doing well. I'm very happy for you."

Thad seemed to genuinely mean it. I thought about all the good times we had.

"Thanks. It's been a blast."

Ross and I gazed at each other and smiled. Thad noticed the look that passed between us. I was certain he guessed we were lovers. I wondered if it made him jealous. If so, he didn't show it, but then Thad was the ice man most of the time. It was never easy to figure out what he was thinking.

Just when I thought things couldn't get any weirder, a good-looking kid of perhaps thirteen or fourteen approached our table.

"You're late," said Josiah when he spotted him.

"Sorry, I spotted an old bookshop and couldn't help taking a look. I lost track of the time."

The kid was an American. I could tell from his accent.

Josiah seemed to have forgotten the rest of us when he spotted the boy, but now he turned his attention back to us.

"Let me introduce Graham Granger," Josiah said.

Introductions were made all around, except Thad who obviously knew Graham already.

"You're traveling with Thad too?" I asked.

"Yes, I've never been to England before. It's awesome!"

I looked at Thad. What the bloody hell was he up to? Traipsing around the UK with two underage teen boys? This wasn't the Thad I knew at all. I'd had the damnedest time breaking through his defenses, largely because of my youth. He told me I was too young for him. I was eighteen! Josiah and Graham were fifteen and thirteen—sixteen and fourteen tops!

Thad stood, and Graham scooted in beside Josiah. Those two seemed rather cozy. Could Graham be Josiah's boyfriend, the one Thad had mentioned long ago? I certainly hoped so. If he was, then maybe there was nothing physical between Thad and Josiah; but who knew? I couldn't ask, and Thad wouldn't answer if I did.

I tried not to be angry, but something about seeing Thad with Josiah pissed me off. I'll admit I was jealous. I had no right to be. Thad and I were no longer a couple, but I didn't like seeing him with someone else. There was also the possibility that there had been something going on between Thad and Josiah while we were dating. I didn't think Thad was the type, but how well did I really know him? I'd long considered him an enigma. Nothing made sense! Thad couldn't possibly date a kid, yet they seemed so chummy, as if they'd known one another for years and years. That wasn't possible unless Thad had been Josiah's babysitter. Yeah, right! I could just picture that!

Ross looked at me with a quizzical expression, and I realized I was sitting there fuming. My eyes met Thad's across the table. A small smile was on his lips. He thought this was funny! I had half a mind to yell at him, but I didn't want to make a scene. Well, that's not true. I didn't care if I made a scene, but I didn't want to have to explain myself to Ross.

"It's a shame we missed your last concert here," Thad said. "We'll probably be in the UK for quite a while. I don't know if we'll make it back home before your tour ends."

"Just how long are you planning to be here?"

"Weeks. I'm not exactly sure. It depends on how long it takes us to get to the bottom of things."

This was getting weirder by the moment. I thought my head might explode. Finally, I forced it all from my mind and concentrated on the food and having fun with Ross. I scooted closer to Ross and leaned into him. He turned his head, and I kissed him on the lips. It probably wasn't the wisest thing to do, but no one could see except those sitting at our table. Neither Josiah nor Graham missed the kiss. Thad might as well have. He didn't react at all. He could have at least shown a little jealousy!

After we finished our meal, Thad, Josiah, and Graham took their leave of us. Ross and I bundled up and headed back toward the B&B.

"So, what was wrong with you in there? You looked as if you were ready to either scream or cry."

I quickly filled Ross in on Thad, Josiah, and my suspicions.

"Come on. Do you really think Thad is messing around with that kid? I'm quite a bit younger than Thad, and I wouldn't even think about fooling around with a fifteen-year old. I don't think he's like that, Cedi. You said yourself you had a hard time getting him interested in you because of your age. You're eighteen; Josiah's got to be fourteen or fifteen."

"I know it doesn't seem like Thad, but they're just sooooooooo chummy."

"Don't get mad Cedi, but I think the real problem is that you're jealous. You think Josiah has replaced you. You're picturing Thad and Josiah doing all the stuff you used to do with Thad. It's probably not like that. Thad said Josiah was showing him around the UK. He's obviously from here, so that makes sense. Doesn't it? Thad writes vampire novels, and Josiah knows all the Dark Age and Medieval sites. That fits in with the kind of stuff Thad writes. Doesn't his explanation make more sense than a sexual relationship that would obviously be illegal? Thad is famous. He has a reputation to protect. Do you really think he'd risk everything to get it on with a kid, even if he wanted to? And, do you really think he'd be interested in someone young enough to be his son?"

"Oh, you're probably right, but seeing them together pisses me off!"

Ross laughed for a moment but quickly reined himself in.

"I'm sorry."

"It's okay. I guess I am being rather stupid, but this whole thing with Thad and Josiah is weird. It was odd enough the first time I spotted them together, but this... Shouldn't he be in school?"

"They're probably on Christmas vacation."

"But Thad said they might be in the UK for weeks! How can he take two teenage boys around with him when they should be in school? Don't their parents think that is odd?"

"I have no idea."

"I guess you think I'm stupid for getting worked up about all this."

"No. I don't. You obviously still have feelings for Thad, so it's hard to see him with someone else. I know all about that, believe me. I do think you're seeing things that aren't there. You know how sometimes people see what they want to see instead of what's actually there? Well, I think you're seeing what you fear. You're afraid Thad will forget about you and find someone else, so when you saw him with Josiah, you assumed the worst."

"Maybe."

"I know this is easy for me to say, but you should just forget about it. If things are as Thad claims, then there's nothing to worry about. Right? Even if Thad is physically involved with Josiah, what can you do about it? Thad's going to do what he wants. Even if your suspicions are true, you still might get together with Thad again someday. The future is always unpredictable. Weird stuff happens. Look at Jordan and Ralph. What were the odds of them meeting? Practically zero, but it happened, and look at them now. I can't tell you what's going to happen. I can't tell you if you'll be with Thad again someday. But, even if you don't get back with him, maybe you'll find someone you like just as well, or better.

"The past is gone. The future is uncertain. The present is what matters. My advice is not to mess up the present by worrying about what Thad is doing. You can't be with him now, no matter what. You should enjoy what you've got."

"You're pretty wise," I said.

"Who would believe it, right?" Ross laughed.

"Oh, I know you're smart, and you're wicked hot in bed."

"Why don't we go back to our room, and I'll make you forget all about Thad and Josiah for awhile?"

"How will you do that?" I asked mischievously.

"Oh, I think you know."

Toby

Mackenzie looked up from the couch and grinned evilly as I entered the front door with Ian. My dad had discovered I had a new boyfriend and wanted to meet him. I had little doubt his discovery was courtesy of my little brother. I knew he couldn't wait to see Mom and Dad's faces when they met my Goth boyfriend. Ian was much more than a Goth, but that's what people saw when they looked at him.

"Dad's going to have a cow," Mackenzie whispered to me as I led Ian toward the kitchen. I tried to ignore him. I was nervous enough already.

Mom and Dad were both in the kitchen. I would rather they had met Ian one by one, but perhaps it was best to get it over with all at once. Mom's eyes widened when she set sight on Ian, but she quickly masked her shock. Ian was wearing his black overcoat. He was dressed in his usual all-black attire. I thought about asking him to tone it down for my parents, but decided against it. Mom and Dad needed to accept Ian just as he was. Ian was wearing his studded leather wristbands, his spiked collar, and the chain that always hung down from his pants. His eyes were lined in black, and his earring peeked out from under his long, black hair. I took a deep breath. This was it.

Ian reached into his coat. My mom's eyes widened, but then relaxed as Ian produced a bouquet of pink carnations and handed them to my mother.

"It's very nice to meet you, Mrs. Riester. Toby said pink carnations are one of your favorites."

"Why, thank you," said my mom, smiling.

"Mr. Riester," Ian said, stepped to my father without fear and firmly shook his hand.

"It's nice to meet you Ian."

I heaved a sigh of relief. So far, so good.

Much to Mackenzie's disappointment, the sweet and loving side of Ian showed through that evening. Ian didn't put on an act for my parents. He was simply himself. I know his appearance frightened my parents a bit at first. I could almost hear them thinking, "Oh my God, who or what has my son brought home?" Mom and Dad quickly got past Ian's exterior. Perhaps they realized that any boy who stole my heart had to be good and kind. The flowers made a good first impression. I kicked myself for not thinking of them. I had only mentioned in passing that Mom loved pink carnations. I had no idea how Ian remembered.

I almost laughed when I thought of what the boys at school would think if they saw Ian handing my mom flowers. Half of the school lived in mortal fear of my boyfriend. Even those who admired him for sending the "ghost" after the bullies found him frightening. If only they knew the real Ian.

Mom created a homemade pizza, and it was incredible. I don't know how she did it, but it tasted every bit as good as the kind bought in a restaurant. It was piled high with pepperoni and mozzarella cheese. Mmmm.

Ian was more relaxed than I. He talked and laughed and acted as if he'd known my family for years. At the end of the evening, my mom actually hugged him.

The first snowfall of the year began as Ian and I walked out the front door. I was already having dreamy thoughts of Ian spending Christmas with me. As cold as it was, we walked to the park and made out in the shadows under the trees. I was out now to friends as well as family, but I still liked to have my boyfriend all to myself.

I was improperly dressed for the cold, and Ian enveloped me in his big overcoat. His body was firm and warm as we held each other close and kissed. I couldn't remember being so happy, even with Orlando.

Ian and I kissed until the cold numbed our cheeks. The snow fell all around us and upon us. At last our lips parted. We hugged once more.

"I'll see you tomorrow sexy," Ian said.

"I can't wait," I whispered in his ear.

I gazed up at the stars as I walked toward home. I smiled. I thought my life was over when Orlando left me, but it was only beginning. I couldn't wait to see what happened next.

Daniel

Josh Lucas had it in his power to utterly destroy Cole's life. Josh knew Cole Fitch was not who or what he seemed. He didn't know that Cole Fitch was actually Caleb Fulton, the boy Josh had once tormented, but that mattered little. Josh knew about Cole's past as a high-priced escort. If he talked, Cole's world and mine would come crashing down.

I was in love with Cole—with Caleb. I was confused about what to call him. Whatever his name, he was the boy I'd sought when I'd gazed longingly into the eyes of other boys before him. It was Cole who had my heart. I couldn't bear to think of losing him. If he had to go away, I was going with him.

Josh's deadline passed. Cole and I nervously waited to see what would happen. Nothing. Nothing at all happened. Josh didn't follow through with his threats. He didn't breathe a word of what he knew about my boyfriend. It was a rather anticlimactic end to the situation between Cole and Josh. I was both relieved and thankful.

Why didn't Josh destroy Cole? Neither Cole nor I could figure it out. Josh said nothing about it. Absolutely nothing. Cole and I began to suspect that he'd actually forgotten what he'd discovered—that somehow his severe reaction to the 'shrooms had wiped the knowledge from his memory or that maybe he'd hit his head so hard he had partial amnesia. We agreed that both possibilities seemed farfetched, but were possible. We thought it far more likely that Josh's second encounter with Martin Wolfe was so terrifyingly traumatic that he simply didn't dare to cross Cole. If Josh had been scared into silence, it was ironic that he surrendered just when Martin Wolfe returned to his grave. Cole had promised there would be no more attacks. I even helped him destroy his mushroom crop myself.

Cole and I thought about confronting Josh, but if the knowledge really had been wiped from his mind, such a move would have been foolish. If he had been frightened into silence, it was just as well left alone. Josh did indeed seem fearful of both Cole and Ian. I noted he avoided them whenever he could.

As the days passed and doom did not fall, I began to relax. I had feared all along that Cole Fitch was too good to be true. I had been right. Cole was not who or what he seemed. His past was disturbing, but he'd left it behind. The ghosts of Cole's past had been revealed and could no longer haunt our relationship. I knew Cole's secrets and I still loved him. Even more importantly, he loved me.

Caleb Fulton had to remain buried in the past. As far as everyone knew, he had died when he was thirteen years old. The boy who now walked in his old hometown was very different from the Caleb Fulton I had known. Cole Fitch was more than just a name. He was who Caleb Fulton had become. Cole had his own birth certificate, Social Security number, and every possible record and document he would ever need. Whatever I thought of Bennie, he had done a thorough job of setting Cole up with a new life.

There were no more ghostly attacks, but Martin Wolfe became a legend. He had long been the school ghost, but he had grown in stature, and there were more than a few who honestly claimed to have seen him with their own eyes—at least so they thought. I began to wonder if there was not more to the situation than even Cole and Ian knew for some of the claimed sightings occurred when Cole was nowhere near. I'm sure those craving attention made up some tales, but a few were told by those I believed to be honest. Had Martin Wolfe truly risen from the grave to give Cole and Ian a hand at revenge? I guessed we would never know for sure.

For a good long while, the bullies thought twice about causing trouble. They especially steered clear of Cole and Ian. Little by little, their fear of Martin Wolfe diminished, but it never quite disappeared. While B.H.S. wasn't a paradise where the bullies feared to strike, it was at least much safer to walk the halls for a good long time.

I'd like to report that Cole and I lived happily ever after, but since we are still both in high school, I can't speak for the future. I have little doubt there are troubles ahead, but I know I can face them with Cole at my side.

Cedi

The jet engines roared as we flew back across the Atlantic. It was a long flight, but sitting beside Ross made it lots better. I gazed over at him while he was napping. I wondered if he'd ever get over Jordan. Probably not. Ross had more than a crush on his band-mate. He was in love with him. Something like that would never go away. I wondered if Ross would ever be able to settle down with someone else instead.

Was I thinking of something more permanent with Ross? Perhaps. We were a good match. I still remembered the first time Kieran saw Ross and me acting crazy together. He said, "Oh, my God. There're two of them." We are a great deal alike and far more compatible than Thad and I. That was for sure. Perhaps Ross and I would get serious someday, but not today and not soon. I wasn't ready and neither was he. I couldn't quite get Thad out of my head and Ross definitely wasn't over Jordan, but I didn't mind. Even if Thad had never been in my life, I didn't think this was the time for me to settle down. My future was so uncertain. When the plane landed, I'd be back in the States. A limo would be waiting to take us into Los Angeles. The next night, we'd be off to another city, then another, and another. The tour would be over in a few weeks, and I had no idea what would happen after.

It was just as Ross said. The past is gone. The future is uncertain. The present is all that matters. The present was about as awesome as it could be. I was on tour with *Phantom*. Ross was my lover. I was living my dream of being a rock star. What could be better than that?

Other Novels by Mark A. Roeder

Also look for audiobook versions on Amazon.com and Audible.com

Blackford Gay Youth Chronicles:

Outfield Menace

Snow Angel

The Nudo Twins

Phantom World

Second Star to the Right

The Perfect Boy

Verona Gay Youth Chronicles:

The Soccer Field Is Empty

Someone Is Watching

A Better Place

The Summer of My Discontent

Disastrous Dates & Dream Boys

Just Making Out

Temptation University*

Scarecrows

Yesterday's Tomorrow

Boy Trouble

The New Bad Ass in Town

*Bloomington Boys—Brandon & Dorian**

*Bloomington Boys—Devon**

A Boy Toy for Christmas

*Crossover novels that fit into two series

Other Novels:

Fierce Competition

The Vampire's Heart

Homo for the Holidays

For more information on current and upcoming novels go to markroeder.com.

CPSIA information can be obtained
at www.ICGtesting.com
Printed in the USA
LVOW12s0205160418
573607LV00002B/155/P